PRAISE FOR
TO SCOTLAND WITH LOVE

"A magnificent triple-hankie debut written straight from the heart, by turns tender, funny, heart-wrenching, and wise. Prepare to smile through your tears at this deft, brave, and deeply gratifying love story."
> —Grace Burrowes, *New York Times* bestselling author of the Lonely Lords series and the Windham series

"Griffin has quilted together a wonderful, heartwarming story that will convince you of the power of love."
> —*New York Times* bestselling author Janet Chapman

"Griffin's style is as warm and comfortable as a cherished heirloom quilt."
> —*New York Times* bestselling author Lori Wilde

"A life-affirming story of love, loss, and redemption. Patience Griffin seamlessly pieces compelling characters, a spectacular setting, and a poignant romance into a story as warm and beautiful as an heirloom quilt. Both heartrending and heartwarming, *To Scotland with Love* is a must-read romance and so much more. The story will touch your soul with its depth, engage you with its cast of endearing characters, and delight you with touches of humor."
> —Diane Kelly, author of the Tara Holloway series

To Scotland
with Love

A Kilts and Quilts Novel

Patience Griffin

A SIGNET ECLIPSE BOOK

SIGNET ECLIPSE
Published by the Penguin Group
Penguin Group (USA) LLC, 375 Hudson Street,
New York, New York 10014

USA | Canada | UK | Ireland | Australia | New Zealand | India | South Africa | China
penguin.com
A Penguin Random House Company

First published by Signet Eclipse, an imprint of New American Library,
a division of Penguin Group (USA) LLC

First Printing, June 2014

ISBN 978-0-451-46829-1

Printed in the United States of America
10 9 8 7 6 5 4 3 2 1

In memory of . . .
Peter Jackson, my brother, my friend.
Janet Hosea Jackson, my aunt, my mentor.
And to you . . . Mom, Dad, and the grandparents.
Gone but never forgotten.

Acknowledgments

Thank you to my husband, James, and my children, Cagney, Mitchell, and Jamie, for cheering me on and for unloading the dishes.

Many thanks to my Critique-Mates—Kathleen Baldwin, Carole Fowkes, and Susan Anderson. Also to Gretchen Craig, Rae-Dawn Brightman, Wayne Hill, and Bill Payne. Thanks for being there along the journey.

Much gratitude to Grace Burrowes, brilliant romance author . . . from stranger to friend. I promise to pay it forward.

A special thank-you to Kevan Lyon, the best agent in the world. And to the wonderful Tracy Bernstein, my editor. There's nothing like being understood.

PRONUNCIATION GUIDE

Aileen (AY-leen)
Ailsa (AIL-sa)
Bethia (BEA-thee-a)
Buchanan (byoo-KAN-uhn)
Cait (KATE)
Caitriona (kah-TREE-na)
Céilidh (KAY-lee)—a party/dance
Deydie (DI-dee)
Macleod (muh-KLOUD)
Moira (MOY-ra)

DEFINITIONS

Gandiegow—squall
Hogmanay—the Scottish celebration of the New Year
Postie—postman
Shrove Tuesday—the day preceding Ash Wednesday

The Quilters of Gandiegow Creed:

Our life is not measured by the quilts we create
but by the number of quilts we give away.

Chapter One

Cait Macleod frowned as the taillights of her taxi sped off into the night. She was standing in a deserted parking lot on the northeast coast of Scotland in the middle of December. All alone. Not new for her, but it sucked all the same.

"Don't worry about me," she said to the now-long-gone cabbie. She kicked snow off her shoe. "I'll be fine and dandy."

A fierce gust of wind caught her hair, reeling it around her head like tangled fishing line. The saying *You can never go home again* smacked her in the face as surely as the wind did. She gazed down at the scant glow of lights rising from the coastal village below and wondered if she was crazy to think she could recapture the happiness she'd once had here. Instead of coming home with her Scottish head held high, she was coming home in defeat.

But there was no time to ponder what was or what might be again as a wintry chill settled into her feet. She grimaced down at her metallic Brian Atwood heels immersed in the snowy slush. Clearly, she hadn't given enough thought to her wardrobe when she'd decided to escape her crappy life in Chicago.

"This is one hell of a birthday," she said into the wind. Thirty-one years today.

She'd forgotten Gandiegow was a closed community— no cars past the parking lot, only walking paths. And here she stood with four hefty suitcases and only two arms to drag them into the village. She yanked two of her bags over to a tree to wait their turn. The other two, she rolled behind her as she awkwardly hobbled into the village, all the while cussing in Gaelic.

Gandiegow had exactly sixty-three houses arcing around the coastline, with rocky bluffs boxing in the village. The way the town snugged up against the sea made it look like an extension of the ocean. But instead of ripples of water, there were houses. She'd been born in this village. She'd watched her mother bake bread in their wood-fired stove. Her father, when he'd cared about being a good da, had taught Cait how to fish just yards from their front steps. Her cantankerous grandmother still lived here in one of the little stone cottages.

Cait sighed heavily at her predicament. How had it come to this? Her cheating husband, Tom, was dead. Her journalism career was nearly a corpse. And her hope for reviving her life was gasping for its last breath, too.

She stopped, pulled out her map, and checked the location of her own newly bought bungalow. It sat farthest away, next to the bluffs, isolated but for one other house next to hers. She'd purchased the cottage sight unseen, based on a few snapshots over the Internet.

It was the craziest thing she'd ever done, selling everything and running away. But, she reminded herself, she wasn't really *running away*; she was *running home*. Her father had been the one to uproot Cait in the first place.

When she was thirteen, he'd dragged her and Mama halfway around the world.

"God, I haven't turned into my da, have I?" she said to the wind.

No. Her rash move had affected no one but herself. It was Tom's deceit, their marriage headed for divorce court, and then the dirt mounding over his grave that had brought Cait to the breaking point. She'd had to get out of Chicago and come home to Scotland. Maybe here she could pull herself together and eventually revive her writing career.

She went back to slogging through the slush, not really thinking about the cold. The tension that had built up over the last few days was getting to her. Now it increased exponentially, making the knot at the back of her neck feel like a burning fist.

Deydie. The only family Cait had left.

Her gran would wring her neck for not letting her know she was coming. Cait had tried—sort of. Before the plane lifted off, she'd called, but Deydie hadn't answered and there'd been no machine to take a message. What kind of granddaughter waits until the last second to let her gran know she's coming? *A stupid one?*

But dang it, Deydie wasn't your typical gran. Cait loved her, but the old gal had issues. Crabby, in-your-face issues. During their last phone call, her gran had made it perfectly clear what she thought of Cait: a chip off the old block—specifically, her father's worthless, good-for-nothing block. Cait knew there'd be hell to pay. She'd never given Deydie a good reason for staying away so long. But what could she have said? *I can't leave town because my husband screws around at every opportu-*

nity? Or, *I lost myself along the way and did everything the cheating bastard told me to do?* How ridiculous Cait felt. Especially now.

What if her grandmother and the other townsfolk rejected her? Cait hadn't visited even when she was an adult and had the means. In Gandiegow's eyes, that was indefensible, regardless of Tom. Cait had slapped her kinsmen in the face, and they would surely repay her by showing her their backs. What would she do then?

The gravel and slush gave way to a cobblestone walkway. Under other circumstances, Cait would've found the winding sidewalk charming, but right now it felt like the devil's path. Her heels kept getting lodged in between the stones, and every few feet, the suitcase wheels got stuck, too. If she had to lug the baggage much farther, her arms were in serious danger of being ripped from their sockets.

Six houses and two turns of the stone walk later, she found Cottage #13. Her heart stopped. There had to be a mistake. This couldn't be the two-bedroom bungalow she'd seen online. That one had been a quaint, one-and-a-half-story, ivy-covered dream. This one was a black, smoky ruin.

"It figures," Cait groaned.

Dangling sideways from a wrought-iron post hung the #13 sign. Judging by the look of the charred wood, a fire had claimed every bit of her new home. The only parts left were the chest-high stone wall surrounding the perimeter of the house and a smoke-stained chimney jutting out of the ashes.

Her house was dead.

It all made sense now. *Death comes in threes.* Wasn't that the old saying?

Well, the Christmas tree back in Chicago had knocked off first. It had turned into a skeleton and dropped pine needles all over the floor. Tom, her lying, cheating weasel-of-a-husband, went next. He'd had a heart attack while inserting his holiday sausage into his mistress. And now her new home was dead, too. A freaking funeral pyre.

A shiver, which had nothing to do with Scotland's frigid December weather, overtook her. "I'm such a fricking idiot." Could life get any worse?

A fat raindrop hit her head. Then another. Just like that, the heavens opened up and dropped a crapload of rain on her dumbass head. She looked up. "Thanks."

She dragged her bags to the house next door with the intent of using her neighbor's phone. While stepping up on the porch, she formulated a few choice words for the online real estate agent—the big swindler!

Before reaching for the knocker, Cait decided to first dislodge the rock from her shoe. But when she bent over, the door suddenly opened. Out of the corner of her eye, she saw a man come through and stop short. She felt pretty sure, even from that angle, he was giving her ass the once-over.

She had every intention of giving him a piece of her mind—she didn't allow men to ogle her like a rump roast—but when she stood and saw who was eyeing her . . .

Omigod! Mr. Darcy. She nearly fell in the ice and mud. She couldn't catch her breath. *Graham Buchanan. It was Graham Buchanan in person.* He was so outrageously handsome, he seemed to glow and shimmer, and she couldn't take her eyes off him. More impressive than he'd ever been on the big screen or in a magazine spread. No glitz, no glamour, no hair gel. Not put together in any sense. And better, so much better—his collar-length brown hair tousled, his beard a two-day stubble, and he wore a Scottish warrior's frown like a badge of honor. Sexy as hell.

She had come to this house to ask for something, but for the luvagod, she couldn't remember what. All she could do was stare at his broad chest and tall frame. She licked her lips. His spicy cologne drew her in.

He took a step back, ready to slam the door in her face.

"Wait," she cried. She still needed a phone. And to smell him a second longer—a tantalizing mixture of ginger, cardamom, and nutmeg.

"You're with the press," he accused.

How did he know? Graham Buchanan must have a sixth sense.

But right now, who cared? His Scottish burr rolled off his tongue like melted caramel. She wanted to lap him up. And the pheromones flying off him were so palpable, they had her wanting to drop to her knees and offer herself up as his love slave, his sex kitten, his everything.

Get it together, Cait.

She straightened herself up and took a deep breath, then lied as if her career depended on it. "I am not with the press." *Not anymore.* Editing *Chicago Fishermen's Monthly* didn't count when it came to journalistic credits.

She looked into his golden brown eyes. Being near him caused her heart to bang against her insides like a wild badger inside a metal drum. She closed her eyes, trying to center herself. It didn't work. She felt like the envy of all ovulating women in the free world. It wasn't every day she stood in the presence of the Sexiest Man Alive.

It hit her then like a wrecking ball—*oomph*. The headline from *People* magazine in her carry-on bag— *Graham Buchanan Gone Missing Again*. According to *People,* no stone had gone unturned, yet she'd stumbled into him, now only three feet away. She'd found the lost actor. Cait Macleod had done it—found Graham Buchanan!

Inside the cottage, another man's voice rang out from behind Graham. "What is it?" He sounded a little perturbed.

Graham's eyebrows furrowed, distrust shrouding his features. "I'm not sure," he called. Any second now he'd slam the door in her face.

Cait stuck her hand in the jamb. "I need to use the phone."

"Then you're not a journalist?" He crossed his arms over his chest. "You look like one of those leeching paparazzi—"

"Heavens, no. I—I—" Her brain faltered, and the stupidest answer came out. "I'm a quilter."

Graham jerked back. "You're a *what*?" He closed the door a bit more.

A small boy saved her. He came up behind Graham and grabbed his hand. The kid looked about six, with dark red hair, sad eyes, and an even sadder mouth. Graham put his arm protectively around him. "Go back to your da, Mattie." Obediently, the boy turned and left.

Graham watched him until he disappeared; then he gave her his full scrutiny again. "Usually, I'm right about these things. I can't believe you're not with the press."

"You're wrong this time, buster." Her Episcopal upbringing had her wanting to make the sign of the cross, a little protection against lying so fervently. And for calling the megastar *buster*. She gestured toward her misfortune. "That's my house next door." She took a couple of deep breaths, trying to regain her composure. "The one that looks like a campfire gone awry." She made sure she looked him square in the face so he wouldn't know she'd lied about her profession. What a bonus that he was so easy on the eyes.

He leaned out and nodded toward her house. "She went up in flames day before yesterday."

Cait gazed over at her cremated house as well. "I knew it was too good to be true. I'm plagued with bad luck."

"Luck has nothing to do with it." He shrugged. "Faulty wiring is what I hear."

"About that phone? My cell's dead." She wiped the rain from her eyes.

He seemed to wake up to the fact that she was soaked. "Come in." He still sounded leery, but stepped to the side and opened the door fully. "Duncan, you have company."

"What?" A young man appeared, the same height as Graham, so much like the actor it made Cait stare at both of them. Two things hit her at once.

The man behind Graham was little Duncan MacKinnon, whom she'd once protected from a bully at Gandiegow's one-room schoolhouse. Shoot, she'd babysat for him a time or two as well. Duncan would be, what, twenty-five or twenty-six by now?

Second, and most unbelievably, Duncan MacKinnon was undoubtedly Graham Buchanan's son. *People* insisted the star had no family. But the resemblance was just overwhelming. And the sad little boy—Graham's *grandson*? She rubbed her temples. It was almost too much to take in.

"Duncan, meet your new neighbor." Graham looked at her quizzically. "Miss . . . ?"

"Caitriona Macleod."

"Caitie Macleod?" Graham said incredulously.

Caitie. Her mother had called her that, and the villagers had called her that, too. Her stepmother, however, had refused, insisting Cait drop the *i-e* from her name along with her other Scottish traits.

The men stared at her, gape-mouthed, in the entryway.

Finally, Graham found his voice. "I knew your mother, Nora, well." Then, a lot sterner, "Does Deydie know you've come?"

"No, but I plan—" she started.

"Are you daft?" Graham took her arm and ushered her into a small but cozy living area. "Call her." He pointed at the black 1960s-era wall phone hanging on the real-wood paneling.

Cait crossed her arms. "It's late. I've been up more than twenty-four hours. I'll see her tomorrow." Graham might be a superstar, but he couldn't tell her what to do. "Listen, I feel too wet, too tired, and my brain too jumbled to deal with Deydie. Is there a hotel in town?"

The men looked at her in disapproving astonishment, like she'd stubbornly sailed a dinghy into a hurricane. *A churlish Deydie hurricane.*

Duncan prodded her, much gentler than his da. "You must call her. She's family. You don't want her upset." It sounded like a warning, the bell of a danger buoy.

He was right about one thing: Cait didn't want to upset Deydie, the most daunting woman in all of Scotland. But there'd be no avoiding it. Cait was the prodigal granddaughter, and that was some powerful unpleasantness she'd rather face when she was dry and when her feet didn't feel like a couple of stumps in her six-hundred-dollar heels.

She tugged at her Barbour trench coat. She'd never tell them the real reason she wasn't asking her gran to put her up. *Rejection.* Cait had had it up to her wool cap with being dismissed, denied, rebuffed, and repudiated. "Tomorrow. I'll see Deydie tomorrow. Tonight, I need a hotel."

Cait got more frowning from Graham. "Gandiegow doesn't have one," he said, irritated.

"True," Duncan said with an edge of resentment. "But *he* can help you out." He gestured toward his da.

She didn't know what was going on between the two of them, but at least someone was on her side. Cait used her best downtown-Chicago scowl to stare Graham down.

Finally, Graham caved with a sigh of resignation. "If you insist on being obstinate, then you can stay in the room over the pub."

She was the one to be circumspect now. "You know this for sure about the room? Shouldn't you speak with the pub owner first?"

The men shared a knowing look.

Graham pulled the handles up on her suitcases and started walking toward the door. "Aye, you're in luck. The owner won't turn you away tonight."

Cait turned to Duncan. "It's nice seeing you again."

"Then you do remember me?" Duncan said.

"How could I forget little Dunkie MacKinnon? I used to babysit you at your grandda's house," she said.

Duncan smiled. "I remember getting extra biscuits when you took care of me."

"We'll catch up later," she said with a genuine smile, then realized that Graham was already out the door.

She stepped outside and found the rain had turned into sleet. "Lovely weather we're having."

Graham shook his head. "What did you expect? It's December in Scotland."

She felt like an idiot and pulled her lapels around her face to block out the *December in Scotland* welcome. "The rest of my bags are back in the parking lot."

"Let's get you to the pub first, and then I'll go for the rest."

"Thanks."

The conversation died, and a million thoughts converged in on her. Was this where Graham went when he disappeared for months at a time? If Duncan MacKinnon was his son, how come the press didn't know? Even more perplexing, why hadn't *she* known? She'd grown up in Gandiegow.

Cait slipped and grabbed for Graham. He dropped the bag handles and reached for her, catching her around the waist with a strong grip. For a moment, they stood toe to toe with her hands holding on to his biceps, *his made-of-steel biceps*. Time downshifted to a complete halt. Before this moment, she wouldn't have given two cents for a muscly man. In a twinkling of an eye, Graham Buchanan changed all that. She looked up into his face and turned into a hot puddle in his capable arms.

Geesh, Cait. Get a grip.

She dropped her hands, made sure she stood on solid ground and then continued on, not looking over at him. Thank God it didn't take long to get to the pub or she might have gone so far as to ask for his autograph . . . or if he needed a warm bod to snuggle up to tonight.

Graham withdrew an old-fashioned skeleton key from his coat, unlocked the door, and held it open for her. "The switch is on your right."

Her own lightbulb went on. "You're quite the joker, aren't you?" She mimicked his baritone voice. "*The owner won't turn you away tonight* and all." She flipped the switch. The place lit up with old-world ambience—all dark wood on the floor, booths, and counter. The chairs had been upended on the tabletops, and the bar and floor had been polished by Mr. Clean. It only lacked a band of rowdy Scots and it would've been perfect.

"Why isn't the place hopping?" Cait asked.

"Renovations. Tomorrow night is the grand reopening of The Fisherman." For the first time, he actually smiled. "Let's get you upstairs and dried off. Over here." He made his way past the bar to a narrow set of stairs. He had to duck his head to make the climb.

She followed him, getting a gratifying view of his man-butt in his jeans. At the top landing, she found a small hall with two doorways.

He pointed to one. "The bath's in there." He opened the other door. "The bedroom. It's not much. It should be enough for tonight, though." He frowned at her, the frown he'd given her earlier. "Are you sure you won't stay with Deydie tonight?"

She shook her head.

"Well, then, I'll be off to get your other bags." He pointed at the armoire. "Towels and linens are in there." Then he was gone.

Cait hurriedly slipped out of her ruined heels and freed herself from her coat. Her Jones New York slacks would never be the same, and she stepped out of those as well. When she dropped her tailored white shirt to the floor and stood in nothing but her lacy white bra and her French-cut undies, the door opened.

Graham stood there, slack-jawed. "I . . . I . . . just came back to tell you I'll leave your other bags out in the hall."

Bless him, he was embarrassed. But not enough to look away. He gave her underthings an appreciative nod. "I'll be going." The door shut.

Cait should've been incensed by him barging in. Instead, her belly warmed with excitement, and adrenaline made her tremble. What was wrong with her?

"What female wouldn't get a little flustered with Graham Buchanan gawking at her underwear?" she rationalized to the wall.

The mirror caught her flushed face and bright eyes. "Oh, shut up," she muttered to her reflection.

Chapter Two

Cait hurried into her pajamas, unpacked her mother's Double Wedding Ring quilt, wrapped herself in it, and reached for the *People* magazine in her bag.

The Graham Buchanan article stretched for four pages even though there was precious little information in it. The sexy actor had a penchant for disappearing for months at a time, sending the press and his fans into a tizzy. "How have you given the paparazzi the slip for so long?" she asked the handsome face so many women adored.

She'd fallen in love with him, too, back when he played the tall and brooding Mr. Darcy in *Pride and Prejudice*. More recently, he'd played Colonel Brandon in a new BBC production of *Sense and Sensibility,* and he was delectable with his long dark hair and piercing brown eyes. He was all Jane Austen's heroes rolled into one.

She ran a finger over his square jaw, strong nose, and sensuous lips. "Yummy. Too bad I'm done with men. Unfaithful dirty dogs."

She flipped the page to a picture spread of Graham at different times in his career. He wore a kilt for *Courage at Midnight*, a sharp suit in *The Last Hour*, and of course, his waistcoat and cravat as Darcy.

It hit her again. She'd found the missing celebrity. Dumb luck, but this could be the big break she'd been hoping for. The way to revive her career. A way to get back some semblance of a life.

Being a journalist had once defined her. And she'd been good at it, the youngest investigative reporter at the *Chicago Sun Times*. She never should've let Tom pressure her into giving up something she loved. She stared out the window, the last few weeks haunting her in vivid detail.

It had been surreal standing over Tom's grave with his mistress parked only a few feet away. She had been decked out in a leather miniskirt and thigh-high boots and wailed as if *she* were the long-suffering widow. As revenge, Cait had gone home and sold Tom's pristine 1968 Ford Mustang to the teenager down the street for fifty bucks. Tom should've thought twice before screwing his whore girlfriend in the backseat of the 'Stang. In their driveway, no less. Didn't he think the neighbors would notice the thing rocking like a martini shaker?

Cait massaged her forehead. Forget Tom. Forget all the other men, including her father, who'd let her down.

Some women might think the best revenge lay in spending the dirty rat's life insurance money, but more than anything, Cait wanted her career back. She could see the first headline:

DOORMAT TRANSFORMED INTO SELF-RESCUING WOMAN

Of course, the same article that would resuscitate her career might hurt Graham Buchanan and his family. Clearly, he'd hidden them away here for a reason. But in this world, it was every woman for herself, and she would be damned if she'd let a man get in the way of her career again. Before she could sleep on it and talk herself out of it, Cait plugged in her adapter and her cell, then looked up the number she'd stumbled upon and stowed a while back—the phone number for the executive editor at *People* magazine.

After two rings, a voice came on the line. "Margery Pinchot."

"This is Cait Macleod. I know where Graham Buchanan is," Cait said, feeling strong and determined and only a little breathless. "I want an exclusive, and I want a big deal."

"Tell me where he is," Margery Pinchot pressed. "I'll send a photographer to you."

"No way. I've got it covered. E-mail me a contract, and I'll send it back if it's all in order." They exchanged addresses.

"You drive a hard bargain, Ms. Macleod," Margery said in conclusion.

"You bet I do." Cait hit the END button.

Shaking just a little and ignoring her travel-weary exhaustion, she went to work, scribbling *Lost Actor Found* on a page of her notebook. She wrote as if her life depended upon it, ignoring the guilt. There was no going back now. The reporting world was small, and her name would be mud if she reneged. So what if Graham was a living, breathing person with feelings? This was the opportunity of a lifetime, the perfect way to jump-start her career. She was sick of playing Ms. Nicey-Nice.

Somewhere in the wee hours of the morning, Cait slipped her notebook under the mattress and spread out Mama's quilt, climbing underneath. She should've passed out immediately, but unfortunately, her doubts snuggled in under the quilt with her, too.

Normally, by this time of year, her house would've looked like Christmas had detonated. There'd be holly and mistletoe, bells and lights, and presents all tied up with bows. Before she'd left Chicago, the only thing underneath her tree had been pots of dead flowers from Tom's funeral. The dried petals mingling with pine needles in the carpet had been a heads-up that Christmas this year was well and truly screwed.

Just like her once promising career, now reduced to editing a beauty salon newsletter, various PennySaver ads, and the local fishing magazine from her kitchen table. How could she have gone from investigative journalism to fish guts and split infinitives? Tom, that's how. He'd wanted her home to take care of him, clean his house, and entertain his business associates. She'd given up piece after piece of herself until she was barely recognizable. Well, the article about Graham Buchanan would certainly change all that.

She smiled with hope at the dark ceiling. But as the wind howled outside, other worries floated in. After eighteen years, would her cranky grandmother welcome her back? Deydie had asked her over and over to come visit, but every time, Tom had thrown obstacles in her path or talked her out of it. Now she knew she had been an idiot for wanting to please her husband.

She pulled the covers up to her chin. Maybe she was still an idiot. Maybe she should turn tail and run back to Chicago, resume her miserable existence in her big empty house before it sold. Her cottage here was charred beyond recognition, an incinerated mess. Dead. A goner. Like her marriage. And her stupid husband.

Cait reached over and touched her mother's urn, which she'd had a helluva time getting through airport security. "What am I going to do, Mama?"

The only answer she got was sleet relentlessly pelting the roof above her head. Running away might not have fixed anything, but at least she'd escaped the coffin of a life that Tom had buried her in.

When Cait awoke, she felt better. The sun was shining high in the sky. She pushed the covers down and immediately pulled them back up. "Jeepers, it's freezing." She waited a few minutes longer, steeling herself against the bitter cold, and then reluctantly climbed out of bed.

She quickly dressed in a chocolate cashmere turtleneck, a brown plaid J. Crew blazer, tan corduroy pants, and leather boots. She still felt cold. She wrapped a coffee-colored scarf around her neck, pulled on a coat, and shoved a dark brown wool cap on her head. Now a little warmer, she went in search of coffee. At the top of the landing, she peered down.

Graham stood at the bottom of the steps, waiting. "I heard you get up." His voice sounded as comforting as the steaming mug he held.

She walked down the stairs toward him, determined that there wouldn't be a repeat of last night. No gushing over him like the president of his fan club. Cait would treat him like anybody else. He might be great looking and a movie star, but he still had a Y chromosome. She was off men, period. "Is there no heat in the pub?"

He shrugged and handed her the mug.

"Just what I needed." She took a sip, and the guilt about the article started to creep back in. Surely there'd be some cosmic retribution for outing him. He'd been nice to her. Let her stay in his pub. Lugged her gigantic suitcases through gale-force winds. And now a hot cup of java. She shoved her self-recrimination to the side and gave him the once-over, committing the facts to memory.

He looked casual in his gray wool sweater and dark chinos. He smelled great and was more handsome in the light of day than he was last night. *Un-freaking-believable.* But the way his eyes bore into her made her think he could read her every thought.

"It's two o'clock in the afternoon," he announced, his brows creasing together. "Deydie knows you're here."

"Crud."

"You'd better hurry over there," he said.

Cait heard the *or else* in his voice and thought about her gran. Was Gandiegow truly the fresh start she needed? Cait had history here. Yes, it was the last place she remembered being truly happy, but it was also the place where her soul had been ripped from her.

She frowned at Graham. "I'm not going anywhere on an empty stomach."

His eyes turned dark with warning. "Deydie expected you first thing."

"I'm sure it'll be fine." Defiantly, Cait sank down into one of the booths.

He shook his head. "It's your funeral."

"Not my first," Cait said into her mug. Then she batted her eyelashes at him. "Any scones in the kitchen?"

Graham walked away, muttering as he pushed through the swinging doors. *Hardheaded* was the only word she caught.

"I like mine warm," she hollered. She relaxed back and gazed out the window.

The wind whipped the sea into a frothy foam and sent

it crashing against the shore. Like friendly barnacles, small crofter dwellings and cottages hugged the rocky coast. A handful of boats bobbed off the long dock to the east. It all felt familiar and foreign at the same time.

Graham ambled back into the room with a plate of warmed bangers and a single scone. It hit her again how surreal this was. Graham Buchanan, her waiter. Last night, Graham Buchanan, her bellboy. What should she tip a zillionaire? He set the plate down and started to walk away.

She patted the seat beside her. "Take a load off and tell me how the fishermen are doing."

He stopped short and slowly turned, tilting his head to the side. "Why should you care?"

"It's my hometown."

Studying her closely, he hesitated a moment longer, then slid into the booth across from her. Finally, he spoke. "The village has all but died. Most people left for Lios or Fairge for work after the Great Storm. Some to Aberdeen or Inverness or farther."

Cait searched his face. "And you? Why are you here?"

He shook his head, staring out at the sea.

Dang it. She'd found Graham Buchanan, but she still didn't have the story.

He turned to her. "What will you do now that you've seen your cottage?"

She gazed out at the sea, too. "It may be a wreck, but it's mine. I'm staying, and I need your help."

He put both hands on the table. "My help?"

"The room upstairs. Let me rent it while my bungalow is being rebuilt."

"Forget it," he said ruthlessly. "Go stay with your gran."

"Can't do it," Cait shot back. "Staying with Deydie in

her one-room cottage? It won't work. There's no room for me. I won't put her out."

"But she's family," he argued. "That's what family does for each other."

She lifted one brow at him. "I'm not budging." *Besides, Gran may not want me there. That old gal knows how to hold a grudge.*

"Ye're putting me in an awful spot." His brogue got thicker as he mumbled to himself. "You are Nora Macleod's daughter." He ran a hand through his hair. "I guess if it's fine with Deydie, it'll have to be fine with me, too."

"Thanks." Cait wanted to hug him, but she stuck her hand out for them to shake on it. When his hand took hers, a warm, electric feeling spread up her arm. She'd been pretty successful at playing it cool earlier, but she was starstruck now, plain and simple. It was the only explanation for why she went all mushy and gooey on the inside when he touched her. She pulled her hand away, reminding herself that she had no use for shallow actors who went through relationships the way normal people go through a bag of Doritos.

She caught the strange look on his face and knew he'd felt it, too. *A connection.*

He rose, turning away. "Are ye ready to go?"

She stood and looked down at her outfit. "Is this good enough for Deydie?"

"What?" He sounded incredulous.

Cait put her hands on her hips. "I haven't seen her in a long time. I need to make a good impression." She smoothed down her pants. "I'd be less nervous if I were having an audience with the Queen."

He scanned her from head to toe, intimate enough to

make her insides crackle. "You look grand," he finally said with a flat frown.

She took the lead and sashayed out the door. "I bet Deydie will find something to criticize. She always does."

"Lassie, don't you think this town and her people can change?" he asked, following her.

"Not Deydie. Not Gandiegow. They'll always stay the same."

The sun from earlier had crept behind the clouds, leaving only a gray December day. The smell of the salt from the sea filled her lungs, a long-forgotten scent. They walked in silence past the storefronts. Three stood boarded up with only two still in business—the GENERAL STORE/ DVD RENTAL and the HAIR SALON/TACKLE SHOP.

A dark-haired young woman ran out and called to them as they passed. "Good mornin'."

Graham smiled and waved back.

Cait cranked her head around as the woman waved at her, too. "That's friendly," she said. "Not something you see in the big city."

"That's Amy," he replied. "One of your gran's quilting ladies."

Next came a row of homes lined up against the coast, some painted bright blue, some red, and some white, but all charming. It was a far cry from the high-rises of Chicago. She had never felt at home there, just claustrophobic. In this moment, her heart took flight and she felt glad she'd come back to Gandiegow.

Her feeling of belonging didn't last. As they treaded farther along the boardwalk, several other townsfolk waved to Graham from their doorsteps. Cait got the distinct feeling that friendly didn't quite cover what was going on here. She suspected they might be using Graham as an excuse to come out and gawk at her. Outsiders weren't easily accepted into the community. And an outsider was exactly what she'd become.

Then real apprehension set in. The closer Cait got to the end of town where her gran's cottage stood, the heavier her feet became. Her grade school teacher, Mrs. Lamont, had described Deydie as "the salt of the Earth." Cait only remembered how ornery the old gal could be. Her gran had seemed ancient back then, and she wondered what she would find now.

They reached the house, a twenty-by-twenty-foot box. Graham knocked on the short wooden door and then stood back.

Cait tried to adjust her stance to be nonchalant, but only achieved awkward.

Deydie flung open the door. "It's about damn time."

My God, she looks the same—short and squat, old and wrinkled. Cait held her tongue. She didn't dare get on the wrong side of her fierce grandmother.

Graham gestured to Cait. "I brought her 'round as soon as . . ." He didn't throw Cait to the wolves, but he did back away farther. Maybe to be out of range in case Deydie threw a ham or something in their direction.

Her grandmother peered at Cait. "Sleeping in, were ye? The day's half gone. Get in here, you two. You're letting out all the warm air." She yanked Cait through the doorway. "Graham, I'll have a word."

"I can only stay a moment." Graham ducked his head as he walked in.

Cait gazed about in wonder. It hadn't changed a bit. Two rocking chairs sat in front of the huge stone hearth. A pot of stew meat roasted above the fire, the smell so familiar and tantalizing that Cait's mouth began to water. Deydie's full-sized bed stood in the back corner layered with quilts, the best way to store the treasures. The same old sewing machine sat in the same old spot on the large wooden dining room table.

On closer inspection, Deydie had changed some. She'd shrunk to less than five feet and was a little more hunched than before. But truthfully, she looked more spry than when Cait had seen her last. *At Mama's funeral.*

Love, strong and powerful, overcame Cait, and she spontaneously hugged her grandmother. Deydie, seeming shocked and embarrassed, turned as rigid as a slab. Cait awkwardly let go.

Deydie inelegantly spun on Graham. "The path from my house to yours is a muddy mess. I told ye to put in more paving stones."

Graham looked like a scolded second grader. "Aye, I've been meaning to do that."

Deydie tapped her foot impatiently. "The bush on the east side needs replacing in the spring. Also, the baseboard heat in the kitchen is glitchy again."

Graham nodded good-naturedly, but Cait thought it odd. What right did Deydie have to speak to Graham in this way?

As if he'd read her mind, Graham explained. "Deydie watches over my place when I'm not here."

He owns a house in Gandiegow?

"The lad needs a lot of watching, too," Deydie groused, but not too unkindly.

Graham peeked at his watch. "I've got to run. A few things need doing at the pub before we open this evening." He looked conflicted. Like he hated to leave Cait and at the same time couldn't get out of there fast enough. He gave her a questioning *You-going-to-be-okay?* smile.

"Thanks for getting me here." She wished he'd stay and be her buffer. Being alone with her difficult gran wasn't Cait's idea of fun.

As soon as Graham shut the door behind him, Deydie lit into Cait. "Too good to stay at my wee place, are ye?"

Cait had prepared herself for this, but it still felt like a good whack on the knuckles. "It was late, Deydie. My plan was to get settled into my *own* house."

"Balderdash," Deydie cursed. "And that Graham. He should've made you come to me straightaway."

"Both Graham and Duncan tried."

Deydie huffed her way to the hearth. "Stubborn lass."

"You know where I get it from—from my tough Scottish gran." Cait had hoped to get at least a smile over that, but it only got her a scowl.

"Do ye want any bread?" It wasn't said sweetly like the cookie-baking grandmothers on television. More like an old grump with a granddaughter who didn't measure up.

Cait decided to accept the bread as a peace offering, although she was still full from Graham's sausage and scone. "Bread sounds good."

She took her old place at the table next to the sewing machine, where she'd sat as a child. Deydie sliced off a hunk of hard wheat bread, slathered it with butter, and set it before Cait.

"Sit with me. I've something to say," Cait said.

"I'm warming up by the fire," Deydie replied mulishly. She stared at a point just above Cait's shoulder. "I've something to say to ye, too. And I'll only say it once." Her gran paused like it troubled her to continue. "I got yere note. It's a hard thing to lose your man the way ye did. At such a young age. I'm sorry for yere loss."

Cait's throat tightened, knowing how hard it was for

Deydie to give any kind of sympathy. The old gal just wasn't that type of gran. Cait could've lied and accepted Deydie's condolence, but she had to tell the truth, no matter how painful and embarrassing. "Don't be sorry. We were getting divorced."

"Divorced?" Deydie growled the word as if Cait had blasphemed.

Cait rose and went to her gran, standing before her like a kid in trouble. She needed Deydie's support in this. "He died in bed with another woman. He'd been having an affair for months. It wasn't his first indiscretion, either."

Deydie stilled so completely she could've become one of the stones in the hearth. Finally, she spoke. "Then good riddance to him." She spat in the fire, and it sizzled.

Relief spread over Cait—Gran understood. "I've come home to stay. But I won't put you out. I've rented the room above the pub until my cottage can be repaired."

"Graham." Deydie hissed his name as if he ranked lower than a beach rat.

"He wanted nothing to do with it. I twisted his arm. I'm stubborn, remember?" Hoping to change the subject, Cait scanned the room, her eyes landing on Deydie's bed. "Show me what quilts you've been working on."

"Not now." Deydie walked away, preoccupied. "You'll be staying for supper." It wasn't a request. She went to the cupboard and pulled out potatoes, carrots, onions, and a cutting board. She set them, along with a paring knife, in front of Cait's place at the table. "Go on, now. Make them good-sized chunks to add to the stew meat."

Automatically, as if Cait were eleven again, she sat down, picked up the knife, and began peeling a potato. As obedient now as she'd been then. One of her earliest recollections was chopping vegetables for Deydie. Back then, her gran had taught her all sorts of things.

It all changed when Cait's mama got cancer. Not an instant change, but small shifts from an attentive gran who'd taught Cait how to sew, to the gran who saw only fault in Cait for looking so much like her absent father.

Deydie resented that Da's life hadn't changed with Mama's illness. He stayed in Aberdeen or Inverness, working in the law offices, returning only on the weekends. The sicker Mama got, the more Cait's father stayed gone. But that wasn't the worst part. When Mama needed Deydie most—when Cait needed her most—he'd accepted a transfer and moved them to Chicago. Only months later, Mama died, and Deydie wasn't there. He'd ripped Deydie's daughter away from her, and he'd ripped Cait from the only life she'd ever known.

Cait's hand began to shake, but she kept on peeling. She dared a glance at Deydie, who stood over the sink, talking to herself. Mostly mumbles, but a few discernible words flew out. "Misguided." "Confounded." "Devilment."

Finally, Deydie set two bowls and two spoons on the table. She stood back and openly studied her. "What have ye done to your hair? Dyed it?"

Cait held up a lock. "No dye. It's just gotten darker over the years."

Deydie made a disgusted grunt with enough vinegar to sour the whole ocean. "Your hair looks the same color as your da's."

As Cait grabbed the onion and peeled off the skin, her eyes filled with tears. She'd come home to Scotland hoping for a glimmer of the happiness she'd known as a child. Instead, she'd stepped into a nightmare. Why couldn't Deydie see that Cait was her mother's daughter, too?

With more force than she'd meant to, she brought the knife down and hacked the onion into two pieces. The floodgates opened and tears fell down Cait's cheeks, blurring her vision. She jabbed the knife into the cutting board, handle up.

Wiping her face, she got up from the table, not meeting her grandmother's eyes. "Sorry. I'm heading back to the pub. To rest. Jet lag has caught up with me." The only thing she wanted to do was to crawl under her mother's quilt and never come out.

Cait slipped on her jacket as she hurried to the door. She wasn't quick enough, though. As she went out, Deydie got in the last word, and it wasn't pretty.

"Go on with ye now. Running away. Just like your da."

Deydie crumpled into the rocking chair, the last eighteen years of bitterness, disappointment, and abandonment weighing her down. She put her head in her hands.

"I shouldn't have done it," she said to her palms. "I'm as bad as me own mother."

That wasn't necessarily true. Mother had been much more wicked, cruelly lashing out because Deydie hadn't been good enough. Even worse, Mother had taken every opportunity to criticize the village for not being as cultured as Edinburgh. Few in Gandiegow had cared when Mother had died of the fever. Mostly, they'd felt sorry for Deydie, losing both of her parents that winter and Deydie barely old enough to fend for herself.

She glanced at her bed with the quilts piled underneath the counterpane.

Dammit, she wasn't her mother. She had friends, most especially her quilting ladies. They loved her. They'd miss her. They would grieve when she passed.

Still, she shouldn't have used her own sharp tongue against Caitie. But certainly, everyone in town would agree that her own granddaughter had shamed her by not coming home when she had the chance. By staying in America even after she was grown and out of her father's house. Deydie gazed around at her meager surroundings, the cottage she'd lived in her whole life. How lonely she'd been. Not a single kinsman left in the whole world but Caitie.

"Those Americans. They love to claim Scotland as their homeland, but they're too good to sleep with the sheep."

Deydie pushed herself out of the chair to go finish chopping the vegetables. Just another meal she'd eat alone. She swiped at a tear on her old cheek.

No sense bawling over spilled milk. Soon enough, Caitie would be wanting to get back to the big city anyway, no longer the small-town Scot she'd been.

No reason to get attached to the lass again. Caitie is just passing through.

Chapter Three

By the time Graham returned to the pub from dropping Caitie at Deydie's, that gnawing feeling had returned. That woman had something up her sleeve and no one could tell him differently. It was no coincidence that she'd shown up at his son's doorstep. How had she known he'd be there? Who'd tipped her off? She had to be a reporter. His instincts were never wrong on that count. This was how he'd kept Gandiegow a secret for all these years.

Last night, he'd tamped down his suspicions. Caitie was, after all, Nora Macleod's daughter. He'd also let Caitie's bum and various distracting parts distract him. But today, when she'd refused to stay with her gran and insisted on staying at his pub instead, it all fell into place. She was a journalist out to expose him—and Duncan, and Mattie, and Gandiegow. Damn her.

Granted, staying with Deydie wouldn't be ideal, but she was family. Family came above all else. Any fool knew that. He passed by the bar and then took the steps two at a time up to Caitie's room, determined to get some answers.

Under any other circumstance, Graham believed in

the right to privacy. Especially since he'd spent a good portion of his life dodging the paparazzi. But Caitie had a sharpness about her that screamed Associated Press. And he had to find out the truth.

He reached the top landing. Maybe for a change, he'd do the rifling instead of the one being rifled through.

When he placed his hand on the doorknob, though, he couldn't turn it. Privacy was sacred, and the guilt for the crime he was about to commit felt palpable, scorched his conscience, slowed his hand, made him grimace and sweat.

But Caitie was a liar through and through. "*I'm a quilter,*" he mimicked. Like that explained everything.

He knew from his own late mother and the other village quilters that few could make a real living on quilting alone. Caitie had fed him a line of bullshit. He paid her back by turning the doorknob.

He stood there shocked. The room looked like Mother Teresa had stayed there. No clothes strewn about. No messy bed. Just a rose-lidded vase sitting on the nightstand and her suitcases lined up in the corner. His new tenant was a neat freak, and somehow this made finding the truth even harder. He didn't know where to start. As he took a step toward her luggage, the front door downstairs opened.

"Graham, are you here?" Caitie called.

Shite. He quietly stepped from the room and pulled the door closed, knowing she could hear his every creak.

He walked down the stairs, getting into character. If he couldn't pull off nonchalance, no one could. He was a bloody actor, after all. He visualized a Hitchcock scene and put himself in it. He'd disarm her by giving her an explanation before she demanded one.

Casually, he laid a hand on the bar. "I was just checking that window in your room. The seal is about shot."

She eyed him doubtfully, which he thought rivaled the pot calling the kettle black.

"I see," was the only thing she said.

Her eyes looked a little red around the rims. Had she been crying? *Bluidy reporters don't cry. You have to have a heart to do that.* He chose to ignore her damned sad eyes.

"Are you hungry?" Another misdirect on his part. "Would you like some tea or hot cocoa?"

She cocked her head to the side. "Why do you look so strange?"

He sauntered over and poured water into the coffeemaker. "I was only working on the window. I'd hate for you to get cold again tonight." He gave her his best mesmerizing smile. It usually worked like a charm, but not on Caitie.

She lifted her eyebrow as if to say his smile couldn't win over a horny nymph. "I don't want anything to eat or drink. I'm going up to lie down."

When she passed by him, he couldn't help himself. He inhaled. She smelled of the outdoors. Of Deydie's stew on the hearth. And of *woman*. God, he was in trouble. It took everything in him not to follow her up the steps to breathe her in deeper.

She turned around, and he was afraid she knew what he'd been thinking. "I'll only rest for a while. Then I want to pick your brain."

He knew it. She was here to get the story on him. He'd been right from the beginning.

But his victory was short-lived.

"I need the name of a good contractor, so I can get started on my house." She went up the steps. He stared after her, not knowing what to think now. Except he'd have to find another way to get the truth out of Caitie Macleod.

As the door closed behind Cait, she leaned against it. She could barely breathe from the polar-opposite emotions bombarding her from all sides.

Depression weighed her down. Deydie's fault.

Her heart raced. Graham's fault.

But he'd always made her heart race. Along with the other 3.4 billion women in the world.

Cait pushed away from the door and went to inspect the window. It looked fine to her, but what did she know about seals? He just seemed too casual about being up here. Even weirder, she could almost feel his presence still in the room. Or at least she could still smell his spicy cologne.

She checked for her journal underneath the mattress. Still there. She pulled it out and sprawled out on the bed. Thank God for this private space.

She wrote down how good Graham smelled. How his eyes hooded when he was up to something. How he knew and understood her grandmother, even cowering from her. Cait wouldn't fault him for that. The Hulk wouldn't be a match for Deydie either when she was in one of her moods.

Graham Buchanan was a bit of a mystery, though, wasn't he? Cait's idea for a story changed from discovering why Graham liked to disappear to what made Graham Buchanan tick.

She heard the door downstairs slam and voices rise up to her. Pretty soon pots and pans clanged in the kitchen. She scooted down further in her bed and closed her eyes.

She wouldn't let Deydie or Graham get to her. Tomorrow would be better. She couldn't expect her prickly gran to change. It was up to Cait to repair their relationship. She'd screwed up today and she'd just have to try harder tomorrow. The wind howled outside and Cait drifted off to sleep.

Cait jumped awake as soon as the bagpipe bellowed its first wailing note. The window shook, and the floor shuddered. She felt dislodged from her senses, not completely certain of where or who she was. When the next note ripped through her, she slipped on her shoes and went downstairs to rip the bagpipe player a new one.

When she got to the bottom of the steps, she couldn't believe her eyes. The pub was packed from front to back and side to side with unruly Scots. Standing on a chair by the door was the man playing the pipes, Mr. Graham Buchanan himself. He had on a black Balmoral cap, an ancient Buchanan plaid kilt, and a codpiece, big and shiny. His eyes were closed as he started the next song, "Amazing Grace." The men in the pub removed their hats and sang along.

Unwilling to interrupt the song played at her mother's funeral, Cait sat on the step and listened to Graham execute the melody with depth and soul. As if he'd been cued, when he hit the last note, he found her with his eyes.

He seemed to twinkle all over and to be on fire at the same time. Strange, he didn't look like the actor anymore; he looked even more alive. She'd found another piece to the puzzle that was Graham. This was his town, his people. He was at home here. They could turn out the light and the room would be sufficiently lit with Graham's glow.

He laid the pipes in the chair and came straight to her.

She wished she'd at least run a comb through her hair or checked for smeared mascara before barging down the steps.

By the look in his eyes, he didn't care. "Did you rest well?"

His words brought her back to her chief complaint. "Yes, until you decided to go all *Brigadoon* on me."

"I don't get to practice much. It's against the rules at my flat in Glasgow."

"Sorry. Can't hear you." She put her hands to her ears. "I'm a bit deaf at the moment."

"Very funny, you. How about a drink? It's on the house."

"It should be," she hollered above the growing noise of the crowd.

She followed him over to the bar, where he pulled out a bottle of Scotch.

"Local stuff?"

"Only the best. MacPherson over there has a distillery near Fairge." Graham poured them both a glass, then held his up to MacPherson in salute.

She stared at the golden liquid, a little skeptical.

"Just down it." He tipped his glass up and it was gone.

She did the same, knowing enough about whiskey to not let it stay in her mouth too long. It tasted smoky and immediately warmed her down to her toes.

"Nice, huh?" He poured her another and she drank that one too.

He had one of those smiles that made a girl woozy. Or it could be the first effects of the whiskey.

Graham handed her another drink. "You wanted to talk about contractors? Sinclair by the back table there, he's our local craftsman. Do you want me to introduce you?"

"No." She downed the next whiskey. "I'd like to see his work first. Which houses has he worked on?"

"The Ramseys', the MacGregors', the other Ramseys'. And of course my house. Would you like to take a look at mine?"

A naughty thought skipped across her brain and warmed her down in her belly. "What?" It took a second to realize he wasn't propositioning her. "Your house. Yes, great."

"Get your coat."

"Now?" she asked. Not to look a gift horse in the mouth . . . but why was he being so congenial? Did he have an ulterior motive for getting her alone?

Like he'd read her mind, he gave her a look of complete innocence. "Bonnie has the bar under control."

Cait moved her eyes to where he looked. A thirtysomething blonde in need of a breast reduction glared back.

Graham put his hand on Cait's back, ushering her to the stairs. "Get a move on. The snow is really coming down."

Bonnie shot her some serious stink-eye daggers, so Cait hurried past her and up the stairs.

When Cait got back from bundling up, Graham was waiting, bundled up himself. He held the door open for her. A blizzard blew outside, the snow coming down almost sideways.

She braced herself and stepped outside. "Bonnie is your barmaid?" she shouted over the gale.

"More than that. She's the pub's manager," he shouted back. "Takes care of things while I'm gone."

"And while you're here?" The scowl on Bonnie's face made Cait wonder if Bonnie was taking care of more personal matters for Graham.

"She takes care of things while I'm here, too."

I bet she does. "What things?" Cait couldn't help asking.

He stopped, and she thought he had a weird look on his face. "Pub things."

She wanted to ask if that was all. But didn't. They walked on.

"The pub is my way of giving back to the community," he added.

They slipped and slid along the path, the snow making it treacherous. At one point she had to hang on to his arm to get over a bit of ice. She got to feel his rock-solid biceps again. And she liked being that close to him. It made her feel safe.

As they approached her gran's house, guilt surfaced. Cait really should stop and see how Deydie was doing. But Graham led her up a path behind Deydie's house. They climbed and climbed up the narrow winding path until they stood in front of a stone mansion.

"You've got to be kidding me." She pushed past him to get a better look. He'd built his place next to the ruins of Monadail Castle. "I played here as a child."

He gestured to the door. "Go on in. I'm off to get a few logs for the fire." He left her and went around the side of the house.

When she stepped inside, it was like walking onto the set of a BBC Scotland film—the dark wood, the ornately carved twin staircases, and the huge coat of arms at the apex.

An old sable sheltie wandered in from the other room with its tail wagging.

Cait squatted to greet the dog. "Well, who are you?"

Graham came through the same doorway as the pooch. "That's Precious, my best girl."

"Well, of course she is," Cait said as she gave the dog a good scratch behind the ears.

Graham got in the dog's line of sight, and Precious lit up. Her backside wagged so hard, she almost knocked herself off her feet. "She's fourteen, just about deaf, but I love her all the same. Come here, girl."

Cait stood back and watched with fascination as Graham took Precious into his arms and murmured sweet nothings into her perked-up doggie ears. *Mr. BBC actually has genuine emotions.* Huh. What would Cait do if he spoke to her like that? Would her tongue hang out, too?

Envy rose inside her. Even the pooch got more love and attention than Cait. She was utterly alone. Cait rubbed her hand over the cool stones on the wall to divert her thoughts and keep herself from sinking into a deep depression.

Graham finally looked up. "Come into the parlor and get warmed up by the fire."

She followed close behind him into the room. "The house is fabulous. I'd love to take some pictures."

He stilled and gently set Precious on the floor. The dog walked over to the fireplace and lay down on the big fluffy bed by the hearth.

"No pictures." Graham's words sounded as immovable as the stone wall she'd touched moments ago.

She frowned at him. "I only want to get some ideas for my own cottage."

He turned to face her. "No. This is my sanctuary. The town is my haven. And my son is my business alone, no one else's."

"Quite a lecture, but what's that have to do—"

He turned away. "No, and that's the end of it."

God, how she hated getting cut off. Tom had perfected it, dismissing her out of hand, and she had lived with it for eight long years. Eight years of him telling her what she could and couldn't do. Because of his edicts, she'd tanked her career and emptied her life of all her close friends. Cait mulled it over in her alcohol-fuzzed brain for a few moments and came to a conclusion.

No man would issue orders to her ever again. Never ever.

Graham slipped off his jacket and hung it over a chair. He went to the antique dry bar in the corner and pulled out two crystal tumblers. While his back was turned making their drinks, she pulled out her phone, clicked off the flash, and took a few discreet pictures of the crown molding, the massive stone fireplace, and one or two pictures of Graham's derriere just for the heck of it. She had her phone back in her coat pocket before he had time to say *That's the end of it* again.

He handed her the drink. "Would you like to see the rest of the house?"

She was still angry with him, but not drunk enough, or fool enough, to miss taking advantage of this moment. "Of course." She took a sip.

Graham placed another log on the fire and reposi-
tioned the screen. "Let's go."

Precious got up to follow them.

"You stay here, girl, and keep warm by the fire." The
dog reluctantly lay back down.

"This place is huge. How many bedrooms?" she asked.

"Eleven. They're nothing special. I'll show you the
main floor, though."

He took her through each room—the professional
stainless-steel kitchen, a small bedroom off the kitchen,
the huge dining area, the library, and a peek at the media
room. She wished she could take more pictures. But as
she followed him from room to room, her irritation with
him faded. It was either the drinks she'd had this evening, or the fact that his voice soothed her into forgiveness. By the time they'd made it back to the parlor, she
felt all warm and cozy. He took her glass and poured her
another one.

"Let's sit by the fire and you can tell me all about
yourself." He looked like the perfect gentleman, but he
could as easily have been the devil for the captivating
look he gave her. He pulled two plush armchairs to the
fireplace, set the bottle between them, and pointed to
where she should sit.

After settling in, she stared at the crackling fire and,
unfortunately, the old dark thoughts crept back in. Suddenly, Cait was back in primary school, her mother recently diagnosed with cancer. She knew what cancer
meant, even at nine years old—Death. And it seemed
everywhere she looked, she found it. The dead bird lying
on the path to school. Billy Kennedy drowning at sea.
And every Sunday, Jesus Christ hanging from the cross
in the stained-glass window at church. Cait couldn't run

away from Death, so instead she had walked toward it to get a closer look. When Mrs. Lamont told the class to memorize a poem, Cait picked "The Cremation of Sam McGee." When she recited the ode to flames and Death to the school, Mrs. Lamont had been both astonished and alarmed. True, most fourth graders weren't obsessed with Death like Cait. But who could blame her?

Graham touched her hand. "Are you okay?"

She pulled it away. "Fine. Why would you ask?"

"You look sad, that's all. Like you'd lost your best friend." Graham glanced down at Precious at his feet.

"It's nothing." It felt like a betrayal, making light of Mama like that, so she told him the truth. "I was only thinking of my mother."

"She was a fine woman, Caitie," he said. "It was a sad day when she left us."

"Tell me how you knew her." Cait's eyes filled with tears.

"She took charity upon me and my da after my mum died. She made sure we were fed during our grief. Organized the village ladies for meals. She made sure I went to church and properly dressed, too. She had sweetness in her. And a bit of the sass, too."

Yes, her mother had had sass. Once, Mama had threatened Da with the business end of a frying pan for tracking mud on her clean floor.

Graham poured them both another drink and lifted his glass. "To Nora Macleod."

"To Mama."

They downed their Scotch.

Cait lost track of time as they laughed about Deydie's cutting remarks and sour looks. Graham opened another bottle, wine this time. They joked about Gandiegow—

how time had stood still while the rest of the world had whirled out of control. He leaned in closer. The coziness of the fire and the old dog at their feet made her feel like they'd known each other for years.

"Would you be more comfortable on the couch?" he asked.

"You're so nice to me." She stared into his lovely eyes.

"Maybe I want something from you," he said.

Her inebriated brain thought he sounded serious. "Surely you're not talking about something naughty?" She reached out and brushed a lock of hair off his forehead. It was nice touching him. He was quite the hunk. And because she could, she went ahead and ran her hand through his hair to the back of his head.

His eyes lit up.

Or it could've just been her imagination.

She slid out of her chair and made her way to the overstuffed sofa. She wanted to ask him something but couldn't remember what. She felt so tired that she lay down. It must've been all right with Graham because he came and sat on the floor near her head. She couldn't keep her eyes open. Right before she drifted off to sleep, she heard him speak, but it didn't make any sense.

"Why are you really in Gandiegow, Caitie Macleod?"

Cait had died. Or at least she wished she had. She tried moving an eyelash, but it hurt too much. An oversized pumpkin had grown inside her head and wanted out.

For a long time, she lay as still as she could, hoping the pressure would go away. After a while, a slow realization hit her.

A warm body lay next to hers. She put her hand out

and touched warm fur. *Precious*. Cait stroked the dog and was rewarded with a gratified groan.

That's when she noticed a movement on the floor below her. She reached over and touched Graham's hair.

Shouldn't the dog be sleeping on the floor and the handsome man be in her arms? Story of her life. Ass-backwards.

From nowhere, a broom hit Cait's backside.

"Get up, you ninny," Deydie shouted. "Why in damnation are ye sleeping in a strange man's house?"

Chapter Four

Ah, bluidy hell. Graham sat up and scrubbed his face. "Seriously, Deydie, a strange man's house? Everyone in the free world knows me."

Damn. He rarely referred to his notoriety. He turned to Caitie and she stared back at him.

He hadn't gotten what he wanted from her last night—answers. He wasn't a single step closer to finding out why she'd landed here. But from the Internet, he'd learned she was a summa cum laude graduate of one of the most prestigious journalism schools in the world. If she wasn't up to something, why would she lie and say she was a quilter? Absurd. Who has a career in quilting? Nobody, that's who. She was a bluidy reporter.

Deydie brought him back to the problem at hand by swatting him with her blasted broom. "That's for taking advantage of my granddaughter," she said.

Caitie's mouth dropped open, and a nice pink blush colored her cheeks as she looked both incensed and ashamed.

"She did nothing wrong," Graham defended, even though she didn't deserve his help. "If anyone took advantage of her loving arms..." He scratched Precious behind the ears. "It's my unfaithful dog. Deydie, you've clearly ruined Precious against male companionship. She used to only sleep with me."

Cait pushed herself to an upright position, her quizzical gaze boring into him.

He explained. "Precious is too old to go on location. When I'm gone, she stays with your gran at her cottage."

"Damn dog's a flea-bitten nuisance." Deydie held her expression as stiff as her broom handle.

"You're not fooling anyone, old bird." He ducked as Deydie took another swing at him.

"Yere sass will get you in trouble one day, wee Graham."

He gave Deydie his best devil-may-care grin. "Until then, how about some breakfast?"

"Get yere arse up and get it yereself." Deydie huffed from the room.

The old gal loved it when he teased her, and he loved her back, regardless of her biting personality.

Cait scooted to the edge of the couch. "You're lucky she didn't sweep the floor with you."

"I can handle your gran." He wasn't nearly as certain he could handle her granddaughter. Caitie looked irresistible this morning, all mussed up. It gave him a glimpse of what it must be like to wake up next to her after a night of rolling around in the sheets together. He got to his feet, nuzzling Precious on the way. Fortunately, or unfortunately, depending on how one looked at it, his nose got close enough to catch another whiff of Caitie. Last night's whiskey wasn't nearly as intoxicating as the pheromones she gave off now. Dammit, he needed a distraction.

"Here." He offered his hand to help her off the couch. "I'll whip us up an omelet."

She ignored his hand. "Another time."

He pulled it back and jammed it in his pocket. He had been raised to have good manners, but women like her didn't appreciate them. It infuriated him. He actually worked hard at being a nice guy. Just last month, *Us Weekly* named him Nicest Man in Show Business. But he wasn't feeling it now. "Something better to do?" It took everything in him to keep the words from coming out as a jeer.

"I have to get ahold of that darned Realtor," she said. "I need to talk to Mr. Sinclair about my house, too." She adjusted her sweater, and it caught his attention, giving him a better idea of the lay of the land under there.

She paused. He looked up to find her giving him the *eyes-up-here* glare and she went on. "The sooner I get my house rebuilt, the sooner I'll be out of your room above the pub." She rose without his help. "Thanks for having me over."

"Another time?" He echoed her words back to her.

She narrowed her eyes. "We'll see."

He needed answers, sooner rather than later. The only thing he'd gotten from Caitie last night was companionship. As great and unusual as it had been for him to spend an evening in lively conversation with a cute, brown-haired firecracker, he hadn't gotten to the truth. It rankled, so he tried another tactic. "How about this afternoon? By the dock. The sun sets at three thirty. I'll bring food."

She shook her head. "Seriously, a picnic? Do I look like a polar bear?" She leaned down and slipped on her boots.

He snatched up her parka as if to take it hostage. "What kind of reporter turns down an offer to spend time with a missing screen idol?"

She stilled at his words. *Aha, got you, Caitie Macleod.*

She pretended to adjust her boot, avoiding looking at him. "I don't know what you're talking about. I told you I'm a quilter."

"Aye. And I'm a bluidy fisherman."

She took a deep breath and finally faced him. "I really must go."

"Yeah, I'm sure there're some urgent quilting matters awaiting you." He held open her coat for her, like a gentleman ought to do. But with her, he felt more like a rogue. As he slipped the coat over her shoulders, he leaned down and whispered in her ear, "If it's any consolation, I enjoyed sleeping with you."

Gooseflesh rose up on her creamy neck. He'd gotten to her, and she couldn't deny it, even if she wanted to.

Ah, hell. A lot of good it'd done. Turning her on had turned him on as well. He couldn't stop himself. He breathed her in and felt a little drunk all over again.

She whipped around, finger raised, snarkiness smeared all over her face, ready to give him a piece of her mind.

But before she could, he dropped one of his disarming smiles on her. Like an anvil. She stopped. Oh, yes, he knew all about disarming women. He spoke with the consistency of honey. "Why, Caitie Macleod, your eyes have grown to the size of camera lenses."

"Oh, you. You . . ."

He smiled because Miss Smart-Mouth Reporter couldn't think of a single comeback.

Like a skittish doe, she lurched for the door.

He let her go. Though it amused him to have an effect on her, the truth was, he wasn't immune to the effect she had on him.

He remembered her mother, Nora, a mixture of kind-hearted and stubborn. Caitie was so much like her. Graham couldn't reconcile the things he liked about Caitie with the idea that she had come here to expose him—his treasured slice of normal life, his family, his town, Gandiegow.

Alone, he went to his laptop and flipped it opened. He had to take precautions. Caitie was attractive, but she might be poisonous as well. Although he couldn't stop thinking about her wrapping herself around him, in the end, he'd prove what she was all about.

As Cait rushed off the bluff back to the pub, her headache increased in size. Last night's alcohol couldn't take all the blame. Her gran's surly temperament had Cait's head close to cracking wide open now. Even more disconcerting had been the rapport between Graham and Deydie. Cait wondered whether she'd ever be as comfortable with her own grandmother as Graham was. How had he done it? How had he endeared himself to the prickliest woman alive?

More unsettling yet was how gorgeous Graham looked this morning—his rumpled hair, the splash of stubble on his face, and that sleepy-eyed look he'd given her. He'd had her close to forgetting the promises she'd made to herself—to never be a man's pawn again.

She'd come to Scotland for a fresh start, not to share a morning omelet or have a cozy picnic by the sea. She'd given up on men. Given up the heartache. Finished with unfaithfulness. Men were dirty, lying bastards, and she had washed her hands of the lot of them.

But instead of being professional and viewing Graham as nothing more than an assignment, she'd let the lines blur between herself and Mr. Gorgeous. She had to rectify that immediately. Any moment now, she'd put aside that off-kilter feeling and kick back into reporter mode. She *would* get the story.

Cait quickened her pace along the path but couldn't outrun the thoughts that chased her. How Graham's breath on her neck had turned her insides into a mushy plum pudding. How the grin he'd given her as she'd left his house had scorched her. Not like burned toast. Or a match that had sizzled and gone out. Instead, it felt like her silly heart had wrapped itself around the wrong end of a hot poker and had gotten itself branded.

When she got back to her room, she forced herself into journalist mode, feverishly writing down everything she'd seen and heard since last night. Graham's mansion, his dog, Precious, how cozy it'd been in front of the fire, how her gran was his housekeeper, how he had a way of teasing Deydie that made her seem halfway lovable. These were all sides of Graham Buchanan that the rest of the world couldn't possibly know. She returned the notebook to its place under her mattress and grabbed her cell phone, ready to deal with the Realtor.

Of course the woman claimed to know nothing about the cottage fire and seemed relieved when Cait said she would keep the house—after an eighty-five-percent reduction in price.

Cait bundled up for a walk and went out. A good granddaughter would be headed off to Deydie's, but Cait didn't have the strength to deal with her gran right now. Besides, Deydie was probably still at Graham's.

Outside, it was gray and bitter. Cait had hoped to make it out to the end of the dock to get a closer look at the sea, but the spray had turned the wood planks into a dangerous icy lump. She stood back and gazed from a distance. She wished for a calm sea to calm her, but it churned violently, definitely unhappy. An angry Christmas sea.

Of course, there would be no tree for her little pub room. No twinkling Christmas lights. Her typical Christmas feast a bust. No husband. No happy family.

Christmas will be peachy, just peachy.

She'd probably spend it with Deydie, sitting by the fire drenched in one of her gran's heartwarming scowls. Cait glared at the sea, and on a childish whim, she flipped it off. "Thanks for nothing, and Merry Christmas to you, too."

She needed chocolate and went to the store to find it. The same young woman from yesterday, the one who'd waved to her, stood behind the counter and chattered away about the latest weather report, how the grand opening of The Fisherman went last night, and how Cait must love to quilt like her gran. Cait didn't get a word in edgewise.

Chocolate in hand, she left the store and walked along the boardwalk, past the other businesses, past the one-room schoolhouse. As if an invisible hand reached out and blocked her path, Cait hesitated outside Saint Henry's Episcopal Church. Darn its bright white exterior and its jutting steeple. As a child, Cait had kneeled and prayed here at the kirk. A good little follower of the faith. But then God took Mama and Cait had a falling-out with the Big Guy. Well, not a falling-out exactly, more like a parting of the ways.

Cait touched the church's door. It hummed with warmth and invitation, but she knew better. A bait and switch scheme. Lure in the sheep and then mow them down with a sickle. She wouldn't be sucked in again. Deliberately, she turned away and trudged back to the pub.

At the top of the stairs outside her room sat a box, the first of her things to arrive from Chicago. This one she'd marked specially: SEWING MACHINE. She carried it into the room, carefully set it on the bed, and pulled out the projects she'd shoved around it to protect her Viking machine.

A nagging feeling tugged at her. She could've sworn it came from the direction of the box. "Fine." She pulled out the machine. "I'll take you to Deydie's, but prepare yourself for some serious unpleasantness."

Cait put on her coat, jammed one of the sewing projects into her pocket, and picked up her machine. When she headed downstairs, the place was again crammed with Scots, but there were no bagpipes and no Graham. A bit of disappointment came over her. She ignored it and slipped out the front door into the cold. It wasn't snowing tonight, but it was bitter. She walked hurriedly toward her grandmother's. Apparently, the business owners had been hard at it this afternoon—multicolored Christmas lights glittered on storefronts, wreaths hung on doors, and garlands, like festive snakes, had wrapped themselves around streetlamps.

Cait sighed and trudged on, trying to outrun the thought of Christmas.

When she got to Deydie's cottage, a front window stood propped open. Crazy Scots, insisting on having a wee bit of fresh air regardless of the weather. Cait heard women laughing inside.

Deydie's irritated voice rose above the others. "Me granddaughter is too good for an ole fishwife like me."

Another woman spoke. "Don't take it personal. I hear American girls are independent sorts."

Cait crawled closer to the window, set her machine on

the ground, and peeked inside. Deydie and three other women sat around the big wooden table, some with sewing machines in front of them, others stitching quilt blocks in their laps.

"A decent girl would've been here with her gran." Deydie harrumphed. "The pub indeed."

Cait lost her footing, slipped on the ice, and knocked over her sewing machine.

"What was that?" came from inside.

Cringing, Cait quickly squatted down, trying to become invisible.

Moments later, an old woman peered out the window and found Cait huddling below the ledge. "I'm thinking your granddaughter has arrived. Come in, wee Caitie."

Deydie swung the front door open. "What the devil?"

Cait stood with as much dignity as she could muster. She wiped off the snow, grabbed her sewing machine, and turned to her badger-faced gran.

Deydie waited in the doorway with her hands on her massive hips. "Why are ye skulking outside me house?"

The others moved forward, gathering around the door. "Come in."

"Get out of the cold."

"We'll make room for ye."

Cait knew what they really meant. *Give us a closer look. We'll judge for ourselves whether you're as bad as Deydie says.*

Even though Deydie was frowning with more vigor than one person ought to be capable of, Cait stepped through the doorway into the overly warm room.

One woman took Cait's sewing machine. Another got a towel and wiped it off. A third made room for Cait at the table. She recognized several of them.

"Go stand by the fire and get warm," said an older woman with the same gray braids wound around her head from when Cait was young.

"Mrs. Lamont?" Cait said.

"Well, of course it's me. I'm still Gandiegow's teacher. But now that you're grown, you must call me Rhona."

"Hi, again." The girl from the shop stepped forward, eager as a puppy. "I'm Amy, remember? I saw you in the store today. I'm from Fairge. I married Coll last spring. He works at the pub. Have you met him yet? Can I get you something to drink?"

Cait wondered if Amy ever stopped for breath. Before she could answer, her grandmother jumped into the fray.

"Caitie's not staying. I'm sure she's got *more important* things to do."

Bethia, Deydie's oldest friend, cleared her throat in warning. "Of course she's staying. She brought her sewing machine." Bethia had withered considerably since Cait had seen her last. But when she finished giving Deydie the *what for* by way of a killer glare, she turned to Cait and smiled, transforming herself into a younger woman. "We get together several nights a week here at your gran's. She has updated electric."

Amy started jabbering again. "My auntie says, 'The more the merrier.' We always have tons of goodies to eat."

"There's always room for one more." Bethia put her arm around Cait. "Ye'll stay. Your gran wouldn't have it any other way."

Not agreeing or disagreeing, Deydie plopped down at the table and started up her sewing machine.

Amy handed Cait a mug of spiced cider. "Sit by me. I sit near the end."

"No," Bethia said firmly. "Caitie will sit next to her gran."

Deydie made a guttural noise akin to a harpooned fish.

Amy happily pulled a chair to the opposite end of the table. "The other three won't make it tonight." She picked up Cait's sewing machine and plugged it in. "What did you bring to work on? I'm making a lap quilt for my auntie. It's a Churn Dash."

Cait didn't know who the *others* were that Amy referred to but pulled her project from her parka anyway. "A potholder."

Deydie *hah*ed loudly.

Rhona put her hand out. "May I?"

The potholder made the rounds, each of them having an opinion: "So many small pieces." "Ah, this is lovely." "It reminds me of yere mother's fine work."

Cait had started it for Deydie for Christmas, her first attempt at making a miniature quilt. She'd assumed Deydie would appreciate that it was both pretty and functional. Wrong again.

When the potholder made it to Deydie, she gave it a cursory glance and then set it aside. Rhona shrugged at Cait sympathetically. "Take your place and get started." Her old teacher patted the chair between her and Deydie as if to say, *I'll be right here beside you.*

Cait threaded her machine, made sure the potholder was lined up correctly, and pressed the pedal. It felt great to be sewing. But she didn't get to do it in peace for long.

"I heard you had a sleepover last night," Amy said.

Cait choked on her own breath and stopped sewing. Everyone in the room sniggered, except for Deydie.

So they'd heard. Small towns were exactly as the

world imagined. Everyone mucked around in everyone else's business. Even in Scotland.

Deydie muttered. "Only in town ten minutes and the girl's sleepin' around like a—"

Bethia cut her off with a *tsk-tsk*.

Amy piped in cheerfully. "I saw you leave with Graham from the pub. I was helping Coll with the sandwiches. Graham put his hand on your back as you walked outside. Are you two—"

"Heavens, no!" Cait shifted uncomfortably in her seat. "I just met him."

Bethia said, "And yet you stayed the night with him."

Cait turned off her machine and gave them her full attention. "Listen. I drank too much and fell asleep on his couch." She turned to her grandmother. "Tell them, Deydie."

Her gran remained mute for so long that Cait wondered if her tongue had been sewn to the roof of her mouth. Finally, Deydie begrudgingly set them straight. "'Tis true what she says." She looked as if she'd downed curdled milk. "Caitie was not in his bed, but on the couch, the dog with her. Graham sound asleep on the floor, *the hound that he is*."

Cow-eyed and gushy, Amy laid her chin in her hand. "Will you be seeing him again?"

Cait huffed, sounding surprisingly like an exasperated Deydie. "Of course I'll see him again. Gandiegow is a small village."

"What we want to know is—" Rhona struck her teacher's pose. "What are your intentions toward Graham?"

Bethia laid her hand on the table, kind of like a judge bringing down a gavel, soft but firm. "He's a son of Gandiegow. No different than if he were me own. It's our job to keep a lookout for him. And Duncan and Mattie. That's why Duncan had the MacKinnon name from the start and not Buchanan. To protect him—and now to protect Mattie. 'Twas Graham's mother's surname. We'll not let any harm come to our own."

Deydie bore down on Cait like a freight train running over an injured dog. "We know ye're a reporter. We'll not be lettin' you hurt Graham. Do you ken?"

As if Cait had dunked her head into hot bubbling stew, heat flooded into her face. *Did they find out about* People *magazine and what's written in my notebook?*

Amy's voice was all sunshiny. "Don't take it personally. They warned me, too, when Coll brought me to Gandiegow after we married. I can't even tell my own auntie about Graham. Deydie threatened to beat me with a broom if I breathed a word to anyone. And, of course, if I didn't treat Coll right."

"And I'd do it, too." Deydie smiled at Amy.

Something in Cait's heart squished together. Deydie's snaggle-toothed grin. When was the last time she'd seen her grandmother smile? Before Mama got sick? Anger surged up inside Cait. Why in the hell did Amy, a chirpy motormouth, deserve Deydie's affection and Cait didn't?

Maybe she'd been too boneless to stand up to Tom and come for a visit. But leaving Gandiegow hadn't been Cait's fault. Gran needed to get over it—quit blaming her and stop acting like Cait had had any say in the matter.

Unlike now. Now it was her choice to write a piece on Graham. After the article came out, well, then she *would* be blameworthy—the village villain.

The tarlike sticky feeling of guilt coated her insides.

Deydie ought to save up her nastiness for later, when she would actually have good reason to dislike Cait.

"Are you planning on coming to the pageant, Caitie?" Rhona asked, her tone a one-eighty from moments ago. "It's next Wednesday night. The children are so excited."

The conversational shift threw her off-balance. But not as much as the flashback that came on its heels, hitting hard enough it would've knocked most women from their chairs.

Her last Christmas in Gandiegow, she'd played Mary sitting in the manger with Donald Elliot as Joseph. She'd loved wearing the white cotton panel over her head and the blue robe. But that's when Jesus had been her friend and she'd been honored to be his mother, if only for an hour. Cait shook off the feeling because it wasn't true anymore.

"Caitie?" Rhona said.

"Yes, Mrs. Lamont, I'll be there."

"I told you to call me Rhona. Makes me feel decrepit when a grown woman calls me 'Mrs.'"

"Yes, ma'am."

Thankfully, the conversation turned away from Cait and onto the gossip of the village. Amy gave a blow-by-blow account of everything she'd heard at the store and the pub. The rest of them commented on the comings and goings of Gandiegow. Relieved not to be asked more questions, Cait worked silently on her potholder.

At five minutes to nine, the quilt ladies packed up their projects, their machines, and notions. As Cait did the same, Bethia came to stand by her.

"Leave your machine on the table," Bethia whispered. "It'll do your gran some good."

"But—"

"She needs a part of you to stay here. That way she'll know ye'll be coming back."

Cait had always thought of Bethia as a wise woman and trusted her judgment. What she didn't trust was her gran. She wouldn't put it past Deydie to chuck her very expensive machine in the sea as soon as Cait was gone.

Cait hurried up and slipped into her parka, not wanting to be the last one out, left alone with Granzilla. She said goodbye to them all, including Deydie, who only snorted and rolled her eyes. Cait opened the door, fled the warmth of the cottage, and got the hell out of there.

Deydie watched her quilting ladies go and shut the door behind them. That all-too-familiar lonely feeling hit her right in the chest. She'd lived alone a long time but had never gotten used to the long nights. Blast Hamish Mc-Cracken! He'd taught her to love and then got swallowed up by the sea, leaving her to single-handedly raise their little daughter, hardheaded Nora. But then Nora had left her eighteen years ago, and the loneliness had become unbearable, a constant thorn pricking her heart—morning, noon, and night. Deydie needed her quilting ladies like she needed fresh water. Of course, she'd never let them know that. The minute you admit out loud you need someone, that's when they up and disappear at sea or die of some hellish disease. No, they were better off thinking she didn't need the lot of 'em, not one tiny bit. And she didn't. Not really. Not much. After all, she had her fire to keep her warm.

She shivered and shuffled around the table, righting it for the morning. But stopped.

Caitie, the little devil, had left her fancy sewing machine.

Deydie slowly made her way over to it, planning to set the blasted thing in the corner, or even better, outside in the snow—anywhere out of sight would do. But as she stood over the machine, she noticed that Caitie had left her work. Deydie grabbed the potholder to get a better look.

It was exquisite, the postage-stamp-sized pieces in a Colorwash pattern that took her old breath away. Nora's fine, detailed craftsmanship had been passed down to her daughter. A bud of pride welled up, and try as she might, Deydie couldn't squash it down.

She gently set the little masterpiece back where Caitie had left it and decided not to toss the extravagant machine in the corner after all. She left it on the table.

But she couldn't look at it all night either, so she grabbed a clean dish towel and threw it over the confounded machine. When Deydie crawled into bed, snuggled under the stack of quilts, and switched off the light, the moon shone through the window. Its rays lit up Caitie's covered sewing machine and the strangest thing happened.

Deydie didn't feel quite as lonely as before.

Chapter Five

On the way home from Deydie's, within a few yards of the pub, Cait heard footsteps running behind her. She whirled around and found Graham, winded.

"Why the hurry?" she asked.

"It's Precious." Worry lines etched Graham's forehead. "I've got to find Doc."

Her heart went out to him. "What can I do to help?"

"Come with me," he said.

They rushed into the pub together and found Doc waiting on his drink. He wore the same square spectacles Cait remembered, but the years had turned his hair shock white.

Graham grabbed Doc by the arm. "Precious is sick," he said, his Scottish burr thick with panic.

Doc laid a bill on the bar and grabbed his ever-present medical bag from the seat next to him. The three of them were off, the snow crunching under their boots as they rushed back through town and up the bluff.

"She wouldn't eat breakfast," Graham said. "And I couldn't get her to drink anything all day. She just lies there. No matter how much I coax."

"This happens with old dogs," Doc soothed, his voice as comforting as a quilt.

Graham wasn't consoled, though. "What can we do?"

"Let me examine her first," Doc said.

They hurried into the mansion, Graham and Doc not even stopping to remove their boots. Precious was lying on her big fluffy pillow in the parlor. When she saw Graham, she raised her head slightly and wagged her tail once. Her head dropped back down as if the weight of it were simply too much. The yearning in her eyes said she wanted to get up, but she didn't have the energy.

"See, Doc?" Graham paced back and forth. "She looks all wrong."

Doc bent down and checked her eyes and belly and listened to her heart. Finally, he rose, laying his hand on Graham's shoulder, not meeting his eyes. A subtle shake of his head brought the angel of death screeching into the room.

"No." Graham shook his own head as if to counter Doc's prognosis.

"You need to prepare yourself, lad." Doc's hand fell away.

"No," Graham said again, quieter this time.

Doc nodded in the way that old men do—patient, tired. He seemed to know enough about Death to know how this dance played out. "I'm sorry, lad. Precious has had a long life. Longer than most dogs." He pulled a vial from his bag. "Give her a drop every hour for any discomfort."

Graham didn't say a word, only nodded his head—a man adrift in a life raft, alone and vulnerable. Cait knew what he was going through, and she didn't want to be there. It felt damned uncomfortable.

Death had been her lifelong companion, but that didn't mean they were friends. Friends shared common interests like gossiping over coffee, shopping for shoes, or constructing the perfect quilt. Death was only interested in causing misery, anguish, and isolation. Death gripped anyone hanging around and doled out lasting sadness and pain.

Doc left, and they were alone.

Cait knew what was coming next and she wanted out. But at that moment, Graham took her hand. *No!*

"Glad I don't have to do this by myself."

But wasn't that the point? Death epitomized loneliness.

He squeezed her hand.

Crap. She had no choice now but to stay.

He let go of her and sat down next to Precious. Those little doggie eyes lit up with complete love and devotion. He unscrewed the lid on the vial and squeezed a drop of liquid into her mouth. "There you go, girl. It'll make you feel better."

Reluctantly, Cait sat down on the other side of the fluffy pillow to keep vigil with him.

Graham put his hand out, and Precious licked it. He tilted his head to the side, his eyes going soft with an old memory. "She was the size of a softball when I got her. All fur. I'd made up my mind to get a blue merle from the litter, but this sable fur ball kept tugging at my shoelaces, trying to get my attention. I picked her up, and that was it. I was in love. She was such a good girl—cute, funny. Never gave me a minute's trouble."

"I can tell." Cait reached out and stroked the dog.

Precious's eyes moved to Cait, then back to her master.

"I couldn't have asked for a better friend," he said, caressing the dog.

It was silent for a few moments, and Cait couldn't stand it. "You said you took her on location, filming." She hoped it was the right thing to do, to keep him talking.

"Aye. She went everywhere with me." Graham smiled. "I even took her to the Oscars. When this obnoxious reporter bent down to pet her, she tried to take a chunk out of him. I gave her extra treats for that one."

They stayed like that for a long while, making a circle with their bodies around Precious, as she labored to breathe. Graham told more stories, his brogue getting thicker with each one. He got up periodically to put another log on the fire, and every hour he gave Precious another drop from the bottle.

At three thirty A.M., Cait awoke. She reached over and laid a hand on Precious. Her fur was warm, but Cait couldn't feel her diaphragm moving up and down, no more air flowing in and out.

The dog was dead.

Graham leaned over and kissed Precious. "Goodbye, girl." His voice cracked, and he pulled in a couple of deep breaths.

A familiar smell reached Cait's nose. The smell of Death.

Graham swiped away a tear. Cait handed him a tissue.

For a long time, they sat on the floor next to Precious's body, both of them silent. Both of them tangled in their own thoughts.

Cait had been alone with Mama when she died. Her father was at work, and the nurse had gone to the kitchen. Cait was sitting next to Mama's bed, working on a quilt block for her while she slept. Without warning,

Mama gasped and jerked. She didn't open her eyes; she didn't say goodbye. Death, the bastard, had strolled into the room and snatched Mama right from under Cait's nose.

Cait looked over at Graham. He wasn't shaking Precious's dead body, screaming for help, or looking as if the walls were closing in on him. He appeared at peace.

He patted Cait's shoulder, then rose. From the sofa, he removed the lap-sized Jacob's Ladder quilt and carefully spread it on the floor. He picked up Precious, who'd started to stiffen, held her close, and then laid her body in the center of the quilt. He wrapped her up gently, lifted her, then carefully rose to his feet.

Still in unchartered waters, Cait followed him up the stairs and into his room—a funeral procession. He put Precious on his bed and laid his hand on her once again. Maybe to make sure she was really gone.

"She was a good dog." His voice was thick and jagged. "I'll take her to Doc when the office opens and have her cremated." He paused a moment longer over the Jacob's-Ladder-quilt bundle.

Cait leaned against the doorjamb, not knowing what to do now. Go? Stay? Death was a lonely business, but grief was damned awkward. Surely, Graham would want to be alone, lick his wounds in private.

He trapped her with four little words. "I'm glad you're here."

God, what could she do now? "Me, too," she finally answered.

He switched off the light and closed the door. She followed him downstairs to the parlor. For several minutes, he stood over Precious's bed, looking at it as if it were a hollow casket. Once again, she didn't know what to do.

How was she supposed to ease his grief? No one sure as hell had ever done it for her. Out of sheer desperation, she wrapped her arms around him, hoping to console.

They stood for a long time like that, holding each other. Finally, they went to the sofa and stretched out together, lying quietly, not speaking. After a while, they both fell asleep.

Cait woke suddenly with Deydie standing over her with her hands on her hips.

"And here ye are again, Caitie Macleod. Do you not care about yere reputation and yere virtue? Ye're as loose as a kindergartener's front tooth. Why aren't ye in yere own bed? Ye do have one, don't ye?"

Cait nodded.

"Then use it," Deydie commanded. "Have you seen that damned dog? I've looked everywhere for her."

Graham gave Cait a sad, knowing look. He got up and went to Deydie, placing his hands on her shoulders. "We've some bad news. You'd better sit down."

"What are ye yabbering about? If you mean to tell me you've had yere way with my granddaughter and she might be in the family way, I've no need to sit."

"It's about Precious." Cait tried not to chew on her lower lip.

Deydie squinted hard at Cait, her mouth riveted shut in an iron frown.

Graham gently squeezed Deydie's shoulders. "Precious passed away in the night."

Deydie's face contorted as if squished between a young child's hands. She pushed away from Graham. "I don't believe ye. Precious? Precious?" she called out.

He looked helpless. "She's gone. I laid her upstairs on my bed."

Her gran bustled away and up the stairs. Moments later, Cait heard the initial sob. Deydie hustled down and out the back door.

"I have to go to her." Cait grabbed her coat.

Graham reached out and clutched her arm. "Your gran wouldn't want it."

"I don't care." Cait tore out the door and down the path.

When she caught up with Deydie, she tried to put her hand on her shoulder. "Gran, wait."

Deydie hurriedly swiped at her eyes before turning to Cait. "Get away from me. I don't need ye. Why don't ye go back to where you belong?"

She might as well have slapped Cait in the face. Her grandmother propelled herself down the path, her large hips bouncing from side to side.

Cait wiped her tears. Gandiegow had promised to be her haven, not her hell. What would she do now?

Graham caught up to Cait. "Your gran didn't mean it. It's the grief talking. Give her time, but not too much. Then go to her, and be with her, whether she wants you to or not."

Graham came back from Duncan's house feeling restless and uneasy. Duncan had taken the news of Precious well enough, but something wasn't right. He was off. He seemed so tired these days. Graham knew that raising a boy on his own wasn't easy, but he worried it was something more.

Everyone in Gandiegow helped with Mattie, babysitting while Duncan made a living on his boat, fishing. If only he could find a wife for Duncan. But few women wanted to live in a secluded village on the northeast coast of Scotland. Mattie's mother had only stayed long enough to drop him off. Graham paced the parlor. He would have to step up his efforts to find Duncan a wife. A fisherman needed help—backup—couldn't be a single da and all alone.

Caitie Macleod came to mind. She loved Gandiegow. She'd shown what a good heart she had by the way she'd handled Precious. Caitie had a nice smile. *An even nicer body.* She smelled like the ocean and spring all at the same time. Being nestled up beside her all night had soothed Graham—she'd been a balm for his grieving soul. She had a lot of good attributes and would make a fine wife.

For Duncan, Graham reminded himself. As soon as he uncovered the secret Caitie was hiding, he would see about bringing them together.

So why couldn't he imagine Caitie with his son, or with anyone else for that matter?

Graham had to put his mind on something else. He grabbed his phone and called his agent.

"Sid, it's Graham."

He held the phone away from his ear while Sid shouted obscenities— Where had he been? Why hadn't he told him he was disappearing again?

After a minute, Graham interrupted Sid's tirade. "I haven't missed any contractual dates. Do you still want me to do the RSPCA public-service announcement or not?" It would be a nice way to honor Precious's life.

Sid gave him an exasperated "Yes."

"I'll be in London by tonight. Keep it low-key," Graham ordered. "No press this time. No stunts." He hung up.

He was too restless to stay in the house, and it was too early to go to the pub. Unless it was to see Caitie. But she was probably napping after their long night.

Graham decided to go back to Duncan's and put up the Christmas tree with Mattie. *Just Grandda and grandson.* Let Duncan rest; give him a breather.

Graham pulled his collar closer around his neck and stared out at the sea. Yeah, he'd be helping Duncan, but he wasn't kidding himself. Right now, he needed them more than they needed him.

Chapter Six

Two hours later, Cait stomped back to the pub. *Things just keep getting better and better.* The meeting with Mr. Sinclair about her cottage hadn't gone as expected. Sure, demolition could take place right away, but most of the rebuilding wouldn't start until spring. Something about concrete not setting up when it's cold, wood and stone orders, and the difficulty of bringing in day laborers from Fairge and Lios this time of year. *Christmas!* Cait wanted to scream it into oblivion. Instead, she marched up the pub stairs and slammed the door.

Where was Graham when she needed him? If he were here, she'd at least have somebody to talk to, a friend who'd listen while she griped, and a shoulder to lean on. And he could lean on hers, too.

She paced about, her emotions bouncing around like racquetballs, battering her insides. Each new thought of Graham caused another jolt. She needed sleep. Instead, she yanked her notebook from underneath the mattress, but found she'd filled it up. She dug out a new one.

Cait wrote down everything that had happened with Graham and Precious and Deydie. Cait was one of those journalists who had to put pen to paper before putting fingers to keyboard.

Her article about Graham had grown into a novella. She flipped through the pages, cringing, feeling awful about betraying him. But writing this story was her salvation, her way back to real journalism and her way out of her dead-end job of freelance editing. Wasn't it more important that she recover her identity, her *self,* than for some bigwig actor to hide out? Yes. She'd submit the story to *People* magazine as promised, and then she'd be able to write her own ticket. Maybe get a regular feature in one of the big magazines.

She lay back on the bed and stared up at the ceiling, the whole room accusing her of being a traitor and a weasel. The more she got to know Graham, the harder it became to separate her personal feelings for him from the business of selling his story. She rolled over and began sifting through her notes of what she'd learned about him so far.

She had a hard time reconciling the Graham she'd discovered here in Gandiegow with the one she'd seen on the big screen. He'd always stayed at arm's length from the media, not a real person but a superstar living a charmed, glamorous life surrounded by a bevy of beauties—usually one on each arm and a few following behind. Here he was an everyday guy who loved his dog, cared for his neighbors, and hurt just like the rest of the world. Just like her.

Damn. It wasn't as if she were one of those slimeballs who'd chased Princess Diana to her death. She'd just be letting the world in on where he hides out. Cait rammed the pages under her mattress and grabbed her coat. She had to get out of here and regain her journalistic perspective, take a walk and clear her head.

The late-afternoon wind barely registered as she tramped along, not getting perspective at all, but worrying about Graham's grief. She found herself walking down the boardwalk, past the businesses, toward his home on the bluff. But outside Deydie's house, her feet stopped.

No windows stood open this time, but there was a light on inside. Cait recalled Graham's advice not to let Deydie be alone for too long. She looked out to the horizon for guidance.

It seemed more enticing to dunk herself in the wintery cold sea than to deal with her frosty grandmother right now.

She kicked a clump of snow. Graham was right. Deydie needed Cait whether the old woman knew it or not.

Cait knocked and waited, hearing slow shuffling steps on the other side of the door. When Deydie opened it, her gran had a crisp clean apron wrapped around her wide body, an irritated glower on her face, and a gleaming butcher knife in her hand.

Cait had seen this movie. It didn't bode well for her, but she pressed her luck anyway. "Let me in. I'm not selling vacuum cleaners or encyclopedias."

Her gran rolled her eyes and stood back, making room for Cait.

The first thing Cait noticed was a green-and-gold Christmas dish towel draped over her own sewing machine. For a moment, she felt her insides went marshmallowy, thinking her normally prickly gran had laid the towel there to protect her prized possession. When she turned to thank her gran, the frown inhabiting every nook and cranny of Deydie's wrinkled face convinced Cait that first thoughts were deceiving.

Her grandmother laid down the knife and put her hands on her hips. "Are ye here to help or not?"

Silence ensued. Cait had no idea what Deydie wanted help with—doing away with one of the neighbors? Gingerly, Cait asked, "Are you feeling better this evening?"

Deydie's jowls folded together, making a menacing grimace. "I don't know what ye're talking about."

"This morning. Precious—"

Deydie grabbed the knife again and jabbed it into the butcher block. "Either help with the supper or go back to the pub."

"Help," Cait said. "I'm here to help." She took her place at the table.

"Good. The chicken's not going to cut itself up." Deydie plopped a metal pan in front of Cait, a scrawny raw chicken lying inside.

Cait hadn't touched a whole chicken since she'd last been in Scotland. Boneless, skinless breasts, perfectly carved and wrapped in plastic, had been the closest she'd gotten to poultry in close to two decades. She peeked at the bird in the pan. This one looked freshly dead, with a couple of feather shoots poking off the wings, the last remnants of life.

Cait stalled, going to the sink, desperately hoping to find a way to tell Deydie she didn't know her way around a chicken. She'd have to be delicate about it or risk losing a wing herself.

"Hurry up. We need to eat before we go. The cookie exchange starts at seven."

"Cookie exchange?" Cait asked.

"Aye. My quilting ladies have one every year at Christmastime." Deydie went to the refrigerator and dug around.

"But I wasn't invited."

Deydie came out with a dozen leeks and a sack of onions, looking chagrined. "You were. I must've forgotten to tell ye. It's at the twins' house this year. Before you go arguing that ye have no cookies to bring, I've made yeres." She straightened up her hunched shoulders. "No more talking. If that chicken isn't in the pot in the next five minutes, ye'll have to go on an empty stomach." Her gran's frown shifted upward for an instant, almost into a furtive smile.

Cait washed her hands and dried them. "About the chicken," she hesitated. "I don't exactly remember how, uh, to dismember one."

With Deydie's half smile gone, her frown reached new heights of scary. "Do ye not have birds in America?"

"Our chicken is prepackaged at the grocery store. Already cut up."

Gracefully, Deydie grabbed the chicken by the back leg. In one smooth motion, she reached for the butcher knife, pulled it from the block, and sliced where the thigh met the body. With a snap, she cracked the thigh bone out of the socket and cut it off the carcass. With another precise placement of the blade, the thigh and leg fell away like friends who'd parted forever. She did the same with the other leg and went to work on the rest of the bird. Part butcher and part Iron Chef, Deydie had that chicken begging for mercy and in the pot within minutes.

Her gran looked up at her. "Chop the vegetables. Surely, they don't have those prepackaged, now, do they?"

No way would Cait admit to buying precut vegetables back in the States. She picked up the paring knife and grabbed the leeks off the counter, settling herself at the table, near her gran. But not too near.

They both filled the cast-iron pot with their fare and then sat by the fire while it cooked. Cait wanted to ask her grandmother what she'd done today, how she'd passed the time, but knew it wouldn't do any good. They sat for a long time with the only conversation between them bubbling in the cooking pot.

There was a knock at the door. Cait got up and answered it, expecting one of the quilting ladies. It was Graham.

He gave her a sad sort of smile. "Hallo," he said.

Deydie shouted from her rocking chair, "I'm not heating the entire coast, Graham. Get yere arse in here."

Cait waited for him to obey before asking, "How are you doing?"

He only nodded, as if the jury were still out on that one. He turned to Deydie. "I came to tell you I'm off to London for a few days. Can you watch things at the house?"

"Of course. I always do," Deydie barked. She pushed out of her chair and shuffled to the refrigerator, retrieving one of the baker's boxes from the top. She gave it to Graham. "Some Christmas shortbread for the trip."

"Thanks. I do love your shortbread." Graham gave her a peck on the cheek.

She batted him away. "Off with ye."

Cait couldn't believe the things Graham got away with. Deydie would've taken the butcher knife after her if she'd tried to give her a kiss.

As Deydie made her way back to her rocking chair, Graham and Cait had a scrap of privacy.

"Did you stay busy today?" she asked.

"I put up Duncan's tree. Then, Mattie and I went to the store and bought candy canes." Instead of Graham looking like he'd had some early Christmas cheer, he seemed bone weary. He might as well have been grave digging all day.

She wanted to reach out and take his hand but couldn't with Deydie only a few feet away. "Will you stay for dinner? I'm sure there's plenty, and Deydie won't mind."

"Can't. The helicopter's on its way. I've already said goodbye to Duncan and Mattie." Graham directed his next comment to Deydie. "Can you check in on Duncan while I'm gone?"

Cait piped in first. "I can do it."

Deydie growled at her. "Do ye believe me not capable?"

Cait cowed. "What I mean is that I'll help. You do so much already." Why did her gran always think the worst of her?

"I really appreciate it." Graham surprised Cait by taking her hand and squeezing it. He gave her a killer smile, looking as genuine as the Rolex on his wrist.

A rush of gooey warmth flooded her, melting her, and she wouldn't have been surprised if she'd dissolved into a squidgy puddle on Deydie's clean floor. Cait had the urge to recite poetry. Cuddle by a romantic fire. Walk hand in hand forever.

Ridiculous drivel. Those thoughts were completely nonsensical. She didn't trust men. Didn't believe that the whole lot of them could be depended upon for anything. Especially to be loyal and faithful. It was stupid to get caught up in Graham's spell. He didn't mean anything by squeezing her hand or *GQ*-smiling at her, except maybe a little gratitude for her offer of help. She couldn't afford to be dumb enough to put her heart in danger again, chance getting it sliced up into pieces, just like Deydie's scrawny chicken.

Cait dislodged her hand from his. "Don't mention it."

He ran his hand through his hair, hesitated for a moment, then slipped a key into her hand. "It's to my house," he murmured. "The electric at the pub is atrocious. You probably have a laptop or cell phone that needs charging. Come and go as you please."

She frowned at him. Did he always go around giving his key to someone he just met? She could be with the paparazzi for all he knew, could take advantage of this situation.

She peered at the floor, the thought hitting her like a story hitting the presses. Two days alone at his mansion. At liberty to ransack his place, dig up all sorts of dirt.

Excitement pumped through her veins. She could investigate the things readers really wanted to know— skeletons in the closet, hinky old tax returns, and of course, the answer to the age-old question: *Boxers or briefs?*

He tipped her chin up and looked her straight in the eye. "Stay there. The pub is loud and cold. The alarm code for the house is seven one one. No one here would ever try to break in, but I worry about the press finding me." He did it again, that troubled expression crossing his face. "It's the least I can do for you. For all you've done for me and Precious and for offering to help my family." It sounded more like, *I'd better not regret trusting you.*

Guilt washed over her, but she tried to keep it from

engulfing her face. She took the key. The way he stared at her lips made her wonder if, or worry that, he might kiss her there and then. But he snapped out of it quick enough when Deydie unceremoniously cleared her throat.

"I'll be off." He turned and was gone.

When Cait returned to her rocking chair, Deydie was eyeing her like an ace detective. "What was all that? My ears might be old, but I'm not deaf."

"It was nothing." But it was. Cait would stay at Graham's. She'd get her story, guilt be damned. After a time, the townsfolk would forgive her for exposing their favorite son to the world. They'd see that one little story wouldn't change anything. It'd be a big deal for all of two days; then Gandiegow would be back to normal.

Wouldn't it?

Holding the box of shortbread close to him, Graham walked toward the beach as the helicopter drew nearer. He almost hadn't given Caitie his house key, feeling a twinge of guilt about the surveillance cameras he had up and running. But he had to know. He'd find out once and for all if he could trust Caitie Macleod.

Trust was key. If he could trust her, everything would fall into place. Caitie would make a good wife—for *Duncan,* of course.

The helicopter blades beat the wind into a fury, the latest snow flying all around him. He did know one thing for sure about Caitie. Most people didn't see *him* for *him*. His fans saw him only as a cutout from a movie poster. The London and Hollywood crowds saw his fame and fortune. Gandiegow saw him as their favorite son.

But not Caitie.

Caitie saw *him*.

He wouldn't let himself go there. He didn't need a relationship. His chest hurt just considering it. *Besides, Duncan needs someone more than I do.* But something niggled at him just the same.

Ah, hell. He just might want to keep Caitie Macleod for himself.

Chapter Seven

Cait adjusted the large box holding all of the cookie exchange containers and tromped behind Deydie in the snow. "You really should hold on to my arm for support," she hollered.

Deydie kept right on walking. "Mind yere own business, *city girl*. I'm doing just fine up here."

As if her gran had willed it, Cait slipped and shuffled. Deydie harrumphed, and for a second Cait wondered if her gran wouldn't stand there and watch as she dropped everything. But then Deydie helped her get the big box settled.

Cait glanced over at her as they continued on. "I don't know what I'm going to do with eight dozen cookies."

"You have friends, don't ye? Send them back to the States."

Cait wouldn't tell her the truth. She had nobody. Under the weight of Tom's demands, she had let her friendships slide away into nothingness. How stupid that had been. What the hell had she been thinking?

They stopped in front of a two-story stone house, one of the larger ones in town.

Deydie held up a gnarly hand. "A word of warning

about the twins. They're a mite strange, but good quilters."

They didn't have to knock. The door flew open, and Christmas music floated into the air. *Let it snow, let it snow, let it snow.*

"Glory be, the newcomer is here," said one of the two women at the door. She was wearing a goofy smile, a green plaid wool dress, and an elf hat on top of her 1960s bouffant. "Come in."

"Come in," the other one parroted, looking identical in features and wearing a matching red plaid dress and a red elf hat.

They ushered Cait in, one taking the big box, the other peeling off her coat. The twins were a bit overwhelming for Cait. She looked to Deydie for buoyancy, but her gran just ignored her.

"I'm Ailsa and this is my sister, Aileen." The first twin extended her hand to Cait. "We're Harry Elliot's nieces. He left us the—"

"House, when he passed ten years ago," Aileen finished.

Cait imprinted their names and their dress color to memory. *Ailsa green. Aileen red.*

The two matronly twins pressed close to Cait while a third woman hung back in the hallway.

Ailsa *green* grabbed Cait's arm and pulled her forward, more toward the heart of the house. "This is Moira. She said you might remember her." Ailsa *green* turned back to the shy, mousy woman. "You said you were, what, two years younger than Caitie Macleod?"

"Aye." Moira looked down at her boots.

Cait recalled her from school—a tall, plain girl who

was so shy she would never meet anyone's gaze. Cait didn't know if small talk would make Moira more comfortable or if ignoring her altogether would be better. "It's good to see you," she tried.

No response, as if her shyness had powers of its own, weighing her eyes down, keeping them glued to the floor.

Cait tried again. "It's been a long time. What have you been up to?"

"Up to?" Deydie snarled as she took off her coat, her pitch rising with each word. "She's been a dutiful daughter, taking care of her sick da. That's what she's been up to."

Moira's cheeks turned a deep red, darker than the Turkey Red quilt on the wall.

Cait's gut took the punch of Deydie's message. *Cait— not devoted like Moira. Cait—neglectful of her family, just like her da.*

Bethia made her way into the hallway and took Deydie's coat. Her kind eyes met Cait's. "Moira's mama had an accident and left us three years ago. Last May, Moira's da got his leg caught in the fishing lines. They had to take it off. He fights infection to this day."

The Christmas music was now playing in the background. "Silent Night" might have been soothing, but to Cait it felt like she'd climbed into a fricking nightmare. Gandiegowans led a hard life of death, illness, and obligation.

"Da is better today," Moira offered, fumbling with a length of garland.

"You're a good girl, Moira." Deydie patted her. "God be with ye and yeres." She gave her a wink. "Now, help me find the whiskey." She toddled off with Moira leading the way.

Bethia took Cait's arm. "Don't let it worry you. Yere gran can be testy at times. Sometimes, ye just have to love her regardless."

"Yeah, like loving a surly pit bull."

Bethia laughed. "Now ye have the right end of the needle."

Before Cait made it down the hallway where the festivities seemed to be, Aileen *red* had come back with a glass of punch for her.

"Just a warning. It's a wee bit strong," Aileen *red* said, her eyes noticeably glassy.

Cait downed the glass. It burned like a son of a bitch, but she welcomed it. Just what the doctor ordered for dulling Deydie's accusations. "I need another."

She followed the noise into the parlor, where a roomful of familiar faces milled about—Rhona, Amy, and Bethia, all the quilting ladies from before, and now Ailsa, Aileen, and Moira. Deydie seemed in her element as the queen bee, with all the ladies surrounding her.

Chestnuts roasted in the inglenook fireplace, and the mantle was decorated with real pine boughs and holly. Instead of twinkling lights, there were beeswax candles. A big Christmas tree sat in one corner, decorated with paper chains and tartan bows. Under the tree lay a quilted tree skirt with the nativity scene in appliqué.

Ailsa *green* tottered over to Cait, apparently a little tipsy, like her sister. "I see you noticing our handiwork."

Cait bent to examine the fine workmanship. "It's beautiful. The stitching's unique—little pine cones. I've never seen anything like it."

"Our signature stitch. Aileen and I invented it when we were teenagers. It goes into all our quilts."

Aileen *red* called out from the cookie table. "Ailsa, come here. You have to see this."

Cait walked with her. The dining room table was stacked with boxes of cookies, each person's grouped together — fancy red ones, plain green ones, blue snowmen, gold plastic containers, all sorts. Aileen *red* stood over one of Deydie's boxes.

Cait looked inside and gasped. "They're exquisite." Deydie had made heart-shaped shortbreads, the top half of each heart decorated with what looked like a delicate string of Christmas lights. Cait gaped at her grandmother.

"'Tweren't nothing," Deydie grumbled.

"It's art," argued Cait.

"What else did you bring?" Aileen *red* opened another box from the pile.

Inside were little individual cheesecakes with a cherry on the top. Cait's mouth watered just looking at them. She'd grab those for herself.

"I knew you could bake, but I sure don't remember these," Cait said.

"There's a lot of things you don't know about me, Caitie Macleod." Deydie huffed away to the side bar, where the finger foods sat.

Using her eyes as laser beams, Cait glared at Deydie's back, hoping to scorch a little niceness into her crotchety old head. *Fat chance.* Ebenezer wanted to completely humiliate Cait in front of her friends. Why? Because Cait refused to stay at her cottage? Deydie should just get over it. It was Christmas, for chrissakes. A holiday truce wasn't asking too much. Couldn't her gran be pleasant for one evening?

Soon Deydie had more than sipped a bit of the juice.

She'd tied one on. She wrangled poor Moira into dancing a jig to "Rockin' Around the Christmas Tree." Deydie had a drink in one hand and a little sandwich in the other, her dress bobbing up and down like a plunger in time with the music. Amy joined in by singing along, a little off-key.

Bethia took a seat in one of the chairs by the fireplace.

Cait joined her. "Deydie seems to be enjoying herself." She said it with more attitude than she'd intended. But dang it, Deydie had bruised her feelings twice since they'd gotten there, and now the old grump was jigging it up like a longshoreman on payday.

"Aye. But would you have your gran moping in the corner instead?" Bethia scolded. "Your gran has had a hard life. At fifteen her parents died, leaving her all alone in that cottage. When Hamish McCracken came along, thinking Deydie hung the stars and moon, I thought her luck had changed. What a hard thing it was when Hamish was swallowed up by the sea, and Nora only three at the time."

"I didn't . . . I mean . . . I never knew." Cait felt the heat rise into her face. She knew Mama had grown up without a da, but no one had ever talked about it. The pain must've been too much. And to think Deydie had been waylaid by Death, too. All alone just like Cait. She hadn't realized the two of them had so much in common. "I'll try harder not to take her jabs so personally."

Bethia patted her hand. "That's a good lass."

Cait spent the next couple of hours working at *enjoying* herself. She let Amy pull her into a long conversation about the comings and goings at the store, which wasn't too bad. Amy's constant chatter was starting to grow on Cait; plus she learned more about the people of the town. Then Ailsa and Aileen took all the ladies on a tour around the house, pointing out their handiwork, most of them appliqué quilts, all of them works of art. Later, she sat with Rhona and Bethia, talking about quilting.

"Freda Douglas asked again if we'd let her join our quilt group," Rhona said.

"'Tis a shame." Bethia shook her head, her old brown eyes sad. "I always say there's room for one more and there isn't really."

"Why?" Cait asked.

Bethia answered. "We don't have the space at Deydie's. We sometimes quilt in Graham's dining room, but it's not the same. And even then, not everyone can join us who wants to. We just don't all fit. Besides Graham's house, Deydie has the only updated electric."

"Aye, Graham saw to that," Rhona added.

"Graham?" Cait questioned.

"He made sure Deydie could have friends over to sew. He worries about her being lonely." Rhona answered matter-of-factly, without a finger of accusation.

Just the same, shame poked at Cait. Hard. What did it say about her if a neighbor cared more about her grandmother's loneliness than Cait had? She mentally kicked herself in the butt for being the all-time loser of granddaughters.

And Graham. Cait didn't know if she liked him *more* because of his thoughtfulness or hated him because he'd done something she should've known to do.

Cait resolved right then and there that Deydie, despite her lean toward unpleasantness, would come first. Cait would spend so much time at the cottage that her gran would be sick to death of kin. Cait would just have to grow a thicker skin to deal with Granny Vinegar.

"Bethia, we should get Caitie involved in the round-robin quilt," Rhona said.

Amy joined them. "What a good idea. The theme is Our Town Gandiegow. You know how a round robin works, don't you? Each one of us sews one row for the quilt. I'm doing a line of paving stone blocks that will be between Deydie's house blocks and Bethia's ocean."

Bethia patted Cait's hand. "We do a quilt every year and auction it off at the Valentine's Day Céilidh, party and dance. Usually draws a hundred pounds. We give the money to the Lost Fishermen's Families Fund."

"Only a hundred pounds? That's highway robbery," Cait said, flabbergasted. "A handmade quilt for that?"

"We're a small village with small means. A hundred pounds is a lot of money to us."

If they'd been back in the States and had the right press, they could get ten times that.

"Will you help, then?" Amy asked.

"Sure. What's left to do?" Cait said.

"The bluffs," Bethia replied.

Rhona gave her a conspiratorial grin. "Aye, the bluffs. You'll have to piece something together for Graham's house, now, won't you, wee Caitie?"

At the sound of a commotion and a shriek, Cait looked up in time to see Deydie grab Ailsa's green elf hat, shove it on top of her own white-haired head, and hustle away.

"Give that back," Ailsa cried. "I'm going to wear it Christmas Eve, when the Urquhart twins come over from Fairge to have dinner."

Bethia sighed. "I think it's time you took your gran home."

Cait followed Bethia to where Deydie played keep-away.

"It's getting late," Bethia coaxed. "Cait will walk you home. I'll pack up your cookies so you can get going."

"Party pooper," Deydie cackled, making everyone laugh.

Cait had never seen her gran like this—carefree and having fun.

Her gran made one more attempt to dodge Ailsa, then finally gave up, shoving the green hat back on its owner's head with a loud "Ha."

As Cait and Deydie went out the door, the quilt ladies serenaded them with "We Wish You a Merry Christmas."

Cait couldn't help but smile as they slipped along the boardwalk. It'd been a nice Christmas party. And in the last couple of hours, no one had died within Cait's immediate vicinity. Old Man Death must be taking a snooze.

When they got to Deydie's house, Cait planned to drop her grandmother off, then go up to Graham's place and start snooping.

But Deydie had different plans. "I expect ye'll be staying." She flipped up the quilts on her bed and pulled out a full-sized trundle. "But first we'll be having ourselves a wee bit of a nightcap."

Cait felt completely confused. Earlier this evening, Deydie had been as disagreeable as a rabid dog, and now she was as playful as a puppy, whistling and clogging to her own tunes. And what about the story Cait was working on? What about combing Graham's house for tidbits and essentials?

The promise Cait had made to herself earlier, the one where she'd vowed to spend every spare moment with

Deydie, felt pretty damn burdensome right now. But it did have her answering her gran. "Of course I'll be staying."

"Good. Then get on to making that nightcap." Deydie went to her rocking chair and creaked back and forth, singing quietly "What Child Is This?" and looking younger and happier than Cait had ever seen her.

Chapter Eight

When Cait woke the next morning, Deydie's bed lay empty and she was nowhere in sight. For a moment, Cait worried her gran had wandered off in the night but then remembered Deydie had duties at Graham's house.

Cait quickly made the trundle bed, sparing a moment to admire the workmanship of the counterpane—a Grandmother's Flower Garden quilt, all hand sewn, using 1930s-vintage fabrics. She slid the trundle back under the bed, deciding to make tea in the pub's kitchen because she needed some things from her room.

When she stepped outside the cottage, she was unprepared for the snow that had fallen by the shovelfuls during the night. She fretted over Deydie coming back down the bluff but saw that the pathway leading up to Graham's had been cleared and salted. But no one had cleared the walkway back toward the center of town, and for Cait, it was slow going. Before entering the pub, she kicked as much snow from her boots as she could. She went directly into the kitchen and put a kettle on to boil. A small flat-screen TV hung near the chopping table. Cait turned it on.

And there was Graham, a media storm over his arrival in London. Even though he smiled graciously, a darkness in his eyes told her he was pissed, close to murdering whoever had ratted him out. Good thing he didn't know she was a journalist, else he might put her on the chopping block when he returned.

Cait filled a mug with the boiling water and dropped in a tea bag.

"Graham Buchanan arriving on the scene after a two-month disappearance. Might I have a word, sir?" The reporter pressed a microphone in Graham's face.

"I'm here to do a public-service announcement for the RSPCA, who are working on the Five Freedoms for animals through legislation," Graham said.

If she were the reporter, her next question would be to ask what prompted this public-service announcement. And why now.

The one-track-minded reporter tried again. *"Yes, but where have you been? Your agent had no comment as to your whereabouts."*

"Sorry, mates. This is my stop." Graham disappeared into the RSPCA building.

Cait lifted a mug to Graham. "Nicely sidestepped." Then she felt guilty for what she planned to do to Gandiegow's superstar. It would definitely knock the air from Graham's sails when he found out she was writing a piece on him. He'd never trust her again. Their comfortable friendship would be dead.

But Cait had to take care of getting her life back on course first and squashed any doubts she had about doing the story. For a moment, she worried his London appearance would affect the salability of the exposé to *People,* but she put the thought out of her mind. Everyone knew Graham disappeared, but no one knew to *where.*

She switched off the TV and went upstairs only to find the hallway nearly blocked with her boxes delivered from Chicago. She wished she'd remembered to talk to Graham about some storage. One by one, she carried each box into her room, stacking them against the wall. When she was done, there was little room to move. She changed into a camel-colored sweater and chocolate wool slacks, then located her tan mittens and matching cap. Before walking out, she grabbed her cell phone and charger, hoping to plug it in at Duncan's house. If not, then at Graham's later.

When Duncan answered the door, he looked paler than the last time she'd seen him. She stepped over the threshold. "I came to play with Mattie and to give you a break, if that's okay."

"My da sent you?" Duncan asked, recrimination in his voice.

"Not exactly. But I'm sure Deydie will be by to make certain you men have enough to eat," Cait said.

"She dropped a stew by first thing this morning," he replied. "I'm glad you're here, though. I planned to leave Mattie at the store with Amy, but he's coming down with a cold."

"Are you getting it, too?" Cait asked.

"No," he said. "But I do need to get going. I have to pick up my da's Christmas present. It'll be my only chance."

"Would you like me to make you some tea before you go?" she asked. "Or are you a coffee man?"

"Aye, coffee." Duncan ran a hand through his hair, looking just like Graham. "You do know that Mattie is mute, don't you? He doesn't speak."

No, she didn't know. And by the I-really-don't-want-to-talk-about-it expression on Duncan's face, she shouldn't ask either. "Don't worry. We'll be fine together," she said.

Six-year-old Mattie peeked around the corner with an old man's somberness masking his child's face.

Duncan walked over and squatted down in front of him. "Caitie is an old friend. I knew her when I was your age. Go show her where we keep the traveling mugs while I get my coat."

Cait followed Mattie into the kitchen and saw a sink full of dirty dishes staring back. The boy pulled out a can of coffee from the fridge and pointed to where the cups were. She quickly got a pot going.

Duncan came in just as she filled his mug. "I won't be long," he said. "My mobile number is on the refrigerator."

"Speaking of mobiles, can I charge my cell here?" Cait asked.

"Make yourself at home. I gave Mattie a dose of cold medicine an hour ago. He should be fine until I get back." He ruffled Mattie's hair. "You help Caitie, son."

Mattie nodded solemnly. Duncan kissed the top of his son's head and walked out the door.

Because Mattie didn't know her, Cait expected to see trepidation on his face. Instead, he looked unchanged, unaffected. She imagined that everyone in the village had watched him at one time or another, and he was used to a variety of people caring for him.

Cait had a brilliant idea. "Hey, Mattie, are you up to helping me with the dishes?"

He grabbed one of the dinette chairs and pulled it to the sink.

Cait was pleased with herself. She'd tackle two things

at once—cleaning the kitchen and keeping Mattie engaged. Intuition told her to keep up a running conversation and pretend like he responded to what she said. She told him all about Chicago, the time she'd caught a cod on Billy Kennedy's boat, and about the potholder she was making for Deydie for Christmas. Mattie remained silent, scrubbing each dish and setting them in the sink for her to inspect, rinse, and dry. Eventually, all the dishes were done.

Mattie looked beat, his eyes drooping, probably from the cold meds.

"I think we should lie on the couch and watch a movie." She pressed a hand to his forehead, checking for a fever.

They went into the parlor, and Cait put on "Rudolph the Red-Nosed Reindeer." Mattie fell asleep within minutes.

She flipped off the television and went in search of other ways to help. She cleaned the bathroom, picked up the parlor, then readied Deydie's stew by pouring it into the Crock-Pot she'd found above the stove.

When Duncan arrived home, Mattie still slept. She put a finger to her lips. "He's napping."

Duncan grinned at Cait and whispered, "Guess what's in the box." He flipped the lid open. Inside was a ball of black, brown, and white fur. "I got Da a puppy for Christmas, a tricolor sheltie."

He is off his rocker! Who in their right mind would get Graham a dog so soon? Cait shook her head and wanted to ask Duncan what he'd been smoking. Did he think Graham would thank him for it? She tried to give Duncan a reassuring smile but wasn't sure she pulled it off. "Is it a boy or a girl?"

"A boy. We're a family of boys. This little guy will fit right in." Duncan's face shadowed. "I don't know what I'll do with him until Christmas, though. I want it to be a surprise, but I've trouble enough arranging sitters for Mattie while I'm out fishing."

Crap. Between another rock and a hard place. Cait had no choice but to offer. It would only be for a few days. "Do you want me to keep the dog until Christmas?"

"Over the pub? Going up and down those stairs to take him out?"

"I'm sure Deydie won't mind if the puppy and I crash at her place." Cait would have to get her gran drunk again before asking permission.

Duncan beamed at her. "Okay. But let me know if it doesn't work out."

"We'll be fine," she said, not sure whether she was trying to convince him or herself.

Deydie could very well turn both me and the pup out in the cold. To counteract that thought, Cait stopped at the store. She'd bet good money chocolate would be just the thing to win over the Grand Pooh-Bah of Crankiness. She nestled the dog in the blanket and made sure the lid was on tight before entering the mercantile.

Amy was just putting the phone down. "I'm glad you're here. We're having an emergency quilt session at Deydie's right now. That was Ailsa—Rhona's had a shocker. Her daughter isn't having just a baby—it's twins. She only made the one quilt, and now she needs another before Christmas. Bethia is on her way, and I'll be closing up in a minute. I'm sure Ailsa has already called Moira, but I don't know if she'll be able to leave her da or not. You'll come and help, won't you?"

Cait looked down at the box. "Of course." Then at the row of chocolate. "Do you know which is Deydie's favorite?"

Amy smiled. "That's easy. Chocolate-covered cherries."

"Great. I'll take two boxes." Cait laid the money on the counter.

Amy rang it up, bagged the chocolate, and grabbed the CLOSED sign. "If anyone needs anything, they know how to reach me. What's in the box?"

"Another shocker," Cait said, knowing it was true. Or at least it would be when her grumpy gran saw it.

Amy shrugged and headed out the door. They set out for Deydie's as a storm came in from the sea.

Amy still managed to talk a mile a minute over the gale-force winds. "I hope Rhona has enough fabric to make another Log Cabin quilt. The babies are due in January. I bet Rhona is cutting out pieces right now. I reckon the rest of us will work on the blocks. I think we can get it done pretty quickly, don't you?"

Seriously, Cait didn't know why anyone would even want to talk in this kind of weather. Her uvula was in danger of freezing. But Cait hollered back anyway, "We'll get it done if we all work together."

It wasn't just the snowstorm slowing Cait down. She hadn't seen or talked to Deydie today. Things were just *okay* between them last night when they'd gone to bed. Not anything said actually—Deydie humming Christmas tunes and Cait careful not to upset her good mood. She wondered how her gran felt this morning. Apparently, well enough to be up at the crack of dawn to leave food at Duncan's and take care of Graham's place. What if Deydie was ticked with her for leaving and not coming back today? Cait would just have to explain that she'd been at Duncan's helping out. She looked down at the carton. This was no box of cookies. How would her gran feel about having extra housemates until Christmas?

When they got to Deydie's, Amy just walked in without knocking. She looked over and must've read Cait's mind. "Your gran told me there's no need to knock." *In other words, Amy is family.* Another little jab at Cait's heart.

"We're here," Amy called out.

The quilting ladies filled every corner of the small cottage. Rhona stood over a card table with a rotary cutter in her hand. Bethia, Ailsa, and Aileen sewed at their machines. Moira stood at the ironing board, pressing small blocks. They all turned their heads and gave their greetings.

Deydie came out of the bathroom and stopped short when she saw Cait. "What's in that box?"

Carefully, Cait set it down on the little table by the door while she slowly took off her mittens and hat, searching for the perfect thing to say. "It's a favor for Duncan."

Deydie eyed her skeptically. "That makes no sense, girl."

"It's a present for Graham, and Duncan needs a place to hide it until Christmas." Cait needed time to ease into the truth, but she would pay for dodging the question. Putting off the inevitable butt chewing would only make the butt chewing worse.

"Ye can set it outside in the storage shed," Deydie said.

"I don't think that will work becau—"The puppy whimpered before Cait could finish.

Deydie cocked her head to the side and squinted at

the box. "What's in there?" She hobbled her way over to the little table. The other women, as if attached to Deydie by a string, gathered around the box as well.

Cait cringed as Deydie opened the lid. She slammed the lid back down. "Get that damned thing out of here."

"I can't," cried Cait.

"Graham won't want it," Deydie said flatly.

Amy pulled the dog out of its hiding place. "It's so cute. Is it a girl?"

"Boy."

"May I?" Moira asked with her hands outstretched to Amy.

It seemed so out of character for Moira to request anything; Cait caught the surprised look on Deydie's face to prove it. Amy gave the fluff ball a kiss and passed the puppy to Moira, who murmured in Gaelic to the dog as she walked over to the rocking chair in front of the fire.

"Well, look at that," Rhona muttered.

They all stared at Moira, gape-mouthed, as she held the dog close and hummed. She didn't seem to notice them. Cait wondered if they'd be able to pry the dog away from her so Graham would get his present on Christmas Day.

"Let's get back to work," Bethia reminded everyone. Everyone except Moira.

"Right," the twins said together.

Deydie grumbled as she went to her machine.

Cait took Moira's place at the ironing board, pressing Log Cabin blocks.

In shifts, the women took small breaks. A cup of coffee with shortbread cookies, a big stretch and a bathroom trip, a turn about the room. Eventually, Moira rejoined them, but only after making the puppy comfortable in his box by the fire. In the company of this group, Cait had completely forgotten about rummaging through Graham's place. As she pressed away, she worried whether she'd be able to steal back up the bluff to his mansion. Because of the puppy, she was no longer a free agent and couldn't come and go as she pleased.

The box made a little shuffling noise.

Deydie scowled at Cait, irritation filling in her wrinkles. "What is your plan for that mutt?"

Cait jumped up. "I nearly forgot. I brought *you* a little present, too."

"Bribe," Deydie muttered.

Cait retrieved the chocolate-covered cherries from her coat. "Not exactly. It's more of a bargaining chip."

Deydie did her usual *harrumph.*

Cait took it as a good sign. "I thought we could do this together as a favor for Duncan," she said firmly.

"We?" Deydie accused.

Cait gave Rhona the last pressed strip to add to the quilt top. "The puppy can't stay at the pub. Graham would hear him. I thought I could stay here at your cottage and *we* could take care of him together."

Deydie stomped over to her rocking chair but didn't sit. Instead, she turned and stared intently at Cait. With the fire as a backdrop, her gran looked every bit the Scottish warrior. Or demon witch. "I knew ye wanted something from me."

Bethia dove in and scolded her like no one else could. "Caitie's family. You have to let her stay with you."

Deydie plopped into her rocking chair. "Bring it to me."

Cait brought over the box. "I'll do everything. But I'll need backup." If Deydie helped with the dog, Cait might still have a chance to search Graham's house before he got back. But she felt the opportunity slipping away. When did he say he'd be home exactly?

Deydie stuck her hand in the box and pulled out the puppy. She held it up and frowned at his face. "You're an ugly-looking mongrel."

The dog wagged his tail.

"He's a purebred sheltie," Cait defended.

Deydie set the dog on the floor at her feet. He stood and took a few wobbly steps, then squatted by her big toe.

"Don't you dare," Deydie barked. The dog stopped and peered up as if he understood—Deydie was the alpha dog. "Moira, take it outside so it can do its business."

Moira grabbed the dog and left. Within minutes, they were back. "He's so good. He went right away." She laid the dog in Deydie's lap.

"It probably has fleas," Deydie groused. The dog licked her hand and rubbed up against her.

Amy came over and knelt beside her. "So can he stay?" She acted as if she had a stake in it. Which she didn't. Deydie was Cait's gran.

"I suppose. For Duncan and Mattie and Graham." In other words, not because Cait had asked her. Deydie set the dog back in the box. "Now, let's get this baby quilt finished."

Rhona pulled the Log Cabin quilt top from her machine. "The top's done. It's ready to pin."

After they cleared the big table of the sewing machines, Cait spread the backing fabric out, right-side down. Deydie, Ailsa, and Aileen taped it to the table. Moira layered the quilt batting on top of that and then Rhona positioned the newly made quilt top over the batting. They all grabbed a container of safety pins and went to work. Because there were so many hands, the quilt was pinned in record time.

"I really appreciate your help." Rhona held up the nearly finished product. "I'll stitch this together tomorrow."

"Nonsense," Bethia said. "We'll take turns doing it now. You have the Christmas pageant coming up."

"We'll get it done tonight," Deydie gruffed. "Amy, get the sandwiches from the icebox. Moira, sit with that dog and make sure he doesn't poop on anything." She turned to Cait. "Set up yere fancy sewing machine and get to work on stitching that quilt."

"Aye, aye." Cait saluted. The other women jumped into action. The twins made them all spiced cider. Bethia and Deydie went to the rocking chairs by the fire while Rhona directed Cait as to what she envisioned.

"It should be Stitched in the Ditch. Make sure you keep the stitch right in the seam. That's it," Rhona coached.

Cait smiled. Her teacher hadn't changed a bit—always the instructor.

"Leave her alone," Deydie called out. "Any granddaughter of mine knows how to Stitch in the Ditch."

Shocked, Cait about ran the needle over her finger. Had her gran actually claimed her as her own? She risked a glance in her direction but couldn't make out her gran's expression with the rocking chair moving back and forth.

After Amy had downed her sandwich, she tapped Cait's shoulder. "Go get something to eat. I'll have a crack at it."

"Are you sure?" Cait asked.

"I've been itching to get my hands on your sewing

machine since you got here. I saw one in Glasgow when I was on holiday. Coll and I could never afford a machine like that, you know, but a lass can dream. You don't mind, do you?"

"Of course not. There's a couple of cool gadgets on here you're going to love." Cait showed her the extras, then went to get a sandwich.

Ailsa and Aileen sat in the rocking chairs now, taking turns holding the puppy. "Do you have a name for the dog?" Ailsa asked.

Before Cait could answer, Deydie spat, "There's only one name for a mutt like that and it surely ain't Precious. We'll call him Dipshit."

The puppy growled.

"Oh, all right," Deydie said with extra emphasis. "I *suppose* Mattie wouldn't be allowed to say Dipshit, now, would he?" She snatched the puppy out of Ailsa's hands and held him up, looking the little guy in the eye. "Yere name's Dingus. And that's that," she declared.

The dog yipped twice in approval.

"That's a terrible name," Cait protested.

"Tough shite." Deydie glared at her. "It's in my house, and I'll name it whatever I want."

"It's not up to you to name him," Cait argued. "It's Graham's dog." A flush came to her face. She felt both embarrassed and warmed just by saying his name. She didn't know why she was defending Graham's rights so vehemently, the same man she planned to betray. The same man who pretended they could be friends. Yeah, right, like a movie star would have any use for a mortal, everyday girl like her. What difference did it make what Deydie called his dog? None. "Call him whatever you want."

As the evening wore on, she showed them all how to use the machine. When they'd all had a turn—except Deydie, who seemed to keep herself busy during switching time—the quilting was done.

While everyone else cleaned up, Rhona worked on the binding. "I'll take this home and hand stitch it down tomorrow evening after school."

"Leave it with me," Deydie said. "I'll have it done and ye won't have to worry about it. Ye've got the pageant. Gandiegow's depending on you."

"All right, then," Rhona acquiesced.

The twins grabbed their coats. "What a lot of fun," Ailsa said.

"A lot of fun," Aileen copied, smiling at them all. "Moira, tell your da we'll be by to see him tomorrow. We're making him a Christmas stollen. Something to cheer him up."

Moira looked down at the floor. "I know he'll appreciate it."

Ailsa handed Moira's coat to her. "It'll give you a chance to slip out if you have any last-minute shopping to do."

Cait thought this strange. It wasn't like there was a mall or anything near.

Moira seemed to appreciate the offer, though. "That would be nice."

The quilting ladies filed out, leaving Cait alone with Deydie.

"*Dingus* will need a bite to eat." Deydie went to the cabinet and pulled out a small can of fancy dog food.

Cait was puzzled until she realized Deydie must've kept it on hand for Precious. She took the can from her and prepared a little of it for the puppy.

The little fur ball ate his fill and promptly fell asleep.

Cait pulled out the trundle while Deydie went into the bathroom.

When her gran came out and crawled into bed, she leaned over and snatched the puppy from Cait.

Deydie settled the dog in her arms. "You'd just crush it," her gran said.

Cait sighed. *And the sweet comments just keep on coming.* She wrapped her arms around herself.

After a moment, she turned off the light, slipped out of her clothes, leaving on only her long underwear and a T-shirt. She fell into bed.

"Good night," Cait said to the darkness.

The darkness remained silent.

Chapter Nine

Cait dreamed she was on a boat, being tossed back and forth belowdecks. Deydie ruled the ship as captain with Graham as first mate. Cait wanted to be out enjoying the fresh air and to find out why there was laughing and singing. But every time she climbed the steps leading up to the deck, the boat would rock, and she would lose her footing and go crashing to the floor. Then more tossing and turning.

Cait woke up, unsure at first where she was. Deydie shook her shoulders. "Get up. That damned dog has had his breakfast. Now take him out." She laid the furry creature on Cait's belly.

But Cait didn't want to get up. It was still dark out.

"There's coffee left in the pot." Deydie's tone made Cait wonder whether her gran meant it to be nice or if Cait was supposed to clean out the carafe.

"Okay," Cait said noncommittally as Deydie whirled out the front door.

She set little Dingus on the floor while she got up. If she could've just lain there a while longer, she might've been able to make sense of the strange dream she was having. Was her subconscious trying to tell her she hadn't gotten her sea legs yet? And what the hell did that mean anyway?

She made the bed and pushed it back under Deydie's. She dressed in her usual brown attire, slipped on her coat, and took the puppy out. Back inside, the coffee hit the spot and she made sure to wash out the carafe and set it in the drainer to dry. She tucked Dingus into her coat and left for the pub to pack a small bag. And grab a clean notebook while she was at it. She'd need it for when she tackled Graham's house.

At the pub, the puppy napped on the bed while she gathered her things together. At the last minute, she remembered her laptop and power cord. She put the dog back into her coat and set off for Deydie's. On her way out, she ran into Bonnie, the barmaid, whose low-cut Christmas sweater showed too much cleavage for her to make Santa's Nice List.

"Haven't seen you around lately." Bonnie certainly didn't sound like she'd missed her.

"Been staying at my gran's," Cait said, hoping Dingus would keep quiet so she didn't have to explain why her breast was whining. "Listen, I'd better run. She's expecting me." Cait turned to go.

Bonnie blocked her path. "You've not heard from Graham, have you?"

"No. Why would I?"

"Good. I'm glad you realize he doesn't answer to you. Or belong to you," Bonnie added with a sneer. "You'd better remember that."

Cait wanted to deck her, but she stepped around her instead. The fact that Bonnie wanted to get her hooks into Graham made Cait want to get Deydie's chicken knife and put it to good use.

And just so Cait could dig the proverbial knife in, she added over her shoulder, "When he gets back, I'll let him know you want to see him. Or maybe I won't." Like he'd call Cait first when he made it ashore.

Bonnie and her considerable rack huffed off. Cait hoped she'd go take a running leap off the pier.

The dog mewed a little then. Cait put her hand in her coat and ruffled his soft fur. "It's okay, buddy. She's a piece of work, isn't she?"

The sun came out from under the clouds and made Cait feel better. She hurried off through the small row of businesses. On impulse, she swung into the store. Amy, like a permanent fixture, was behind the counter, arranging receipts. "Hey, ya," she said.

Cait put a hand up in greeting. "I thought I'd pick up some groceries." A brilliant idea lit up her brain. "Do you know if Moira and her da have any plans for Christmas?"

"Kenneth won't be leaving the house right now. The doctor said he has to stay in bed until he's stronger," Amy supplied.

"If I give you a list of things, can you have them delivered to their house?" And because Amy was a bit of a friendly blabbermouth, Cait added, "Without letting anyone know? I mean absolutely no one."

"Mum's the word." Amy gave her a big grin. "You're a nice woman, Caitie Macleod. I know all of Kenneth and Moira's favorites, if that'd be a help."

"That would be great." Cait unzipped her coat to give the pup some air.

"Oh, you've got the wee one with you." Amy came around the counter. "Can I hold him while we work on that list?"

Cait handed over Dingus.

It didn't take long to come up with enough food to last Moira and Kenneth a good month. At the same time, Cait filled a sack full of nutritious items for her and Deydie, then took Dingus back from Amy and set off.

When Cait got to her gran's, she took a page from Amy's book and didn't knock, but walked right on in. She left her backpack by the door.

Deydie looked up from her rocking chair. Rhona's baby quilt lay across her lap along with a needle and thread. "Where's the cur?" she growled.

"Right here." Cait pulled out the fur ball and put him in the box near Deydie's feet.

"Hmmph," Deydie said, plunging the needle into the binding of the quilt.

While Cait unloaded the groceries, she chewed the inside of her cheek. She needed to go to Graham's and she needed an excuse. Her laptop wouldn't do. She could charge it here, using Deydie's powerhouse electric, courtesy of *Himself.*

"When yere done there, ye're off to Duncan's," Deydie commanded. "It's time for him to check the nets. Put that roast in the oven while yere there."

I can't. There's something I need to do, Cait shouted inside her head.

Without so much as an *Is that okay with you?*, Deydie spoke again. "Get on. And leave that mutt here."

Later, Cait promised herself. Later she'd get to Graham's and work on that story. Margery at *People* magazine would want it soon.

She headed out into the cold and walked at a brisk pace. She nearly froze her butt off waiting for Duncan to open the door. Both he and the boy had their coats on.

Duncan pulled a wool cap over his head. "I was just on my way to drop Mattie at Ailsa and Aileen's."

Mattie hung back in the hallway, as quiet as wallpaper.

She looked directly at him. "I'll stay with him, and we'll have some cocoa. If that's okay with you?"

No response from Mattie.

"Are you sure you don't mind watching the little monkey?" Duncan squeezed Mattie's shoulder.

"You go. Take your time." She turned to Mattie. "Do you have any Christmas music?"

The boy pointed to the parlor and she followed him as Duncan slipped out the door.

Once in front of the CD cabinet, she prompted Mattie. "Any suggestions?"

He didn't budge.

"I know it's silly, but I like the *Chipmunks Christmas.*" She pulled it from its slot. "What's your favorite?"

He pulled out the *Highland Christmas* CD.

"Excellent choice. We'll put yours on first." She looked at the complicated stereo system. "Do you know how it works?"

Mattie removed the *Chipmunks Christmas* from her hand and popped it into the player. He hit two buttons and Alvin came on. He opened his CD case and loaded his music in as well.

She smiled at him. "Promise this'll be our little secret, that I like the *Chipmunks Christmas,* okay?"

He just stared at her.

In the kitchen, they sat at the dining room table eating shortbread cookies and drinking cocoa. Afterward, Mattie watched her put the roast in the oven.

When the *Chipmunks Christmas* finished on the stereo, the Celtic music came on. Mournful bagpipes filled the house with an eerie wail. *Death music.* She caught Mattie staring desolately out the window toward the sea. Too young to be so sad.

Maybe she'd take him down to the coastline to take his mind off his sorrows.

"Get your coat, kiddo," she said cheerfully. "We're going for a walk."

Mattie slipped soundlessly out of his chair, moving like a ghost as he retrieved both of their jackets.

Outside, the sun made a rare appearance, sneaking from behind the gray clouds in the sky. Two large white gannets, their black-tipped wings stretched outwardly, sailed above them.

She peeked over at Mattie, who was watching the elegant birds. "So, your da is a fisherman. Do you go out with him often?" She didn't expect an answer, so she went on. "I bet you're a right good fisherman yourself." She stared out at the waves crashing violently against the rocks.

She stepped up on the pier and noticed Mattie stayed on the ground. "Come on, pokey. Let's go all the way to the end." Someone had scraped the ice off and salted the planks clear.

Mattie didn't move, his face turning as pale as the whitewashed deck.

"Come on, Mattie. There's nothing to be scared of." She hopped up and down on the wood planks. "It's been here a hundred years. It'll be here a hundred more." She took his hand and pulled him onto the pier.

She started walking, holding his little hand. "Yesterday I saw three fishing boats just there beyond the rocks. Maybe we'll see your da's boat coming in."

Mattie stumbled. When she righted him, she found him

trembling, his eyes transfixed to the spot she'd pointed to just off the rocks.

She saw nothing there except the splash of waves. "What's wrong, Mattie?"

His eyes grew wide as life preservers. He opened his mouth in a terrified scream. Except nothing came out. He pointed off in the distance, the silent scream going on and on.

Panic gripped her. She grabbed him and wrapped her arms around him. "It'll be all right, honey." Then she gave him a gentle shake, praying he'd snap out of it.

From the walkway, she heard urgent cries and the footsteps of two people hurrying onto the pier. Moira sprinted full-out on the planks with Deydie lumbering as fast as her plump body would carry her.

"Get him away from there," her gran shouted. "Have you gone crazy?"

Cait turned toward Deydie, whose face was a sea of rage and fury, anger seething from every corner of her wrinkled face.

"A walk," Cait cried. "That's all. We went for a walk."

Moira snatched Mattie up, cooing at him. "Shh, shh. It's all right," over and over. Mattie buried his face into Moira's shoulder as she whisked him off the pier and onto higher ground.

Deydie slammed her hands on her hips, blocking Cait's escape. "Why did you bring the boy out here?"

"I thought we'd watch for boats."

Deydie eyed her with accusation. "Or were you meddling, trying to making him face his fears?"

"W-what?" Cait stammered. "I don't know what you're talking about."

"The *Water Dawn*. It sank and drowned six men."

Deydie glared out at the rocks. "Out there. Last spring. When a sudden storm came up. Mattie and Duncan were standing right here when it happened. Duncan took that blue dinghy and tried rowing out to them, shouting for Mattie to go for help. Mattie froze. The ship sank, and we're lucky Duncan didn't go down with them."

"I . . . I didn't know." Cait's eyes stung. "I'm so sorry."

Deydie harpooned her with a killer glare. "Sorry don't fix a damn thing, missy. Have you no sense? Didn't you wonder why the boy doesn't speak?"

The wind sent a spray of salt water up, smacking Cait directly in the face. After what she'd done, Cait doubted Mattie would ever speak again.

Deydie despises me. And Cait deserved her scorn. When the townsfolk heard what had happened here today, they'd hate her, too. Including Duncan. And Graham. She ran off the pier.

"Of all the devilment," Deydie shouted after her. "Go on, now. Get yereself back to the cottage."

Cait ran to the pub instead. She burst in and dashed past Bonnie's gaping bloody-red lipsticked mouth, past gawking men with the stink of dead fish on them. Cait ran up the stairs with Father Death sailing right behind her, laughing, mocking, torturing her once again. She threw herself on the bed and cried for herself and for Mattie, so utterly defeated.

Death was such an asshole.

Hours passed. Cait didn't ever want to leave the pub again. Embarrassment and guilt almost had her packing for Chicago.

But she came from tougher stock—north coast Scottish stock. She'd also made a pledge to stick with Deydie come hell or high water. Even if her grandmother told her to shove off.

Cait pulled herself out of bed and splashed water on her red, puffy eyes. She'd go back to Deydie's and face her.

When she walked through Deydie's door, the old woman hollered at Cait, not about Mattie, but an errand. "Run up to Graham's and get my sewing basket. I finished Rhona's quilt but forgot the damn basket. I need to darn a sock or two after dinner."

Great. Finally the chance to ransack Graham's place and her heart wasn't in it. She needed to clear the air with Deydie first. But Deydie was acting like nothing had happened.

Cait fingered the cell phone in her pocket, hoping it was charged up enough to take photos for the story about Graham. The ticket to her new life. A life that didn't include so much pain and involved a little less contact with Old Man Death. "Where's the basket?"

"In the parlor, next to Precio—" Deydie stopped herself. "Next to the fireplace. The key is on the hook by the door."

"I'll be back," Cait said, grabbing the key, even though she had her own, and went out the door.

Hurrying, Cait wound her way up the path and noticed her gran had left a few lights on. She unlocked the door, but when she swung it open, Graham stood there. The headline flashed before her eyes.

WOMAN FOUND DEAD OF FRIGHT
ON FAMOUS ACTOR'S PORCH

She grabbed her chest, trying to breathe, and at the same time, noted how good he looked. Damn good. He wore a tweed jacket, black turtleneck, and jeans that hugged him perfectly. The concern on his face, though, looked out of place.

"Are ye all right?" His Scottish burr came out as thick as warm fudge. He took her arm and helped her over the threshold.

"You scared the bejeebers out of me, that's all." She liked him holding on to her, and he didn't let go.

"Sorry. Got home a bit ago. I flew into Inverness and drove back." He did let go of her then and went to the laptop on the desk and shut the lid. It seemed an odd thing to do, but she didn't question him.

"So, have ye been staying here like I asked?" he said.

"No. I've been at Deydie's. She got a little tipsy at the cookie exchange, and the next night we had an emergency quilt session. We've been busy, busy, busy."

"Haven't come up here at all?" he asked.

"No." She shook her head, maybe overdoing it a bit, so she stopped.

"Hmm," he said. It almost sounded like, *We'll see about that.*

Cait tried to act as nonchalant as possible, but her cell phone in her pocket felt mighty heavy with guilt right now. "Deydie needs her sewing basket. Left it by the fireplace. Do you mind if I get it?"

"*Mi casa es su casa,*" he said.

She dug in her pocket and produced the key he'd given her. "Here." She hated offering it back.

He waved her off. "Hang on to it. It might come in handy."

She smiled to herself and put the key away.

"How about staying for a drink?" he offered, giving her a slow, easy smile.

It should've been a no-brainer—either spend a few moments with Mr. Darcy or rush back down the bluff to Cruella De Vil. "Deydie has socks to darn." She tried to move past him.

He touched her shoulder, infusing more than a little sizzle into her bones. "At least let me show you what I got Duncan for Christmas," he said.

What was it with the Buchanan men that she had to keep their Christmas secrets?

"Sure, but only for a minute," Cait said.

Graham walked down the hallway with Caitie trailing behind. He had to do it now, had to talk to her about Duncan before things went any further. He spun around to her.

He must've stopped too quickly, because she was right there, her hands landing on his chest. He liked it. *A lot*. With her standing so close, he could smell her shampoo—some sort of flowers or something. He breathed her in. She tilted her head back and looked up at him with dazed eyes. After a moment, she slowly pulled her hands away. He didn't miss the blush forming on her cheeks.

"Duncan needs a wife," he blurted. Not exactly how he'd intended to approach the subject, but it was on the table now, for better or for worse. And no matter how wrong it felt, he would make this sacrifice for his son.

"You're not interested, are you?" he said.

She flinched like his words had pricked her.

"I had to know before . . ." He stepped forward and brushed a loose strand of her hair behind her ear.

She shifted nervously away from him, looking like she was gathering her thoughts. "Graham, if you're trying to play matchmaker . . ."

He waited, watching her, maybe even holding his breath. Was she going to say she wanted to be with his son?

She turned to him with her face screwed up in pain. Or was it confusion? "I like Duncan, I do. And Mattie, well, he's a sugarplum—"

Graham cut her off, taking a step back. "If you're worried about romantic love, well, it's overrated. Love doesn't fade over time. Reality snuffs it out."

She gave a harsh laugh. "And here I thought I had cornered the market on emotional baggage. Listen, about Duncan: I used to babysit him. I'm not interested in your son in that way. And for your information, I'm not marrying again. Period."

Like a rogue wave, he was slammed, almost knocked from his moor. A variety of emotions hit him. Relief that she didn't want Duncan. Disappointment that she would never marry again. And shocked at himself that he was distressed by her declaration. He stepped closer to her.

"It's like this." She put her hands on her hips, Ms. Bad-ass now. "Love is a freaking fairy tale. And I'm no longer nine and want to marry Prince Charming. This princess doesn't need a man to take her to the ball. I'm going stag."

"Whoa. I'm the one who's supposed to have issues." He laughed, laying his hands on her shoulders. It was settled. Things would go on the same. But then several things happened at once. Time stood still. Her tough girl act fell away. As they gazed into each other's eyes, he saw something there. *Is it a future?* Then her pupils dilated, and he knew he was going to kiss her.

Part of Cait was dying to find out what it would be like to kiss Graham Buchanan. But her heart couldn't chance it. And her mind knew without a doubt that kissing him would be detrimental to this new life she was trying to forge for herself.

She wriggled out of his arms. "Back off, hoss. This show pony wants no part of your rodeo."

He tipped her chin up. "Your eyes say differently, lass."

Even if she'd wanted to shoot him down with a snarky remark, she couldn't muster one, especially since he was wrapping her up in that sultry gaze of his. She was under his spell and didn't stop him as he leaned down and deposited a small kiss on her lips. And in response, an inferno lit up inside her, burning downward into her lacy underwear. God, what a delicious ache. She went all Julia-Roberts-for-Hugh-Grant soft, wanting more, even leaned in for it, but he stopped and pulled away.

"Is that the best you can do?" She only said it to keep him from seeing how embarrassed she felt. *Who in their right mind gets so hot and bothered by an innocent kiss?*

He took her words as a challenge, though, and wrapped his arms around her, crushing her to him. Before she could tell him she'd only been kidding, he was kissing the hell out of her. Not some milquetoast BBC kiss. An R-rated, no-holds-barred kiss.

Every molecule in her pulsed for Graham. It had been so long since she'd been with a man. Cait had all but forgotten what lust felt like, but she damn sure knew now.

He set her away from him at that moment. He stood back and grinned at her like the kid who'd won the triple-dog-dare bet. "Was that better for ye, lass? I can try harder if it wasn't good enough."

She wanted to smack him. He knew exactly what he'd done to her. She'd have to go sit in the snow to cool off her panties. She put her hand up. "Nope, I'm fine. All good, hoss." *Go back to the ranch and leave this sad cowgirl alone.*

She backed out of the doorway and stumbled her way down the path. When she got to Deydie's, she slung the door open. She must've been a sight, because her gran looked alarmed.

"Caitie?" Deydie rose from her chair. "Ye look as if ye've encountered a banshee."

"Fine. I'm fine," Cait practically yelled. "Just need a little snack, that's all." *To take the edge off.* She headed for the mini cherry cheesecakes in the fridge.

And ignored how her hands shook as she opened the box.

As she took her first bite, Deydie asked the question that Cait had forgotten all about. "Where's me sewing basket?"

"Crap," Cait mumbled under her breath. She couldn't go back to Graham's tonight. Or ever.

Deydie snarled. "Are ye daft? That's the reason ye went up there." She snatched her coat off the hook. "If I want something done, I'd just better go do it meself."

There was a knock on the door. Before Cait could process who it might be, Deydie swung it open. There stood Graham, holding the sewing basket and looking like the devil himself.

Chapter Ten

Graham should've taken pity on Caitie, but he couldn't help himself. He had to witness her frazzled condition again—the one he'd put her in. She still looked disheveled and frustrated, like the kind of woman he wanted to see naked in his bed.

"I believe you forgot this." He held up the basket, not cutting her any slack.

Deydie snatched it from him. "What the devil are ye doing home? I thought ye were in London."

"A cheery good evening to you, too." He leaned down and gave Deydie a quick kiss on the cheek.

"Git off me," Deydie said as she took a swing at him with her sewing things. "Ye're so fresh."

"I came home early," he explained. "Got back an hour ago." It'd been just enough time to fast-forward through the surveillance tape. Caitie hadn't been on it. Which he didn't understand. If she was a reporter, wouldn't she have jumped at the opportunity to scour through his things and get the *ungettable* story?

Unless he'd come home too early. But he'd finished up in London and had missed his family.

"Would you ladies like to join Duncan, Mattie, and myself for a Christmas movie and popcorn?"

"Which movie?" Deydie eyed him shrewdly.

Graham shrugged like he had no particular one in mind. Finally, he gave her one of his full-on grins. "You know which one, ye ole bird."

Deydie clapped her hands together. "*White Christmas*. Caitie, get the things ye need from the icebox to make that spaghetti you've been talking about."

Graham looked over at Caitie. She was stuffing a piece of cheesecake into her delectable mouth. He dared her with his eyes to turn down his offer.

She narrowed hers back at him and swallowed the rest of her bite. "You'll have to help."

"I make a killer spaghetti," he said.

"You'll be my sous chef. I'll be in charge."

He liked it. Her feistiness. But she had it all wrong. He was the one in charge. He could have her sizzling like garlic in a hot pan, right here, right now, if he wished it. It might be fun to show her who had the upper hand, but then he remembered they weren't alone.

Deydie bustled around, pulling out two Christmas lap quilts, a red one and a green one. "For me and Mattie," she announced. "I told him these were our special movie quilts." She looked over at Caitie. "Ye'll have to bring yere own."

Graham came to Caitie's rescue. "Don't bring a thing. I have a cupboard full of quilts and a refrigerator full of food. Everything you need for spaghetti."

"Okay." Caitie grabbed her jacket, and as if it were a last-minute thought, she grabbed her laptop, too. "Needs charging."

He helped her into her parka. She didn't say "thank you" or even look up at him. He liked that he could affect her with just his presence.

Blocking Graham's view, Deydie bent over a box by the fireplace and shoved a bundle under her coat.

"What are you hiding there?" he asked.

Caitie turned to her gran, panicked, her eyes growing to the size of serving platters.

"Never you mind," Deydie groused. "Go on, now. I need to stop by Moira's first." She squished her face together and glared at him. "Don't ye dare start Bing Crosby without me."

"Wouldn't dream of it." He turned to Caitie. "Ready to go?" He held his arm out to her and she ignored it.

"I was born ready," she said.

She didn't look *born ready*. She looked frightened to be alone with him. Again.

It's going to be okay, Cait kept telling herself. Everyone would be at Graham's. It wouldn't be like before, alone with him in his house. This time Duncan, Mattie, and Deydie would be there as chaperones, keeping her safe.

When they got to his house, though, no one else had arrived yet. Cait felt as jittery as a doe being circled by a hungry wolf.

"Let's put your coat in here." Graham grinned, unnerving her more.

She cautiously followed him into the spare bedroom off the kitchen. It was pretty, straight from *Better Homes and Gardens*, decorated in blue—indigo paisley on the comforter, cobalt-striped curtains, and blue-and-white plates hung in an interesting pattern above the bed. The neutral color on the wall pulled it all together nicely.

But it didn't help her feel better. Being with him alone, next to the inviting bed, added to her unsettled feeling. She wanted out.

He acted like he didn't see her distress. "If I had a maid, these would be her quarters. There's a small sitting room through there." He pointed toward an arched doorway. A plaid blue love seat and a white oval coffee table sat under the window. He walked farther into the room. "The view from here is amazing. Come see."

She felt paralyzed and didn't move. Her eyes flitted to the bed. For a crazy brief moment, she could visualize the two of them there, doing *the deed* with the blue paisley comforter twisted around them. She shouldn't think such things. She was much too wise, and wary, to entertain those kinds of irrational thoughts anymore. No more falling for guys just because they had a pretty face. No more exposing herself to the lying, cheating half of the population.

What about scx, pleasure, and orgasms?

Shut up, Lust, she told herself.

He cleared his throat. "Coat? Closet?" He had his hand held out to her.

She slipped out of her parka and saw him zero in on her chest. Her tight brown turtleneck betrayed her, showing her stupid *hello-there* nipples. Embarrassed, her first instinct was to cover her breasts with her hands, but she wasn't one to back down. She straightened up and stood tall, her chest more in his face than ever. His eyes widened. It felt good turning the tables on him. *Who has all the power now?*

She handed him her coat. Their hands brushed, and more than a little crackle buzzed between them. Just that quickly, the power had shifted back to him.

And he knew it. He smiled at her like he loved being in control and she was the helpless damsel. Darn him.

He swept his gaze over her chocolate-colored turtle-neck and dark brown cords. "Why do you always wear brown?"

With a sniff, she defended herself. "Brown's my color."

"No. That's not it. I think you're trying to fade into the woodwork."

"Kitchen," she demanded. "Now."

"You're prickly tonight, my Caitie. What's the matter?" he teased.

"Don't worry your pretty face over it." She stomped out.

He followed her. "Plug your laptop in over there next to mine." He pointed to the table, and she did as he said.

From the pantry, he pulled out several packages of whole wheat pasta and jars of sauce. "There are home-made meatballs in the freezer. There should be enough for us all."

She opened the bottom drawer of the stainless-steel industrial-sized refrigerator and found perfectly labeled containers of soup, homemade bread, and a large bag of meatballs. "Did you make these?"

"What do you think?" He smiled, showing his Ultra Brite teeth.

"I think you fly in a personal chef once a month to fill up your freezer. I've seen *Oprah* and how she runs her kitchen."

"Ah, that's where you're wrong. No one knows I'm from Gandiegow. They think Glasgow is my home. The truth is, most of the food in my freezer is from your gran and the other women in town. But the meatballs are my own recipe." He gave her a wicked grin. "Not completely my own. It's adapted from an Italian friend of mine."

"Friend? Ha!" She glared at him. "Everybody knows about you and Antoinette Rossellini."

"Antoinette and I never had a thing." He pulled out a huge pot.

"All the tabloids said you two were going at it like rabbits."

He filled the pot with water. "Didn't happen."

"I saw you on *Entertainment Tonight.* You were giving her tongue."

He opened the pasta package. "Publicity. It was in our contract. I don't approve of it, but the studio insists we use the press to sell tickets. And the audience eats that stuff up. It worked. The film was a hit." He took the bag of meatballs from her. "As a sign of friendship, Antoinette shared her mother's special recipe with me—but not all of it, though. She left out her secret ingredient. I improvised, and these babies turned out pretty well. You'll see."

Cait still saw green. "Why didn't you sleep with her? She's beautiful."

He frowned at her like she should know better. "Beauty's in the eye of the beholder."

"Well, you're not blind."

"I never thought of Antoinette in that way." He shrugged, looking totally sincere. "Most of my *extracurriculars* have only been PR fabrications."

"I see your point. You'd have to have one hell of a libido to have bedded as many starlets and supermodels as they say you have."

He cocked his eyebrow as if offering to show her the extent of his sex drive.

She shook her head. "You don't need to prove your manhood with me, buster."

He stopped and became serious, as if this important point needed to be made. "I've had my share of relationships and I've come to an inescapable conclusion."

"What's that?"

"I'll never have the great love and subsequent happy marriage my parents had." He shrugged again, looking oddly apologetic toward her. "I've found it's best to keep things casual."

She frowned. Two things gnawed at her. Why did she feel so let down by the "keep things casual" statement and why did he look so sorry?

But her inner reporter wanted the details about all those failed relationships. Or was it her own curiosity? Either way, he looked closed on the subject, like he'd sealed the vault and destroyed the combination.

As if on purpose, he changed his expression to the happy chef. "I brought back fresh tomatoes from London. Lettuce, too, for a salad. What else do you need?"

She needed her freaking head examined for getting sucked into liking this man, the same man she meant to expose. But she shouldn't feel bad. He used the press to get what he wanted. Why couldn't she play his same game from the opposite end of the field? "Green peppers and parmesan," she said sweetly but not really feeling it.

"Got them." He pulled out a chopping board.

Cait poured the sauce into a pan and dropped the meatballs in. She put Graham to work, dicing and slicing. There was no more intimate talk between them. But cooking together like that felt pretty damn cozy.

Thirty minutes later, Duncan knocked at the back door. Graham answered it. "Why didn't you just come on in?"

"It's not my house," Duncan said coolly.

"It could be," Graham snapped. "I built it for all of us."

Graham had gone from pleasant to irate in three seconds flat. Other than on-screen, she had never seen him furious, and it was powerful, but Duncan didn't back down.

"I told you, I'll not be taking your charity," he said as he helped Mattie out of his coat.

Mattie looked from one to the other of his male relations, his sad eyes welling up with tears. Cait wanted to smack both for being idiotic enough to argue in front of the boy.

"Hey, Mattie," she said. "Go put those coats in the room off the kitchen."

As soon as the boy was out of sight, she spun on the Buchanan men. "You two had better get your act together. You have a child who needs you united, not bickering like a couple of primary-school girls. Now, put on your happy faces before he returns."

"She's got a tongue," Duncan said to his da.

"I know," Graham agreed, glancing toward her mouth.

"Get your mind out of the gutter," she hissed as she walked by.

Obediently, Graham handed Duncan a loaf of bread as Mattie appeared in the doorway. The kid looked afraid to come in the room. Graham put his acting skills to good use. "Do you mind, son," he said to Duncan, "slicing the bread?"

Duncan poured it on thick. "Sure, Da."

Cait smiled at them both as Mattie wandered all the way in and sat at the table. She handed him a head of lettuce. "Can you tear this up for me?" She set the colander in front of him.

He nodded his head once and got to work.

Duncan buttered each slice of bread. After a while, he spoke to Cait. "I put the roast in the refrigerator. Mattie and I'll enjoy it for dinner tomorrow."

Graham looked at her questioningly.

"No biggie," she said. "I helped out, that's all."

Duncan disagreed with her. "She was a huge help. Showed up just when I needed her."

Mattie finished with the lettuce and wandered from the room.

Duncan nodded in his direction. "I really appreciated that you stopped by."

"Don't mention it," she said, knowing she'd have to own up to what she'd done to Mattie by taking him out on the pier. "Your little guy is awfully special."

Graham gave her a queer sort of look. Like she was harder to crack than the *New York Times* Sunday crossword. Then his eyes softened, doing serious damage to her resolve to never fall for anyone again.

He came over to put the pot on to boil and in the process spoke quietly only to her. "Thank you for helping my family while I was away."

There was no suggestiveness in his voice, but her deprived body responded anyway. She melted like snow set before the fire. Then she hid her feelings by stirring the sautéed veggies into the sauce a little more fervently than need be.

Deydie came in through the back door. "Duncan, you look as ragged as my aunt Aggie's quilt, and she's been dead fifty years. Is dinner ready yet?"

"Go sit yourself down and we'll call you when it's done," Graham commanded.

Deydie paraded from the room, speaking over her

shoulder as she went. "I'll do it because I want to and not because ye're telling me to. I'll be in the media room with me feet up."

Duncan pushed himself off the stool he'd been sitting on. "I'd better go check on Mattie."

Graham put his hand up. "You stay. I'll take care of Mattie. Caitie, watch the pasta for me."

When he left the room, Cait touched Duncan's arm. "Hey, I'm sure you heard about what happened with Mattie out on the pier. I'm sorry."

"No, it's my fault. I should've explained the situation to you." Duncan gave her a sincere smile. "No harm's done. Forget about it." He took a sip of his coffee. "Before da gets back—where's the puppy? Is he okay?"

"Deydie took him to Moira's. Moira has a huge crush on that dog. Are there any left in the litter?" She'd been toying with the idea of getting one for Moira and her da.

"Several. I'll get you the number," he said.

She thought out loud. "I'd have to be sneaky. I could arrange food and vet care without Moira and Kenneth finding out. You won't tell, will you?"

"Never." Duncan laughed, sounding so much like his da. "You're a good person, Caitie Macleod."

"Why, thank you, Duncan." She did a little curtsy for him.

Graham cleared his throat. "What's going on in here?" He sounded aggravated, as if Duncan had played with his favorite toy without permission.

"Geesh, Da. Nothing's going on," Duncan said defensively. "I'm going to join Deydie and put my feet up, too."

Graham decided it was time to make things perfectly clear to Caitie. About what, he wasn't sure.

That she belonged to him? *Certainly not.*

That he didn't want her flirting with anyone else? *Maybe.*

The only thing he knew for sure was that he needed to have her alone. *Now.* He turned to her and pointed the way. "Come to the wine cellar."

He was a man on a mission, wound tight. As she passed, his eyes glued themselves to her ass. Down the stairs, he stayed mesmerized by her sashaying hips in those tight brown trousers. With just enough stretch to drive him crazy.

That she'd been chatting up his son while Graham was out of the room made him that much more determined.

When he reached the bottom step, he about ran into her—the minx didn't have any rear brake lights.

She came to a standstill. "This is amazing. Did you do all this yourself?"

"Aye." He looked about the room, trying to cool his jets. He'd designed the large game room for his family. Three pinball machines, an arcade basketball hoop game, a pool table, foosball, Xbox, and a bouncy ball pen for Mattie. The remainder of the room he'd filled with guy seating—beanbag chairs, gaming chairs, and an extra-large sectional sofa. "Follow on through to that hallway."

When she turned to look back at him, he was awe-struck by her simple beauty. This lass wasn't Hollywood; she was an ocean sunset. It took everything in him not to reach out and fondle the brown curls that rested on her shoulders.

"In there." His voice sounded husky. As they walked through the doorway, he tried to pull himself together, but he felt himself unwinding.

"It's an old English pub. I love the wooden bar," she exclaimed.

With Duncan in mind, Graham had stocked it with every imaginable beverage. His hope of his son using this space for parties or poker nights with friends faded soon after Graham finished the house. There was plenty of seating, stools against the bar, tables scattered about the room. Duncan could've had a grand time here. But, no.

Graham took the lead to where an old wooden door stood. He'd reclaimed the wood from his father's cottage and used it for this entryway and for other pieces of furniture about the house.

She reached out and ran a slender hand down the worn mahogany. "This looks ancient."

Never in his life had hands looked sexier. The way hers slid on the door, gentle and soft, made blood rush downward to his aching groin.

He'd explain about the damn door later. Right now, he had to get her inside. He grabbed the old key from the top ledge of the doorframe, unlocked it, and flipped on the switch. "In," he commanded.

He saw her take in the expanse of his wine cellar, which spanned aisle after aisle, using up a good portion of the lower level. He reached around her and slammed the door shut.

"Sorry. Temperature controlled, right?" She had nervous excitement in her eyes, and it drove him wild.

"To hell with the temperature," he hissed, and backed her up against the door she liked so well. He kissed her. Hard. It was an *I don't want you flirting with another man, even if it is my son* kiss.

She grabbed onto his shirtfront, clinging to him for dear life. It only made him tighten his hold. He didn't know why he had to have her in this way. He never lost control, always the reserved gentleman. But kissing Caitie Macleod brought out his inner brute. He shouldn't be so attracted to her, and he shouldn't be sending out mixed signals either; but he couldn't help himself. He had her here now, and by God, he meant to properly take advantage of it.

He tugged at her clothes and she tugged back. *Thank the heavens, he would have his release.* But in the next second, she pushed away from him and stumbled from the room, not looking back.

Chapter Eleven

Graham sat on one of the kegs and put his head in his hands. He never should've done it. If she hadn't gotten up enough strength to stop them, he would've been convulsing inside her right now.

On so many levels, she was wrong for him. He was the guy who kept it loose with women, clear from the start that he'd never commit.

With Caitie, though, it felt like all bets were off.

He'd have to stay away from her or, at the least, stop kissing her.

Shite. That wouldn't be possible. He *would* kiss her again. And again. As much as he damn well pleased.

Just this once, he'd break his own rule and not be so honorable. He'd lead her on to get what he wanted from her. *Complete satisfaction.* He was male, after all, and wasn't that what men did?

He grabbed a bottle of red wine and went back upstairs. She stood over the meatballs, stirring the heck out of them, mumbling to herself loudly.

"What gives him the right to kiss me like that? I have a box of sympathy cards to remind me that Y chromosomes are nothing but a heap of trouble."

"What?" Graham said, even though he'd heard every word clearly.

She spun around and glared at him. He tried looking innocent, but he'd been the tomcat and she'd been the canary. Well, it'd tasted damn good.

She flipped a meatball at him.

He ducked, a little sauce landing on his shoulder.

"What was that for?" he said, giving her more of his innocence.

She glowered at him as if her brain waves were lethal. "No more kissing." She paused for a moment, looking a bit perplexed. "Without my permission, anyway."

He conjured up his most effective smile. "My only excuse is that I couldn't help myself."

"I don't want to talk about it anymore. End of story." She turned back to the sauce.

He grabbed paper towels and cleaned up the splatted meatball from the floor. "I should've left this for Deydie. And when she asked who'd done it, well, you'd be sorry then."

"I am sorry, but not for what you think. I should've catapulted a steak knife or two in your direction instead. Now, get back to work," she ordered.

Cait felt flushed—not from standing over the stove but from the searing kiss in the cellar.

As Graham drained the noodles, he got serious with her. "How do you think Duncan looks today?"

She laid the spoon down and turned to him. "Truthfully? I think he looks a little under the weather. Maybe it's the short winter days," she suggested. She was glad they were discussing a safe subject.

"I've never seen him like this." Graham frowned

while running water over the pasta. "After the New Year, I go on location. I'll be gone for a few months. If he still looks tired when I get back, I'm going to insist he see a doctor in London. He's a stubborn man, my Duncan, but I'm stubborn-er." He poured the pasta onto a platter and looked satisfied to have come up with a plan. "Let's serve supper."

Cait looked at him and he beamed back. In that moment, her resolve slipped a fraction. Staying close to him, she might slip further. "I'll get Mattie and the rest," she said as she hightailed it out of the kitchen.

She found Mattie in the parlor all alone, standing over Precious's empty fluffy bed. He was breathing hard; then he sniffed and wiped his nose. She wanted to go to him and wrap her arms around his small frame, but the moment seemed too intimate to interrupt. She stepped back out of the room quietly. "Mattie," she called from down the hall. "Go wash your hands. Dinner's ready."

When she went back into the kitchen, she quietly spoke to Graham. "Go find Mattie and give him a hug. He's missing Precious."

"Bluidy hell." Graham sighed. "They had a special bond. I should've thought about it when he got here. Sometimes I can be a selfish prick." He squeezed her hand before he walked out of the room.

She gathered up the plates and silverware and made her way to the smaller dining room. It took only a few trips to fill the table with their food. One by one, they all made their way in and sat down.

Dinner, despite Duncan and Graham's tiff earlier, turned into a huge success. There was a lot of laughter, except from Mattie, who remained quiet and thoughtful.

When they were done, Deydie insisted on getting

Mattie upstairs to his bath and Graham cajoled Duncan into resting before the movie. Cait worried Duncan would fight his da on it, but he didn't seem to have the energy. By the time Graham and Cait had finished cleaning up, Mattie was in Spiderman footy pajamas.

They all went into the media room and sat down. Cait settled in next to Deydie, but her gran shooed her away. "Give me some room here. I intend on stretching out."

Cait chose a recliner in a row of eight. Mattie, with his green plaid quilt in hand, crawled into one of the recliners next to hers. She situated the lap quilt over him. He smelled of baby shampoo and freshly scrubbed boy. He relaxed back, sinking into his chair like a favorite pillow. Nonchalantly and without looking at her, Mattie reached out and took her hand.

An inexplicable peace overcame her. He was such a tender little boy, and her heart ached for him. A small voice inside of her said, *You need one of these. A child.* Once she sold the article about Graham and got her career ironed out, she'd seriously consider having a baby of her own. In the meantime, though, she was content with holding Mattie's hand.

Duncan settled into a beanbag chair, stretching out, looking ready for a nap.

Graham shut off the lights and the big screen lit up with *White Christmas.* A second later, he claimed the recliner on the other side of her. He reached over her and caressed Mattie's head for a moment.

"He's a great kid, isn't he?" Graham whispered.

Before Cait could answer, Deydie turned around and gave them both a "Shhh."

Cait felt like she was on a first date, wondering if Graham meant to hold her hand, too. He didn't disappoint her. Before the wall fell on Danny Kaye, Graham had taken her hand.

She got butterflies that made their way down and fluttered into her panties. Almost immediately, Mattie began snoring softly, and his hand slipped from hers. She tried concentrating on Bing Crosby singing and not on the warming sensation pulsing through Graham's hand to hers. Then he really messed with her by rubbing small circles into her palm.

She tried to pull her hand away, but he tugged back. She leaned over. "Stop."

The word had barely left her mouth when he kissed her, very softly, very quickly.

Deydie turned around again. "Don't make me take the broom after ye two. Now, be still."

Graham laughed and brought Cait's hand to his lips.

Her heart pounded, and for a moment, she couldn't think clearly. Then she wanted answers. *Why is he doing this?* His heart wasn't available—he'd said so. And she'd already told him she wasn't interested.

Determined this time, she tugged her hand free and sat on it. She chanced a glance at him and he was smiling at the screen, but she knew he was laughing at her.

For the rest of the movie, she was acutely aware he was there, but he didn't try to touch her again. As the credits ran, Graham got up and leaned over as if to pick up Mattie. He whispered into her ear, "You look at home with a bairn next to ye." He gently picked up the limp boy and turned to Duncan. "I'll lay Mattie down. Do you want to stay also?"

"No," Duncan said gruffly, like his da should've known the answer to that one. "I'll be up to get Mattie as soon as I'm done with the nets in the morn."

"I'd like to go with you," Graham proposed. "I haven't been out on the water in a while."

"No," Duncan said unequivocally. "I like to do things on my own."

The air had become dense with tension. With those two at it again, Cait felt uncomfortable. She wanted to say something, but then Graham spoke up.

"All right, then," he conceded. "But don't worry about rushing back here. Let me keep Mattie for a while. I'll return him after lunch."

"Fine," Duncan said and left the room.

Deydie stretched. "That boy is hardheaded. He needs help with those nets."

Graham looked at Cait. "Would you stay in the guest room tonight? I'm going to help Duncan anyway. You don't mind, do you?"

Cait looked to her gran.

"I don't know why ye're looking at me," Deydie complained. "Ye've spent several nights here already. I didn't have a say *then*. Why would I have a say *now*?"

"Aye," Graham said, not giving Cait a chance to answer. He nodded toward Mattie in his arms.

"Oh, all right," Cait said, a little worried about her resolve. She turned back to Deydie. "What about that thing we're watching—"

Her gran cut her off. "Never you mind."

Graham walked to the door of the room but turned at the last minute. "Deydie, *Holiday Inn* next or are you done for the night?"

"I'm no spring chick, but I can stay up for more Bing." Deydie had a mischievous grin on her wrinkly face.

"Caitie, meet me in the kitchen. We'll make snacks."

Graham left with Mattie, and she stood there looking after him.

What a presumptuous man. She had two choices—be obstinate and go to bed upstairs alone or stay downstairs and watch one of her favorite movies. Cait found it hard to hold to her principles when her favorite part of Christmas was watching and rewatching all the holiday flicks.

Cait grabbed Mattie's green plaid quilt and laid it over Deydie's feet. For her thoughtfulness, she got little more than a grunt.

Then, just as she was leaving the room, Deydie placed her order as if Cait were the waitress. "Bring me back some cheese and crackers. The white kind."

"Yes, your hiney-ness."

"That cheek," Deydie warned, "will get ye in trouble."

Cait left and found Graham at the counter in the kitchen, filling a tray with fruits and veggies. He looked up and gave her a lazy smile.

She hurried to the refrigerator. "Deydie wants cheese and crackers." She hated that she was so flustered. That one smile unnerved her. And excited her. She grabbed the fridge door for support.

He came up behind her. "The Manchego's in the dairy drawer. I keep it for her."

"You're good to my gran. I'm grateful for everything you've done for her." Cait could actually feel the heat coming off him. Or maybe it was just the refrigerator cooling her front. She was so confused.

"I'm the one who's grateful," he said. "Because of Deydie, Duncan was able to stay here in Gandiegow and have a normal life. Between my da and your gran, they convinced me to leave the boy here while I worked.

When Da was out on the boat, before Duncan was old enough to go with him, Deydie and the quilt ladies worked in shifts to change his nappies, bandage his scraped knees, and spank his backside when he needed it. They did a great job and deserve the credit for the man Duncan is. And they did the same when Mattie's mum dropped him off as a wee one, only days old."

Cait didn't know where to start with the questions. "Where is Mattie's mother? Who is she?"

"Her name doesn't matter. Duncan met her on holiday in France before he started university. She's one of those women who likes to jump out of planes and climb mountains," he said, a cross between disgust and being distraught.

Cait started to object that women could be thrill seekers, too. But Graham put his hand up.

"I'm not being sexist," he explained. "Selfish is selfish. She's older than Duncan by ten years, besides. She liked her life as it was and didn't need him. When she got pregnant, she wanted an abortion. Duncan dropped out of university and kept Mattie. I told him I'd get him a nursemaid and a house in Edinburgh, but he's always been independent and didn't want my help. He's a fisherman, through and through. Like my Da and his da before him. I'm glad of the choices he's made. But I've had the means to make his life easier, and he simply refuses. I wish at times . . ." His voice trailed off as he looked out the window, even though it was frosted over. "Anyway, Mattie's mother relinquished her legal rights, dropped him off, and disappeared on a 'round-the-world trip. Duncan's never heard a word since."

"Oh," was all Cait could say. She wasn't the only one who'd been used and discarded.

"Are you okay?" Graham asked.

"Yeah." She straightened up and put a smile on her face. "Where're the crackers?"

"The pantry, left side," Graham said. "I'll grab a knife for the cheese."

Back in the media room, Cait leaned back in her lounge chair, thinking. Graham set the tray in front of Deydie, who looked half-asleep.

He filled a plate for himself, turned on the movie, and faded the lights.

"Is this seat taken?" he asked.

"Such a gentleman, huh?" she remarked. "What if I told you it was?"

"Not such a gentleman then." He sat beside her, balancing the plate between them. "Orange slice?"

She shared from his plate as Bing sang, and Fred Astaire danced. Deydie began to snore. Loudly.

"Romantic, isn't it?" he teased. "Do you have a remote for her?"

"Shh," she chided.

They watched some more, as Bing worried over the success of his Holiday Inn, but the snoring became unbearable.

"Let's go into the parlor," Graham suggested.

They snuck out from the room and relaxed on the sofa in front of the fire. Precious's bed still lay there, and Cait wondered if Dingus would be allowed to use it.

"How are you adjusting to being back in Gandiegow?" he asked. "It's a much slower pace than you're used to."

She laughed. "Do you know how busy I've been? I haven't had a moment's peace since I arrived."

"Why don't you have that moment now? Come here." He pulled her to him and put his arm around her.

She should've relaxed, but she couldn't. Surely, he'd guessed by now that her nerves unraveled the closer his body got to hers. She started prattling. "There's so much I need to do. I haven't checked my e-mail. I have boxes to unpack. Which reminds me. Do you know of any place to store my things until my house is rebuilt? It might be a long time, since Mr. Sinclair can't really do much until spring."

"My outbuilding is nearly empty. And anything of value, like photos or anything else, you can store in one of the bedrooms upstairs."

Okay, when he said bedroom, she went straight to sex. And dammit, it conjured up the movie he'd done with Antoinette. She'd showed her boobs in that one. Big fleshy double D's like Bonnie's. Those love scenes had been hot and heavy. Cait saw green, and it wasn't the green plaid from Mattie's quilt. She pulled away from Graham.

"What's wrong?" he asked. "There are locks on the bedroom doors and on the outbuilding. I promise not to rifle through your personal belongings."

She couldn't make that same promise to him. In fact, the next chance she got, she planned to pick through his home as if she were an archaeologist on a dig. "Nothing's wrong. Just thinking about Antoinette. She's gorgeous, and I hate her. Tell me she's stupid." Normally, Cait wouldn't be so frank, but it was late and the coziness of the fire made it easy for her to loosen her tongue.

"Sorry. Antoinette's a Rhodes Scholar. Brilliant in mathematics. She couldn't pass up making millions with her looks and acting skills. She says when her acting career is over, she'll get her doctorate and teach."

Cait rolled her eyes. "Figures."

He pulled her back to him. "Ye're beautiful, too, lass."

"Now you're just being ridiculous." But she stayed under his arm and leaned her head back. "Some of us are just passable. We can't all be beautiful like you and the marvelous Antoinette." She turned her head to look at him, which was a big mistake.

He stared at her lips like they were juicy orange slices and he wanted to suck on them. He moved in and did. Very tenderly and carefully. She tasted him back.

Then he eased away from her. "We'd better wake Deydie so she can get home."

Cait's foggy brain cleared. "Maybe you should just leave her." It'd be safer that way, with eagle-eyed Deydie as chaperone. Keep Cait from doing something foolish. Like climbing into Graham's bed.

"No," he said. "She won't stay. She'll shoot me if I don't wake her."

On the big screen, Bing had sung "White Christmas" to his girl, and they'd made up. Graham stirred Deydie. "Time to go home, ole bird. I'll walk you."

"Ye'll do no such thing." Deydie pushed herself up. "I'm not an invalid."

He looked at Cait and shrugged.

Her gran trundled toward Cait and wagged a finger in her face. "Mind ye stay in yere own bedroom or there'll be hell to pay."

"Yes, ma'am," Cait said without a moment's hesitation.

"I'll see ye in the morning." Deydie snatched her coat up and waddled out the door.

Graham took the tray and Cait turned out the lights.

As they put everything away in the kitchen, Graham spoke. "Tomorrow we'll figure out how to get your boxes here. Leave the dishes," he added as Cait started to fill the sink with soapy water, "else Deydie will go Rambo on me. I've put her on my payroll, and she feels like she has to earn every penny. We'll leave the rest to soak." He went to the stairway. "I'll show you to your room."

She followed him, getting a perfect view of his butt in his Dolce and Gabbana's. She would've loved to put her hands on those jeans, but she told her lustful body to get real. All men were the same, hounding after double D's, like her pig of a dead husband. They had no interest in brains or commitment, only in breasts and sex. Graham Buchanan was no different from the rest.

At the top of the stairs, Graham pointed to the first room. "Mattie's in there. I should be back before he gets up in the morning. You'll be in here." He opened the door to a Victorian paradise.

It had a queen-sized canopy bed covered in delicate pink flowers. The wallpaper and draperies matched the bedspread. It was like she'd been sent to court to inhabit one of the ladies-in-waiting chambers. The only thing that broke up the pink was the white dressers. "Don't tell me you have women's clothes in there? I refuse to wear Antoinette's nighties."

He shook his head. "Get over the whole Antoinette thing. I don't bring women here. The dressers are empty. I'll give you one of *my* shirts to sleep in." There he was again, giving her that possessive look.

"Bonnie wants to see you," Cait blurted out. "I ran into her earlier."

No spark ran over his features. "It's probably the imported rum. I told her to tell me when it came in. It can wait."

"Good," she mumbled to herself. "Then you aren't stupid."

"What?" he asked.

"Never mind."

He disappeared and came back with the top half of a pair of expensive men's pajamas. "Go change in the en suite. I'll be back in a few minutes to tuck you in."

"I'm not five," she retorted.

With hooded eyes, he gave her a steamy, sexy, slow once-over. "Aye."

"Stop it." She stomped toward the bathroom with his jammies in her hand. She heard him laughing as he went down the hall. She knew he was playing with her.

As quickly as she could, she slipped out of her clothes and into his shirt. She ran back into the Victorian room, got under the covers, and turned off the light. That should stop him from thinking he had to tuck her in.

A few minutes later, the hall light went out. She heard him making his way back to her room, the darkness not deterring him.

Until she heard a *thud* and then, "Bluidy hell." He hopped the rest of the way to the bed.

"I know you're not asleep," he said.

Cait remained as quiet as a pillow, hoping he'd go away.

The bed shifted with his weight.

Her naughty mind wondered if he were naked. It would take only one wandering hand to find out. She clasped her hands together instead and then clamped them between her legs to make doubly sure her hands didn't go exploring.

He scooted under the covers. "I just want to lie next to ye for a while."

Yeah, and she had an air conditioner she wanted to sell him for the middle of winter.

He moved closer to her, enough so that she could feel his warmth.

"'Tis hard for me that Duncan won't stay in this house. I spend so very little time in Gandiegow, and he feels he has to keep more than walls between us."

Dang it. Just like that, he'd brought her defenses down. She reached out and found his hand among the covers.

"At least he lets me be with Mattie." Graham squeezed her hand back.

She turned toward him, barely making out his features from the half-moon's glow. "It's not easy to forgive parents." She still had a huge chip on her shoulder when it came to her dad and stepmother, Evelyn. Her dad hadn't even been loyal to her mom's memory for ten minutes before he was off hunting for wife number two. And Evelyn, she had made sure Cait was shipped off to an East Coast boarding school before the wedding bouquet had wilted. "Believe me. I know a thing or two about not forgiving."

He laid a hand on her cheek and stroked it.

She laughed nervously.

"Calm down, Caitie. I'm not here to ravish you." He gave her a chaste kiss on the lips. "I just want to be near ye for a bit."

"Deydie would beat us both to death with her broom if she saw us right now. I promised her."

"Ye promised not to sleep in my bedroom." He motioned to the floral room. "This is definitely not my room. I'd have to return my *Man Card* if it were."

She smiled into the dark, knowing under the covers lay the bod of Mr. Darcy. This room couldn't change that. She had the urge to know for sure. She wriggled up against him, and sure enough, she discovered what she wanted to know. He was fully dressed. And hard.

He groaned. "Don't do that. Unless you want me to *not* keep my word."

"Sorry," she said, trying to sound contrite. She wasn't really. Her husband had blamed her for *his* sleeping around—that she hadn't been sexy enough. Yet here was Mr. Darcy, with a woody that would've frightened the pantaloons off Elizabeth Bennet. "We should get some sleep. You have to get up early if you're going to crash Duncan's fishing party."

"Aye. He'll be angry."

"You're a persistent man," she said. "You wouldn't let a little resentment stand in the way of making things right with your son."

"I am persistent." He pulled her to him and kissed her.

She should've pushed him away. But the inside of her lit up like the northern lights, tingling in places she didn't even know she possessed. She deepened the kiss by opening her mouth to him, and her tingles turned into a slow burn, flowing through her, devouring her from the inside. She found the bottom of his shirt and put her hands underneath to get to him. It wasn't enough. Her skin ached for his. She started unbuttoning his shirt. He was unbuttoning hers. When she reached pay dirt—that lovely chest of his—she pushed him onto his back and made a slow exploration of every inch of his uncovered territory. That didn't stop him from doing his own assessment of her with his hands.

"You're so soft," he said.

"And you're so hard." She meant his broad chest, but he growled and rolled on top of her.

Apparently, the fun and games were over. And this was really happening. As she was wondering if she should stop and think it through . . .

Mattie cried out.

They froze.

"God, I'm sorry," she said, as she pulled her shirt together.

He got out of bed. "I've got him."

She felt so ashamed of herself with Mattie in the next room. She shouldn't have tempted Graham after he'd promised not to ravish her.

Graham came back in the room with Mattie sobbing on his shoulder. "I can't get him to stop. I don't think he's awake."

She sat up. "Put him here between us. I'll rub his back."

He laid the distraught boy down carefully. Cait adjusted the covers over him and caressed his back. Graham climbed in next to him, their two bodies cocooning Mattie.

He began a low Gaelic lullaby, and Mattie calmed a little. By the end of the song, he no longer sobbed, but gave out small gasps, remnants of a bad dream.

"How long has this been going on?" she whispered. "Since the accident?"

"Aye." He took her hand in his. "I tried to get Mattie help, made several appointments with professionals. But Duncan wouldn't hear of it. He's sure Mattie will come around in time on his own. I'm not so sure. When I told Duncan what I thought, it only gave him more reason to be mad at me." Graham sighed. "Therapy has helped a lot of people."

"Firsthand experience?" she asked gently.

"Aye," he said. "When Duncan was a teenager, he was so angry. He seemed to change overnight from wanting my complete attention to resenting me. I had no one to turn to. No one knew I had a son. I found a therapist I could trust to keep my secret. He helped me to deal with the guilt of being away so much and to try to come up with strategies for dealing with Duncan as well."

"Has it worked?" She thought about the small outbursts before and after dinner tonight.

"No, but at least I'm not beating myself up over it as much. It is what it is. Even if I wanted to, I can't quit acting. A lot of people are depending on me." Sadness had gripped his voice.

"Like Deydie?" Now Cait felt guilty.

"She's a small fish in a very large pond of people my acting supports. I have a production company. I have obligations," he said. "Let's not talk about it anymore." He got up and walked around the bed, then crawled in beside her. "Good night, Caitie."

He settled in and she relaxed, falling asleep against a bona fide heartthrob.

Somewhere in the early hours of the morning, she heard him get up. He kissed her before leaving the room.

Fishing was the most dangerous job in the world. The boy lying next to her had been witness to that.

For the first time in a long time, she offered up a prayer. *Please keep Graham and Duncan safe.* Even though she couldn't remember the last time she had talked to God, she sure hoped to hell He was listening now.

Chapter Twelve

Cait woke up to the tantalizing aroma of Deydie's coffee and bacon making its way upstairs. She sighed and opened her eyes. Mattie stared back. No smile. No frown.

"Good morning," she said. "I bet you didn't expect to see me here."

No reaction in those big sad eyes.

Cait kept right on talking. "Have you ever wondered why I talk funny? I lived in America for a long, long time. That's why my Scottish burr doesn't sound like anybody else's in Gandiegow." Even Evelyn's speech coach couldn't eliminate it completely. "Well, your grandda's accent is a little different, now, isn't it? That's because he's lived all over the world. But I've heard him get very burrish when he's emotional." No response. "How about we get up and see what Deydie's up to?"

The boy slipped out of bed and went downstairs.

This kid will be a hard one to crack.

Cait dressed in her clothes from yesterday, located a comb in the bathroom, then went to find the coffee.

She found Graham instead, sitting at the kitchen table

with Mattie on his lap. He looked windblown and exhilarated. A rush pulsed through her, waking up her senses. When Graham's eyes met hers, she saw gratitude. He nodded to the boy to acknowledge the source.

She nodded back. Her cheeks got hot remembering how they'd kissed yesterday. It wouldn't happen again. Graham would be leaving soon, back to his glamorous life. She needed to get a grip and stop being drawn into his persuasive arms.

Determined, she went to her laptop and powered it up. "Where's my gran?"

"Went home. Said she had things to care for," he said.

"Oh." The puppy, Dingus. "And Duncan?"

"Home taking a nap. I told him Mattie would spend the day with us."

Her eyebrows went up. "Us?"

"I thought we'd make some Christmas cookies. Decorate them like we're Americans. Climb up in that chair, Mattie, and pull down the copper container from the cabinet." Graham pointed to the one next to the stove.

Mattie slipped off his lap and did as he was told.

"Take the lid off and look inside," Graham encouraged.

Mattie's eyes got big as he pulled out each cookie cutter—a candy cane, a stocking, a bell, a star, a gingerbread man, and a reindeer. He looked up at Graham, his eyes saying, *Wow*.

"There's dough and icing in the refrigerator, compliments of Bethia and Moira."

"How about Mattie and I eat breakfast first?" Cait believed if the little boy would talk, he would've argued with her. "Let's wash our hands."

Mattie pulled the chair over to the sink.

Cait went to Graham, king of the kitchen, and touched his cheek. "You're a good grandda, Mr. Buchanan."

He grabbed her hand and pulled her down for a quick kiss.

The three of them had a fine time making cookies and messing up the kitchen. Dozens of cookies lay on waxed paper, haphazardly decorated.

When Cait went to sit down, she realized she'd forgotten about her booted-up computer. She jiggled the mouse and brought up her e-mail. The most recent note was from her boss at Write Chicago.

You're fired!

Cait broke into a cold sweat and frantically scrolled down to the previous message.

If you don't respond by midnight, you'll be replaced. I understand you've had unusual circumstances, but that's no excuse for not doing your job.

That is dated two days ago. Desperate, Cait scrolled down again.

Your nonresponse has forced ME to do YOUR job for YOU. If you want to stay employed, call me.

Hadn't she asked for time off? Hadn't that request been accepted? Almost hysterical now, Cait scanned all the e-mails from Write Chicago and went to the oldest one.

I know I approved a short leave of absence, but half of the freelance editors have come down with the flu, and we are backed up with jobs. Your time off will have to wait. Attached are four articles to edit.

Cait slumped over the screen, stunned.

Graham came up behind her. "What's wrong? You look like your best friend just died."

"I've been drop-kicked off my job," she said, feeling lifeless.

He planted himself beside her. "You said you were a quilter."

"Quilting's not my day job." She put her head in her hands. Fired? Sure, she had committed to do the *People* magazine article, but there were no guarantees for future work. Write Chicago was her backup if nothing came afterward.

He rested a hand on her back. "Mattie, run in and turn on 'Frosty the Snowman.'" The little boy left the room with a worried eye on Cait.

"He's anxious," she said, starting to rise.

"He'll be okay for a few minutes. Tell me what happened," Graham urged gently, taking her hand.

"I haven't checked my e-mail since I got here. Haven't listened to my voice messages either. I assumed they'd respect that I was in mourning and leave me alone."

"Mourning?" He looked both sympathetic and horrified. "If I'd known, I never would've . . ." He trailed off and searched her face. Finally, he asked, "Who?"

"My husband," she said sheepishly.

He got up and stomped over to the dirty dishes, throwing them in the sink like he was launching missiles at the enemy.

"It's not what you think."

"It might've been a relevant piece of information, Caitriona. Considering I almost, well, *took advantage* of you last night."

She slammed the lid down on her laptop. "My *husband* had been cheating on me for years. Most recently he'd shacked up with a twenty-two-year-old silicone-enhanced model. *Surgery I probably paid for.* The divorce wasn't final yet, but it had sure as hell been filed. He saved me a lot of money by dropping dead. Do you know how much divorces cost these days?"

He looked stunned, as if she'd just Tasered him.

She put her hands on her hips, feeling more like her heavy-handed gran every moment. "*I'm sorry* you regret last night. But you shouldn't on my account. You did nothing wrong. And for that matter, neither did I."

He didn't back away from her as she expected. Instead, he came to her and wrapped his arms around her, laying his chin on top of her head. "I'm sorry for yere loss just the same. I know how ye feel. Duncan's mother cheated on me as well. I never got over it."

Cait's stomach dropped. *He's never gotten over his ex?* Figures. She tried to pull away.

"What's wrong?" he asked, tightening his grip.

She wiggled free and started pacing the length of the kitchen. "Now I'm the one who feels stupid. You're not over Duncan's mom." She stopped short, inches from him. It made sense he would still care for the mother of his only child, but still. Then all her worries burbled out. "You've been using me. All you men are the same. As long as you get your rocks off, you don't care who you hurt along the way."

He grabbed her upper arms. "Ye're wrong. I met her

on my first shoot, when we were both nobodies. I fell head over heels for her. When she got pregnant, I begged her to marry me. She thought it would hurt her career if anyone found out about the baby, and she had no intentions of marrying. When Duncan was just a wee babe, I discovered she was cheating on me. She left me with Duncan and said she never wanted to see either of us again." He gave Cait a shake. "She kept her promise. We never saw her again. A year later, she died in a plane crash with some Hollywood producer." He dropped his hands from Cait, looking more miserable than ever. "I know now it never would've worked between us. I wanted a marriage like my parents'. One that lasts forever. Instead, Duncan had to grow up without a mother. And now Mattie, too. What a legacy I've started for my family."

"Don't beat yourself up." She caressed his arms as if he were cold. "It's not your fault. One thing I finally learned from my husband is that I couldn't control him. Just like you couldn't control your ex. And Duncan couldn't make Mattie's mom be a mom. It's not your fault; it's a circumstance beyond your control. No one blames you. Who knows? Maybe some good will come out of all this."

"Hmm." He sat down at the table, seeming to let the idea soak in. He laid his hand on her laptop, and when he did, he brought his gaze up to meet her. "Maybe the same can be true about you getting fired. I've got a thought." He jumped up. "Follow me."

She trailed after him up the stairs and into the den. He opened the bottom drawer of his desk and pulled out a thick manuscript. "How'd you like to work for me?"

She took a step back. "No way."

He held the papers up to her. "I need a second pair of eyes. Will you read this script? I need to know what you think about it." He dropped it on the desktop.

"Maybe as a favor. But not as your employee." She picked it up and scanned the title. "I read an article about this book. Some predict it's the next Harry Potter."

"The studio wants to get rolling quickly. I'd be playing the headmaster," he said. "Let's go back to what you said a minute ago about good things coming out of bad things. It would mean a lot to me if you'd take a look at this and give me your honest opinion." He looked so anxious, she couldn't say no.

"I guess I have plenty of free time now. When do you need it?"

"An hour ago." He laughed. "I'm holding everyone up."

"Sure. Why not?" she said.

"You go get settled in the parlor, and I'll bring you a cup of tea. Mattie and I will tell Deydie not to expect you today," he said. "You're busy."

"No," she blurted. He'd see Dingus. "I'll talk to her. You know how persnickety she can be."

"Aye. Prickly as a hedgehog. Run along now while I clean the kitchen. You still have your key?"

She nodded.

"I'm taking Mattie to the city to buy his da a present before returning him home. I'll be back late this afternoon. You'll stay, won't ye?"

She was playing with fire. The more she was with him, the more she wanted to be with him. And every time she looked into his brown eyes, the harder it became to ignore the guilt about the article.

"Yes, I'll stay," she finally acquiesced. "If my gran will let me."

As soon as Caitie left for Deydie's, Graham went to her computer and did some snooping. He opened the most recent e-mail from WriteChicago.com. "So, I was right. Our Caitie Macleod is a journalist."

He opened her documents folder. None from the past few weeks. "It doesn't make any sense," he said out loud. "It's an opportunity of a lifetime, to rat me out. And why didn't she nose around my house when she had the chance? What kind of journalist is she?"

A small hand tugged his shirtsleeve. Graham looked down and saw his mute grandson frowning up at him, disappointment in those young eyes.

Shite. "I know." Graham put the lid down. "I shouldn't have been poking through her laptop. I won't do it again."

More frowning from the six-year-old.

Graham put his hand up. "Promise. Grandda just had a weak moment, that's all."

The boy seemed to understand weak moments and laid his head against Graham's arm. It broke his heart to see Mattie so sad. "Let's get you dressed. We're going to Inverness, lad, to do some Christmas shopping. What do you want to get yere da?"

Mattie said nothing. Graham led him upstairs, wondering if he'd ever get his grandson back. Or if the sea in all its glory—and horror—had swallowed up Mattie's voice forever.

"Mind ye get home tonight." Deydie rocked back and forth with Dingus curled up in her arms. "My quilting ladies are coming over for a sew. We're finishing up our Christmas projects."

Cait bit her lower lip. "I'll try. I promised I'd wait for Graham to get back and give him my take on the script. He has to make a decision right away."

"Watch yereself with him," Deydie warned. "That Graham is a charmer. No man will buy the goat if he can get the milk for free."

"Gran, I don't plan on getting milked anytime soon." Cait held her breath, waiting to see if Deydie would notice that she'd called her "Gran" for the first time in a long time.

"Ye better keep yere teats covered then," Deydie mumbled.

Cait grinned and left the house. She didn't want to ponder too long about getting "milked." She had a growing ache inside of her that needed fixing and wondered if there were any free men within a hundred miles of Gandiegow who could be her "handyman." Or would she have to order an electronic device to take the place of a man in her bed?

The path to Graham's house stretched up before her. She chose her steps carefully so as not to stumble. A sinking feeling took hold, almost overwhelming her. What if Graham was the only one who could satisfy her?

She wrapped her scarf tighter around her neck and let herself into his house. A message had been posted on the refrigerator.

Make yourself at home. Tea is in the teapot and there're extra logs by the fire. My mobile number is on the refrigerator. Call me if you need anything. G.

She ran her finger over his handwriting, tracing the letter *G*. It was stupid how dreamy she felt. She wandered over to the fridge and found his posted number. For kicks, she programmed him into her cell under *Mr. Darcy* but didn't call. This would be the perfect time to snoop around his house, but she'd promised to read for him. She grabbed the manuscript and went into the parlor and curled up on the sofa.

After some quiet hours in front of the fire, she closed the manuscript, laying her hand on top. It was good.

As if on cue, Graham came in the back door, and she went to greet him. He met up with her in the hall with rosy cheeks and windblown hair. She wanted to warm him up by using her body as a blanket but remembered herself.

"The verdict is?" He acted as anxious as if he'd auditioned for a part.

She held up the script. "It's a much different character than you've played in the past."

Graham took off his gloves. "I've never done fantasy. I don't know how the audience will react."

"You'll make an awesome headmaster." *A much sexier headmaster than I ever encountered at boarding school.* "It'll widen your fan base." She stopped herself and put on her journalist hat, storing away these tidbits for when she got back to her article about him.

"Then I should accept the part?" He looked both excited and unsure.

"They'll love you. Like always," she added sincerely.

He looked over at her with his eyebrows knitted together. His unspoken question hung between them. *And you, do you love me?* But surely she'd imagined it.

She ducked her head and squeezed past him, heading

for the kitchen. The sack on the counter gave her the diversion she needed. She struck a light tone. "Now, let's talk about more pressing matters. What did you bring back for dinner? It smells delicious." She pointed to the sack.

"Who said it's for you?" he teased. "It might be for one of my other script readers."

"Not buying it." She grinned at him. "You're smart enough to understand that while I refuse to be paid for my services, I do expect to be fed. Good choice on picking up Chinese. Tell me you brought chicken lo mein."

"That and everything else on the menu." He took small white boxes from the sack. "If I'd had your cell number, I would've called to find out your favorite."

He beamed at her, and they shared a moment—one where time stood still, both of them grinning at each other, crushing like a couple of idiots, making her forget to feel self-conscious. But feeling so comfortable with him made it uncomfortable for her. "I have to hurry home. Deydie needs me. Quilting."

"I was hoping you'd stay awhile. Duncan didn't want to come back up to the house tonight. And Mattie is pooped." Graham laughed. "He picked out a vanload of toys for Duncan as Christmas presents." He stared at her for a second longer and then spoke, his voice pouring out, smooth as fine Scotch. "And you, Caitie Macleod, what do you want for Christmas?"

It should've been easy to answer, but the question seemed too personal. And she felt too vulnerable. The things she truly wanted couldn't be bought and were too much to ask for, so she mentally marked them off instead.

1. A family. All she had left was Deydie, and at every turn her gran hindered her plan to get close.
2. A career. Journalism was her ticket to fulfillment. But until she had the gumption to finish the *People* magazine article, her career was dead.
3. Happiness. She wasn't ten years old anymore and knew the score. Happiness could be elusive. But since returning to Scotland, she'd had a few rare moments of utter contentment.

And all of them had been with Graham.

Panic washed over her. She couldn't, and wouldn't, rely on a man again to give her what she wanted. She grabbed her coat and ran for the door.

"Where are you going? You haven't eaten yet." He came toward her, looking concerned.

She backed away from him, recalling clearly what had happened when she'd allowed another man to cast a spell over her. Loads of heartache. Then death. "I'll take the lo mein with me."

When she reached out for the container, he grabbed her hands and searched her eyes. "Why are ye running away?"

"Deydie will skewer me if I'm late." She tried to ignore the seductive tingling that had electrified her hands where he touched her.

"I don't believe you." His eyes implored. "Why is it so hard for you to come clean with me?"

She pulled away from him. "Listen, Mr. Sensitive. Life is full of shitty things. Getting fired is only one of them. And I have to deal with my stuff on my own. End of story."

He pushed a lock of her hair behind her ear. "No, you don't. You have all of us to help you through it."

"What is that supposed to mean?" she practically yelled. "My only family is a gran who can't stand me. I've been on my own for most of my life. The only person I can count on being there *for* me, *is* me. And sometimes even I'm not that reliable."

"What about me?" he said, his voice sounding strong and steady, reminding her of the oak in her backyard in Chicago. Every time she felt beaten down by Tom, she'd lean against the tree and soak up its strength.

"Nope." She shook her head. "You're that good-looking guy from the big screen. Even I'm not stupid enough to believe that you're real. Besides, I don't want *or* need a man in my life. God has given me a do-over, and by God, I'm going to take it. This time, though, I'm not going to think I can have it all. I just need my career. And even though I might've blown it these past couple of weeks, I'll get my foot back in the door."

"How do you plan on doing that?" he demanded, angry this time.

"None of your business." She grabbed the lo mein carton and stomped out the door.

It took only a few steps down the path before she realized how unfair she'd been to him. Guilt, and not the cold wind, made her shiver. Why had she taken her dreadful life out on Graham after he'd been so nice to her? He didn't deserve her bitchiness. As soon as she got to Deydie's, she'd text him and tell him she was sorry. Yes, it was the chicken's way out.

She ran the rest of the way down the path, half slipping, half stumbling. At Deydie's, she didn't hesitate but threw open the door. The quilt ladies turned to her. Bethia and Rhona rocked in the chairs in front of the fire, hand stitching. Deydie and Moira sat at the sewing machines. Amy sloshed tea over the side of a mug as she placed it beside Deydie.

"Shut the damn door, lass," her gran shouted. "Ye look like you've seen a kelpie."

"I've seen nothing." Cait closed the door and set the lo mein carton down. "Where's Ailsa and Aileen?"

"Not here yet," said Rhona.

Cait dug around in her pocket for her cell phone. She had to text Graham now or she would lose her nerve. But she didn't get the chance.

Deydie got up and shuffled toward her, holding Dingus at arm's length. "Take him out. The little bugger got into the oatcakes. He'll have to shite from here to next Sunday."

Cait took him and held him close. "You've grown, little guy."

There was a knock at the door.

"It's probably the twins," Deydie announced and opened it.

Shocked, Cait almost dropped Dingus, but she regained her wits enough to shove the dog inside her coat without Graham seeing.

He ducked his head and came in with the brown sack. "Anyone interested in Chinese food?"

The women ran to him like cats on catnip. Cait slipped past him. Before she made it out the door, though, he grabbed her arm. "Don't go because of me."

"Don't worry. Take a load off. I'll be right back." She tried to smile at him, knowing she'd have to apologize in person now that he was here.

He let go of her, and she slipped out of the house.

While Dingus did his business, she rehearsed what she would say to Graham. She let the dog sniff around longer than usual, trying to put off the inevitable. Finally, she hid the dog under her coat once more and headed back to the cottage.

Once inside, though, Cait got a momentary reprieve. Amy gave her a pointed look and nodded toward the bathroom. Mr. Eagle Eye caught it all, but Cait couldn't do anything about it. As nonchalantly as she could, she snuck off to the restroom. Dingus's box sat in the bathtub with his little blanket fluffed up and ready to go. "You be quiet." She knelt down. "Your new daddy doesn't know about you yet." She gave him a kiss and settled him inside. She pulled the shower curtain in case Graham decided to make a pit stop in Deydie's loo, then went out and joined the rest.

They were all devouring the Chinese food, including Mr. Movie Star. Before she could take one bite, Ailsa and Aileen walked in.

"What did we miss by coming late?" Ailsa pulled out a half-finished Crazy Quilt.

Aileen grabbed for it. "Give it to me, Sister."

"No." Ailsa tugged back. "I have more embellishments to add before we move on."

It was almost comical, two menopausal women playing tug-of-war like kindergarteners. Cait noticed that Graham was openly laughing.

"For heaven's sake, don't start again," Bethia said. "It's almost Christmas. Sit down and have some Chinese food before it's all gone."

Cait grabbed a rangoon and joined Graham, who lingered with his food by the fireplace. It was a brave move on her part. All the ladies were watching, and she was sure to take some flak for it later, but she owed him that apology.

"Sorry about earlier," she said, half whispering. "I'm a little off-kilter right now. You know, the job thing and a million other worries. I hope to have my life figured out before I'm Deydie's age. Forgive me, okay?"

"What are you saying over there?" Deydie snapped. "Speak up. The rest of us want to hear."

Graham winked at Cait. "She agreed to come back to the house tonight and help me wrap presents. You don't mind, do you?"

Chapter Thirteen

"I never agreed—" Cait cried.

Graham cut her off. "You ladies wouldn't be able to help wrap presents, for the obvious reason." He wagged his eyebrows like Groucho Marx and, at the same time, gave them all his beguiling smile.

"Aye, we understand." Deydie beamed. "Do you have any sewing to do, Caitie?"

"Almost done." She'd argue with Graham as soon as she got him out the door. "I can finish tomorrow."

"Then go on," Deydie commanded. "Take yere food with ye back up the bluff."

Cait zipped her coat and headed out the door. It was barely closed when he pulled her into his arms—right outside Deydie's front door! Boy, was he asking for trouble. She let him kiss her anyway, which was the least she could do for going bitchy on him earlier.

When he pulled away, he took her hand. "Let's get out of here."

"So do you really have presents for all of them, or were you making that up?" Cait asked, their hands still linked.

"Aye." He nodded. "New sewing machines. Dougal—

you know him, our postie? Our postman," Graham clarified. "He should have them unloaded by now. I heard Deydie talking about your machine and, well, I had them ordered."

"You bought *them all* machines? You'd better bring along a defibrillator when you deliver them or else you're going to have drop-over-dead seamstresses on your hands," Cait ribbed. "Are you always so extravagant?"

"No, not always. You know you have to be careful with a Scot. If you do too much for any one of them, they get upset. Scots don't handle the thought of taking charity very well." He shrugged. "This year I had to do something special. Those ladies have been good to me and Duncan and Mattie."

He stopped then and stared at her, the moon their only light. "I didn't get anything for you. I wanted to, but I just didn't know what."

"Your friendship's enough." She dropped his hand and hurried up the path. "And that's all you're going to get from me, bucko," she called over her shoulder.

"I'm not interested in being yere friend," he said, his strides getting longer.

He caught up to her at the entrance of the house and pulled her inside, taking her into his arms again. "Tell me you don't like kissing me." He leaned in and teased the hell out of her lips, then pulled away, apparently waiting on an answer.

She had to let the fog clear from her brain first before speaking. "Kissing you is like kissing my cousin."

He unzipped her coat and slipped his hands inside. "Most unconventional family." He kissed her again, this time tantalizing her with his tongue. She couldn't help the moan that slipped from her lips.

She forced herself away from him. "Okay, I concede. Maybe kissing you is a *little* fun." She touched her swollen lips. "But it has to stop. I'm not an affair-type girl. In fact, my Dating Card has been revoked. By me," she added.

"Relax," he said—the Big Bad Wolf to Little Red Riding Hood.

"Yeah, *relaxing* before got me into an atrocious marriage."

He rubbed his nose against hers. "Put it out of your mind." He kissed her again. This time his hands roamed over her, running up her sides, over her breasts. "If you want me to stop, I will. But I hope ye don't."

Deydie's lecture on teats and milk came back to Cait, and she laughed. She put her hands on his chest and pushed him away. "Time-out. I need to regather my convictions."

She wasn't the only one affected—he breathed hard himself.

"We need a diversion," she said. "Let's get to wrapping those Christmas presents."

"Ye're no fun at all," he groaned.

"That's not what you said a few minutes ago." She turned and sashayed up the stairs.

The den had been packed full of sewing machines. A mound of overflowing sacks sat in one corner. On the desk lay rolls of wrapping paper, ribbons, bows, tape, and scissors.

"This is going to take all night," she exclaimed from the doorway.

The Big Bad Wolf breathed down her neck. "I hope not."

"Don't get any ideas. I'm here to help with the presents. Not for you to get into my goodies."

He laughed. "We'll see."

She walked to the center of the room with the boxes surrounding her. "You could've fed the whole town for what all this costs."

He gave her a pointed look. "From what I hear, I don't need to."

She put her hands on her hips. "What did Amy tell you?"

He shrugged. "I don't know what you're talking about."

"I'm going to duct tape that girl's mouth shut," Cait mumbled. She tossed him a roll of wrapping paper. "Come on, Mr. Generous. Time to get to work."

He tossed it back. "I'll go get us something to drink." And left.

"Men," she complained to the room. "Always making themselves scarce when it's time to wrap presents." She sat on the floor and started with the first machine.

She'd finished with two before he returned with two steaming hot cocoas.

He set hers down beside her. "It's the salty caramel kind. I hope you like it."

"What I'd like here is some help." She took a sip. "It's delicious, though."

He crossed over to the mound of sacks. "How about I get these organized into piles? Most of it's for Mattie and Duncan." He looked over at her. "I never got around to showing you what I got Duncan."

"Because you were accosting me," she whispered to her cocoa as she brought it to her lips again.

He pulled out a package. "It's the latest satellite phone for the boat. I want Mattie and Duncan to always be connected."

"What's the story with you and Duncan?" she said. "Since I'm doing all the work here, you have to spill it."

"In a nutshell? You know how kids are. When they're young, you're their hero; then they hit adolescence, and suddenly you're the devil. But I think things really got complicated when Mattie came along. Ever since then, Duncan's been really angry about me not being around when he was a kid." Graham sat beside her and picked at the carpet. "I can respect he wants to be his own man. But he could give me a chance to make up for not being there. I don't think he'll ever forgive me." Graham sighed.

She took his hand. "Anyone with half a brain can see that Duncan is a hell of a man, which means you've been a hell of a da."

He gazed at her. "I was determined to never raise a child in the limelight. Those kids can get pretty screwed up. My own da kept Duncan here, and I got back as often as I could. When I was younger, though, I stayed very busy, one job after another. If I had to do it over, I would make different choices."

"Such as?" she prompted.

"Long ago, when that producer discovered me and told me I'd be great on the big screen, I should've told him to go flush himself. I was so full of it back then. So cocky. I had no idea what I was getting myself into. And it was a lark at first. I thought I'd do it for a while and then come home. But starring in *Pride and Prejudice* changed the course of everything forever. I had expected to parallel my father's life—live here, be a fisherman. As it turned out, I became his polar opposite. I'd walk away from it all if I could, but too many people depend upon me." He tilted his head, his eyes creasing with sadness.

"I know what would help," she said seductively.

."Yeah?" He perked up. "Some serious necking?"

She held out the wrapping paper. "A little manual labor."

He chucked her under the chin. "Always full of sauce, aren't ye?"

"Yup," she replied. "I come by it honestly. Deydie's my gran."

Cait actually made it back to Deydie's that night and into her trundle bed. The next morning, the day before Christmas Eve, she woke to the smell of coffee, the aroma of fresh-baked scones, and Dingus licking her face. "Stop it," she chortled. "You're not my alarm clock."

He wagged his tail in reply.

Deydie hovered over the table with her hand made into a fist. "Ye better get yere arse up." She punched the dough in front of her with the force of a sledgehammer, making Cait glad she wasn't the flour and yeast. "We've got to get the baking done today."

Cait rolled over and snuggled with the puppy. "Don't you ever enjoy a little lie-in?"

"Not when there's work to be done." Another *oomph* to the dough. "And there's always —"

"Work to be done. Yeah, yeah, I know." Cait chanced a glance at her gran.

Ever consistent, Deydie delivered one of her withering glares.

Cait pushed herself into an upright position. "No need to get your panties in a twist. I'm getting my arse up." The dog barked happily.

The morning and early afternoon flew by, her gran taking Christmas baking to a whole new level—an obsessive-compulsive one. It wasn't so bad spending time with

Deydie, working side by side. They made enough butter-laden baked goods to clog the arteries of the whole northern coast of Scotland. They'd gotten into a sort of rhythm with the flour, the sugar, the shortening, coming together to make something special from the separate ingredients.

While Cait braided the last fruit-infused dough into a Christmas stollen, she wished she and Deydie had become like the dough, weaved inexplicably together, become a real family. But they hadn't.

By late afternoon, the table was covered in loaves of fresh bread, mounds of decorated cookies, and a line of Christmas stollen that Santa would've been proud of.

"Mind now, we'll be up early," her cranky gran commanded, as she handed Cait the plastic wrap. "We have a lot to do."

Cait tore off a sheet. "And today was a respite?"

"Don't be fresh," Deydie growled.

They had a light supper, and before Cait knew it, the old woman was ushering her off to bed like she was six years old again.

Even though Cait was exhausted, she lay in bed for a long time thinking about things she shouldn't. At odd times throughout the day, she'd had these unbearable twinges of hope come over her, a sweet and sappy anticipation, wondering if Graham would make an appearance. Just to see his face would've been enough to keep her from missing him, the handsome dog. How he'd weaseled his way into her life and into her thoughts was beyond her. But as the sky darkened outside and no one had knocked on the door, her twinges had faded into a dark despair. Cait punched her pillow and rolled over, determined to get some much-needed sleep.

In the wee hours of the morning, Dingus whined and

Cait got up and took him out. No sooner had she gotten back into bed than Deydie was poking her awake.

"Up with ye. We've got calls to make today," the old woman said.

Cait's groggy mind didn't understand. "Phone calls?"

"No, ye silly girl." Deydie's voice was barbed. "Calls to the infirm and homebound. We're sharing our Christmas joy."

Christmas joy? It sounded like six months' hard labor. Cait just wanted to sleep a while longer, but she dragged herself out of bed anyway. "I need caffeine."

"I'll make tea while you dress. Hurry now," her gran nagged.

"All right already." Cait dressed in her chestnut wool slacks, mocha turtleneck, and walnut-colored mukluks. The browns made her light blue eyes stand out. By the time she'd finished, Deydie had a mug ready for her. Breakfast consisted of one cherry scone from yesterday's cooking frenzy and half of a banger.

They started Christmas Eve morning by dropping off the puppy with Moira, along with a fresh loaf of bread. They spent the rest of the day going from house to house. Deydie insisted Cait pull the wagon with the boxes of goodies, her gran cackling every time the wagon slipped off the icy path. Some of the people they visited got lap quilts and loaves of bread, others only Christmas cookies. It seemed to Cait that Deydie was an unlikely Santa, but she took her job seriously, barking orders at her elf, Cait, every chance she got. The more her not-quite-five-foot gran ordered her about, the happier she seemed.

Christmas Eve had awakened all of Gandiegow. Normally, the streets were empty in the middle of the day, but not today. Everyone was out. With the number of people coming and going to the store, it should've had a revolving door. Others hung garlands as last-minute decorations outside their homes. Even more folks stood about calling, "Happy Christmas to ye," to passersby, the harsh weather not stopping their cheer. A real Norman Rockwell Christmas.

But it was all bittersweet. Everywhere they went, Cait felt her mama. The folks of Gandiegow talked about Nora as if she were making Christmas cookies in the cottage around the corner with the bright blue door. Didn't these people know that her mama was dead? Hearing Nora's name both hurt and soothed at the same time. After Mama died, her father had never mentioned her again. Cait, so alone and new to America, had sometimes wondered if she'd only imagined the mother her father had forgotten. But here in Gandiegow, Mama was remembered. And remembered fondly. Was it hard for Deydie to face her dead daughter's memory day in and day out? Or did it make her feel better? Cait began to feel it was almost too much. She wanted to hide under one of Deydie's quilts and never come out. Instead, she walked on behind her gran, pulling the wagon.

Deydie Claus ended her route back at Moira's house. The twins had arrived and were sitting with Kenneth. Deydie and Cait stayed only long enough to make sure they weren't needed and to get Dingus. But before they left, Cait felt compelled to hug Moira. She wanted to tell her everything would be okay, except she wasn't sure it would.

On the way back to the cottage, Cait once again longed for Graham. It'd been two whole days, and she wanted to see him, talk to him. She wished he'd been there to see Deydie hold the sick Bruce baby or hear how Deydie had sung Christmas songs with the tone-deaf Mr. Menzies. Or see how the townsfolk had stepped outside for a kind word or a wave as they passed with their Christmas wagon. She could almost see Graham's eyes twinkle with the telling. Cait's erratic brain had gone into automatic journalist mode, cataloging little snippets for him all day long. How stupid. She should give herself one hell of a shake for being so foolish. Why would he care how her day went, anyway? She was nothing to him, and he was nothing to her.

By the time they got back to the cottage, it was already dark and it was only three thirty. Cait tried to unwind in front of the fire while Deydie warmed the leftover Cullen skink soup for their dinner. Cait took deep, relaxing breaths, recentering herself as she'd learned in yoga class.

No surprise, her gran didn't cooperate with Cait's mental health moment.

"Get that last loaf of bread," Deydie demanded. "We'll need to hurry through our dinner to get to Mass and the Christmas pageant by five."

It'd completely slipped Cait's mind. The thought of entering the church made her stomach churn even worse. The last time she'd walked into a church was the last time she'd seen her mama. Nora had lain in a plain wooden casket, dressed in white, looking like an angel taking a nap, not dead at all. But when her da made her kiss her mother, she'd felt nothing but cold; none of Mama's warmth and softness was there. That's when it hit home. Mama was gone forever. Cait didn't hear one word of the service that followed. She simply stared at the cross, wondering why her beautiful mother had to die and nobody was doing anything about the pain she was feeling.

"Caitie?" Her gran snapped her fingers, waiting for the missing loaf. "What's got into ye?"

"Nothing," was all Cait said. She'd have to glue her game face on for Gandiegow tonight, or else all would know she had no intentions of cutting God any slack.

Graham got back to the house empty-handed and frustrated after spending a good portion of the day in Inverness. He'd been there for an hour, going from shop to shop, before he realized what he was doing—hunting for a present for Caitie. He started kicking himself for acting like a pining fool until he figured out his motive. He wanted a present for her only because she'd been so good to his family. And when he found that present, it would be from all the Buchanan men and not just him.

The last two days, he'd stayed away on purpose. He'd wanted to prove to himself he didn't need her. Caitie made him laugh, sure, and he wanted a physical relationship with her—who wouldn't? God, she was sexy as hell. It was okay to enjoy her company, the way her smile comforted him and how her smart-aleck cracks made him feel like a normal guy. Not something he experienced out in the real world. But it wasn't like he depended on her. He was just fine by himself.

He made himself a Scotch on the rocks and took it upstairs to the den. If it had been anyone else but Caitie, he would've bought a piece of jewelry and that would've been the end of it. But Caitie only wore a small locket on a chain around her slender neck and a pair of simple stud earrings. Both seemed to be part of her, like the mole on her right forearm or the dimple on her left cheek when she smiled. Generic jewelry for Caitie just wouldn't cut it. Maybe he would order her something special from the Internet. But he just didn't know what.

The den looked empty now with all the wrapped presents downstairs in the parlor. He pulled a photo album from the shelf and sat at the desk. He still had a few minutes before he had to get ready for the Christmas pageant.

Many of the pictures were of his da and him, ones his mother had taken with their old camera. Others were of Gandiegowans—Deydie, Bethia, Freda, Kenneth, *The McDonnell,* Pippa, and Claire. Some of these townsfolk were still here, some gone to other locales now.

And there it was. Graham had almost missed it. A Christmas present for Caitie.

He pulled the album closer and examined the photograph: Caitie and her mother—a young Nora smiling, holding a toddler with mischief written all over her face. Graham carefully removed the picture and walked around the house, searching for a frame from his own collection. He found the perfect one—an antique mahogany that held a photo of him at eight, holding up a nine-kilogram cod, one that had given him a hell of a fight.

He removed his picture and positioned Caitie's photo in the matting. On a whim, he returned his boyhood picture so it sat behind hers. After locating the wrapping paper Caitie had liked best, he gently wrapped up the present.

For long minutes he sat at the desk and sipped his drink, staring at the gift. He'd had a successful day. Besides finding her the perfect present, he had finally figured out what he was about. He wasn't some lovesick pup or attached to Caitie in any way; he was just attracted to her, nothing else, and the same was true of her. He felt confident they could keep it loose between them. They could have the physical relationship he'd been fantasizing about, and nobody would get hurt. He walked from the room and turned out the light. It was time to get ready for the service at the church and spend the rest of the evening with Caitie.

Chapter Fourteen

Cait laughed at the sight of Deydie hurrying to Saint Henry's Episcopal Church as if rushing to witness the actual birth of Jesus.

"I need to get there early for Rhona," her gran called over her rounded shoulder. "Now stop yere lollygagging."

Cait would've liked to skip church. It would've been nice to sit this one out, just stay by the fire with Dingus instead of torturing herself by going. She caught up with her gran anyway.

Deydie elbowed her. "Now, listen up. I know we're an Episcopalian community and all, but that doesn't mean that we don't accept outsiders."

"What are you talking about?" Cait asked, pulling her bronze scarf tighter around her neck.

"It's Ailsa and Aileen. They're *Catholic*." Deydie lowered her voice, as if the word were a bit daring to utter. "But they're good quilters. And because we don't have their church here, they come to our Mass." Her gran looked over at Cait as if she might do something rash, like block the doorway when the twins tried to enter.

Deydie added, "I just thought ye should know."

"Okay. Thanks." Cait realized this was the most her gran had said to her that didn't involve biting her head off in the process.

When they got to Saint Henry's, two bundled-up boys stood out front with bulletins in their hands. "Happy Christmas," they said, handing each of them one and opening the door.

The narthex was nearly deserted. Deydie slipped out of her wool coat and shoved it at Cait. "Here," she said and shuffled off to talk to a small group of women by the sanctuary's entrance.

Not having attended church for the last eighteen years, Cait felt like a mackerel out of water. She stood there for a moment, trying to get her bearings.

She slowly gazed around and saw nothing had really changed except for a new coat of white paint. The church boxes were still lined up against the left wall. They were nothing more than cubbies for each family in the parish, but they served as mailboxes of sorts, invaluable to a small community as a means of communication. An old memory flooded her senses.

"Caitie, run to the church and put this recipe in Pixie's box. She said she'll pick it up tomorrow." Her mother had been standing in the kitchen of their cottage, wiping her hands on a yellow-and-blue dish towel. "While yere there, check our box to see if anything is in it." She had felt like a big girl for being entrusted with such an important task as checking the church box.

She forced herself out of the memory as Moira walked over to join her.

Cait pointed to the bulletin board on the right-hand wall. "It all looks the same. The flyers, the lone glove, and has that key been hanging there since I left?"

Moira smiled. "Saint Henry's Lost and Found. It's the first place I come if I've lost anything. Did you see we have a bigger box below now for the larger lost items?"

Cait nodded at the hoodie hanging over the side.

A hand tapped her shoulder. She spun around and found Father Gregory, the Episcopal priest of her childhood. He was old now, but his kind eyes remained unchanged. "Ah, Caitie Macleod, how good to have you home. I'd heard you'd come."

She received the underlying scold as if she'd skipped his confirmation class. The only thing absent was a *tsk-tsk*.

"Deydie's been missing you, child." Another veiled reprimand.

Cait couldn't say what she really thought in God's house. "Aye," was her only reply.

He patted her on the arm as if he understood and shook his head. "Deydie's quite the . . ." He seemed to be searching for the right word.

"Character," Cait provided.

"One of God's finest," the good father added.

Rhona called to the priest. He and Moira said good-bye and went to help Rhona.

Cait went down the hall to find the coatrack. As she hung up Deydie's coat, another hand laid itself on her shoulder. At first she assumed it was Father Gregory again, but then Graham's aftershave teased her nose.

"Caitie." That deep voice she'd grown so used to. It melted her like a marshmallow over a warm fire. "How are ye this Christmas Eve?" he continued.

She turned around and saw Graham wearing an Italian suit with a charcoal gray overcoat slung over his arm. And he looked better than good. She tried to play it cool and slip out of her jacket as nonchalantly as she could. But he took over, spinning her around and slipping the coat off like she was his marionette. His breath was on her neck and goose bumps rose all over her. She bit her lip. Surely somewhere in the Bible it said not to entertain intimate thoughts within the confines of a church.

"How've you been?" To anyone else, his voice would've been perceived as interested or concerned, but her delighted heart chose to hear it otherwise, as flirtatious and seductive.

She had planned to lambast him and demand to know why he'd left her alone the past two days. Instead she just gazed up at him, captivated not only by his good looks but by what made him Graham—that boy-next-door quality in the hard body of a warrior. The way he studied her with intensity made the quiet, dark hallway turn from a cozy respite into a sexually charged opportunity.

We're in church, for heaven's sake! She tried to counter what was going on between them by answering his question. "I've been good." Except for the naughty thoughts she'd been having about him.

He surveyed her brown sweaterdress. "Aye." Judging by the eager and lustful look in his eyes, he should be struck down for his erotic thoughts as well.

He leaned down, and she wondered, and worried, that he'd kiss her in front of God and anybody who might peer down the passageway at them.

But Mattie appeared, thank goodness, and put his hand into Graham's. *Such a tender kid, such a tender act.*

Cait automatically knelt down and brushed the hair out of the boy's face. "Hey, Mattie. Happy Christmas."

He gave her no reaction except to look into her eyes. He reminded her of a portrait she'd once seen of a solemn Amish boy. That boy's eyes, like Mattie's, held a wisdom beyond his years, his whole demeanor guarded.

She didn't know how to get through the barricade that Mattie had built around himself. How could she assure him the world could be a safe place when he'd witnessed otherwise? She had the urge to march into the sanctuary and demand God do something—take back the boat from sinking, let those drowned men live, or just let Mattie go back to being a kid again.

Graham looked from her to Mattie. "I'm ushering. And running a little late. Do you mind getting Mattie to Rhona? He's in the pageant as a shepherd."

"I'd love to." She smiled down at the somber-faced boy.

"You're a doll," Graham said, while hanging up his coat. Before he walked away, he ruffled Mattie's hair. "Knock 'em dead, lad. Do Grandda proud."

Mattie nodded.

"I'd better get to work." And Graham was gone.

Cait stared after him, trying to wrap her mind around that man. A world-famous movie star seating the lowly people of Gandiegow. But she knew that he wasn't doing it to lord it over the townsfolk or to put on a show of being a "regular" person. He did it as a service to his community.

And she felt humbled by it. "Wow," she said aloud, a mixture of warmth and giddiness filling her.

Mattie studied her face, taking everything in with his big eyes and big heart.

"I know. I'm such a mess." She put her arms around him, and he responded by standing as still as one of the planks in the manger by the altar. He smelled of Christmas cookies, pine trees, and the cold wind outside. "What am I going to do?" she said to the universe.

Mattie lifted one hand up and patted her back. Twice.

"Come on, you. Let's find Rhona." She led him away.

After leaving Mattie with the other pageant players, Cait headed back to the narthex. Graham held his arm out to her.

"Will ye be sitting with me this evening?" He might have been behaving like a perfect gentleman, but she caught the gleam in his eye—one that undressed her and had her in his bed, begging for more.

"No. I'll be with my gran." Cait peered into the sanctuary.

"Not likely," he added.

Of course he had seated Deydie, so he would know. Cait looked and saw it, too—the quilting ladies taking up a whole pew with her gran in the center.

"Come." He took her hand and tucked it into his arm.

And, bold as brass, he marched her down the aisle. With all Gandiegow's eyes on her, she felt as hot and ruddy as a red Christmas stocking hung too close to the fire.

He led her to the nearly packed pew behind the row of quilters. "Save me a seat," he said, then retreated back to his post by the entrance of the sanctuary.

No way. She stood up and moved herself farther down, squeezing herself between two families until she was directly behind Deydie. *There*, she said to herself.

But it didn't work. A few minutes later, Mr. Christmas Charm himself excused his way down the pew between the two families just as she had and squeezed in beside her. He took her hand.

"No handsies in church," Cait hissed out of the side of her mouth.

"Just hanging on so ye don't slip away, that's all," he whispered back.

Deydie turned her head and shushed them both.

Cait glared at Graham and he shrugged. The lights went down, except the one over the altar.

A fair-headed teenager came out in a white shirt, tie, and black trousers with a microphone in his hand. "And it came to pass in those days, that there went out a decree from Caesar Augustus, that all the world should be taxed. Joseph also went up from Galilee, out of the city of Nazareth, to be taxed with his espoused wife, Mary, who was great with child."

Two other teenagers, a boy and a girl dressed in period clothing, entered. It was the same Christmas story being played out all over the world. The same one Cait had been in for so many years long ago.

Until finally, her last Christmas here, she was old enough to have the part of Mary. It had no lines to learn—then as now, there were no speaking parts except for the narrator who told the story while others acted it out. But she remembered being Mary, and how, in those moments, utter peace had surrounded her, even though her young life was spiraling out of control. To be part of a bigger story—the story of birth and ultimately the story of forgiveness—had left her with some hope that her own life would turn out okay. Now, eighteen years later, the fact that the Christmas story hadn't changed was comforting. And despite what Jesus had done to her and her family, Cait's uneasiness unraveled just a hair.

She looked at Graham's hand holding hers. It was big and strong, a confirmation that she had landed in a safe place.

Mattie came onstage then wearing his brown shepherd's costume, and all the shepherds were visited by an angel who was perched high on a ladder, close to the cross. Cait saw the Jesus's feet with the nails in them and looked away. A curious mixture of guilt and pity came over her.

Mattie crossed over to where the cradle lay. In years when there wasn't a new infant in their parish, like this one, they used a doll. But the way Mattie stood over the crib, solemn as a pastor at a funeral, one would've thought he'd witnessed the miracle for real. One of the other shepherds had to move him along, he was so transfixed.

This gave Cait courage to look up at the full-grown Jesus hanging over the altar. He didn't look coldly indifferent, as she'd imagined him all these years. He looked accepting of the things that had come to pass. A peace came over Cait and she knew who to share the feeling with. She reached over the pew and laid her hand on Deydie's shoulder.

Deydie turned her head slightly for a second, then went back to watching the play. Cait kept her hand there a moment longer, then sat back feeling content. It had been a long time since she'd felt truly connected to anyone. But here she was, knotted into the same net as her gran.

Two blocks in the long-lost quilt of their family.

Graham leaned over to her. "You all right?"

"Yes," Cait whispered. "Now, shhh," she said gently.

After the pageant, Father Gregory said the Mass, the people had their Communion, and then all of Gandiegow gathered in the narthex for cookies and punch. Children ran between the tables, shoving goodies in their mouths, as the adults chatted, the buzz deafening. Cait hung out with the quilt ladies, Moira and Amy on either side of her. Graham had gone to find Mattie, and Cait could see him now across the room, standing with Duncan. Soon they made their way over to where she stood.

Graham held Mattie's hand. "Can I have a minute, Caitie?" he asked her.

Duncan took Mattie, lifting him up over his shoulder like a sack of potatoes. "We'll be going now. I'll see you back at my house later. The couch will be made up for ye."

"Sounds good." Graham turned to them all. "I'm spending the night at Duncan's so he can set the nets in the morning."

"Isn't that grand," Rhona said. The other quilting ladies agreed.

"We'll see what Father Christmas brings to his house before heading up to see what the old elf left at mine." Graham winked at the ladies, who seemed almost giddy at the prospect of Christmas morning themselves. He took Cait's elbow. "If you'll excuse us?" He ushered her away, toward the coatrack.

From this close, she could smell his familiar aftershave again. And God, he looked great. So sexy. And where he touched her, she sizzled.

"Will ye come back to the house with me now for some eggnog before I go to Duncan's?" The candlelit church made his eyes smoky and alluring.

"Let's go back to Deydie's instead." *It's safer there.*

His wolfy grin surfaced. "Ye're not scared to be alone with me, are you, Caitie?"

She glared at him. "Of course not. You're harmless."

"Right," he drawled, not sounding harmless at all. "I thought we could sit by the fire. And talk," he added as an afterthought.

Except she could read his mind. The two of them on the sofa, shagging.

She couldn't—wouldn't—be destructive with her life again. Tom had played her, known how to make her succumb, like he'd read her instruction manual. He'd wooed her, cajoled her, and convinced her that they were two halves of one soul. But they were only empty words. He was incapable of real love. Like her da. Like all men she knew.

But even though she'd never fall in love, her body burned for Graham in a way she'd never felt before. Literally burned. If she went outside and sat in the snow, the white stuff would melt and go to steam in seconds.

"Deydie will expect me home at the cottage."

Her gran, with her superpower hearing, made her way over to them. "Go on, now, but watch yereselves. I'm off to see Kenneth and have a wee bit of a nightcap with him and Moira." Deydie yanked her coat off the hanger and Graham helped her into it. When she was sufficiently garbed, she turned to Cait. "Don't be long."

He pulled her coat from the rack and slipped her into it. "I need to have a quick word with Father Gregory. Shall I meet you outside?"

"Sure." To her own ears, her conviction sounded about as firm as the cotton batting in a soft quilt.

As he walked away, she said a small prayer. *Please give me strength.* But she was weak. And couldn't help falling just a little bit for the luscious man sauntering down the hallway.

She should just make her excuses and head back to Deydie's cabin alone. But when she stepped outside and Graham came toward her, any resolve she'd had got swept away with the wind.

Graham gazed into her eyes, and as if on cue, the wind died down and his wolfish grin faded. What was left was sincerity. He kissed her hand. "Ye are safe with me, Caitie. I promise."

She tugged her scarf more securely around her neck. "Since you promised." The problem was, could she trust herself?

Graham led them down the boardwalk, then up the path to his house. "You go in and sit by the fire."

In the parlor, the first thing she noticed was that Graham still didn't have a tree. "Surprising," she said aloud. He'd helped Duncan with his earlier. She wondered for a moment if Graham had an aversion to pine needles strewn all over his mansion. Her next thought was that it was way too intimate in here. She went around the room, turning on every light and even bolstered up the fire with extra logs. The place looked as bright now as if it were midday instead of Christmas Eve.

He returned, shaking his head. "Caitie, shame on you. Ye've doubled my carbon footprint." He handed her a glass mug. "Let's just enjoy the firelight."

He turned off the switches himself and came toward her.

She was one of those rabbits caught in the sights of a predator—too scared to make a run for it.

He reached out and gently took a lock of her hair, examining it as if it were a petal of a delicate flower.

It was a strange sensation, standing by the fire so—one side of her heated to the extreme, the other side chilly. Kind of how she'd felt about coming back to his place.

He leaned down and kissed her. It was all flame then—her insides skipping the pleasant middle ground and kicking straight into full-on desire. She could feel him holding back, and she knew it was for her benefit. He'd promised her safety. But her inner naughty girl took his restraint as a challenge. What harm was there, really, in playing with fire? She deepened the kiss, slipping her tongue inside his mouth and exploring like she had something to prove.

He moaned, and her desire intensified. She held him tighter. Just to up the stakes a little, she found his waistband and tugged out his tailored shirt. Her hands traveled up his body to his warm chest.

"Caitie," he moaned into her mouth. "What're ye doing to me?"

"Shut up and take it like a man." Her wicked hands caressed their way to his back and downward to his waistband, this time moving into the lower region.

"My promise." His plea came out a bit strangled.

"Screw yere promise." She was surprised at how thick her own brogue had become. Her hands went downward, to the place of no return.

"Are ye sure about this?" he asked.

She kissed him back, hard. "It's Christmas," she finally answered. "What the hell."

Chapter Fifteen

That was all Graham needed. Still kissing her, he scooped her into his arms. He had a hard time of it making his way up the stairs, trying not to trip or bump into a wall. He used his elbow to switch on the lights and lay her on his bed.

"*Now* you want the lights on." She said it playfully and looked smoking hot at the same time. He could've lit a firecracker with her. And if he didn't get inside of her soon, he'd go *bang* just at the sight of her lying on his bed.

"Ye're driving me crazy, lass." He ran a hand through his hair. He wanted her to strip so he could revel as every bit of her came into view.

"Turn off the light and come here," she answered, rising up. She looked completely sure about herself now, none of the worry he'd seen earlier. She'd crossed some hurdle, and he was glad of it.

He hit the switch, thankful for the full moon and the skylight positioned over his four-poster mahogany bed. "God, ye're beautiful," he said.

He went to her, and she kissed his neck while she unbuttoned his shirt. He stood very still, taking her torturous loving caresses, knowing instinctively she needed to be the one who took this first step, be the one in charge. *Only for now,* he consoled himself.

She made a path down his chest with her mouth, his hard-on straining upward against his pants. She undid his belt and slipped it off. There was no time for teasing with this woman. Next she went for his zipper and pressed his pants to the floor. He stepped out of them, but she wasn't done with him yet. She slid her fingers under the waistband of his boxers.

"Ye're killing me," he groaned.

"I know." She laughed and ran her tongue over his hard nipple. She pushed his boxers down and wrapped a hand around his dick.

And the game was up. He put his hands around her face and pulled her lips to his, working hard at kissing her tenderly. Only it came out as much more. Every emotion he'd felt for her since he'd met her went into that kiss. He burned for her. Not some little matchstick flame but a full-blown bonfire, out of control.

But all of a sudden, something shifted in her. She pulled away from him and got into bed resolutely, and he wasn't quite sure what he'd done wrong. She no longer looked like an eager lover but a dutiful one. For a second, honor had him close to throwing on the brakes to find out what had changed with her. But blood surged through him on testosterone overload. *No, Graham. Don't you dare miss this opportunity.* He let his hormones win out, and he joined her on the mattress, rolling on top of her, careful not to squash her.

But he was naked and she was fully clothed.

"There's something wrong here," he said lightly, not wanting to distance her further. "Yere clothes."

She wriggled beneath him until he felt the coolness of her bare legs against his.

"I'm ready," she said.

He couldn't ignore her strange mood this time, but he tried once more. "That's all I get? Those tights off?"

"My panties, too. That's the important stuff," she defended. "Are we going to do this or what?"

Pride had him close to redressing himself.

His penis, though, would never forgive him for throwing in the towel.

"Do you have anything?" For as sexy as it sounded, she could've been asking for a fucking Band-Aid.

"Fine." He sounded like a prat, but he didn't apologize. He retrieved a condom from the bedside drawer.

"Can I help you with that?" Like offering to help tie his shoes.

"I've got it," he hissed and slipped on the rubber. He might be peeved at her, but his pecker was still hard as a hammer. And he had some banging to do.

No! He stopped himself. This was Caitie. Except she hadn't been herself in the last few minutes.

He rolled on to his side, finally acting the gentleman instead of a horny bastard. "What's going on here?" he said gently. "I thought you wanted this."

"I'm cold." She pulled the covers up over her nearly clothed body and lay as stiff as a corpse.

"It's my job to keep you warm." He took off the condom and pulled his boxers over his disappointment before joining her under the covers. "Come here." He slipped his arm around her shoulders.

"I don't know what's wrong with me," she whispered.

He didn't know if she'd said it to him or the darkness.

"Nothing's wrong with you. Apparently, it wasn't the right time." His dick would've begged to differ.

"No, it's me. You're perfect." Her thick Scottish burr had vanished, becoming a sort of forced American accent. "The timing is fine. I'm just damaged good-ds." There was a catch on the end of her voice.

"Nonsense." He pulled her close. "Ye're a piece of work, Caitie Macleod. I'll give you that. But it's not damaged goods that ye are." He kissed her temple. "You're a masterpiece. Do ye hear me? A masterpiece." A warmth came over him and woke something deep inside, a fierce beast. If it was her dead husband who'd done this to her, Graham only wished the motherfucker were still alive so he could make him pay. Maybe it was something else. He only knew that he'd do everything within his power to make this woman happy.

"A masterpiece," Graham repeated to the night.

She began to cry and curled into him. He felt helpless. He did the only thing he could do—held her closer. "I promise you, Caitie—"

He stopped himself—threw the throttle in reverse. He'd almost made a fucking declaration. Was he crazy? He did not make pledges or vows.

Even worse, he actually had no idea what it was he so desperately wanted to promise her.

Cait heard the words but didn't respond. Her heart was broken. This wonderful, amazing man thought she was a masterpiece, while she'd spent most of her life believing she was a bit of dust gathering in the corner.

She felt awful that she had led him on and then put on the brakes. She couldn't believe he wasn't furious with her. Taking care of her emotional needs when his carnal needs hadn't been met? Graham was an extraordinary man. Hell, Tom wouldn't have cared.

They lay entwined in each other's arms until she got her emotional breakdown under control.

He kissed the top of her head. "Are ye all right, then?"

She looked up at him from the crook of his arm, his face a mixture of helplessness and stoicism in the moonlight. She sat up. "I'd better get back to the cottage. Deydie wouldn't approve of me in your bed."

"Ye're probably right." He sighed. "I'll walk you home. I need to get to Duncan's anyway." He slipped out of bed.

She searched for her discarded tights and undies, finding them in the folds of the comforter. Embarrassment swept over her, and she was grateful he hadn't turned back on the lights. After they were both dressed, they walked back down the hill in silence.

Outside Deydie's darkened cottage, Cait put her hand on his chest. "You can't come in."

"I know." He kissed her on the forehead.

She slipped into the cottage without a backward glance.

Because the lights were out, Cait expected to find Deydie in bed. Instead, she found her gran sitting in her rocker by the fire. "The little one needs to go out," Deydie said without looking up.

That was the nicest thing she'd called the puppy since he'd come to stay.

"I'll get him," Cait said.

"Ye do that. And keep an eye on that scoundrel. I need to run up to the big house. I forgot to check on the turkey." Deydie grabbed her coat and left.

"Oh God," Cait said to Dingus. "Lucky we didn't get caught." *The bed, Graham, Cait's tights in the sheets.*

She picked Dingus up and ran her hand over his plump wriggly back. "I guess it's just you and me."

The dog yawned in reply.

"Or not," she said. But she wasn't truly on her own anymore now. She had her grandmother. She rubbed her cheek on Dingus's fluffy fur, then took him outside. When she got back in, she quickly set up her sewing machine and grabbed the quilted potholder. It took only minutes to put the finishing touches on Deydie's Christmas present. She hid it in the small Christmas bag she'd brought with her just before her gran returned.

Deydie took off her coat and sat by the fire again.

"Tomorrow—" Cait started.

"Now, tomorrow is a busy day." Deydie said it like today had been one of idleness. "Most of the day we'll be preparing the Christmas feast."

"And where are we celebrating it? Here, just the two of us?" Cait asked, not sure what to expect, especially after the "checking on the turkey" comment.

Deydie eyed her closely. "Ye're not getting all squidgy over Graham, are ye? He's one who'll never marry again." She glared a moment longer, then sighed. "We tried, ye know. We wanted Duncan to have a proper mama, not us old ladies watching after him. But our Graham declared he'd never wed again and he's held to that promise."

"Who's talking about getting married? That's the last thing I want or need," Cait defended. "I was just asking about Christmas. Are we having it here or not?"

"Not." Deydie looked like a churlish child with a secret.

Cait put her hands on her hips. "Fine. Then I'll assume we'll be at Graham's."

There was a long silence while Deydie creaked back and forth in her rocker. Finally, she looked up. "Watch yere heart, Caitriona Macleod," Deydie warned. "It's a hard thing to take back once ye've given it away." By the fierceness on her face, she looked like she could've written the book about love lost.

Cait eased into the other rocking chair beside Deydie. She wanted to reach out and touch her but didn't.

"I know something about giving my heart away," Cait said. "Believe me. I know what a mistake that can be." But her heart seemed to have a mind of its own. Graham had called her a masterpiece. He'd been nothing but wonderful to her. And despite all of Cait's rational reasons for not wanting to get tangled up in a love affair, her heart had a mind of its own.

It wanted to defy everything and wrap itself in pretty paper and give itself to Graham as a present on Christmas morning.

Christmas Day started at five A.M. with her gran rushing around like she'd downed a case of Red Bull. Deydie bossed Cait from one end of the cabin to the other. But Cait occasionally caught her gran stealing moments alone with Dingus, sitting in her rocking chair and holding the little guy close. If Cait even looked their way, her gran would harrumph and put the dog back in his box.

Before they left, Deydie dug a red ribbon from her sewing box and tied it around the puppy's neck. "Not a word from you, missy," she growled at Cait. "I'm doing it for Graham."

Cait raised her hands. "I didn't say anything."

Gran put the dog back in his box. "Take yere nicest clothes. We'll be dressing for dinner."

"Okay." Cait had anticipated this and dug around in her suitcase for an outfit.

"Hurry up, now," Deydie complained at the door. "We've things to do."

Cait rushed to Graham's as sweet anticipation flowed through her. *It's Christmas,* she told herself, and her butterflies had nothing to do with a possible crush on a certain someone.

But when they arrived at his house, Graham wasn't there. It felt like the Grinch had stolen her Christmas. At least the turkey smelled good.

Cait put a cap on her feelings lest Deydie get the wrong idea about her relationship with Graham.

"Put these in the parlor." Deydie stacked the gifts into her arms.

Cait took them there but had no tree to deposit them under.

She heard the back door open, and her heart skidded to a stop. Deydie started caterwauling from the kitchen like a near-murderous fishwife.

"Watch yere feet. Not on my clean floor." Her gran's frantic voice got closer and closer, her pitch higher and higher. "Oh, Graham, stop."

Mattie, still bundled up, appeared first, his cheeks glowing from the outside. Then came Graham, dragging a tree behind him. Deydie followed, ranting about her floors.

"Ye're making a mess. Look at those pine needles. If ye'd warned me. Oh, dammit." Gran huffed back to the kitchen.

Cait smiled at Mattie and stood beside him. "Now *that's* a tree."

The boy laid a possessive hand on one of the branches

and ran it along the length. When he looked up at her, she saw a little pride there.

Graham propped the eight footer in the corner. "Mattie found it and cut it down with my da's saw. You should've seen him." He turned to his grandson. "Run out to the shed and get the tree stand."

The boy raced from the room, snow dropping from his soles, his boots echoing as they thudded across the hardwood floor. Graham and Cait were alone.

She raised her eyebrows at him. "Cut it down *all* by himself, did he?"

"With a little help." Graham stalked up to her, playfulness and determination etched into his grin.

Signals were sent out to her nether parts to prepare for an invasion. It warmed her through and through.

He stopped directly in front of her. "Is Duncan here yet?"

The question threw her, since the only thing she could really concentrate on right now were the golden flecks in Graham's brown eyes.

"Haven't seen him." Her voice sounded hoarse. Probably from lack of oxygen.

"Good." Graham took her arms and adjusted where she stood. "Mistletoe," he said as way of explanation. "Making it legal."

Before she could protest, he'd pulled her to him and kissed the dickens out of her. She was so shocked by the electric heat roiling through her that she didn't have time to relax and enjoy it.

"My turn," Duncan said from behind.

Graham pulled away and shielded her with his arm. "Forget it."

"You know it's bad form." Duncan's tired eyes lit up

mischievously the same way that his da's did. "Ye're the one who taught me the importance of sharing."

"Don't forget, wee lad, I'm one of the famous ones." Graham squeezed her a little tighter. "I don't have to live by the same rules as you do." Teasing or not, he wasn't giving her up, his hold on her feeling like a pair of vise grips.

"Oh, good grief." She unlatched herself from Mr. Possessive and put herself back under the mistletoe. "Duncan, get over here." When Duncan leaned down, she caught the scowl on Graham's face. She gave Duncan a chaste peck on the cheek. "There. Everyone happy now?" Neither one looked it.

"I'd better go help Deydie in the kitchen." Cait escaped from the room.

Deydie had everything well in hand, standing over the stove. She spoke without turning around. "Wash yere hands and pull the potatoes out."

Cait went to the sink. "What do you have, Beelzebub? Eyes in the back of your head?"

Deydie cackled and gave the Christmas soup another stir. "Get over here and give the turkey a baste."

Cait put her hands on her hips. "Seriously, I'm only one person here. I can only do one thing at a time."

"Stop yere sassing and get it done," Deydie ordered.

"Slave driver," Cait mumbled as she grabbed the potatoes from the bin. "And Merry Christmas to you, too."

At the oven, she squirted juice over the bird and pondered her grandmother. Only a few days ago, she'd taken Deydie's tone and bossiness personally, as if the old woman had it in for her. Now Cait understood that maybe after all her losses, her gran just needed to feel in control. Cait glanced over at her. Deydie looked like the master and commander of the kitchen, a fair bit of contentment squashed between the wrinkles of her old crabby face. It made Cait's heart soften.

"Get that floor cleaned up," Deydie barked, breaking Cait's reverie. Gran gave another stir and spoke to the soup. "Graham and his damn tree."

"I'll get right on it, Ebenezer." Cait grabbed a rag and started to rub back the sparkle to Deydie's clean floor.

"You missed a spot," Deydie spat out.

"Nag, nag, nag," Cait replied and wiped the floor all the way back into the parlor.

Graham and Mattie stood admiring the lighted tree. Over by the sofa, Duncan rummaged through a box, pulling out ornaments. The poor guy looked bone tired.

"Here. Let me help you with that." She grabbed a wooden snowflake from the box.

"That'd be great," Duncan replied, collapsing onto the sofa. "I could use a breather."

Graham turned to his son and gave him a vexed glance. "Why do you look so tired all the time? You're in the prime of your life."

"Leave it go, Da." He nodded his head in Mattie's direction. "Not on Christmas."

The worry line between Graham's brow deepened. "Then go get yourself a tea, Dunc. I'm sure Deydie will allow you in her kitchen by now."

Cait, determined not to let her own uneasiness show, forced a grin for Duncan. "Yeah, good luck with that, buddy."

"Tea does sound good. Save the star for me." Duncan plodded from the room.

Cait caught Graham's eye, shared a concerned look with him, and then tried to let it go. "So what's next?" she said lightly. "I'm here to help."

"Get the video camera running." Graham busied himself with adjusting the tree. "I should've had it going earlier."

She found the camera on the writing desk, flipped it open, and started filming. "Mattie, do you know how to turn on your grandda's stereo? Can you put us on some Christmas music?"

Surprised, Mattie's eyes grew big, as if he'd been told to play with matches. He gave her his most-devoted-servant nod before running from the room.

"I don't allow anyone to mess with my sound system." Graham grinned even though she knew he was still apprehensive over Duncan. "But I guess I'll make an exception since it's Christmas. Did you see the look on Mattie's face?"

"I got it on film. Recorded for all posterity," she said proudly.

"Ye're right handy to have around, Caitie Macleod." Graham came over to her.

"So I've been told." She kept the camera running.

He leaned down, his chest covering the lens as he gave her a hard and quick kiss. There was power behind it, as if he wanted to reassure himself that everything was going to be all right.

Deydie's voice bellowed throughout the house. "Everyone get yereselves dressed for dinner."

Graham patted Cait on the rump like a teammate. "Go on now and put on one of your *brown* outfits." He laughed and shook his head as if it was a private joke.

But the joke would be on him. Cait made her way to the room off the kitchen where she'd hung her clothes.

Deydie had just finished adjusting her McCracken

plaid around her shoulders and was clasping a brooch to hold it.

"You look nice," Cait remarked.

"Hesh up, now. The food's getting cold." Deydie hustled from the room.

Cait slipped on the only *non*brown outfit she owned as the butterflies in her stomach kicked up a storm. The red sweaterdress clung to her curves like a Porsche on the Grand Prix. She finished the ensemble with gray tights and Prada heels. Graham would have to eat his words when he saw her in this. She checked herself one more time in the mirror, then went to help put the food on the table.

As she walked into the formal dining room with the last dish, the two Buchanan men sauntered in, wearing their matching kilts and tucked-in white peasant shirts. Cait nearly dropped the mashed potatoes on the marble floor. "Damn," she drawled.

Between their sporrans, knee-high socks, and those cocky grins on their faces, they were too gorgeous for their own good. And they knew it, too. Their testosterone filled up every molecule in the room.

Then Mattie stepped out from behind the two and stood in front, decked out in an identical outfit.

Her heart melted. "Oh, Mattie," she cooed, going down on one knee to be at his eye level. "You look grand."

Though it was completely out of character for Mattie, an air came over him, like he knew he'd be the future laird of the Buchanan clan. Just as self-assured as the other two.

Graham took her hand and pulled her back to her feet, letting go with a low whistle. He gave her the once-over, twirling her around, taking her in from head to toe and from breast to breast. His eyes hooded like he'd seen exactly what he wanted for Christmas. He'd be put on the Naughty List for thinking it. That seductive smile of his spread over his face as his eyes continued to eat her up. "I see ye've been holding out on me, Caitie. *Red* is your color."

Deydie bustled into the room with a basket of bread and elbowed Graham. "Stop ogling me granddaughter and sit yere pretty arse down. Ye too, Duncan."

Duncan nudged his son. "Go on, now, and be a gentleman."

Mattie took Cait's hand and led her to her chair, pulling it out for her.

"Why, thank you, kind sir," she said.

He sat beside her. Duncan next to him. Graham took his place at the end of the table on her right. Her gran plopped down opposite Cait, frowning.

"Everyone put yere hats on," Deydie barked.

Cait passed around the ridiculous paper hats, smiling at the Scottish tradition. Graham took a sparkly black top hat, Mattie a homemade sailor hat and Deydie a flashy pink one. Duncan produced a Santa's cap for himself. Cait grinned at the motley crew as she adjusted her choice, the purple paper crown.

"Graham, say grace," Deydie ordered, reaching out to him.

They all clasped hands, completing the circle, and bowed their heads. Graham's prayer was simple and sincere—for the meal, for the fishermen's safety, for those less fortunate. Cait hadn't known it until this moment, but she'd missed this tradition—the family praying. She couldn't help but soften a little more toward

God. She took a silent moment to be truly grateful. Graham squeezed Cait's hand when he said, "Amen," and held on maybe a little longer than he should have.

Deydie kicked Cait under the table.

"Ouch." Cait rubbed her shin. "What's that for?"

Her gran sneered at her. "Get yere head out of yere nether parts and pass me the pudding."

"Violence, especially at Christmas, is never called for," Cait retorted. *Not to mention "netherparts" at the table.*

"I feel right bad about it. Now, pass the pudding," Deydie said.

Mattie's Christmas music played in the background, and they all ate until they were stuffed, like the cooked-to-perfection turkey. When they finished, Duncan showed a burst of energy, getting up and grabbing the dishes.

"As soon as we get these done, we can open presents," he said. "Right, Mattie?"

Mattie jumped up and stacked their dirty plates together.

Graham removed the turkey platter and turned to Cait. "We do things differently in the Buchanan household," he explained to her. "Most families in Scotland unwrap their gifts on Christmas Eve." A mischievous grin filled his face. "But we like to wait, don't we, lads?"

"Da has a thing about torturing people," Duncan said with his hands full. "As a kid, I always thought he was the cruelest of parents. Still do."

"Get over it," Graham said. "You turned out just fine."

"Hurry up." Deydie balanced three dishes in her ample arms. "I want to get to me presents."

Graham laughed. "You know the rule. The one who insists on being first will be last."

"Hogwash," Deydie said, hustling from the room.

With all of them helping, even though Duncan looked like a worn-out Santa with circles under his eyes, they got the kitchen back in shape in no time. Then they made their way to the parlor.

Mattie got a present first, a remote control car, and Duncan got his satellite phone next. Graham got a tie from Duncan. Then Cait gave Deydie her present.

With zeal, Deydie discarded the tissue paper covering the potholder. Then she froze. There was a long pause as the gift lay limp in her hands. Deydie's eyebrows folded together like flaps on a box. "For me?" she whispered to the perfectly pieced fabric. Cait thought she saw a tear form.

"Do you like it?" Cait asked, desperately trying to catch her gran's eye.

Deydie flinched. Instead of her gran coming to Cait and giving her the expected Hallmark-moment-hug, her gran harrumphed. She shoved the potholder into her dress pocket as if she'd been given a pair of men's briefs for Christmas.

It felt like an anchor had landed on Cait's chest, and she wanted to slip from the room for a good cry.

Just then, Deydie rocketed out of her chair. For a moment, Cait's hope returned. Maybe they'd share that hug now.

But ole crabby pants wouldn't do thank-yous or hugs. Gran trekked from the parlor, speaking over her shoulder. "Duncan, I'll get yere da's present from the room off the kitchen." Her voice sounded strange, like she was trying to keep it steady.

Cait stared at the frosted window, hoping to purge her hurt feelings. Graham came and stood beside her, laying a hand on her shoulder, but said nothing. He didn't have to; his presence was enough to help her feel somewhat better.

Within minutes, Deydie returned with the lidded box, no sign of the emotional turmoil of moments before. She set the present in front of Graham.

"What's this?" He smiled at his son, kneeling down to the box. He opened it, and his smile faded, his back stiffening.

Cait had known it was too soon to replace Precious. Men were so stupid.

"His name's Dingus," Deydie announced.

"Call him whatever you like," Cait interjected. "He's your dog."

Graham just frowned at the pup. "No. Dingus is fine."

The dog growled.

"What do you think, Da?" Apparently, Duncan was blind to body language. "He's a sheltie, too. I thought he'd make a great replacement for Precious."

Graham's face tightened. Cait knew he couldn't trust himself to speak.

Duncan finally got a clue. "Ah, bloody hell. If ye don't want him, all ye have to do is say so." He opened his mouth to say more, except Cait laid a hand on Duncan's arm to stop him.

That's when she noticed Mattie, who was making his way trancelike across the room.

Dingus yipped at him as he got nearer. The boy looked at his dad for permission. When Duncan nodded, Mattie picked up the dog. Dingus wagged his tail and licked Mattie's face.

Deydie plucked a small can of dog food from her other pocket. "How about ye feed the pup?" she said to Mattie as she popped off the lid. "Get a bowl from under the counter."

Mattie took the can and left with the dog.

Duncan cleared his throat, getting his father's attention. "Seriously, Da, I'm sure we can find the wee pup a home since you don't want him." His hostility brewed just below the surface.

Graham's frown deepened into resignation. "It's a fine gift. Thank you, son." But the accomplished actor didn't pull off his lines.

"Ye two stop yere bickering like a couple of old ninnies and get me my present," Deydie declared. "Where is it, Graham?"

He sighed, seeming to be straightening out his emotions, while across the room, Duncan, red-faced, deliberately flipped through the instruction manual to his satellite phone.

Finally, Graham reached around the back of the tree and produced a large box. "I'm sure you're not going to like it." It was obvious he was working at being playful, trying to behave more like himself. He slid the box over to her. "I can always take it back."

With gusto, Deydie ripped into it, paper flying about like an origami tornado. She froze so completely when she saw it that for a second Cait feared her gran had stopped breathing.

Graham started explaining excitedly, like he was the one who'd gotten an amazing present. "It's like Caitie's. I thought you might want to have one, too. I got one for all the quilting ladies."

"But . . ." Deydie started. "It's so . . ." She didn't finish. She jumped up and threw her wide body at Graham, wrapping her pudgy arms around his middle in a bear hug.

Cait slumped against the couch and bit her lower lip. *That hug should've been mine, not his.* It stung.

Then Deydie smacked his arm. "Ye're too extravagant for yere own good, Graham Buchanan."

"But you love me anyway, ole bird," he said with affection.

Deydie turned to Duncan. "Help me get this thing out of the box. I want to take a look at it."

Mattie wandered back in with the sated puppy hanging under his arm like a football. He sat down and rolled the dog into the hem of his shirt, ready for more presents. Dingus snuggled against the boy, his tongue hanging out like a pink flag.

Graham pulled another gift from the tree, much smaller this time. "How about one for you, Caitie?" He placed it in her lap. "It's from me and the lads." He nodded toward Duncan and Mattie.

She stared dumbfounded at the plaid wrapping paper and gold ribbon for a moment. Finally, she looked up at him. "Don't tell me you actually wrapped a present all by yourself," she said.

He gave her a soft, gentle smile. "Go on, now. Open it."

She peeled back the paper, and her breath caught in her chest. She smoothed her fingers over her mother's image. "Mama," she managed, before tears filled her eyes.

"Do ye like it?" he asked, his eyebrows raised, his face anxious.

She held it to her heart and gazed at him. "It's the best gift I ever got," she said honestly.

"What is it?" Deydie rose from behind her new sewing machine.

Cait swiped at a tear and smiled up at him. "It's a picture of me and Mama."

Deydie waddled over to her. "Let me see that."

"I found it in my mother's photo album," Graham explained. "My ma and yours were friends. Did you know that?"

Deydie studied the picture, her voice hoarse. "Ye were a wee kipper back then, Caitie. A handful, like Nora at that age." She ran a craggy finger over Cait's small image. "Nora had made ye that little yellow pinafore and dress from some fabric of mine." Her gran didn't give the frame back to Cait, instead carefully propping it on the end table. "I haven't given ye my gift yet."

With her voluminous rump up in the air, Deydie dug under the tree. She produced a package wrapped in white tissue paper with a piece of cotton fabric tied around it.

Cait carefully undid the makeshift ribbon and pulled off each piece of tape, savoring the anticipation of getting a gift from her gran.

"Ye're too slow." Deydie snatched it away and ripped it open. She dropped it back in Cait's hands.

It was a simple patchwork lap quilt.

"It's all I had time to make on short notice," Deydie complained.

"It's beautiful." Cait recognized several of the fabrics—a piece from Deydie's curtains, a swatch from her comforter, a bit from her apron.

Deydie pointed at a yellow gingham quilt block. "That's the fabric from your pinafore. And the blue floral next to it is a piece from Nora's dress in that picture." Deydie stepped back. "I put all the rest of Nora's scraps in that quilt there. To clean out my stash," she added, making it sound as if she hadn't taken love and care in creating for her granddaughter the most special quilt ever.

Cait held it up, her eyes filling with tears once again. Warmth wrapped around her like she'd been swathed in a blanket fresh from the dryer. "Oh, Gran." She jumped up and grabbed Deydie into a hug before her gran could stop her. "Thank you so much."

Graham leaned against the wall. "And I only got a thank-you."

Cait kept her arms around her gran for a moment longer. "You can wait," she said to him.

"Off with ye." Deydie pushed Cait away. "I have to figure out that contraption Graham gave me."

Deydie lumbered away, not meeting Cait's eyes. That was okay. Cait had gotten her hug.

"Is the lovefest over?" Duncan stood. "I think there's another gift or two for Mattie under the tree." He went and sat next to his son as they pulled out presents for the two of them.

Cait cuddled up on the sofa with her legs tucked underneath her new quilt and put the framed picture of her mama in her lap.

Graham waded through the ever-growing pile of discarded boxes and ripped-up paper to where she sat. "Scoot over."

"Santa doesn't like bossy Nellies," she quipped.

"I have a whole year to be bad before it matters again." He sat close beside her and quietly spoke to her. "Having a nice day?"

"Perfect." She felt as content as Dingus looked, tucked in Mattie's arms, taking a snooze. "It beats being alone in my big empty house back in Chicago, surrounded by all those sympathy cards."

He nudged her with his shoulder. "Do you want to talk about it?"

She shook her head. "There's nothing to say." She stared at the fireplace, Christmases past bombarding her memory. Last year, Tom had sneaked out without saying a word. Undoubtedly to slip his yule log into his latest squeeze. At the time, though, Cait had convinced herself he'd gone to the office to get some urgent work done. She'd been left alone with a dirty kitchen as her only company. He hadn't even opened the gifts she'd bought for him.

Graham, that astute bugger, slipped his hand into hers. He had such a lovely way of comforting her.

"Keep yere hands where I can see them," said eagle-eyed Deydie.

"Yes, ma'am." Graham pulled his hand out in the open.

Soon all the presents were unwrapped. Graham helped Mattie clean up the paper with Deydie following behind them, bellowing orders.

Duncan took the chair next to Cait. "I delivered your package to Moira's house this morning. I felt right juvenile for ringing the doorbell and hiding." Cait noticed a large black-and-blue bruise on his arm.

"So she got it, then?" Cait asked, deciding not to ask about the bruise.

"Aye. You should've seen it. Moira gasped, she was so happy," Duncan whispered. "It was a good idea, Caitie. The pup will be a blessing to both of them." The telling seemed to drain all of his energy from him. He withered before Cait's eyes. "I wish Da had had the same response."

"Give him time." She laid a hand on his upper arm. "He's still grieving for Precious. Once he sees how adorable Dingus is, he's going to love him."

There was a *grrrr* from behind Deydie's sewing machine. One end of Graham's new tie was caught underneath the machine and the other end was in Dingus's mouth, a makeshift tug-of-war taking place.

"*Adorable*," Graham said mockingly. He stood behind Cait, leaning in the doorway with his arms crossed.

"Toss him out in the snow, then," Duncan grumbled, rising. "I'm going to have a lie down. Send Mattie to get me when it's time to roast chestnuts."

With a frown on his face, Graham ambled over and removed his tie from the floor. The dog shot a series of rapid-fire barks at him.

He exhaled loudly. "What am I going to do with this damn dog?"

"Give him love and attention?" she offered sarcastically.

"I told you I'm going on location right after Hogmanay. I'll be gone at least the whole month of January. Probably longer."

A pit formed in the middle of Cait's stomach. Even though she wouldn't admit it under the threat of torture, she'd miss Graham when he was gone. She wanted to offer to watch Dingus to help out, but that would only make her more connected to Graham. And she might've become too attached to him already.

He picked up the dog and looked him in the eye. "Ye're no Precious."

Cait defended the cute mutt. "He's a sweet little fellow. You took Precious with you while you traveled. You can take Dingus, too."

"Precious was well trained."

Dingus chose that moment to cut loose and pee on his new master, a long stream arcing out and soaking his white peasant shirt.

"Dammit! Here. You take him." Graham thrust the dog at Cait.

"No way. He's yours." She jumped up, getting her quilt away from the residual dribbles, and joined Deydie in the dining room, where her new sewing machine had been moved. She spent the next hour helping her gran get acquainted with the features of her Christmas present.

When Duncan got up, they all gathered back in the parlor around the fireplace. Graham had changed into a T-shirt and a gray utility kilt. He sat in his wingback chair by the fire. Duncan instructed Mattie on how to roast the chestnuts while Deydie hovered above them, belting out instructions.

Graham leaned over and whispered to Cait. "I taught Duncan how to roast chestnuts when he was about Mattie's age. It's all in the wrist."

When it was done, they filed into the media room to watch the Queen's speech. Then the movie marathon began, Mattie falling asleep during *Little Drummer Boy*.

Duncan bundled the limp boy into his arms. "Do you mind, Da, letting him stay? I'll get the nets early and then be back to get him."

"You stay, too," Graham said.

"Nah. I like my own bed," Duncan replied. Cait knew it was more than that.

"After you tuck Mattie away, come back down. I want to talk to ye," Graham said.

Duncan glowered at his father and left the room.

A few minutes later, he came back in, looking dead on his feet.

"Out with it," Graham said. "What's going on with you?"

"Don't worry yourself over it. I've got it under control," Duncan retorted.

"What? Like when you broke your leg and couldn't fish?" Graham paced back and forth. "If Rhona hadn't called me, you would've lost your boat."

"It's my life," Duncan said.

"You're wrong." Graham had a sad look on his face. "We're all connected. When you hurt, I hurt. Now, out with it. Is your business in trouble again? Is that why you look so tired all the time? I hate to say it, son, but you look like shite. Do I need to get a doctor in here to take a look at you?" Graham reached for his phone.

"I've seen a doctor." Duncan paused for a long moment. "Another opinion isn't going to change anything." He looked squarely at his da with both belligerence and sadness written on his face. "I have leukemia. Merry Christmas."

Chapter Sixteen

"No!" Graham bellowed so loud that the family portraits shook on the wall.

Deydie hobbled from the room, tears winding through the wrinkles on her cheeks.

Poor Duncan, thought Cait. Death and sickness had stalked her all the way to Scotland and found its next victim.

Graham paced in front of the large screen. "Ye're only tired, Duncan. That's all. Rest more."

Duncan looked wilted. "Da, the tests were conclusive."

Graham stopped suddenly. "We'll see another doctor. A better doctor. Get a second opinion."

Duncan shook his head. "The second and third opinions agreed with the first."

"You haven't seen my physician. I'm going to get Dr. Jackson on the next plane here."

Cait went and stood by Graham. When he reached for his phone, she laid her hand over his. "Duncan, what is the prognosis?" she asked.

Graham looked at her as if she'd betrayed him. "Prognosis?" He spewed the word like it was poison.

"Acute-blast phase," Duncan said flatly.

"What does that mean?" Cait asked.

Graham turned his anger on her. "It means nothing. We're not even sure he's sick." He turned to Duncan—a desperate man, clinging to a rocky precipice.

"It means I'm very sick."

Graham stared at him in disbelief. "Stop saying that. We'll get you to Mayo Clinic or Guy's and St. Thomas.'"

"No, Da. I'm off on the morrow. For a week. I got into a study—an experimental trial at the University of Aberdeen. It's the only treatment available to me at this point. Rhona has agreed to stay with Mattie."

"Rhona?" Graham yelled. "Why not his own grandda?"

"You said you're going on location on Wednesday."

Graham did hit speed dial then. "Sid?" A pause. "Cancel all of my commitments for the next month." There was a longer pause. "I don't care about contracts. Just do it." He pocketed his phone.

The two Buchanan men glared at each other.

Cait stuck herself between them. "Duncan, I'll help out, do whatever I can."

Graham spoke before Duncan opened his mouth. "Yes, good. Caitie, you'll take care of Mattie." It wasn't a question. "I'll be going to Aberdeen, too."

Duncan tried to speak, but Graham beat him to it once again. "I'll take no argument from you," he said.

Duncan hauled himself from the room, scowling at his father on the way.

Cait put her hand on Graham's arm. He didn't look at her, his eyes glued to the doorway his son had just passed through. "Go home," he finally said.

She stared at his face. She knew that look. He was ticked off—at God, at life, at the whole universe. When

Mama died, Cait had cornered the market on that look. Cait tried one more time. "I should stay." It wasn't about the two of them. She just wanted to give him comfort.

But when she moved to put her arms around his waist, he sidestepped.

"I mean it. Go home, Caitie."

Dingus, who'd been lying quietly on Precious's fluffy bed, perked up his ears at his master's terse tone and whined. It was the wrong move on the puppy's part. Graham grabbed a throw pillow from the sofa. For a second, Cait worried he might lob it at the dog. Instead, he let it fall near the fireplace. He picked up the dog and unceremoniously plopped him on the throw pillow. Dingus growled.

"Stay," the master said, assuming the dog would do as he was told. Graham began switching off the lights.

Dingus stuck his nose in the air and pawed his way defiantly back over to Precious's pillow. He circled three times and dropped into a puppy *C* in the middle of the fluff. He was asleep before his master turned off the last light.

Cait didn't know what to do. Graham shouldn't be alone.

He stood in the doorway of the parlor, glaring at her. "Deydie needs you." The underlying *I don't* came through perfectly clear.

She gathered up her new quilt and took Mama's framed picture from the table. "Thank you for this."

He stared right through her and then walked away.

When she went to fetch her coat from the room off the kitchen, Deydie sat there motionless on the bed.

"Are you all right?" Cait asked.

Deydie glowered at her, the red around her eyes the

only sign that she was upset. "Of course I'm all right. But ye should stay here tonight for Mattie's sake. I've made up the guest bed. I'd stay meself, but me back is *killing* me." She shuddered at her own choice of words. "I need me own bed."

"I can't. I'm going back to the cottage."

Deydie stood up and put her wide body in Cait's personal space. "Rebellious lass. How many nights have I told you to come home to the cottage and instead your skinny arse stays up here on the bluff? Now I'm telling you to stay here and you insist on coming home."

"Graham doesn't want me here."

"That's rot. He's in no condition. He needs you here for Mattie." Deydie shook a knobby finger at her. "Mind ye stay in yere own bed and don't sneak into Graham's."

Cait *ha*ed. "No chance of that."

The back door slammed.

Deydie unfolded herself from the bed. "He's gone out now for a walk. Get yereself to bed before he comes back."

Cait couldn't help herself. She hugged Deydie fiercely. Her gran stiffened like a week-old corpse but didn't immediately push her away.

"Bring Mattie to the cottage tomorrow for Boxing Day. The quilting ladies will be there. We'll make a party of it." Deydie's old face fell and she spoke to herself. "Or at least it's been a party in the past."

As Cait climbed the back stairs to the bedrooms above, she heard Deydie letting herself out of the house. As Cait opened the guest bedroom door, Mattie cried out, making her jump.

She quietly slipped into Mattie's room and found the boy sitting up stiffly, trembling, his eyes blank. Cait knew he was reliving the horror of the accident. She climbed in beside him and put her arm around his shoulder, shushing him, coaxing him into lying back down.

Mattie relaxed and slumped against her. She slid farther into the bed and held him close, her heart aching for him. He'd already endured so much, and now his own da was in mortal danger. She kissed his forehead and closed her eyes.

Sometime later, the bedroom door opened. Graham stood there a long time. Finally, he turned off the hall light. At first she thought he might join her and Mattie in the bed, but instead the bedroom door closed, shutting him out.

The next morning, when she awoke, the other side of the bed was empty. In the kitchen, she found Mattie and Graham sitting on barstools at the peninsula, eating pancakes.

Graham barely glanced up. "I see you stayed anyway. Coffee's in the maker."

Mattie shot his grandda a questioning frown.

"Caitie is going to watch you for a few days while your da and I go to Aberdeen. We're going to see a man about building your da a new boat. Isn't that grand?" Graham's blatant lie sounded hollow, and Mattie's eyebrows narrowed.

"Really," Graham assured him. "Isn't that right, Caitie?"

She avoided the question. "You'll help me take care of Dingus, won't you, Mattie? He'll have to learn the ropes around here. You'll have to show him where your grandda keeps his favorite slippers. Dingus needs to become acquainted with them, give them a right good chew before Grandda returns home."

That earned her a small smile at the corners of Mattie's mouth.

"Keep that fur ball away from my things. Or else," Graham threatened.

Cait raised her eyebrows and gave him a scathing look from across the room. *Tell Mattie his da is going to see the doctor,* she tried to convey.

Graham turned away from her. "I'd better get a shower. I expect yere da to be here any minute."

When he'd left the room, Mattie came over and took her hand with his sticky syrupy one and led her back to the table. He put a plate and a fork in front of her.

"Thanks, kiddo. I am hungry." She couldn't meet his imploring eyes. It wasn't her place to break the news to the boy, but she wanted to. She remembered clearly the lies she was told when her own mama first got sick. Her father said Mama had gone away on holiday, but Cait knew better—she'd gone to the hospital for surgery. Illness wasn't something to be swept under the carpet. It was better to tell the truth, and she planned to tell Graham so. Right now.

She pushed herself away from the table. "Save those pancakes. I'll be right back."

She steamed up the stairs and straight into Graham's room. The bathroom door stood open, the shower running, and she decided this wasn't the time for niceties. She marched into the bathroom and closed the door behind her.

The shower was one of those roman showers, no door, just a big open room, big enough for a soccer team. Graham turned toward her and she got quite a view.

"Have ye come to join me?" Sarcasm pricked at his burr.

Cait's anger had her stepping into the tiled shower, no hesitation, no embarrassment. "I'm certainly not here to scrub your back. I've come to rip you a new one."

"Well, if that be so, you might want to take yere clothes off first." He turned around, giving her a perfect view of his perfect muscular ass, and stuck his lathered head under one of the oversized showerheads.

This was no time to ogle. She grabbed a wet washcloth and threw it at him. "You're making a big mistake. Lying to Mattie is not doing him any favors. Tell him the truth. He may be a little kid, but he isn't stupid. He knows something's wrong."

"*There is nothing wrong*," Graham said through gritted teeth.

"Lying to yourself is not helping anyone either." *Especially your family.* "I know what I'm talking about. Tell him. It will help alleviate his fears."

At *fears*, Graham's head fell.

Without thinking, Cait stepped farther in and reached out, touching Graham's shoulder.

It was as if she'd burned him. He jerked around so fast that lather from his shampoo shot out and smacked her cheek. By the fierce grimace on his face, she knew he was about to yell loud enough to knock the tiles off the wall. But in an instant and without warning, pain washed over him, making him raw and vulnerable. He pulled her into his arms and kissed her roughly as the water showered over them both. She knew what he felt. She felt it, too. He was alive and he needed to prove it.

Then he pulled away from her, anger replacing his vulnerability. "Get naked or get out."

Hard words that cut her like a knife. He turned his back on her, those perfect buttocks and the rest of his body fully in the water again, protecting him from the real world.

Defeated, she stepped out of the shower and grabbed a towel, scrubbing it fiercely over her scorched lips and face. But she wasn't done with him yet. "I mean it, Graham. Mattie will never forgive you for your lies. I've never forgiven my father for his."

She walked out of the bathroom and grabbed a long-sleeved polo shirt from Graham's walk-in closet. She slipped off her wet shirt and replaced it with Graham's, tying up one corner to make it fit.

Back downstairs, Mattie sat on the kitchen floor with Dingus in his lap. He looked up when she came in the room.

Not meeting his eyes, she reached down and scratched the dog behind the ears. "Dingus, have you had breakfast yet?" She went to the cabinet to search for food. Sure enough, Deydie had left puppy food in the pantry. "Here you go." She handed the can to Mattie.

By the way he kept petitioning her with his eyes, she knew he wanted her to spill the beans. And she might've caved if Duncan hadn't saved her by coming in the back door. "Hey, you're up." He picked up Mattie and squeezed him. "Where's yere grandda?"

Mattie pointed up.

"I see." Duncan scrutinized her, waving at her wet appearance. "Squall?"

"Yeah," she said. "Something like that."

He didn't probe her any further. "Are there any pancakes left for me?"

Cait grabbed a fresh plate. "Sit down, and I'll get you some coffee, too. Mattie, run upstairs and let *his highness* know your da is here."

Mattie gave her a knowing frown. He understood she was trying to get rid of him. He set the dog food on the counter and grabbed Dingus before heading up the stairs.

Cait got right down to business. "Graham lied to your son. Told him you're off to talk to a boat builder. Somebody had better tell the boy the truth or I will."

Duncan shook his head. "I know it's time. I'll talk to him."

A few minutes later, Graham appeared at the foot of the steps with Mattie in his arms and Dingus in the boy's. "I found these ragamuffins upstairs. Does anyone know who these two belong to?" He fake-smiled at the room until his eyes landed on Duncan. He set Mattie down and then glared at Cait.

Duncan put his arms out. "Mattie, come here a moment. I've something to say to ye."

Mattie walked solemnly toward his da.

Avoiding Graham's sharp, piercing stare, Cait busied herself by preparing Duncan's breakfast.

Duncan pulled Mattie onto his lap. "Lad, ye know how tired yere da's been lately?"

Mattie nodded.

Duncan continued. "I'm off to Aberdeen to see some good doctors."

Graham exhaled exasperatedly.

Duncan ignored him and went on. "Ye're not to worry. I'm hoping these doctors will make me better. I need you to stay here with Caitie and help take care of things at Grandda's. Can ye do that for me?"

Mattie patted Duncan's cheek, then laid his head on his chest. Duncan kissed the top of his son's head and then set him on his own feet.

Graham yanked his coat from the back of the chair.

"We should get going." His words sounded like bullets. With stiff, jerky movements, as if poles had replaced his arms, legs, and spine, he walked across the kitchen.

Man, was he ticked at her, and at Duncan, and at the truth.

She silently sent up a plea to heaven. *Please heal Duncan.* But judging by Duncan's tired body as the door shut behind him, it was going to take more than a prayer to make him better. It was going to take a miracle.

Chapter Seventeen

After the guys left, Mattie played quietly in the parlor with Dingus. Cait told him she'd be upstairs making beds, but mostly she stared out the window. Or gazed at her shoes. She felt weighted down. Death had taken up residence and was squeezing the life out of her. She felt crushed, miserable, and depressed. Once again, she wasn't in control of her life.

Her phone tweeted. A text message from Margery Pinchot, *People* magazine's editor.

Where's the story? it read.

For the last few days, Cait had worked hard at pretending she hadn't committed herself to writing that article. She shoved her phone back in her pocket without answering and haphazardly threw the comforter over Mattie's bed. Who gave a damn whether the bed was made correctly? In the vast scheme of things, it didn't matter. The only thing she had to do today was to live. And to take Mattie to Deydie's, as ordered. Another day of going through the motions.

As she walked from the bedroom, she stubbed her toe.

"Damn! Damn!" She pounded the wall, the pain real

and excruciating. And suddenly, she felt liberated—mad as hell, and she wasn't going to take it anymore.

No longer would she be at Death's beck and call. She'd defy the bastard, stop giving him the deference he expected. Instead, she'd grant herself permission to write them all off. Death couldn't hurt her if she didn't give a crap. Even about Deydie, her own family. Too soon, he'd be whisking Gran away to oblivion anyway. Cait could see the handwriting on the wall. Death was going to take Duncan, too. It had been useless to protect him as a little boy against the bullies who threatened him. A waste of time. All of Gandiegow stood defenseless and weak, waiting for Death to suck the life from them.

"Not me." Cait rubbed her sore toe. "I'm going to live. And I'm going to live well." It felt so much better to be angry than to feel helpless.

The only way to keep her sanity in the midst of Death's cruelty was to pledge allegiance to herself. Screw trust. Screw this town. She didn't need any of them. She'd finish writing the exposé about Graham and get the hell out of Dodge.

Back downstairs, she wrapped Mattie up in his coat, thrust Dingus into his arms, and marched the boy down the bluff. He kept looking over at her, but of course he didn't say anything. His intent gaze upon her face almost had her caving, but Cait was on a mission—to live her life away from all this damned pain.

When they got to Deydie's cottage, the door swung open before Cait could reach for the handle. Her gran ushered them in.

"Here now, Mattie, give me that fleabag." Her gran took Dingus and at the same time hugged Mattie to her ample bosom.

I never get any hugs, Cait wanted to yell, *and I'm yere freaking granddaughter. Oh, screw it.*

Cait looked around the cottage with disgust. Deydie must've spent the whole night scrubbing it from top to bottom—everything sparkled. Irritatingly, a clean cloth rested upon the table, all the dishes were stacked away on the shelves, and fresh logs sat by the fireplace. Didn't her gran know that she was going to die? They were all going to die.

Deydie eyed her, giving her a worried frown. "The ladies will be here any moment. Caitie, go put on fresh clothes and then help Mattie set out the food." The old woman took Mattie's coat and hung it by the door. "Hurry up, now."

Begrudgingly, Cait pulled out her suitcase and rolled it into the bathroom. In the mirror above the sink, she glowered at the dark circles below her eyes. She poked a finger at the puffiness. "Fabulous. Great. I look like a raccoon."

As she pulled on her brown cable sweater, Cait heard the quilting ladies arrive. She didn't want to see any of them. They'd be all nice to her, and Cait wasn't in the mood. She had no use for Gandiegow's small-town charm right now.

When she came out, she saw Mattie trapped in the midst of the first of the quilting ladies, all of them hugging the breath out of him.

A small bit of sympathy got through Cait's defenses and she went to his rescue. "Mattie, I need you to help put out the food. Come on, now."

Looking relieved, he unglued himself from the crowd.

At the refrigerator, Cait pulled out the leftover turkey

and the Christmas pudding from yesterday. Mattie dutifully set each item on the table. When they were done,
Cait took pity on the boy once again. "Take Dingus and
sit with him on Deydie's bed. I'm afraid the quilting ladies are going to trample him to death."

Mattie snatched up the puppy from the pillow by the
hearth and climbed on the bed. Cait laid a bag beside
him, the one she'd filled with toys from Graham's. For
the first time ever, Mattie gave her a real smile—lips
curved upward, no teeth showing, but it was a smile all
the same.

Her hardened heart wasn't happy to see it. *Too little,
too late,* Cait thought. *I'm out of here. I'm leaving as soon
as I get my story.*

Amy pulled Cait off to the side. "Is it true, then, about
Duncan?"

Mentally, Cait rolled her eyes. Amy had the tact of a
branch banging against a window.

Bethia shushed Amy, quietly chiding her. She pulled
out a quilted apron, making a big performance of showing it to them, covering up what was really said. "Little
ears," she reminded them.

Cait sighed, frustrated she had to talk at all. "It's true.
Duncan has leukemia." Dutifully, she *ooh*ed and *ahh*ed
over the apron, but in reality, she didn't give a rat's ass
about the quilted work of art.

Bethia patted them both. "We'll all get through this
together. We always do."

Not me. I won't be here.

Cait glanced at Deydie, who appeared to be having a
good time among the ladies—laughing, smiling her
toothy grin. *Appearances can be deceiving.* It aggravated

Cait that she'd come to know her grandmother so well—
the worry lines in her wrinkled forehead told the real
truth of how Deydie felt.

Bethia folded up the quilted piece. "It's hard for your
gran. She's seen a lot of illness. She feels like a mama to
Duncan. We all do." Determination crossed her face.
"I'm going to light a candle for him."

Cait thought she meant the next time she went to
church. Instead, Bethia grabbed her coat and announced
she'd return shortly. Cait didn't even get the chance to
tell her she was wasting her energy. God wasn't paying
attention. He'd turned a blind eye.

Just as the door shut behind Bethia, Ailsa and Aileen
arrived.

"We've brought handmade socks," Ailsa said. "For everyone," Aileen finished.

The twins unloaded two bags, giving Mattie his dino-
saur fleece socks first. Dingus thought it grand fun and
ran away to the bathroom with one of the socks.

When Mattie went after him and was out of hearing
range, Ailsa shook her head. "Poor little dear." She
pulled out more socks, a different color for each one of
the quilting ladies.

Cait got a rosy pink pair, too bright and cheery for her
dark mood.

She sat beside Moira while putting them on. "How's
your father this morning?"

Moira answered gravely, "He had a good night's rest."
Like that was an anomaly. Moira had a clue when it
came to illness and uncertainty. Cait just wished the rest
of them would wake up and smell the coffee.

There was a bustle at the door and Rhona came in.

She went straight to Mattie for a hug and then gave him a new picture book.

"Now that everyone is here," Deydie said, "our Boxing Day celebration can officially begin."

Cait didn't feel like celebrating. She felt like punching something instead.

Deydie waddled over to the big white mound in the front corner and whisked off the sheet. There stood the sewing machines Graham had delivered before he'd left.

"Santa was damn good to us this year," Deydie cackled.

All the ladies squealed and ran to their loot.

Cait dodged them and headed for the opposite corner of the cottage. She watched the women in antipathy as they ripped into their presents. And suddenly, it was all too much. The joy. Suffocating.

Cait grabbed her coat. "I'm going out for a while."

No one paid attention, except for Mattie, who cocked his head to the side. Cait slipped out the door.

It was a dirty trick using Graham's absence and Duncan's leukcmia to get her story, but she didn't care. What did it matter whether she threw Graham to the wolves or not? In the end they'd all be dead anyway. All that mattered was that she get out of there and start living. Live until she wasn't living anymore.

Besides, if it came down to Graham Buchanan or Cait Macleod, she'd choose herself every time.

Cait slogged up the bluff. "I don't care if I'm betraying Duncan or Mattie. Or Deydie. Or the whole damn village. Trust is overrated. Having roots is overrated, too."

Cait let herself in through the back door. And just to

seal the deal, she pulled out her cell phone and called Margery Pinchot at *People* magazine.

"The story on Graham Buchanan is almost done," Cait said with barely a quiver in her voice. "I'll send you the final soon."

"Good. I was beginning to worry that you'd changed your mind," Margery said.

"No. My mind is made up." Cait said goodbye and signed off. The deed would be done and would no longer hang over her head.

"First things first." Cait went to Graham's office to pick through his finances. She tested the filing cabinet and, sure enough, he'd left it unlocked. "Stupid man."

"Graham?" she said as she pulled the top drawer open and lifted out the first file. "Prepare yourself. I'm going to go through your stuff." She kind of singsonged it, cockylike, which helped to ease her nerves. She pulled out bank account statements and contracts, spreading them over his mahogany desk.

With cell phone in hand, she took several pictures of the documents as she mentally cataloged the information. Statement after statement, she found what he'd kept hidden. Anonymously, he'd funneled money year after year into this freaking town. He'd financed ventures from initially stocking the store and repairing the fishing docks to helping to repave the road leading down into the village, even paying some of Kenneth's medical bills.

Oh, crap! Graham had buoyed them all at one time or another. Right down to the sick little Bruce baby.

Cait could hardly breathe.

"Holy shit," she exclaimed. When she outed Graham to the world, the town wouldn't understand that she didn't have a malicious bone in her body; this was a matter of self-preservation. Of course they'd never, ever forgive her. They'd string her up like a bloody carp. Earlier she hadn't cared, but now . . . she did.

She dropped her cell phone. When she bent to pick it up, she knocked over a digital frame. A small device fell off the back and rolled along the smooth desktop.

"What the hell is that?" she said to his office. She picked it up and peered at it closely.

It couldn't be. She'd seen something like it when she'd worked at the *Sun Times*. Only this was tinier. A spy camera. She turned it over and an itty-bitty LED light shone green. "Oh, God, no." She dropped it like it was hot coal.

She gave the room a hard frown, remembering all the sideways glances he'd given her since she'd arrived. As if she was the head paparazzo. "I thought we were beyond this, Graham. I thought you trusted me."

Like a drug dog, she went from room to room, sniffing for cameras. And found them. To find the rest, she booted up his computer. It was all there. The location of each camera and its status. All were running. She played back the footage of her phone conversation with Margery Pinchot. She watched herself ransacking his office.

Without a moment's hesitation, she deleted all the recorded video and brought all the cameras offline.

"Thanks for installing an easy-to-use system."

She put all his papers back into the filing cabinet exactly where she found them and turned off the light.

As she headed toward the pub, she felt conflicted, no longer the hard-ass of earlier. Did she have the right to destroy Graham to take care of herself? She didn't know anymore. The only conclusion she came to was to emulate Scarlett O'Hara and think about it tomorrow.

When she got to the pub, Bonnie stood behind the bar, preening in the oversized mirror. When she saw Cait, she came at her like a downhill boulder.

"What have you done with Graham?" Bonnie hissed.

"I didn't shrink him and stick him in my pocket, if that's what you're thinking."

Bonnie put one hand on her hip and glared at her.

Who could argue with a floozy stance like that? "He's gone out of town."

Bonnie reached for her phone. "I'd better give him a call. We need to order more whiskey."

"Don't," Cait said firmly. "He doesn't want to be bothered."

"Why, you little gold digger." Bonnie advanced on her, coming toe to toe. "Who left you in charge? Certainly not Graham. I have more right to him than you."

Pathetic. Cait shook her head. "He took Duncan to the hospital in Aberdeen," she said flatly.

That stopped Big Boobs short. "What for?"

The news was already out, so Cait wasn't breaking a confidence. "Leukemia treatments. Leave them be."

Cait figured she could try to smooth things over for Graham's sake. Maybe Bonnie wouldn't hassle him if she softened her tone. "Graham told me you're a very capable manager. That he never worries with you looking after the pub." A bit of a stretch, but she could see Bonnie's ruffled feathers smooth down. "Can you handle whatever it is this time?"

"Of course I can handle it. I've been working at the pub since I was thirteen."

Is Bonnie another of Graham's near charity cases? Cait only replied, "Thanks."

That was the wrong thing to say. "I'm not doing it for

you. I'm doing it for Graham." Bonnie spun on her four-inch heels and sashayed her tight-ass jeans into the pub's kitchen.

Cait ran up the stairs and made sure everything was in order. She packed the few things she needed and left, heading back to Deydie's to get Mattie. Deydie didn't ask where Cait had been and she sure as hell didn't tell her.

Over the next few days, all of Gandiegow did their best to keep Mattie busy. Amy had him help out at the store, dusting off shelves. Moira had Mattie and Dingus over for a playdate with her puppy, Snoozer. Ross, Duncan's best friend, came by to play checkers with Mattie while Cait worked on dinner. And every afternoon, Duncan called Cait's cell phone and asked for the boy. The first day, Duncan sounded like himself, but as the week wore on, Cait thought he sounded frailer. "The treatments are rough" was his only explanation. Duncan never mentioned Graham, and Graham didn't call to see how any of them were doing.

As company every night, Mattie would drag Dingus into bed with him. And every morning afterward, Cait would find Dingus, not in Mattie's room, but sound asleep in the center of Graham's bed.

Cait hadn't returned to her snooping, still processing what she'd found. She didn't know why she wasn't eager to go back to her search, but she told herself she had plenty of time to nose through the rest of Graham's things while he was gone. She was wrong. The guys arrived on New Year's Eve afternoon, two days earlier than expected.

When they came through the door, Cait didn't recognize Duncan at first. He'd aged twenty-five years and looked ten pounds lighter. His skin was sallow, and he ran to the bathroom as soon as he made it through the door.

Thank God Mattie was upstairs with Dingus.

While Duncan was in the bathroom, Cait decided to hit Graham up for information.

"Tell me what—" she tried.

Graham put his hand up to stop her. "I'm not in the mood, Caitie."

The wall he'd built between them was so palpable she could've reached out and touched it—solid stone, impenetrable. It shouldn't have hurt like a son of a bitch, but it did. *Stupid, stupid, stupid,* she called herself over and over. Why did she expect anything different from him? He was a man, wasn't he? If only she was immune to the charms of the gorgeous Graham Buchanan.

"I'll just go check on Mattie, then," she managed, before running out of the room.

She ran into Duncan instead.

"Where's Mattie?" he asked.

"Upstairs," Cait answered. "I'll get him. Tell me what happened first."

Duncan sighed, a man defeated. "Turns out, I'm not a good candidate for the study. My system is rejecting the experimental drugs." He looked like he might run to the bathroom again.

"What do we do now?" Cait was mad and sad at the same time.

"There's not much to do. This was my only real option."

Poor Mattie. Cait touched Duncan's arm and felt bone.

Mattie came bounding down the stairs with Dingus hot on his heels. The boy stopped short on the bottom step, staring at Duncan.

"Mattie, come to your da," Duncan said.

Mattie shook his head, running to hide behind Cait.

Duncan looked down. "I'm a fright, aren't I? I'm still your same da though, Mattie."

Mattie peered around Cait.

Duncan pasted on a smile. "Why don't you and Caitie make me some hot cocoa?"

Mattie took her hand and led her into the kitchen.

Graham walked in moments later and put a sham of a smile on his face. "Can I have a mug, too?" He scooped Mattie up and gave him a bear hug.

Cait caught Graham's sad desperation as he squeezed his eyes shut, holding his grandson tight. Finally, he loosened his grip and Mattie went to help Cait.

Duncan walked in and lowered himself into a chair at the table right before Mattie carefully brought him a mug, sloshing only a tad over the side. He grabbed the marshmallows and gave Duncan extra. For a moment, the boy stood next to his da, then laid a tiny hand on his shoulder.

Duncan tilted his head toward him. "I love you, monkey."

Mattie pulled a chair closer to his da, and Cait brought him his cocoa.

"What do you say, Mattie?" Graham started. "How about you and your da stay up here at the big house tonight? We'll have a big party for our Hogmanay."

Cait couldn't help but feel invisible. This wasn't her family. But part of her wanted to belong, just the same.

Before Mattie had time to shake his head yes or no, Duncan answered for the both of them. "No, Da. Mattie and I will head back to the cottage."

Graham flushed. "Mattie, go upstairs and find Dingus." He waited until the boy was out of earshot. "I built this damn mansion for you—my family."

"I'm worn-out, and we're not doing this," Duncan said, both exhausted and angry.

"Fine," Graham said.

Cait put the dirty mugs in the sink as Mattie and Duncan got their coats. She went to the room off the kitchen and grabbed her own. She heard muffled goodbyes, the door shut, and it was quiet.

She should head out too, but she had to confront Graham before he figured out his surveillance equipment had been tampered with. She found him in the parlor, sitting in front of the fire, staring at it blankly.

"Graham?"

He looked up, surprised to see her still there.

She took one step into the room. "I have some bad news."

"Great," he said. "Just what I need."

Because he hadn't exactly bitten her head off, she took another step closer.

"You were bugged," she announced.

"Bugged?" He looked as if he didn't understand the word.

"As in someone was spying on you." She'd go to hell for the lie she was about to tell.

"Someone spying?" he asked.

"Are you going to repeat my every word? I'm trying to tell you something important."

"Go ahead."

She stepped all the way in but didn't look him in the eye. "You don't have to worry about it, though."

"Caitie?" His voice had a warning in it. "What did you do?"

"I took care of it," she said.

"How, pray tell, did you do that?"

"I found all the cameras and deleted all the recordings," she answered.

"You what?"

"And the backups," she added, as innocent as the morning dew.

"Why would you do such a thing?"

She shook her head emphatically. "The nerve of some people. Videotaping you in your own home."

He rubbed his chin. "Did you look at any of this video?"

"No. I wouldn't dream of invading your privacy."

She saw his sly smile.

"No, I guess you wouldn't," he said.

"I'll see you later." She hightailed it out of the room, feeling vindicated and dejected all at the same time.

When she got back to the cottage, Deydie wanted to know what she'd done with Mattie.

"Duncan and Graham are back," Cait told her.

Deydie said nothing but looked worried. Cait guessed it had to do with Duncan.

But when Deydie did speak, it had nothing to do with the Buchanans. "I'm off to Kenneth's to sit with him tonight so Moira can go out and do a wee bit of New Year's celebrating. You should go with her to the pub. Knock back a few. You deserve it."

Great. Just when Cait had decided *to hell with it all*, her crotchety gran had opted to be nice.

"I think I will," Cait said. Drowning her sorrows in a pint or two might be just the thing.

For the next hour, Cait and Moira sat companionably at a table inside The Fisherman while all of Gandiegow celebrated around them. Amy popped over every little bit to say a few words and then went back to serving the rowdy crowd. For the hundredth time, Cait's thoughts strayed back to Graham, wondering and worrying over how he was doing. She took another sip of her ale.

As if she'd finally conjured him up, Graham wandered in, his mood made clear by his bowed shoulders. Cait held her seat but had a strong urge to rush to him and lift his burden—if only she could.

Moira elbowed her. "Do you see who just came in?"

Before Cait could answer, Amy, from across the room, gestured to her and inclined her head to indicate that *Himself* had just arrived.

"Yes, I see," Cait said.

Moira smiled at her warmly as Graham made his way to the bar. Bonnie, the annoying gnat, flew over to him with a bottle of Scotch and a shot glass. Cait's hackles went up. Then Bonnie leaned across the bar, practically pushing her boobs in his face, as if she expected him to reach out and fondle them.

Moira stood and pulled Cait up, too. "You'd better go tend to Graham. Don't worry about me none tonight. I'll go help Amy and Coll with the serving, and they can walk me home later."

"Why does everyone think Graham is my responsibility?" Cait asked. He didn't want anything to do with her. And she didn't want anything to do with him.

Moira shrugged. "He might not be your responsibility, but I think he's taken a shine to you. He's been alone far too long."

Amy sidled up to them and joined in their conversation. "Moira and I are on the same page. Graham needs a good woman."

"You're both a couple of ridiculous romantics," Cait said.

Amy jabbed her thumb in the direction of Deydie's house. "You know I love your gran, Bethia, and Rhona, but they seem to have given up on Graham finding anyone." She winked at Cait. "But I think he already has."

Cait rolled her eyes. "Your overactive imagination is at it again. I'm the last person Graham wants."

Moira touched Cait's arm. "Graham deserves love. He's a good man."

This was nuts. Neither one of them was listening to her.

Amy tilted her head in Bonnie's direction. "If you don't step in, our friendly bartender is going to take advantage of Graham. He'll hate himself in the morning if it happens. Something has to be done." She paused, which was unusual for her; silence was not her forte. "I've never seen him like this. He's as vulnerable as a baby seal."

Cait glanced over. Bonnie, indeed, had a determined gleam in her eyes, which Cait wanted to scratch out.

Moira squeezed her arm. "You'll get him home safely?"

Cait shook her head but said, "Aye," anyway.

Both of the romantics hugged Cait before she made her way over to Graham. She could feel Bonnie's glare on her forehead like the crosshairs on a gun. Cait ignored her and leaned against the bar next to Graham so he could see her.

"Hey, sailor, want to buy a girl a drink?"

"No. I'm not sure I'm staying." He looked so exposed and helpless that it broke her heart. She laid a hand on his shoulder.

Bonnie snorted like a wild boar. "Off with you." She

pushed a shot in front of him. "Graham, darling, here's your drink."

Cait moved it away. "He said he's not staying."

Bonnie puffed up, her face turning ruddy. "Why, you little conniving . . ." she hissed. "He's better off staying here with me than being with the likes of you."

Graham glanced up but said nothing. He didn't seem to care what he did.

Cait was prepared to make a scene—pull a little of Bonnie's hair if need be—but thank goodness, Doc walked over and intervened.

"Do you need help getting him home?" Doc asked.

Graham rose. "Nay, I'm fine." He looked anything but.

As Cait walked Graham to the door, she caught sight of Moira and Amy beaming at her. Bonnie stood behind the bar giving poor Doc an earful as Graham and Cait slipped out into the cold.

She walked beside Gandiegow's favorite son through the village, wanting to put her arm around him, to do something to comfort him. "Do you feel like talking?"

He made a harsh, throaty noise, which she took as a *no*. It was okay. There were no words anyway for what he was going through and the pain he felt.

They climbed the bluff in silence. At the mansion door, Cait glanced up at him with a sad smile. "Well, I'd better get back to Deydie's." She turned to go.

Graham reached out and snagged her arm. "Stay."

"But—" she tried.

"For a while," he said.

She couldn't turn him down. She followed him inside to the parlor and slipped off her coat while he laid more logs on the glowing embers.

She didn't know what she was expected to do. Graham was hurting, and he'd made it clear he didn't want to be comforted.

He took off his coat, too, and threw it over a chair before going to the dry bar.

She spoke to his back. "Is alcohol the answer?"

He lifted the whiskey decanter. "I need something so I don't think about . . ." He let the words trail off.

She didn't hesitate but went to him. She wrapped her arms around his waist, hugging him to her, letting him know he didn't have to carry the burden all alone. He set the decanter down and slumped.

"God, Caitie, what am I going to do if—"

She twisted him around and pulled him close. His head dropped to her shoulder and she rubbed circles into his back.

"I could lose him," he choked out.

Pain racked him, and it nearly undid her to see him so sad. She lifted his head and saw his despairing eyes. She needed a way to let him know she was there for him, so she kissed him—for a distraction and to comfort. It was a lifeline that he took. He kissed her back desperately, crushing his lips to hers, holding her tight. She gave in to his need. She understood. There was nothing like the threat of death to make a person feel like they had to prove they were alive.

Unabashedly, she kissed him back, sending her tongue into his mouth, making sure he understood she'd use everything she possessed to help lessen the pain.

He moved to her neck and kissed it hungrily. "Caitie," he rasped, "I want you."

"I know," she said in consent. She wanted him, too. But most of all, she wanted to help him.

As he gazed into her face, he slipped his arms under

her legs and carried her to the oversized sofa. Anguish still haunted him, but as he searched her eyes, she saw something more intimate burning there, a longing she recognized. She didn't know if he meant to tell her he cared for her deeply. Or that he desired her greatly. Or maybe it was just gratitude. She didn't care which it was. As long as she could erase his torment and make him whole again with her body.

He kissed her, and the moments stretched out. Maybe time stood still. She didn't know. The only thing for certain was that she lost herself in him. As she did, her objective shifted. No longer was this only about Graham; this was about her, too. Together, they both became more in the most primal way, in sensation and in touch. She arched toward him as his hands found her breasts through her clothes and his fingertips woke her neglected nipples. She moaned.

"Don't," Graham growled. "You're driving me crazy."

"I can't help it," she whimpered. She wanted more.

He pulled back. She started to complain, but then he laid his forehead on hers.

"Are you sure about this?" he said huskily, breathing hard.

The appropriate answer would've been *hell yeah*. But action spoke louder than words. She gently shoved his chest, pushing him away so she could stand. With a slow smile, she unzipped her dress and let it slide to the floor.

He liked her answer. His eyes turned smoky, heat transferring from his gaze to her bra. She undid the clasp and let it fall to the floor, too. He gave a suppressed groan as he took her in his arms once again. Mr. Darcy was no gentleman, and she'd have a fling with him, screw her past reservations.

As he kissed her, she did her best to get his clothes off his body. She needed his skin—now. He laid her down and pulled off her shoes and tights, leaving her with nothing but her red-checked panties. There was no doubt now that they were both teeming with life, not just existing, but impatient for each other.

She watched with eagerness as he stepped out of his jeans and could hardly wait for Graham to come to her so they could be together. Almost from the first, she'd wanted this but had ignored the chemistry between them. Or at least tried to. Right now, she would own the truth— she was going to make love to him and it would be the gift she gave herself. Later, she might pretend that she'd done it for him, to make him forget or to help him to feel better. But that wasn't true; she was doing this for herself.

He pushed down his boxers, glorious in his nakedness. He peered at her red-checked undies with keen interest. "We definitely don't need these." He pulled them off and tossed them. They landed on the chair by his coat.

She started to giggle. It could've been nerves. But then he scooted in beside her and wrapped his arms around her once again. The sensation was heady. His closeness made her feel warm, consoled, and reassured. He positioned himself over her, using his arms as supports, and gazed into her eyes. She felt the shift; the game had changed again.

He seemed to be searching her, looking into her soul, trying to puzzle her out. Then, as if he'd made his decision, he threaded his fingers into her hair and kissed her more deeply than before. This kiss wasn't about foreplay, sex, or proving he was alive. This kiss was about claiming her.

The shock of it sent her reeling, and oh God, it turned

her on. Knowing she belonged to him, even if only for right now, sent her heart soaring. As she kissed him back, she gave everything to him— heart, soul, body—not withholding even a piece for herself. She was peeled back, exposed, knowing she was safe to do so.

He seemed to know that she'd given it all to him in spirit. He rewarded her by entering her in one smooth motion. She gasped with the pure pleasure of feeling him inside of her. As he kissed her, he began to move. She could feel his restraint and was glad he gave her the time to savor their joining.

"Caitie, my love," he said. Then, in Gaelic, he murmured sweet nothings as he made love to her, thrusting gently, pulling her to the surface and then backing off. It was both delicious and cruel to make her wait for a release. And at the same time, she could stay like this forever—in his arms, feeling him above her, feeling him in her. From nowhere, she fell apart, a near sob coming from her lips. He kissed her as the world became perfect. Then he slid into her one more time, deep, ever so deep, and he shuddered as well with sweet undoing.

As their breathing became normal again, she felt utterly content. At complete peace with the world, with what they'd done, and how she felt about him. He rolled over and pulled her on top of him, dragging the lap quilt over their bare bodies.

She didn't regret it, feeling so happy it had finally happened. But then she saw remorse in his eyes.

"I'm so sorry." His brow collapsed together into a serious line. "I never should've done that."

Chapter Eighteen

Caitie rolled off and threw the quilt at his crotch. "Bastard."

Graham saw the hurt in her eyes, and it killed him. Shit, he'd never meant to upset her. But his emotions were in an uproar. "I mean, I didn't intend for this to happen."

Now she looked even more pissed off. With exaggerated movements, she grabbed her bra, wrapping it around herself and mumbling loudly, "Fricking stupid. That's what I am."

He wanted to go to her and wrap his arms around her, but in truth, she scared the shit out of him. He couldn't tell her that he'd never experienced anything like that before. How he'd felt connected to her, like they belonged together. A frightening, forever kind of feeling. Besides, making declarations wouldn't be fair. He was in no position to offer her anything right now with his life spinning out of control—Duncan's leukemia, his demanding career. Everything. "It was a mistake. It's my fault."

She glared at him as she snatched up her dress. "You could've just said thank you for the pity screw." She paused. "Idiot." Her tone was harsh, but it wasn't clear whether she was speaking to him or to herself.

In a different time, hell, in a different life, he would've taken her to his bedroom and kept her there, possibly forever. But right here, right now, that would be a selfish thing to do. Almost as selfish as making love to her a few moments ago to take his mind off his miserable life. God, he hated himself.

"I don't want to hurt you," he tried.

She picked up a throw pillow and hurled it at his head. "Hurt me?" With one hand, she seized her red-checked panties and shook them at him. "You didn't hurt me. I'm fine. Never better."

She pulled them on and then cursed violently. "You didn't even use a fricking condom."

"Oh, Christ." He couldn't get her pregnant. Not on top of everything else.

"Relax, Graham." She sounded anything but relaxed. "My period ended yesterday. There's no way you knocked me up. Hell, I could probably sell these undies on eBay for your stupid DNA."

He stood up and started yanking on his pants. "Caitie, wait a second. I can't let you leave like this. Let me just explain—"

"Forget it, Graham. You've made yourself perfectly clear." She grabbed her parka and hurried from the room.

He let his head drop, and there on the hardwood floor, lay her tangled tights. He picked them up and went to catch her at the back door.

She about plowed into him as she came out of the room off the kitchen. She swiped at a tear.

"You forgot these." He held up the tights.

She snatched them from him as though she wouldn't deign to leave anything of herself behind. Then she fumbled with the door handle and slammed out of the house.

*   *   *

Cait stood for a minute outside the mansion, not knowing what to do. She couldn't go back to the cottage; she was a mess, her emotions all over the place. She was furious with herself for sleeping with Graham when she knew full well he didn't want to be in a relationship with her. Of course, she didn't want a relationship, either, so why was she so upset? On the other hand, how *dare* he call it—call *her*!—a mistake? She was tired of him yanking her around. He couldn't come on to her anytime he pleased. He had no right. And she was going to tell him, give him a piece of her mind right now!

She opened the door and went back inside. She made it to the parlor's doorway before spying him on the floor with Dingus in his lap. He was talking to the dog, and she stopped to eavesdrop.

"It's like this," Graham told the pup. "I did a lot of praying while I was waiting at the hospital. I made a deal with God. Told him if he'd fix Duncan, I'd be a better da. No more arguments. No more trying to bend him to my will. I'd be more of a blessing instead of a hindrance."

The dog licked his hand, then looked up at him.

"I'd willingly take Duncan's place. Mattie needs him, and God knows how much anger builds up in little boys when they don't get the attention of their father." Graham ran a hand through his hair. "You understand what I'm saying, don't you?"

The puppy nuzzled his arm.

"Of course you do." Graham scratched him behind his ears. "What I'm afraid of, little fellow, is that God doesn't bargain with mere mortals." He stretched out in front of the fire, and the dog cuddled into his chest.

Cait felt limp, her anger now only a memory, drained

away into nothingness. And in its place was pain. She ached for Graham and what he was going through. Quietly, she backed up and went down the bluff to Deydie's. When she got there, she pulled out the trundle and fell into it. If she were lucky, she'd sleep through the New Year.

But for a long time she lay awake, her brain unable to switch off. Over and over, she replayed making love to Graham, still able to feel his kisses and caresses on her frustrated body. She tried working up a little regret for what had happened, but it wouldn't come.

The next morning, when Cait woke, Deydie was sitting at the dining room table with a pad and paper in front of her.

Cait rubbed the sleep from her eyes. "What are you up to?"

"It's for Duncan and Mattie. A schedule for everyone to follow. Ye better get yereself up and dressed. You're off to put Duncan's house in order."

Cait rolled out of bed and went to the list. The whole village, not just the quilting ladies, were scheduled for cleaning, cooking, and shopping. Plus Duncan's boat duties were divvied up among the fishermen.

"Have you ever thought about a career in logistics?" asked Cait.

"Stop yere yabbering and get going. I'll need you to post this at the store on yere way to Duncan's," Deydie said. "Graham's off to Italy this afternoon."

Cait stopped short. "I thought he canceled his engagements."

"He did try. But if he doesn't make this movie, he'll be sued. The bastards," Deydie muttered. "He said he won't be gone long."

"Oh." Cait plopped down at the table.

Deydie got her coat. "I need to get going now. I have to make sure his things are washed and ready for his trip."

Irrationally, Cait wanted to be the one helping Graham instead of her grandmother. And how come Deydie knew what he was up to and Cait didn't?

Her rational brain answered that one. *Because it's none of your business. And in his eyes, you don't count. Not a shilling.*

Unbidden, her womanly bits squeezed in delicious remembrance of what they'd done last night. She blocked the thought. She'd known at the time it didn't mean anything. She had just better get over what little crush she had on him and stop thinking about his manly parts and how he wielded them.

"Snap out of it," Deydie barked. "Ye've work to do."

As nonchalantly as she could, Cait dared to ask, "How long will Graham be gone?"

Deydie glared at her. "I've been crystal clear about Graham from the get-go. You're not to get involved with him."

"I'm only asking for Duncan and Mattie's sake."

"And I'm a bluidy movie star." Deydie bent her head and added one more thing to the list. "Graham should be done in four weeks. At the latest, he'll be back for the Valentine's Day Céilidh. Now, stop asking questions and get cracking."

"Fine." Cait pushed herself out of the chair, accepting she wouldn't see Graham again until the village dance and celebration.

"Wait," Deydie said. "Do you know anything about a load of groceries delivered to Kenneth and Moira? It's enough to feed them for a month or more."

Cait struck an innocent pose. "Not a clue. What good fortune for them, though."

Deydie eyed her closely. "Aye, good fortune, indeed."

Cait did as she was told—dressed, went to Duncan's, and got busy cleaning the house. She hadn't been there long when the phone rang. Duncan was in bed, so she answered it.

The line was silent for a moment. Finally, Graham spoke. "Is that you, Caitie?"

"Aye. And what's it to you?"

Another long silence. "I wanted to talk to Duncan about Mattie. Can you put him on?"

Trying to ignore Graham's smooth-as-butter voice, Cait became as professional as an executive secretary. "I'm sorry. Duncan's not available right now." Like he was in a meeting or something.

"What do you mean, not available?" Graham demanded.

Cait gave up and sat down in the chair by the phone. "He's resting."

"What are you doing there, then?"

"Scullery maid," she explained. "Deydie's orders."

"Maybe it's good I got you instead of Duncan." He had the nerve to speak to her like she was his confidante. "I'm worried about leaving him. And dammit, I don't know what to do." Graham breathed heavily. "I'm going to call Sid to see if the shoot can be postponed."

"Don't do that," Cait said, trying to calm him down. "Deydie has it all worked out. A master list. Everyone's going to pitch in."

Graham gave an exasperated sigh. "What about the nights, though? What if Duncan gets ill with only Mattie there with him?"

"I can stay with them," she offered. *For Duncan and Mattie's sake.*

"There's not enough room at Duncan's house. You know that. If only he'd listen to reason and stay up here on the bluff. There's plenty of room for several people to be here at all times. But when I suggested it, he went a little crazy."

"I'll talk to him," Cait said, even though it would once again put her in the middle of the Buchanan feud.

"Would you?" Graham sounded anxious.

"If I can't convince him, I'm sure he'll listen to Deydie and her broom."

He sighed in relief. "Thank you. You've taken a great weight off my shoulders."

"Yeah, I'm a regular Atlas," she said dryly.

He chuckled. "Caitie?"

"Yes."

"I'm going to miss that sharp tongue of yours."

"You sure know how to sweet-talk a gal," she shot back before hanging up the phone.

Damn. She shook her head in disgust. A few well-placed words from him and he had her wanting him again.

That afternoon, without too much of a fight, they got Duncan moved up into the big house. It didn't take as much persuading as Cait had thought. He seemed to have reasoned it out for himself.

Deydie had Dougal move Cait's things up to the big house as well.

"One of us has to stay up here," her gran said. "And it can't be me. That damn mattress in the guest bedroom was stitched together by the devil himself. You go and be my eyes and ears when I'm not there."

To Cait's surprise, Graham hadn't left yet. As she put her things away, Graham was across the hall packing for his Italy trip. When she finished, she peeked in on him. His inner glow, that special quality that made Graham the man that he was, seemed to have dimmed at the prospect of leaving Gandiegow and his son.

Cait leaned against the doorjamb. "I promise we'll take good care of them both."

He didn't look up. "I'm counting on it."

"One of us will call if anything changes," she added.

He did look up then, pinning her to where she stood. "It'll be you. I know you'll cut through the bullshit and tell me the truth."

She saluted him. "Always at your service."

Her quip didn't stop the sizzle he'd sent through her.

He'd made it clear he didn't want a relationship. She didn't want one either. Unfortunately, she was weak. So weak. She wanted him. Just one more time. One more walk in the orchard before he left. Let him pick her peaches until she was bare.

Her face went warm and she turned away.

He came up behind her. "Are you all right, Caitie?"

His breath on her neck made her tingle even more.

"Absolutely," she said and walked quickly from the room.

Within the hour, Graham was gone. And the house, though crawling with helpful Gandiegowans, felt desolate.

The next morning, a large helicopter landed on the beach. Three doctors and two nurses disembarked, toting various medical equipment. Duncan called Graham and gave his da an earful. Cait overheard, as did the rest of village, no doubt. In the end, Duncan acquiesced, letting the medical entourage stick him with needles, prod him with instruments, and bugger the hell out of him with questions. By early evening, the doctors and nurses had left the village the way they'd come.

"Deydie," Duncan said from Graham's recliner in the media room. "Harpoon the next helicopter that tries to land."

"What if it's yere da returning?" Deydie asked.

"Then definitely shoot it down." Duncan laid his head back and closed his eyes.

Mattie climbed up on his lap and laid his head against Duncan's chest.

Cait's cell phone rang. It was Graham.

"Is Duncan resting?" he asked.

"Who is it?" Duncan called out with his eyes still shut.

"Now's not a good time," Cait whispered into the phone. "The weather's still a little testy."

"Then go into the other room. I need to talk to you," Graham said.

Cait strolled out of the room, putting her hand over the phone. "I'll be right back," she said to Duncan.

"Tell Da I said to sod off," Duncan called.

"I heard that," Graham replied.

"Oh, good grief." She leaned against the wall just outside the room. "Why are you calling me?"

"I don't want to disturb Duncan while he's resting," he said.

"And it's okay to disturb me with this bickering back and forth? You two are like a couple of old women," she carped.

"You can expect a lot of calls from me. Now, tell me, how did it go with the doctors?"

"I don't know. They wanted to talk to Duncan alone, so Deydie and I took Mattie for a walk."

Duncan hollered from the other room, "Tell him to mind his own business."

"Did you get that?" she asked Graham.

"Tell him it'll never happen," Graham said.

"I'm not your mediator. Do you want to talk to Duncan yourself?" she challenged.

Graham's voice softened. "No. I want to talk to you."

If she didn't know better, she might've sworn she heard a hidden meaning in Graham's words: *I need you. Hearing your voice makes me feel better.* She shook her head, erasing that ridiculous thought from her addled brain.

"Why did you do it?" she asked, trying to change the subject. "Why did you send those physicians here? You were with Duncan in Aberdeen. You knew the diagnosis was correct."

"I needed the top experts to take a look at him. And because Mohammed wouldn't go to the mountain, I brought the mountain to Mohammed."

"The only thing you succeeded in doing is pissing Mohammed off. He's worn-out," she added.

Graham cut her off. "I'm sorry for that. Hey, I've got to go. I'm getting a call. It's probably the doctors."

"Yeah, sure, go ahead." But he'd already hung up.

That night, Mattie and Dingus went to bed with Duncan, but soon afterward, Cait found Dingus asleep in the middle of Graham's bed again. She lay down next to him and scratched his ears.

"Are you missing your master?" she asked the puppy.

He sleepily licked her nose and shut his eyes. She wanted to say, *Me too,* but she wouldn't allow herself.

And to counteract her longing for the master of the house, she tried to focus on her mission—finishing the story on Graham Buchanan, movie star.

But of course she couldn't ransack Graham's house with Duncan ill in the next room. It wasn't the right thing to do. When Duncan felt better, she'd seize her chance.

As if a chilling breeze swept over her, she felt the cold grip of Death come into the room. Down in her bones, the truth clutched her like ghostly icicles. *Duncan will not get better.*

"No," she whispered. And fled the room for her own salvation.

The next day, Deydie organized a sewing bee in Graham's formal dining room. Instead of turkey and stuffing, the table groaned with the new sewing machines.

"Ladies," Bethia said, getting all of their attention, "it's now or never. It's time to complete our round robin for the raffle. I've finished all the shoreline blocks. Caitie, how are you coming on the bluff blocks?"

Crap. She'd forgotten. She'd wanted to be included in the quilting group. But then she'd let them down by not doing her part.

"I'll get right on it," Cait said.

Deydie stopped sewing. "Moira, get my basket from the other room and give it to Caitie. I picked out some fabrics she might want to use."

Was this Gran being thoughtful and nice? Cait waited for the other shoe to drop—a snide remark was sure to follow. She looked around at the quilting ladies to see if they'd noticed, but they seemed to take it in stride.

"Eight-inch blocks," Rhona instructed Cait in her

schoolteacher voice. "You'll need to make nine for the row."

Deydie smacked the table. "Caitie's been busy. Hasn't had a moment to work on the quilt."

The other women's jaws dropped open. A jet could've crash-landed on the long table and their eyes wouldn't have shifted from Deydie.

Bethia regained her composure first. "Rhona wasn't lecturing."

"Just saying, that's all." Deydie caught Cait's smile. "Don't glean nothing from it, lassie."

Cait shook her head. "Wouldn't dream of it." But it felt good that Deydie might be warming up to her a bit. A little bit.

"Let's get on to the quilting," Deydie ordered.

Amy sat behind her machine. "Have you heard about the Lynches? Little Mary had to be taken to the hospital. I don't know how they're going to pay for it with Mr. Lynch dying like he did over the summer. Mrs. Lynch hardly has enough to feed those six sweet bairns. And now this."

Bethia sighed. "If only we could make more money on the quilt raffle."

"It's hard times for everyone," Moira said as she set the fabric basket on the table.

A glimmer of an idea came to Cait. She'd seen the movie *Calendar Girls* and wondered if something like that would work for Gandiegow. Not naked quilters, but something. "It would have to be longer-term, though," she said to herself.

"What are you rattling about?" Deydie said.

"Just an idea." Cait picked up the basket and held it to her chest.

"Get to working on those blocks," Deydie huffed.

"What idea, child?" Rhona asked.

"A way to make more money for the Lost Fishermen's Families Fund," Cait said.

Bethia came to stand by Rhona. "Speak up, then."

"Why don't we try to auction the quilt on the Internet? It would certainly bring in more than the projected one hundred pounds. I could use my contacts to get some press. We could use eBay or sell it on Etsy.com."

Of course, Cait knew they could get a hell of a lot more press if the world knew the quilt came from Graham Buchanan's hometown. She could start by informing his fan club about the quilt, then do a full press release to all the major publications. The quilt could bring in thousands, maybe tens of thousands. A good reason if she'd ever heard one for writing the *People* magazine article about him. She'd be helping the town. They'd thank her. *Hell, they'll probably throw me a parade.*

"You check into it, Caitie," Ailsa said.

"See what you can find out," Aileen added.

"Yes," said Amy excitedly.

"Right now ye better get yere head out of the clouds and get those damn bluff blocks done," Deydie said.

"I'm on it." Cait pulled out five shades of brown and several gray pieces of fabric, her mind buzzing.

More could be done, besides auctioning the Our Town Gandiegow quilt. She just didn't know what it would be yet. She could—and would—make a difference to this community.

For one brief wonderful moment, Cait felt Death stepping back into the shadows and Life stepping forward toward her.

*   *   *

Deydie left the dining room and headed to the back of the house to the bedroom off the kitchen. The Valentine's Céilidh would still need a quilt to raffle and she had a Pinwheel quilt started that would be just the ticket.

Caitie's idea to sell the quilt on the Internet was a good one. Deydie had heard tell of how high some of those auctions could go. Her granddaughter was a smart one, just like her Nora. Had a way with numbers.

Deydie pulled the quilt top from her sewing bag. The only thing left to do was to add a border and do the quilting. The ladies could work on this while Caitie finished her blocks. Pride swelled in Deydie's chest. Her granddaughter had turned out to be a hell of a quilter.

A ringing sound came from Caitie's coat, which lay across the bed.

"Probably Graham again." Deydie dug around until she found the phone. She hadn't used one of these contraptions but had watched how Caitie had done it. Deydie slid an arthritic finger over the green line.

"Hallo," Deydie shouted into the phone.

"Yes, it's Margery Pinchot with *People* magazine. Is this Cait Macleod?"

"No. I'm her gran." *You ninny.*

"Please give her a message for me. If I don't get the Graham Buchanan story soon, the deal is off."

Deydie's old breath stopped and then rage filled her. Red, boiling-hot rage.

"Hello? Are you there?" said Margery.

"Aye," Deydie spat into the phone, seething. She did her best to hold back the obscenities that threatened to jump off the end of her tongue. "Let me make sure I have this right, missy. My granddaughter, Caitriona Macleod, has promised to write an article for your magazine about Graham Buchanan."

"Yes," Margery said.

"I see," Deydie answered, spitting-nails mad.

"And I need it ASAP," Margery said hesitantly. "Will you tell her I called?"

"You can bet your last sheep on it," Deydie said sarcastically.

"Thank you," Margery added and hung up.

Deydie threw Caitie's phone on the bed. "Me granddaughter doesn't have a lick of sense. She's as bad as her damned father."

Chapter Nineteen

For the rest of the afternoon, the quilters worked on the Pinwheel quilt that Deydie had started while Cait set up the blocks for the bluff. She used chunks of the gray fabric to construct a small castle block that would represent Graham's mansion and inserted it among the brown blocks representing the bluff above Gandiegow.

After being almost nice to her earlier, Deydie now shot lethal glares in her direction. Cait wanted to ask her what her problem was, what had happened between now and then, but decided not to rock the boat. Deydie had stood up for her earlier, had acted as if she halfway liked Cait, and she wasn't going to do anything to jeopardize her gran's newfound affection.

Ailsa and Aileen headed off to the kitchen while Bethia and Amy went to check on Duncan and Mattie in the media room.

Cait held up the castle block. "What do you think, Deydie? Did I do a good job on Graham's house?"

"A hack job, that's what ye're doing," Deydie muttered and put her head back down, sewing the border to the Pinwheel quilt.

What stick had gotten up Deydie's backside? Would it kill her gran to be nice for two minutes in a row?

Moira looked embarrassed. "I think it's wonderful, Caitie. It'll really add to the Our Town Gandiegow quilt."

Graham's landline rang. Cait picked it up and took the cordless in the other room. "Hello?"

"Why didn't you answer your mobile?" It was the big house's owner.

Cait looked down at his castle block in her hand. Then patted her cargo pockets. "Must've left my cell in my coat pocket. What's up?"

"Shooting is delayed and I just needed someone to talk to." Graham sounded dejected.

Part of her wanted to tell him to go jump off a cliff for hanging up so abruptly yesterday. The other part of her wanted him to come home and cuddle up next to her for the rest of his life. Every time she heard his voice, she fell for him a little more. And each time, when he backed away, it broke her heart a little more, too.

"Are you there?" he asked.

"Yes, of course, I'm here." *I'm always here for you, you bozo.*

"Duncan's results came back positive," he said.

"Does that mean you'll finally accept your son is truly sick? I think he needs your support, not your denial," she said.

"You're right. I just had to find out for myself." He sighed. "I hate being away from him and Mattie."

Graham hesitated a moment longer and she wondered if he meant to add one more person to the list—herself. But he didn't.

He went on. "You know the script you read?"

"Aye," she said.

"I turned it down," he said, sounding even more depressed.

"Why? It was a great part. I told you—you'd be perfect for it."

"I know. I was excited about it until I found out the shooting schedule." He paused again. "I decided it wasn't the right time. Filming begins in March."

Yes, she understood. "And you couldn't be away from your son. I know." She tried to console him. "You want to know something? I think you're an amazing father. Duncan is lucky to have you."

"He doesn't think so," Graham said.

"Well, I know you're an amazing father, and that's all that matters," she said.

He laughed, and it sounded good to hear a bit of cheer in his voice.

"I like a woman with a healthy ego, Ms. Macleod," he said. "You do have a way of brightening my day."

"I'm a little piece of sunshine," she boasted.

He chuckled again. "A piece of work, that's what ye are."

She remembered—*a masterpiece*.

He stopped laughing and went serious all of a sudden. "I am grateful for you. You know that, don't you?"

He didn't say *grateful to you* but *for you*. She shouldn't put much stock in a word choice, but the distinction made all the difference to her. Her heart swelled.

She had to bring them both back down to earth. "Yeah, I'm grateful for you, too. Especially when you walked around in your boxers in *Passage to Manchester*. Ooh-la-la." She shouldn't have relegated him back to the movie star realm. But if she was going to safeguard her heart and maintain her sanity, she'd have to keep them firmly in their respective places.

"Aye, I'm just a pretty face. Thanks for reminding me," he grumbled.

She'd hurt him. Her own heart wanted to tell him the truth. *I see you. I know who you really are.* But her heart had been stupid before, so she bit down on her lip to keep from saying it.

"I'd better get going," Graham said. "Let Duncan know I called." He hung up.

Cait looked down at the castle block in her hand. It was crushed in her fist. "Why do I have to be such an ass?"

Because you have to protect yourself, her rational brain answered.

Cait returned to the kitchen and found Duncan alone, Mattie nowhere in sight.

"Your da called," she said to Duncan.

"So, what did he have to say? That he was too busy to be bothered with us mortals?"

Something in her snapped, and she didn't care that Duncan was sick.

"Don't you dare bad-mouth your da," she said. "You have no idea the sacrifices he's made for you."

"I think I know better than you what he's done and not done," Duncan retorted.

"A regular Oliver Twist, were you?" she sneered. "Were you sent off to boarding school to live among strangers?"

Duncan remained silent.

Cait went on. "Or were you left in the care of family and friends?"

Duncan shrugged. "'Tis of no matter."

"I know your da has done some stupid things, like sending those damnable doctors to examine you. But do you know why?" she said.

"To torture me."

"No. He can't accept that his lovely lad is sick. He had to have the best-of-the-best look into it and to hear it from them. He loves you so much, Duncan."

"He has a strange way of showing it," Duncan jabbed.

"Listen, *Dunkie*." Because he was acting like a spoiled brat, she'd use his childhood name. "Your da just gave up the role of a lifetime for you. I read the script. It's going to be a huge hit. Your da didn't even think twice about it. He told them no on the off chance that his boy might need him. What do you have to say about that?"

"I never told him to give up any role."

"But have you ever been grateful for anything that your da has done? Do you have any idea the money he shells out to help this town? He would've loved to be living the life that you've had. He only wanted to be like his own da, a fisherman. The fact that you've been able to live out his dream gives him great satisfaction. If he weren't an actor and done the things that he's done, you wouldn't be here raising your son in this village. And without your da's help, it's possible this community would've been washed out to sea a long time ago." Quite a speech on her part and maybe a stretch. She was thankful Duncan didn't ask her how she knew all this.

He hung his head, perfectly ashamed.

"Good. I'm glad you're getting the right of it. Your da is a good man, doing the best that he can with the abilities that he has." She plopped down on the barstool next to him and laid a hand on his shoulder. "All I ask is that you give him a break."

"We'll see," was all he said.

Warily, Mattie walked into the room and mirrored Cait's action, putting his hand on his da's other shoulder.

She felt bad that he'd heard that whole lecture, but she guessed it wasn't terrible that the kid knew the truth.

"You know, Mattie," she said to him, "you have a terrific da, too."

Mattie looked up and nodded. Cait expected him to hug Duncan, but Mattie came over and kissed her cheek instead.

"I'll leave you two alone," she said. "I'm sure the quilting ladies are wondering where I've run off to."

Cait found her phone on the bed in the room off the kitchen and gave only a passing thought as to why it was lying out before shoving it back in her pocket. She rejoined the others in Graham's dining room, but they were winding up, all their sewing things being stowed back in their bags. It was just as well. Deydie was really in a snit now, and Cait was grateful for her guest room upstairs so she didn't have to go back to her grandmother's cottage with her.

As everyone filed out, they said goodbye. Except her gran, who only made a grating noise. Deydie's revived contempt reminded Cait of her mission.

When she got to her room, she sat on the bed and laid her head in her hands. She just *had* to do this story. Not for herself, but for Gandiegow. *Big star in little town.* Tourists out the wazoo. They could sell Graham Buchanan souvenirs. Then maybe Gandiegow could stand on its own two feet without the help of Mr. Charitable. Whether or not any of them understood, Cait would be doing them all a favor by exposing Graham.

Focusing on the village made Cait more determined than ever. Tonight, when everyone slept, she would get back to working on the story. There was plenty of this house she hadn't searched yet.

*   *   *

Later that night, after Duncan and Mattie went to bed, Cait slipped out of the guest bedroom and snuck across the hall to Graham's room. As usual, Dingus lay in the center of his bed. He perked up when she came in and gave an excited yip.

"Shh," she said as she closed the door behind her. "If you're quiet, Caitie will give you an extra treat after she ransacks Master's room." Guilt welled up, and she squashed it down.

The dog ran to the edge of the bed, jumped off, and followed her into Graham's closet.

"What little secrets do you have hiding in here?" she whispered.

She started at the top with an ancient red hatbox and pulled it down. When she took off the lid, she found pictures—black-and-white snapshots. She took the box to Graham's bed and got comfortable, the dog cuddling up against her while she pulled out a handful of photos.

Graham had been a cute little boy, and she could see a lot of Mattie in him. Except Graham always had a smile on his face. It was like he was born to be in front of a camera, still or otherwise. Cait could've spent the rest of the night going through these pictures but decided she'd take this box back to her room and go through it later. Maybe there'd be more pictures of her mama in there, like the one Graham had given her for Christmas.

She squashed down the pang of guilt that rose up. Cait would write an article that painted him in the best of lights. He was a good guy and the world should know it.

She went back to the closet and pulled down a shoe box that held only a cruddy pair of worn work boots. They had to be important to Graham or else they wouldn't be there. She took a picture of them with her cell phone and slipped them back on the shelf. As she was pulling down the next item, an old quilt, she heard Graham's bedroom door creak open.

"Caitie?" Duncan whispered. "Are ye in here?"

She started to slip in among Graham's suits but knew she'd been busted. She came out from the closet.

Duncan stood there drenched in sweat. "Can you help me?"

She ran over to him. "Are you all right?"

"Can you put Mattie into his room? I need to change the sheets. They're soaked. I must've had a fever when I went to bed."

She moved the red hatbox to the floor. "Here, lie down. I'll take care of Mattie and the bed. Do you need something to drink?"

"No. I'll be fine." He'd already stretched out and closed his eyes. Dingus tentatively crawled up beside him and lay down.

"I'll be back in a flash." Cait shut the door behind her.

If Duncan had been a little more cognizant, he would've demanded to know what she was doing in his da's closet.

She went into his room and saw Mattie, the boy she loved so much, lying in the bed. This beautiful child had been through hell. He was still going through hell with his da so sick. Her heart ached for Mattie. She wished she could take his pain away. She would never do anything to hurt him. Never.

In that moment, Cait had clarity, the unmistakable truth now blindingly clear. She couldn't do the story on Graham. God, how could she have been so dumb for so long? He and his family had come to mean the world to her, everything she held dear. It would hurt him, and to hurt Graham would hurt everyone. She'd stupidly been lying to herself to think that she could expose him. And Duncan. And Mattie. But she couldn't. Not for the good of the town. Not for *any* reason.

She moved Mattie to her bed in case he had a bad dream and kissed his forehead before leaving. For a long moment, she watched over him, knowing she was finally on the right path. Next she changed Duncan's sheets and then helped him back to his bed. After a few sips of water, he was back to sleep before she left his room.

"When are you coming home, Graham?" she said to herself just outside Duncan's door. "We need you."

But Death was the one who answered. She could feel him laughing at her efforts to keep him at bay, tendrils of dread pricking at her spine.

Deydie busied herself with binding the quilt, avoiding Bethia's gaze.

"Something is on yere mind. And don't tell me it isn't," Bethia said as she sat down at Deydie's wooden table. "What is it ye're keeping from me?"

Deydie waved her hand in the air, not looking up. "Nothing's going on. Yere powers are off, that's all." Except Bethia's instincts were square on, as always.

Deydie was fuming mad over Caitie and that story, enough to take a stick to that girl. She felt damn near ornery enough to tell Graham, her quilting ladies, and the whole town what tomfoolery her granddaughter had been up to.

But she hadn't.

Graham was like a son to Deydie, and she'd protect him from the devil himself. But every time she thought she might break the bad news, she couldn't. There was something about Caitie's face. An expression. Especially when she looked upon Graham. Her eyes shone bright then. Deydie didn't know a damn thing about romance; too much work to be done to worry over that nonsense. But that look haunted her. That look spoke of love.

Deydie sighed heavily. Where there was love, there was always hope. Hope Caitie would do the right thing and not write that story. Besides, no need preparing the tar and feathers if the lass had second thoughts.

"I'll just watch and wait," Deydie mumbled.

"Speak up," Bethia scolded.

"I didn't say anything," Deydie spouted. "Maybe it's time you got one of those hearing aids."

Cait walked up and down the seashore at dusk, trying to work up her nerve to call Margery Pinchot. She'd put it off for most of the day. The cowardice in her wanted to send a text message and be done with it. But Cait was no coward. Besides, Margery deserved to hear Cait's voice. Finally, she pulled out her cell phone and dialed.

When Margery answered, Cait swallowed her pride and told the truth.

"This is Cait Macleod. I'm sorry I didn't get back to you sooner."

"Is the story done?" Margery sounded frigid.

"I can't do it," Cait confessed. "I never should've said I could, and I'm sorry I kept you hanging." She took a deep breath and plowed on. "I was mistaken."

It was the truth. Cait was mistaken about a lot of things. Mistaken that she could write a story about Graham and think it wouldn't hurt anyone. She was mistaken to think she could keep a professional distance from a town that she loved so much. And she'd been mistaken for some time now that she could betray anyone. Even to save herself.

Margery handled it as well as could be expected. Obscenities flew through the cell phone towers between New York and Scotland. When she was done, Cait apologized again and hung up.

The deed was done, but the guilt still lingered. Her only consolation was that no one else knew what she'd been up to. She trudged to the big house and found she was still in a load of trouble with Deydie. The ole gal didn't give her two civilized words in a row but kept an eye on Cait as if the silverware and candlesticks would go missing.

Over the next several weeks, Cait concentrated on doing her best to take care of Duncan and Mattie to atone for nearly writing the story. Duncan called Graham every day now, and because Graham's schedule had gotten hectic, the incoming calls from Mr. Movie Star to her had dwindled. Between her gran's newfound contempt and Cait's infrequent contact with Graham, she felt alone all over again.

Mattie, though, was the one bright spot in her life.

In the evening, Duncan started going to bed earlier than Mattie. Cait dug out all her favorite books from Graham's collection and read to Mattie with him cuddled up on her lap. *Winnie-the-Pooh* was first, followed by *The Wind in the Willows*. It was their special time together where outside worries didn't intrude and the moments were magical. She could tell Mattie had come to care for her, too. His face lit up whenever she came into a room, and his smiles were easier, too. And for her, Mattie was everything. There was such a peace inside her when she held Mattie, and it healed that part of her that had wanted a child of her own for so long.

The quilting ladies hadn't been back to the house for a sewing bee since that day when Cait had started on the bluff blocks. When she finished the row and handed it to Deydie, she posed the question she'd been burning to ask.

"So . . . when are the ladies coming back up to Graham's place to sew? I'd love to help with the Pinwheel quilt now that I'm done with my part of the round robin," Cait said.

Deydie harrumphed. "They'll not be coming back up here. Ye'll not be helping with the Pinwheel quilt either. 'Tis already finished."

"Can't they come here to put together the Our Town Gandiegow quilt?" Cait knew the answer by the fierce frown on Deydie's face.

"Gandiegow doesn't need yere brand of help." Deydie shoved the stretch of fabric in her pocket, wrinkling it.

Suddenly, Cait could read it in her gran's eyes—she knew. She knew Cait had been planning to write an article about Graham. *Crap!* That was the reason for her recent scorn. Cait opened her mouth to tell Deydie the truth. That she hadn't been able to go through with it. That she couldn't expose Graham and betray Gandiegow.

But Mattie ran into the room and stopped her confession. He tugged on Cait's hand, the dog barking wildly at his side. Mattie had such urgency in his eyes that she hurried away with him, Deydie rushing after them both.

When they got to the media room, it seemed empty. Mattie pulled her in farther and then she saw.

Duncan had collapsed.

Chapter Twenty

Cait ran around the recliner to where Duncan lay on the floor. "Help me get him in the chair," she said to Deydie.

Duncan put his hand up. "I stood too fast, that's all. I'll be fine." They had to help him to his feet anyway. "There's no need to rat me out to Da."

"Here, lean back." Cait reclined his chair.

"I'll get you a wee bit of tea," Deydie said. "That should fix you up."

Duncan turned toward Mattie's anxious face. "Don't worry, monkey. Your Pops is all right."

Mattie took his father's hand and held it to his chest.

"Climb up there, Mattie," Cait said. "And keep an eye on him."

"Ah, Caitie, I'm fine," Duncan complained, but Mattie did as he was told, cuddling close to his da.

Duncan's cell phone lay on the floor and "We Are the Champions" rang out.

"Hand the phone to me," he said. "It's Da."

Cait picked it up, and instead of relinquishing the phone, she stepped just outside the media room. "Impeccable timing. Duncan has taken a spill. Mattie found him on the floor, but I think he's okay. He said he got dizzy when he stood up too fast."

Graham sighed. Cait could almost hear him running his hand through his hair.

"I'll be home tonight. Wait up for me," Graham said.

"Sure. But everything is under control here," she assured him. "I don't think you need to come home."

"I have to see him. I won't be able to stay long, but I need to come."

"I understand," she said.

"Good." Graham hung up.

Cait walked back into the room and saw Duncan's color had returned.

"Good news, fellas." Cait handed the phone back, trying to sound the epitome of optimism. "Grandda is making a quick visit home. How about bangers and mash for breakfast?"

Mattie nodded his head, but Duncan only frowned at her.

Cait put her hands on her hips. "Hey, I promised to keep your da apprised. You wouldn't want me to be negligent in my duties, now, would you?"

Duncan shook his head. "Hand me the remote control."

He wasn't happy with her, but tough noodles.

Deydie brought the tea in and perched near Duncan, keeping her eagle eyes on him while at the same time working on some hand stitching.

With everything under control, Cait slipped out and stood against the wall in the hall, trying to calm the butterflies hopping around in her stomach. *Graham coming home. Wanting her to wait up.* She tried giving herself a good talking to, repeated her mantra about *self-preservation* over and over again, but nothing worked. She almost ran upstairs to take a cold shower, but instead went to make the promised bangers and mash.

At one twenty A.M., Graham came through the door. Cait sat in her pajamas on a barstool with a magazine in her hand, but she hadn't been able to read a word. She was wound way too tight, not knowing where she stood with him. Did he care about her even a little, or was she just a convenience? It took everything in her not to jump up and run into his comforting arms.

Graham shocked her by dropping his overnight bag and making a beeline for her. He wrapped himself around her and kissed her. When he ended the kiss, he pushed a lock of her hair off her cheek.

"Let me check in on Duncan and then we'll go to bed," he said.

Okay, there was a whole lot of ambiguity going on in that sentence. Did he mean separate beds? Or *Let's make mad passionate love all night long?*

She opened her mouth for clarification, but he only gave her another kiss. When she opened her eyes again, he was on his way upstairs.

She had no choice but to follow. She still didn't have any answers as to where she stood with him, but she wanted to make him feel better. And she knew if she did that, it would make her feel better, too.

She could give herself to him fully and still protect herself, couldn't she?

When she got to the top of the stairs, Graham was stepping back out into the hall, pulling Duncan's door closed. He took her hand and guided her into his room.

Well, that answered at least one of her questions—his bed, then.

As soon as Graham shut the door behind her, he pulled her into his arms and burrowed into her neck. "God, Caitie, I need you. I've needed you every night since I left."

"I need you, too," she admitted. She pulled away to look into his eyes. "But I have to know one thing first. Are you going to regret us being together like you did the last time?" She gazed upon his face, searching for the truth.

"I was an idiot before. You gave me a gift and I threw it back in your face. I'm so sorry." He brushed back her hair. "You have to know, lass, I treasure our time together."

That was exactly what she needed to hear. She could spend the rest of the night analyzing everything he did and said but chose to switch off her brain and live in the here and now.

She put her hands on either side of his face and kissed him back, putting all the emotion she felt for him into that one moment.

He slid his hand into her hair and pulled her head gently back, making her open more to him. And like that, *she was his*. Bare, vulnerable, his for the taking.

For as much as they were both turned on—Graham's erection pressed into her—he seemed to want to make their time together last. He peeled back her clothes with care and gentleness, kissing every bit of exposed flesh along the way. She did the same to him. Every once in a while, he would stop and gaze into her eyes. He cared for her, and she knew it all the way to her heart.

When they were naked, he steered her to the bed

and stretched out beside her. They touched, caressed, kissed, and joined together like forever lovers. It was sweet and lasting, a memory she would hold close to her always.

Afterward, they held each other for a long time and then made love again. When they finally fell asleep, she was spooned into him, his arm protectively around her waist, the puppy lying at their feet.

Early in the morning, Mattie crawled into bed and climbed on top of Graham.

"Hey, sport." Graham tickled him, pulling the sheet tighter around Cait so her bare ass and other essentials wouldn't be exposed.

"Why don't you two go start the breakfast?" she said to them. "I'll be down in a minute."

Graham shooed Mattie out while he dressed. Before leaving, he kissed her nose. "See you in a minute, lass."

Deydie would broomify Cait if she caught her buck naked in Graham's bed. Quickly, Cait crawled out, hugging the sheet to her, and zipped off to the guest bathroom with Deydie nowhere in sight. Cait quickly showered, hyperaware of her body, everywhere Graham had touched. Her belly turned warm and full just thinking about their night of loving.

But no words of love had been spoken. And no matter what she saw in his eyes in the heat of passion, she had to stop this nonsense. Stop casting them in some stupid fairy tale. They were having an affair, plain and simple. It didn't mean a damn thing to Graham; he had affairs all the time. She certainly hadn't fallen in love or some ridiculous drivel like that, and she'd be damned if she let him think that she had, too. To prove it, she didn't get all dolled up for him but dressed in her grungiest jeans and put no makeup on. She was still Cait Macleod, single and proud of it. She headed downstairs.

Graham looked up as she came in the kitchen, gazing at her with sappy eyes. "You look more beautiful this morning than you did last night."

Cait turned to Mattie. "Grandda needs a pair of glasses." She helped herself to a banana.

Mattie gave her a small grin.

Graham put a hand on his little shoulder. "Don't listen to her, Mattie. Caitie is one of a kind."

She sat there quite dazed—how easily he could derail her. Even with a corny compliment.

He poured her a cup of coffee, adding cream and sugar, and set it in front of her on the counter.

Duncan came in the kitchen, scrubbing his face. "I'll take one of those." Sleep hadn't helped his coloring at all.

Graham surveyed his son for a moment, then did the darnedest thing. Gave Duncan a hug. It shocked the hell out of Duncan, too.

"Aw, Da, I'm right as rain. Caitie blew it out of proportion."

She put her hands on her hips, but stopped. These two were making up. If she had to be the scapegoat—well, so be it.

Graham let go of his son and grabbed a mug. "Milk and sugar, too?"

"That's how I like it," Duncan replied, smiling.

Mattie looked from one to the other of his male relations, and for one glorious moment, he wasn't the sad little boy but had transformed into a normal kid with a contented glow on his face.

They spent the day playing board games with Mattie

and shooting the breeze in front of the fire. Every time Cait tried to slip out to give them privacy, one of them, usually Graham, would pull her back into their midst, so she finally gave in—they sincerely wanted her around.

Deydie made a short appearance in the morning. She delivered a list of grievances to Graham, then announced she'd be spending the rest of the day with Amy and Moira working on the Our Town quilt. Cait knew better than to ask to help. Besides, the clock was ticking. Cait shouldn't want to spend as much time with Graham as possible before he left, but dammit, she did.

Before she knew it, Graham was shoving clothes into his overnight bag, preparing to head down to the beach to meet the helicopter.

In the doorway of the parlor, he stopped and turned to Duncan. "Son, don't get upset, but I've hired a couple of nurses to keep watch over you."

"Da," Duncan warned. "I'm too old to have babysitters."

"I didn't do it for you. I did it for me," Graham said. "I worry. Having them here will ease my mind. Besides, I believe the pressure has been too much for Caitie and Deydie."

Cait started to argue but didn't get the chance.

Graham went on. "You're not too upset with me, are you?"

"Asking permission first would've been grand," Duncan said, not sounding too angry.

"That's an idea." Graham smiled. "I'll take that under advisement."

"Thanks," Duncan said. "You're a real team player."

"Dunc?" Graham went all serious. "You will take care, won't you?"

Duncan forced a smile. "Sure, Da."

*   *   *

The nurses arrived the next day and handed Cait two nondisclosure agreements. "We were told by the agency to give these to you."

"Thanks." Cait took the signed papers, then set the two nurses up in the rooms on the third floor.

Deydie made certain the Florence Nightingales understood the newly revised volunteer list hanging on the refrigerator and promptly left. Cait still needed to set her grandmother straight that she hadn't written the story on Graham. She just couldn't get her alone to do it. And whenever she thought they might get that moment, Deydie would disappear, acting as if being near Cait was the last thing in the world she wanted.

Graham's home turned into a regular Four Seasons. He should've installed a revolving door for as many people who traipsed in and out each day. When Mattie wasn't at school, she played with him while Duncan rested. On Thursdays, Ross, Duncan's closest friend, took Duncan to his doctor's appointment in Aberdeen. After returning home, they'd sit by the fire, sipping Scotch that probably wasn't what the doctor had ordered.

Duncan continued to call Graham every day, but now Graham called her every night as well, usually very late, sometimes waking her up.

"We're having long days here," he'd tell her. "I just need to hear a voice from home."

He's homesick for you, her irrational heart sighed. And then it would pound away at her chest like a slaphappy clogger.

Her reasonable self knew better: Any voice from home would do. She wasn't anything special. Just his Gandiegow friend with benefits.

The days without Graham passed pretty slowly. But whenever the nurses e-mailed reports to him about Duncan, Cait was sure to get an extra call to confirm what the nurses had said.

On February 2nd, Cait brought Groundhog Day to Scotland. She and Mattie celebrated by printing out pictures of the cuddly creature and pasting them to paper crowns to wear at dinner. Duncan wasn't up to sitting at the table, so Mattie ate with him in his room, both of them wearing their crowns.

"When are you coming home?" Cait asked Graham that evening.

"I don't know. The weather hasn't cooperated for the outdoor shoots."

"You will be home by Valentine's Day, won't you? Mattie is counting on it. He's been decorating your office with hearts," she confided. "But you didn't hear it from me."

"I'll get home as soon as I can. It's the only promise I can make."

"Everyone misses you." The truth was that she missed him the most—his stupid cocky grin, his übergood looks, and the way he held her close in the darkness of his bedroom.

"I miss you, too," he said.

On Shrove Tuesday, two nights before the Valentine's Day Céilidh, Graham came in the back door. He hugged Mattie, Duncan, Deydie, and then headed for Cait.

The pancake she was making flipped onto the stovetop.

"Don't I get a welcome-home hug from you?" Graham asked Cait.

Cait smiled but held up a blocking hand. "I'm busy. It's Pancake for Dinner Day. Go get washed up."

They had a nice evening together, though Deydie kept glaring at Cait and muttering. Cait breathed a sigh of relief when it came time to clean the kitchen and her gran headed out the back door to her own cottage. Peace fell over the house. Unfortunately, along with it came some time to think.

Where was she supposed to sleep now that Graham was home? Nothing had been said, and now it was late.

Everyone disappeared one by one for bed—Duncan, Mattie, and the nurses. Only Graham and Cait remained.

"Will you have a nightcap?" Graham said, walking to the dry bar.

Cait attempted a fake yawn. "I'm bushed."

She fled the parlor, hightailed it up the stairs, and got into bed in record time.

She needed to regain her senses. She wouldn't get her heart broken again. She wouldn't be tempted by him tonight.

Her door opened. She hoped it was Mattie needing a glass of water. It wasn't.

"Caitie, come to bed with me. Please."

Her resolve crumbled and swept itself under the bed.

"Well," she huffed, getting up and going to him, "only if you make it worth my while."

"Don't worry, love." He patted her on the rump as she passed by. "I've been saving up just for you."

The next day, Ash Wednesday, they all went to church, kneeled and prayed, leaving with ashes on their foreheads. Cait left with something else—a decision. It had been a long time since she'd given up anything for Lent. In the past, she'd given up something like chocolate or

Dr Pepper. This time it would be much harder to live without—she'd give up Graham.

Graham and Mattie headed to Duncan's place to pick up some things. All alone, Cait walked up the bluff, prepared to put her new plan into action. It was easy making a decision. Following through was a whole other matter. He was an exquisite lover—inventive, playful, and intent on getting the job done right. Her intimate bits lit on fire just thinking about their moments wrapped in the sheets. She undid her scarf and unzipped her jacket to cool off.

The only way to stay out of his bed would be to get out of his house. She couldn't go back to Deydie's. Her gran hated her. So much for new beginnings and starting over. Their relationship was in the crapper, flushed down the proverbial loo. Not even Roto-Rooter could get it flowing again.

Cait's only choice was to move back to her drafty room over the pub. She shivered and zipped her jacket again.

She didn't falter at Graham's doorstep. She slipped into the mansion, hurrying upstairs to be packed and gone before Graham got back. She emptied her drawer into her suitcase without worrying over wrinkled clothes. Time was of the essence.

"What are you doing?"

Cait jumped.

Duncan rested in the doorway of the guestroom. She'd forgotten that he was home because he hadn't felt well enough to attend the church service.

She zipped up the luggage and set it on the floor. "I thought I'd get out of everyone's hair now that your da is home."

Duncan came farther into the room. "Ye know he's not going to like it."

Cait ignored him and went into the bathroom to clear out the shower.

Duncan blocked the bedroom entry. "Don't leave until you tell him what ye're doing. He's come to depend upon you."

Cait frowned at Duncan harshly until she realized that was how Deydie had become so wrinkled. "Graham Buchanan is rich and famous. He can hire someone to take my place." A housekeeper, a babysitter, a hooker. Oh God, what had she reduced herself to?

From behind Duncan, a deep voice rang out. "Hire someone? I'm a frugal Scot. I can't find someone who'll do what you do for so little."

Duncan turned and smiled at Graham. "It's about time you got here. I'll leave it to you to sort it out. Make her stay. She makes me smile."

Cait stomped her foot. "Dang it, Duncan. You stalled me on purpose."

"Aye." Duncan left the room, leaving Cait and Graham alone.

He leaned against the doorframe. "Why are you leaving?"

"I'm giving you up for Lent." She stood her ground, slipping her toiletries into another bag. "Nothing you can say will make me stay."

"If you won't stay for me, then do it for Mattie."

"You're not playing fair."

"I never do," Graham replied.

And then came the final nail in her coffin—the six-year-old bugger stepped out from behind his grandda. She was sunk.

"Fine." She sighed. "But get out while I unpack." She grabbed Mattie. "You can stay."

Graham shot her his victory smile. "I'll be working on tonight's meal."

"You do that," she called over her shoulder.

Deydie came to the mansion for the meal of bread, wine, and soup. Her gran didn't glare as much at Cait, which was helpful. But all wasn't well. Cait caught sight of the purplish bruises covering Duncan's arms before he pulled down his sleeves to cover them up. He looked more tired than usual and headed to bed right after he nibbled on a little bread.

She wished she could tell those two connivers, Leukemia and Death, to rot in hell. It wouldn't do any good. Hell had sent them in the first place to take up residence in Gandiegow.

She went upstairs to her room and started writing a piece about what family and the community go through when one of their own has the dreadful disease. She typed it up and sent it off to *Woman's Day* to see if it might work in their human interest section.

She put on her cuddly pajamas, crawled into bed, and turned off the light. She felt terrible for Duncan, sad for Mattie, and pity for herself. Why couldn't she find true love? Or at least someone who would stick? Graham had told her point-blank he liked to keep things casual. The problem was she simply wasn't a casual kind of girl. She didn't just want incredible sex; she wanted more. Oh God, how she hated to admit it. She wanted the whole shebang.

Sometime later, she woke up to her bed dipping down on one side. Graham pulled her into his arms. He didn't try to put the moves on her, but did something much more devastating—held her close. For a long time, he was quiet and then entwined his hand with hers.

"Tell me it's going to be okay, Caitie," he whispered into the dark.

She laid her hand on his chest and decided this wasn't the time to lie. "I don't know, Graham. I just don't know."

Chapter Twenty-one

The next morning, first thing, Cait headed to Deydie's house with her camera to take pictures of the Our Town Gandiegow quilt. All the quilt ladies had assembled.

"Hurry it," Deydie barked at her. "We've got loads to do for the céilidh tonight."

"Fine," Cait said. "But I need to get some good pictures for the online auction. The more personal we can make it, the better."

"Are you going to write up an article?" Rhona asked.

Cait's head shot up in surprise. Had Deydie told everyone what she'd planned to do? But the look on Rhona's face held no accusation in it, only curiosity.

Cait wiped the worry from her face. "Yes. I thought I would take a crack at it. Make it a story about you, the quilters. If that's all right?"

"Asking? Now, there's something new," Deydie mumbled.

Amy piped in, all excited. "Are you going to interview us separately or together? I have some funny stories I could tell you about my auntie."

"I'm going to write about you as a quilting community. I'll let you all approve it before I post it online. Is that a deal?" Cait said.

Deydie looked dumbfounded, and Cait knew why. They were both thinking about the other story.

Cait put her mind back on the task at hand. It took some doing, but she snapped several pictures of the women holding the quilt by the sea, by the bluff, and crouched outside Deydie's cottage.

"Caitie, will ye be helping us with the decorations for tonight's party?" asked Moira.

Cait was about to say yes, but good ole Gran got her two cents in first.

"No," Deydie barked. "Caitie's got that quilt to get on the Internet."

Cait was left to watch them as they headed off to work on the céilidh.

Alone, she went back to her room at the mansion to put together the article and get the ball rolling on the auction. As she typed, she couldn't help but wonder at the amount the quilt would bring if only Graham would give his permission to use his fame to sell it.

Knowing him, though, he'd probably just bail out the town again, outbid legitimate buyers to make sure the quilt brought in top dollar. It was best not to tell him anything about it. She wanted the town to be able to help itself, to stand on its own. She wondered what else she could do to help.

Suddenly, her door opened. She looked up and slammed her laptop lid down.

Graham looked perturbed.

"Sorry to interrupt." He seemed unhappy to find her on her computer. "Just wondered if you wanted to take a walk over to your cottage."

Cait wiped the guilt off her face. She hadn't been do-ing anything wrong. *Like writing a story that would di-vulge everything he wanted to keep secret.*

Graham stepped farther into the room. "I ran into Sinclair. He has a group at your bungalow, cleaning up the area, preparing for the remodel. What were you do-ing?" He pointed to her laptop, looking embarrassed for asking.

"Just working on a piece about quilts," she said. "Nothing special."

"Are you coming or not?" He squinted in her direc-tion like he had a lie detector aimed at her head.

"Sure." She got up and grabbed her coat.

When they got downstairs, Graham stopped at the back door. "Oh, darn." His fake exclamation put her on guard. "I left my gloves upstairs. I'll be right back."

"I won't move a muscle," she said, smiling to herself.

Go ahead, snoopy. You won't find one incriminating thing.

Quilts, my foot. Graham was sure she'd been writing a story about him, sure he'd caught her in the act. And it was surprising how disappointed that made him feel. But now he stared at the screen, dumbfounded. It was only a story about a quilt and the ladies of Gandiegow. So why in the world had she acted so strange?

God only knows, was the only conclusion he could come to.

He'd never been so happy to be wrong. She hadn't come here to expose him. He suspected she had been sent by a higher power to help him get through this, to be a comfort to him. But she'd become so much more. She'd taken his somewhat fake and shallow life and brought depth and realness to it that he hadn't experienced since he was a boy. She gave meaning to his existence beyond what he made in box office sales. She made him feel like a superhero in his everyday life. He wasn't completely sure what it all meant, but he knew he cared deeply for her. He was exceedingly grateful she was in his life. Even more important, he felt like Caitie had somehow brought an extra layer of protection to Gandiegow, too. If the vultures knew Graham lived here and got wind of Duncan's illness, the press would be picking at their carcasses, making a painful situation unbearable. Thank God he had Caitie, and thank God he still had his privacy.

Caitie hollered from the bottom of the steps. "Are you coming or what?"

Graham shut the laptop lid and hurried down the stairs.

Caitie stood there all flushed and cute in her brown parka. He had the urge to kiss her, but he opened the back door for her instead. "Let's be going, Ms. Macleod."

Outside, the sun broke through the clouds, and he began to whistle.

Suddenly, Caitie stopped walking and turned to him. "There's something I have to talk to you about. It's about you and your stardom."

He felt confused. Hadn't he just resolved this whole issue and decided she didn't want to write a story about him? "All right," he finally answered, bracing himself.

"There's been this idea floating around in my brain for some time and I've just figured it out. I've been wondering what to do about you."

Maybe she wasn't talking about writing a story. Maybe it was about having an honest-to-goodness "relationship."

Funny, the thought didn't make him want to hop a plane and get the heck out of Scotland.

"Go ahead," he encouraged.

"It's the quilting," she said as way of explanation.

"What?" he said. She had a way of making him crazy. "I'm lost. What are you talking about, lass?"

She picked at her scarf, not looking at him. "It's this idea. I'll need your help. Your cooperation to make it work."

"What does that mean?" *What is she up to?*

She faced him fully. "If I buy two of the empty businesses on the boardwalk, I could renovate them and turn them into a retreat for quilters, something catchy."

He felt like he was on a roller coaster tossed from side to side and up and down. He got his bearings, then touched her arm. "If you need the money, lass, all you have to do is ask. I don't mind helping the town."

She pulled away from him. "I don't need your money. Aren't you listening? What I need is your cooperation."

Tentatively, Graham asked, "How, then?"

"This quilting spot wouldn't just be for the locals. I want it to be a profitable business that will positively impact Gandiegow's economy. I thought if we turned the town into a quilting destination—"

"A what?"

"A quilting destination. A quaint and charming tourist spot for quilters. People could come from around the world and soak up some local flavor while doing what they love. We could teach classes. When I say we, I mean Deydie and the group. I'm only thinking out loud here, but we could bring in Fons and Porter or Eleanor Burns to do some workshops."

"Who?"

"Famous people in the quilting world." She put her hands on her hips. "Seriously, Graham, you haven't heard of Fons and Porter?"

"I see where you're going with this, but where would the quilters stay? We've only the one room over the pub. I'm certainly not turning my house into a hotel for a bunch of women with scissors."

She broke into a smile. "Don't worry, Mr. Generous. I thought we could turn my cottage into the lodging area. Make it dormitory style. Maybe build an extension off the back. Since Mr. Sinclair hasn't started yet, he could revise the plans."

Graham felt like a heel. "You'd give up your privacy for this venture?"

"Sure."

"Where did you say you're getting the money for all of this?"

She leaned in to him and whispered, "Don't tell anyone, but I'm loaded."

He grinned at her. "Aren't you just full of surprises."

"So you'll help me?"

"You keep turning down my help. I'll do whatever you want me to do."

"Good," she said, looking relieved. "I need you to co-ordinate your visits to Gandiegow so you're gone when we have our retreats."

A new path had appeared to Cait out of thin air. A better path. One with fewer moral dilemmas and challenging turns. One she could embrace with all her heart. Instead of restarting her journalism career, she would dedicate herself to the Kilts & Quilts venture. She loved quilting. She loved this town. Gandiegow, her home.

He broke her reverie by tucking a lock of hair behind her ear. "Why are you doing this?"

She shrugged. "To give back? To help?" She gave him a hard look. "Scratch all that. I just want to be as big a martyr as you are."

"What?" He acted like a rat caught in a cage, then relaxed. "Oh, yes, the pub. Right."

She raised her eyebrows and stared him down, letting him know she knew everything he'd done for everyone in secret. He finally turned away.

She went on. "I thought a share of the profits could go to the Lost Fishermen's Families Fund."

He gave a low whistle. "You'll get sainthood for that one."

"Not if they don't know about it." She lightly punched him on the arm. "I'll keep your secrets if you keep mine."

He rubbed his arm as if she'd hurt him. "Fine."

"Can you do it?" she asked.

"What?"

"Work with me on scheduling. And I'll work with you to preserve your privacy."

He shook his head, not as an answer but in wonder. "You're quite a woman, Caitie Macleod. Sure. I'll do it." He reached out to take her into his arms.

She sidestepped him. "And you, sir," she said in her best queen voice, "take too many liberties."

He placed her arm in his. "Yes, it's a grievous fault, but it is Valentine's Day. Happy Valentine's Day, Caitie." He kissed the top of her head. "Now, let's go talk to Sinclair about your grand scheme."

The little peck of a kiss got her all hot and bothered.

"I hate Valentine's Day," she complained. "There's

too much expectation and not enough delivery as far as I'm concerned." She looked to him to see if he agreed.

He gave her a wolfy grin. "I'd show you delivery if you'd let me."

She shook her head. "I told you, I've given up all of that for Lent, so don't try anything, buster."

"I wouldn't dream of it." He wasn't fooling her. That hooded gaze he gave her said he'd jump her bones right here right now in the middle of the path if she'd let him.

She glared at him. "We've got a lot to do today, so keep your mind out of the gutter, will you?"

He only laughed, not promising a thing.

They found Mr. Sinclair directing a small group of men cleaning up Caitie's burned-out cottage. She told the contractor of her new plans for the house and the businesses downtown.

She ticked the items off one by one. "For the quilting building, I want plenty of electrical outlets, a nice kitchen area, a big hearth, and room for comfy seating."

Mr. Sinclair said it could all be done and he would be by later in the week with new plans for everything.

"Listen, Graham," Cait said as they left. "I've got to get some stuff done before the dance tonight."

"No problem," he said. "I'm going to check on Duncan's house and then go over to the pub. I promised to see Bonnie today."

Cait went incinerator hot. "Tell her to keep her paws to herself," she blurted out.

"Why, Caitie, I do believe you're jealous."

"I am not. I just know her fingernails should be registered as lethal weapons. You'd better stay three feet away from her at all times lest she poke an eye out or something."

He gave her a squeeze. "I'll not be letting anybody touch me but you."

A warm sizzle shot up Cait's spine. She pulled away and hurried off, trying to get her hormones—*the little sluts*—under control.

She made her way to the other side of town to the mansion. Once at Graham's, she finished the quilting article and made copies for the quilt ladies to proofread. Cait's stomach began to roil like a ship tossed about, knowing she'd have to face Deydie's scathing comments and glares soon.

She headed to the old wool factory that was one of the buildings she planned to buy for the quilting retreat. Tonight, though, it would serve as the location for the dance.

She found the quilt ladies and many others decorating the interior with hearts and streamers while young boys lined up chairs around the edges of the room. Amy was hanging a disco ball from the ceiling in the center. Cait went to her first.

"Hey, Amy, here's what I wrote about the quilt." She handed her one of the copies.

"Awesome." Amy climbed off the ladder. "I'll look at it now."

Cait went around to all the ladies, but it was Bethia who had other things on her mind.

"Why have ye not been quilting with us?" Bethia nagged. "Deydie says you're too busy, but I'm not believing it." The old woman touched her arm. "What's going on with you and your gran?"

"A misunderstanding," Cait said. "We'll work it out in time." At least she hoped so.

"You'd better, lass," Bethia said. "Your gran is hurting."

Deydie didn't look like she was hurting at all. She was in her element, acting the drill sergeant, shouting out orders to everyone and smiling with satisfaction when they snapped to attention.

Cait walked over to her, having saved Deydie's copy for last.

"Here's the story I wrote." Cait held out the sheet, but Deydie didn't take it.

"I'll not be reading it." Deydie gave Cait a scowl, then her back.

Since they couldn't be overheard at the back of building, Cait pleaded to the old woman's hunched shoulders. "It's the quilt story, Gran. Not the other." Cait looked at the floor. "I started to write it, but never sent anything in. I couldn't do it."

Deydie spun around so fast, she should've given herself whiplash. And if Cait thought there would be gratefulness about her, boy, had Cait been wrong.

Deydie slammed her fists on her hips with her eyes burning like a Scottish warrior. "It doesn't matter one whit that you came to your senses, you stupid girl. Changing your mind doesn't erase the fact that you were going to do it. It's still a betrayal."

"But—"

Deydie marched away.

Cait stood there a moment, her eyes stinging, her face hot, then fled the building before anyone looked closely and saw her shame. She ran back to the big house.

Mattie met her at the door with a hug.

Thank God for this little boy.

They spent the rest of the day working on Valentine's Day cards. Cait tried to help him with his, but he kept shoving blank red construction paper at her, thumping his pointer finger on it. Like she had valentines to complete for herself. Yeah, right.

Finally, she acquiesced and made one for Deydie, which Cait had no intention of giving. She made one for Duncan, making it extra cheery. She made one for each of the quilt ladies. When she was done with that, Mattie stared at her expectantly. He pushed another red piece of paper at her, a shiny one, a special piece.

"Fine," she barked, sounding a lot like Deydie.

Mattie grinned at her.

She cut out three hearts—two big ones, one little. She pasted them together with the little heart between them. There was no way she was writing *Be Mine* on it. She wrote only, *Happy Valentine's Day*.

Mattie frowned at her.

"Okay," she said and wrote, *Love, Caitie*. "Are you happy now, you little monkey?"

Mattie got out of his chair, walked around the table, and gave her a sloppy kiss on the cheek.

When he wasn't looking, she stuck another piece of paper under the others, planning to get his card done in the privacy of her room before the gathering.

After cleaning up their Hallmark mess and stacking their cards in piles by the back door, Cait went to work on the homemade chicken soup for dinner. When it was done, she sent Mattie to pick up his room while she took a tray to Duncan.

He sat propped up in his bed, reading *Fish!* magazine. If he hadn't appeared so tired, he would've looked like a man at leisure.

Cait tapped on the doorjamb. "Can us non-fishing-people come in?"

He brought his head up and grinned. "Only if you have food."

"I'm in luck, then." She set the tray in front of him. "Will you be up to going to the céilidh tonight?"

"Wouldn't miss it." He attempted a good-humored smile. It fell a little short. "I'm only resting now so I can party later."

She pulled a napkin from her back pocket and gave it to him. "I'm sure you'll knock 'em dead." She cringed at her word choice. It was never a good idea to bring Death into the conversation.

Duncan winced and closed his eyes, looking like he was trying to ignore her slipup. "Caitie, I want to thank you," he started.

She shook her head. "The soup? 'Tis nothing. No need to thank me for that."

"Not the soup. For setting me straight about Da." He reached out and took her hand. "Your nasty temper came into good use."

"Nasty temper?" She tried to look shocked. "Is that your way of complimenting me?"

Duncan went on. "Things are much better now between me and Da. It makes Mattie happy when we get along." He squeezed her hand. "You've been good to our family, Caitie. I'll never forget it."

Foreboding came over her—Death had just taken a step into the room. She shook her head and shrugged it off. "It sounds like you're bidding me farewell. I'm not going anywhere."

"I know you're not," he said.

She refused to let him get gloomy on her. "I'm needed too much around here. The dishes, the laundry, even my nasty temper would be missed." She pushed the tray closer to him. "Now, eat." She turned to go.

"One more thing," Duncan said. "Send Mattie in to see me."

After Mattie had been in his father's room for a long time, he came downstairs and found Cait in the laundry room, pulling her red dress from the dryer.

"What is it, little bug?" She squatted down to get a better look at him. His eyes were red and watery like he'd been crying.

He reached out and gave her a hug, clinging to her as if his little life depended upon it.

Chapter Twenty-two

Even though Deydie didn't want her to, Cait went to the dance early to see if she could help with any last-minute preparations. The wool shop had been completely transformed into Cupid's corny, cotton-candy land of love. Most people would've found it adorable. Not Cait. Red and pink hearts made her want to puke. Saint Valentine's Day could go jump off a tall cliff as far as she was concerned.

On Cait's first Valentine's Day with Tom, he'd given her fifteen million excuses why he hadn't planned anything special—no flowers, no chocolate, no fine dining. She'd gotten him the complete collection of the Beatles—something he'd wanted. A box of turtles—his faves. And a slinky teddy for her—what a waste. After that, Valentine's Day went downhill. He spent most of them "working late at the office."

Cait walked her homemade cards to where the paper sacks sat lined up against one wall. Each bag had a villager's name on it, and they were organized alphabetically. She deposited her cards into their respective bags and went to help Moira fill cups with red punch. Slowly, people trickled in, and Cait found herself watching the doorway intently.

"Are you waiting for someone?" Moira asked.

Cait hated to lie, but she did it anyway. "No. Just making sure the door isn't left open. Don't want all the warm air to escape."

"I see," Moira said straight-faced. "Are you sure you're not waiting for a certain film star?"

Amy popped up from nowhere and elbowed Moira. "Is she looking for Graham?" Then she turned to Cait. "I'm sure he'll be along soon."

Cait's cheeks burned, and she felt like crawling under the table. "Will you two stop it?"

They smiled at each other and shrugged.

Rhona joined them, and Cait was glad when she went into teaching mode, even though she wasn't keen on the subject. "Did you know Scotland is world renowned for its romance?" She ticked them off on her fingers. "Gretna Green for eloping. Robert Burns for romantic poetry. Rob Roy for his great love."

Moira looked interested. Cait wasn't. Romance and Valentine's Day were for those who believed in love.

"And your gran, Caitie," Rhona continued, "met your grandda on this very day, many years ago, at a céilidh very much like this."

"What?" Cait asked, her interest finally piqued.

"You haven't heard the story?" Rhona asked.

Bethia joined them. "I'll tell it. I was there. It was a game. One that was played for many years. All the single men of the village wrote their name on pieces of paper and put them in a hat. The single ladies chose a name from the hat, and he had to stay with her for the whole evening. Deydie pulled out Hamish's name."

"Deydie, my gran, played a Valentine's Day game?" Cait said incredulously.

"Now, listen here, lassie," Bethia chided. "Your gran was quite the beauty, like yourself, but pragmatic. She didn't have time for courting in the normal fashion. She needed a man to help with the chores, so she chose a name from the hat."

"So that's how Deydie got a husband."

"Behave yourself, wee Caitie, or I'll be telling your gran." Bethia chuckled. "Anyway, Deydie didn't count on falling in love with Hamish McCracken. Before the night was through, those two were thick as thieves. Married a month later."

"I never knew." Cait squeezed Bethia's round shoulders. "Thanks for telling me."

"It never hurts to be forewarned," Bethia said. "These things run in families. Deydie fell in love on Valentine's Day. You might, too."

"Not a chance," Cait declared. "I don't need a man. I have you ladies. Who could ask for anything more?"

Bethia and Rhona shook their heads, but it was Rhona who spoke.

"Sometimes we don't have a choice in these matters, wee Caitie," her teacher said. "Just remember I told you so."

But Cait had come well armed. Before leaving the mansion, she'd tacked her resolve firmly back in place and wouldn't be swayed. No matter how much Graham begged and pleaded, she wouldn't dance with Mr. Wonderful tonight. Holding him close and swaying to the music was only asking for trouble.

And sex.

If she let him, she'd be putty, pliable and willing, in his

hands, letting him take her over and over again in his bed, making her hot and sweaty and satisfied.

Cait waved a napkin in front of her face. "Is it warm in here?" she asked Moira.

"Nay, but I believe you'll be wanting to see who just came through the door."

Cait jerked her head up and found Graham gazing at her. "Damn."

"Are you all right?" Moira asked.

"Sure."

But she wasn't. Graham looked better than wonderful. He exuded sex like the sun gave off rays. And every woman in the room knew it. They'd all turned in his direction and, whether they were conscious of it or not, were drawn to him. The females walked toward the door in a trance, like pheromone-starved zombies. Except for Bonnie, who sashayed up to him, draping herself on his arm, her nearly exposed boobs within licking distance of his tongue.

Cait's resolve seriously faltered. She hadn't foreseen this happening, hadn't figured Bonnie and all the other women into the equation for the night.

Moira reached out and stopped Cait from hopping over the table and shoving Bonnie into the special heart-shaped cake.

"She's not in your league, Caitie," Moira said. "Ye've nothing to worry about."

Moira is at it again. "You should give up this amateur matchmaking." Cait filled another cup.

Moira shrugged. "I have eyes, 'tis all. And by the looks of it" — she inclined her head toward Graham — "he only has eyes for you."

"If we're going to be grand friends, Moira Campbell, you'll have to stop being such a romantic."

"I'd like us to be grand friends," Moira said.

"Then you'll have to stop seeing things that aren't really there." Cait smiled at her all the same.

The music started, a Scottish reel, and the crowd whooped and hollered as the dance floor filled up quickly. Cait walked two steps from behind the table before she saw the exchange by the door. Without warning, Bethia and Deydie extracted Graham from Bonnie's tentacles and pulled him out on the floor.

Cait smiled. "Those two are a couple of peaches, aren't they?"

Moira smiled, too. "Why don't you go dance with Mattie?"

Moira was right. Mattie stood next to Duncan, gripping his hand.

Cait made her way to him, trying not to bump into the hyperactive dancers. When she reached him, she knelt down. "Can I have this dance, kind sir?"

Mattie looked up to Duncan for approval.

"Go on, now, and have a good time," Duncan said. "I'm going to go sit by Doc. Remember, Mattie, women don't like it if you step on their toes."

Cait gently squeezed his arm, then took Mattie's hand. They danced an alternate version of the waltz. When the song was over, a little girl, five or so, asked if she could dance with him next.

Mattie looked pleased, so Cait went back to the punch table to help Moira. It gave her a clear view of the action on the floor.

Freda Douglas had snatched the next dance with Graham. Then Rhona. A teenage girl. Amy. Ailsa, then Aileen.

Good, Cait tried convincing herself. *I'm glad he's*

dancing with the town's women. But when he asked her to dance, she'd have to refuse.

The next song started, and Bonnie snatched him up for a slow dance. She clung to him like cellophane and gyrated her hips as if she were practicing her Hula-Hoop.

Just when Cait couldn't take it any longer, the song ended.

The lights came up, and Rhona started the auction of Deydie's Pinwheel quilt. Graham got in one bid before Bethia captured his arm, keeping him from jacking up the price. The quilt sold for one hundred twenty-five pounds to Coll, Amy's husband.

"Happy Valentine's Day, Amy," Coll shouted, holding the quilt over his head.

Never-shy Amy ran and jumped into his arms, plastering a kiss to his lips.

The music started again. While handing a punch cup to Mattie and his new lady friend, Cait glanced up and saw Graham weaving his way toward her.

This is it, Resolve. Be brave. Be firm. Be ruthless.

He smiled and then held his hand out to Moira. "Would you like to dance?"

Moira gave Cait an *oh well* shrug and grinned, succumbing to Graham's charms without a backward glance.

Cait changed her mind. *Moira sucks at being a friend.*

Cait couldn't take her eyes off them, the jealousy bug taking hold again. She didn't know if it was Graham or the music or just Moira's natural talent, but the shy woman came alive—smiling, laughing, graceful on her feet—a different person.

After the song hit its last note, Rhona announced the last dance of the céilidh. Graham deposited Moira back at her post with the girl glowing like a sunflower. Cait glared at her, a wee bit of animosity seeping in.

Graham put his hand out to Cait. "Will you do me the honor of the last dance?"

Cait opened her mouth to say no, but nothing came out. She tried again. "I—I . . ."

He grabbed her hand. "I'll take that as a *yes*." He led her out on the floor and twirled her into his arms. He whispered Gaelic into her ear as he cuddled her close.

She closed her eyes, going with it, letting the music sway them into their own little world. She was caught up in his net, her emotions tangled up in him. For all Cait knew, they were alone in his bed, making love, becoming one. It felt so good and so right. She wouldn't let herself think about how exposed her heart was. She'd deal with that later.

The lights came up. The music had stopped. A minute ago, judging by all the eyes on them. She extracted herself from Graham's embrace and felt branded by the heat rising in her cheeks. Across the room, Cait caught Deydie's fierce frown. Cait ran for the door.

Outside, it was cold, especially without her coat. She couldn't go back to the big house—Graham's home. She couldn't go to Deydie's.

Cait fled to the little room over the pub.

Cait had to start over. Had to get a grip. Had to get a restraining order against Graham to keep him away from her heart.

From the outside, looking in, the pub was dark. She let herself into the building and ran up the stairs. Her room was still wall-to-wall boxes, but at least she had a bed. Fully clothed, she kicked off her dancing shoes—a pair of Kate Spade red leather heels—and climbed into bed. She missed her mama's Double Wedding Ring quilt, but this one, an Around the World quilt, would do. She pulled it up to her chin, a tear slipping down her cheek.

Maybe she could move to Fairge until her house was livable. It wouldn't be forever, just enough time to pull herself together and bolster up her resolve. But what if Mattie and Duncan needed her?

Sometime later, the door opened to her little room. She wasn't scared. She'd known he'd find her. Footsteps creaked across the floor.

"Scoot over," his deep voice said.

"No," she answered back, sounding like a petulant teen. "I don't want you here."

"Tough." He gently slid his large frame beside her. She was sure he had to be hanging off the twin bed.

He put his arm around her. "It's not all that comfortable here."

"Nobody asked you," she shot back, even though he smelled great.

"Caitie, I can't sleep without you nearby. I was a veritable grump in Italy." Graham sighed. "Mattie needs his grandda in a good mood. Duncan, too. So here I am." He squished her up against the wall. "We'd have more room in my king-sized bed back at the house." He bounced up and down. "It's pretty lumpy here, too. If we're going to be sleeping at the pub from now on, I'd better replace the mattress."

She did her best to ignore him, but it was damn near impossible. Her hands ached to run themselves all over him.

He went on. "I do worry about Mattie. What if something happens in the night and the boy needs us? I know the nurses are there, but Mattie has grown awfully attached to you." He exhaled dolefully. "Oh, well."

"Fine." She sat up. "You're such a drama queen." She scooted off the bottom edge of the bed. "I have to find another jacket to wear. Mine's at the party."

He chucked his coat at her. "Let's get you home."

"No," she said. "It's not my home. I'm just the help. When the cottage is completed, I'll be out of your hair. Duncan will be free to call me night or day. Do you understand?"

Through the light of the full moon, he studied her. "I understand. But I don't think you do."

Graham's thoughts kept him from feeling the winter wind as they walked back to the mansion.

Big words he'd given. Like he had all the answers. Shit, he didn't understand a thing either. The only thing he knew was that he needed her near. She made him feel sane. Real. Right. When she was around, he was more of what he should be, more of what he wanted to be. Was that love? He didn't know.

He glanced over at her as she huffed along. He didn't know why she was unhappy. He wanted to make her feel better. But he couldn't even do it for himself.

"I know I'm being selfish," he started.

"Damn straight you are," she shot back.

"I just need someone to talk to," he said honestly.

She stopped and looked down at the ground. "I'm sorry. I'm the one being selfish. You're going through a lot with Duncan. I'll always be there for you if you need to talk."

What about letting me touch you and hold you? He didn't say it, but he wanted to.

When he reached out to her, she took off at a clip on the boardwalk.

Graham followed. "Did you think Duncan looked bad tonight? The nurses talked to me about getting a hospital bed. Said he'd be more comfortable. One is coming. And tomorrow, I'm going to see about a doctor coming to stay at the house as well."

She stopped again. "If I were in your position, I would."

Guilt over the past had him walking away. "I should've been a better da. Duncan grew up without me. I've spent most of his life working on too many damn films. If I'd been a fisherman, we would've been poor, but at least I would've been there for him. He would've known that I loved him."

She yanked his arm, stopping him in his tracks. "First of all, Duncan knows you love him. Haven't you noticed he's forgiven you for not being around? He doesn't blame you for making a living." She let go of his arm. "You need to cut yourself a break. Look at all your career has given you. It's helped Duncan with his boat when he needed it. The pub for the town. And all the other things you do." She made a sweeping gesture.

He opened his mouth to deny it.

She put her finger to his lips. "In the last six or seven weeks, your career has provided something very special for Duncan. It's given him the best possible care, from the comfort of home, with his son beside him. How many people in the world can afford such a luxury? Don't be cursing your career, Graham. Your career's been a huge blessing."

"Blessing?" He looked out at the dark sea, her words taking root in him.

Finally, he took her hand and examined it closely by

the moonlight. So petite to his large one. He brought it to his lips and kissed it. "You're right, Caitie. I don't know why I didn't see it sooner."

"Because you're a thickheaded, whiny actor?"

He laughed a genuine laugh. "I think you're pushing it, Macleod. Now, let's get you home."

Deydie waited at the house for them. Cait held back while her gran gave Graham the report.

"I helped the nurses get Duncan into bed," Deydie said. "He just doesn't look right to me."

Graham squeezed Deydie's shoulder. "I agree. We're going to get some more professional help here. Will you stay for a nightcap?"

"Aye." Deydie sighed. She glanced over at Cait and seemed resigned to the fact that she was a part of all this.

"Is Mattie in bed as well?" Cait asked.

"If you hurry up now, you might get to say good night." The civil words from her gran were surprising but welcomed.

Cait nodded and headed up the stairs.

Mattie lay in his bed, staring at his lighthouse night-light. Cait crawled in beside him.

"Are you okay, monkey?"

He cuddled close to her.

"Do you want me to stay in here with you tonight?"

He nodded.

"Let me go get my pajamas on and tell the others good night." She started to get out of bed, but Mattie grabbed her arm.

"What is it?" She knew he wouldn't talk, but the fear in his eyes was easy to read.

"Listen, sweetie, Grandda is going to hire a doctor

tomorrow to come stay here. I know you're scared. And with me and Grandda, you can be afraid all you want, okay? But around your da, we're going to have to be brave for his sake. Okay?"

Mattie's eyebrows furrowed while he mulled it over. Then he nodded his head.

"That's my boy." She smoothed back his hair and kissed his forehead. "I'll be right back."

Mattie didn't have nightmares that night, but he was right to worry. The next day, Duncan was worse.

Graham brought a tray up to Duncan's room, setting it on the side table. Duncan looked like he was sleeping, so Graham tried to sneak out.

"Da?" Duncan's voice sounded like he'd swallowed gravel. "Stay for a minute. I've things to say."

Graham's hair rose on the back of his neck. He wouldn't talk with his only child about last wishes. He just wouldn't.

"Humor me," Duncan said.

"Fine." Graham helped Duncan sit up, positioning a couple of pillows behind his son's back. He pulled over a chair to sit close to the bed.

"It's about Mattie," Duncan said. "When I'm gone, I want—"

Graham cut him off. "We're not going to speak of it."

Duncan's face turned red. "We are," he said forcefully.

Graham took in the stress lines showing between Duncan's brows and backed off. "Don't worry about Mattie. I'll take care of him. You must know that!"

Duncan shook his head, irritated. "You've got it all wrong. I want Caitie to be a part of Mattie's life and share guardianship with you."

Stunned, Graham couldn't say a word.

Duncan reached out and touched his arm. "Can you think of a better person to watch out for him?"

Graham found his voice. "How about his own grandda?" he growled.

"What's my son going to do when you're on location?" Duncan sat up straighter, the propped pillows falling. "Be passed from house to house like a stray dog?"

Silently, Graham counted to ten. "Have you discussed this with Caitie? Has she agreed to take Mattie?" *From me.*

"No. I wanted to talk to you first." Duncan fell back, his shoulders slumping.

"It seems I have no say in it," Graham shot out. "You've already made up your mind."

"Aye, I have." Duncan pursed his lips together. "Now that that's settled, I want to talk about what's to be done with my house." He was silent for a moment. "I want to give it to Caitie to use for her quilting venture. It's right next door to hers. Maybe she'll turn it into a dormitory as well."

Graham's irritation bubbled over. "Is there anything else you want to give her? Seems like she's the only one who's been on your mind."

"Da?" Duncan reached out again. "Ye've been on my mind. You deserve to be happy."

"I am happy, dammit," Graham snarled.

"I'm going to tell you my last request now, in case I don't get to do it later," Duncan said.

"Don't be so maudlin," Graham said, exasperated.

"I want you to marry Caitie."

Chapter Twenty-three

"What?" Graham bellowed. It wasn't as if Caitie had been anything but good for him. But neither one of them would ever marry again. She'd said as much. They'd been having a bit of fun, that's all.

"Seriously, Da. Marry her."

"You're being unreasonable, Dunc. Caitie won't marry me or anyone else." That got Graham off the hook.

"If you marry her, then Mattie would have a family. A real family." Duncan paused. "Plus, it would make an honest woman out of her."

So Duncan knew what'd been going on behind Graham's closed door.

Duncan gave Graham a sad smile. "She makes you happy."

Graham remained silent, his hands clenched in his lap. "Marriage is out of the question. At one time, I wanted to marry your mother. Total failure. You didn't have much luck either."

Duncan peered out the window. "Caitie's different. We both chose women who didn't belong here. Caitie loves Gandiegow. She's one of us."

Graham ran a hand through his hair. "I don't know."

Duncan smiled. "Give it some thought. And then for once, do what *I* want."

Cait spent a portion of the morning standing by the unusually calm ocean. The lack of crashing waves made her feel uneasy. Like she'd gotten away with something and shouldn't have. As sure as the sun had risen this morning, she knew she'd have to come clean with Graham. She would have to tell him how she'd planned to write the article and show him the notebooks filled with the facts she'd gathered about him. It was the only way to rid herself of the guilt. And Graham deserved to know the truth about her.

She wandered over to Quilting Central and checked on the progress. Mr. Sinclair had removed the adjacent building's wall, installed a new support beam, creating an open area the size of a large ballroom. Cait could visualize rows of tables with sewing machines on top. At the front, they'd have a projector for teaching classes. Maybe a long-arm quilting machine or two in the far corner. Some couches on the east side by the fireplace, the kitchenette on the back wall. It would be grand. When she finished at Quilting Central, she visited Amy at the store and then hiked to the top of the bluff for some exercise and exploring. When she finally made it back to the mansion, she met Rhona coming out the back door.

"Duncan's been asking for you. He'd like to have a word." Her old schoolteacher pointed in the direction of the parlor.

"Thanks," Cait said.

She found him sitting in front of a roaring fire, his legs draped with an Hourglass quilt.

"I hear you're looking for me," she said.

"Aye. Have a seat." Duncan looked tired, but she

didn't mention it. His pallor resembled white paper, the bruises on his arms standing out like inkblots.

She took the chair across from him.

"I wanted to talk to you about Mattie," he started. "It's a really big favor, and I want you to take your time in answering."

"Sure. I'd do anything for the little squirt." She smiled at Duncan, but he was so serious.

"Caitie, I want you to be Mattie's coguardian, along with Da."

It took a moment for the full impact of his words to register. "What?"

Duncan went on. "I know it's a lot to ask. But Da needs backup when he's out filming. Do you think you could do this for me? Be the mother that Mattie has never had?"

"I'm speechless, Dunc." She leaned back in the chair, thoughtful, the weight of what he asked almost a one-two punch. To be Mattie's mom would be the most precious gift anyone could ever give her. She twisted her hair. "Why?" *Please don't say you've given up hope of getting better*, she pleaded silently.

"Do you have to ask?" He lifted a black-and-blue arm as evidence and gave her a sad smile. "You are so good to Mattie. I just want him to have continuity. Someone who will be there for him when Da is away." He paused. "But you don't look happy about this. If you don't want to do it, all you have to do is say so."

"That's not it." She frowned at him. She wanted to yell at him to keep the faith! She, who had lost all faith herself, had taken to praying for him every day, religiously. He just needed to hang on, to give prayer a chance. The problem was, he wasn't improving. He knew. She knew. They all knew. She finally answered him.

"What you're asking of me is not the problem, Duncan. Of course, I would do it, in a heartbeat. But I'm afraid when your da finds out about this, he'll wring my neck like I'm one of Deydie's helpless chickens."

"Da already knows," Duncan said flatly.

"And he's pissed?" she added.

"That's an understatement."

"Then why do it?" she asked. "Aren't you done yet making your da pay for his past mistakes?"

"It's not him I'm thinking about." Duncan adjusted the quilt. "I'm trying to do what's best for Mattie. If I'm gone, he'll need a full-time parent. A mother. I know Da will do his best to take care of Mattie, when he can, but he still has his career to think about." He beseeched her with his dark-circled eyes. "What do you say, Caitie?"

"Dammit, Duncan." She wanted to tell him, *Yes, of course*, with no hesitation. But she couldn't. "Let me talk to your father first." She touched Duncan's arm and tried to give him an encouraging smile. "I don't want you to worry on this, though. There's time."

Duncan grasped her hand. "For my sake, don't put it off. Speak to Da soon."

The next day, Duncan's headaches got worse. Everyone breathed a sigh of relief when Dr. Tsang arrived to stay in Gandiegow to be Duncan's personal physician. He was efficient and caring and fit right in with the crew at the big house.

Graham spent the next two nights away, to do a cameo he'd promised in the new Julia Roberts film being shot in Monte Carlo. When he hurried back, Cait met the helicopter on the beach with a picnic lunch.

"I hope you're hungry." She wanted to make sure he

had a full stomach before broaching the subject of Mattie's guardianship.

"What's wrong?" Graham looked so tired that a picnic might not have been the best idea.

"Nothing's wrong. I just thought we could check out Quilting Central together. You could ease back into Gandiegow before going up to the mansion. The big house has become a bit of a madhouse."

"Duncan's all right, then?"

"Dr. Tsang is with him, along with half of the town. Moira took Mattie to the store to pick up groceries. Deydie is organizing another quilting bee for your dining room."

Graham ran a hand through his hair. "It's hard being away."

"Come on. I made you chicken potpie and held the vegetables."

"Just the way I like it."

"Yeah, I know."

When they got to Quilting Central, Cait unlocked the door and was awed with the transformation. The walls had been painted a pale, calming blue and the floors redone in a rich hardwood. There was no furniture yet, so she laid an old blanket on the floor and spread out their feast, the potpies still piping hot.

As Graham dug in, Cait worried her napkin. "There are things for us to talk about," she hedged. "And I'm afraid you're going to be angry with me."

He put his hand up to stop her. "Duncan already told me what he wants." He frowned at his potpie.

"I'm sorry. I should've waited until after you ate."

"That's okay," he said. "Did you also bring my favorite dessert to butter me up?"

"Aye," she said sheepishly, pulling out a gooseberry pie she'd made that morning.

Graham stuck his fork in a piece of chicken. "Listen, I've had some time to think on it. What Duncan is asking makes a lot of sense. But Mattie is my grandson."

"I know. That was my gut reaction as well. I love Mattie, but I have no right to him."

Graham put down his potpie and stared at her intently. "Unless we marry."

Cait felt rocked, like she'd taken a rogue wave — unexpected and hard. "Excuse me?"

"It's just an idea. *Duncan's idea*," Graham emphasized.

Duncan's idea. Of course. Graham didn't want to get married, much less to her. This was for Duncan's sake. But even if she wanted to say yes — which she didn't — what about love? Was there any hope for a marriage otherwise? She busied herself with straightening up the picnic basket, not meeting his eyes. "I don't know why Duncan chose me in the first place. The whole idea's crazy. He's going to be fine. We're all going to be fine."

But she knew better. Duncan wasn't going to be fine. Nothing would be fine ever again. She felt like a leaf caught in gale-force winds. Tossed about, tumbled, pulled almost to pieces.

"Duncan wants an answer from us," Graham said. "Wants assurances. He says it will alleviate his fears if the worst happens." He ran a hand through his hair again. "God knows I don't want to think about it."

Cait knew Graham meant he didn't want to think about death claiming Duncan, not about marrying her, but now they seemed inexplicably tied.

"Please, Caitie, for Duncan's sake. If it does turn out badly, promise me you'll say yes and be Mattie's mother."

They were kidding themselves to think there was more than one possible outcome. It was just a matter of time. But she wouldn't be the one to say so.

"For Duncan's sake, I will." But she wasn't exactly sure what she'd just promised. Was it only to be a mama to Mattie, or was it to be a wife to Graham as well?

When he woke up, Duncan felt like he'd been drifting on his boat. More days now than not, he teetered between two worlds. He so wanted to stay on earth and be there to see Mattie grow up, but he felt drawn to the other side.

He no longer wanted his morning coffee. He was content to stare out the window and watch the sea. Often, he'd fall into a slumber and not even know it. If this was what dying was like, it wasn't so bad. He wanted to explain it but didn't seem to have the energy to do so.

The villagers revolved around him, and he saw the sadness in their eyes. Duncan would smile at them and assure them he was content.

No, he didn't need anything. No extra pillows. Not another quilt. He needed only to stare out at the sea and have Mattie come visit every now and then.

The next five weeks were hell. Cait felt numb. Just going through the motions. But as the days wore on, something began to happen. A little shift here and there. Not until this morning could she pinpoint what was really going on.

Like most mornings, Father Gregory showed up with his missal and Duncan's room filled up with the usual suspects—Deydie, Graham, Mattie, and Cait—plus a few of the townspeople, in this case, Ross, Amy, and Coll. But this time when Father Gregory went through the cere-mony of Communion, Cait felt her whole world tilt. Then a crack formed in her outer shell.

The coming together, the prayers, the readings—it turned and twisted on her, becoming more than the church ritual she'd grown up with. These people, Gandiegowans, believed in the power of God, their tradition, and the com-munity. Believed they could get through anything if they had one another. Cait stood back and watched in wonder, maybe rediscovering a piece of herself that had been lost. Death lingered close by, but Cait didn't feel alone any-more. She felt part of the community. The beating, bleed-ing heart of them. These people who clung to their faith and to one another. It seemed weird and terrible and won-derful all at the same time that while Duncan got worse and slipped away, Cait inched toward getting better.

Graham noticed that Duncan spent more and more time in silence, looking off into the distance, and less time con-versing with others. He no longer wanted to go to the parlor or to have rowdy conversations with Ross. He had no appetite, not even for his morning coffee. He seemed to slip further and further away from them.

One day at the end of March, Duncan seemed to come back to them, more like himself, pleading with Graham to take him to his boat.

"Da, just a little jaunt around the cove is all I'm ask-ing. Will you do it? Will you take me for one more ride?"

"Dunc, I don't think it's a good idea."

"If the doctor says I can go?"

"Aye, lad. If the doc gives permission," Graham said, giving in.

Dr. Tsang granted his son's wish. "I think at this point

we have to do whatever Duncan wants to make him happy and comfortable. Take him. Just keep him warm. It'd probably raise his spirits," Dr. Tsang said.

Graham wanted to argue but didn't.

Doc, Ross, and a few of the other fishermen went with them on Duncan's boat. With a blanket wrapped around his shoulders, he sat on the bench in the front as they maneuvered into the bay. Duncan looked back and smiled at Graham, who drove the boat. Soon Ross took over, and Graham went to sit with Duncan.

"It's a fine day we're having for a ride," Graham said.

"It's grand, Da. So grand. I only wish Mattie were here with us." Duncan looked off to where the fateful boat had gone down and those men had died. "But I guess that's asking too much. He will be all right, won't he?"

"Mattie? Aye, he'll be all right."

Duncan clutched Graham's arm. "Da, I don't want you to mourn me. I'm happy. You know I've had a wonderful life. My only regret is that I wasted part of it being angry with you. I'm not anymore. You've been a great da. I love you so much."

Tears welled up in Graham's eyes. He hated Duncan talking like this, but the doctor had told him to prepare himself. His son wasn't getting better, and it was important to acknowledge it. "I love you, too, lad."

Duncan patted Graham's arm. "Just try to be happy for me. And I'll do my best to not worry about Mattie. I know I'm leaving him in the best of hands."

And because Duncan needed peace of mind, Graham assured him, "Caitie and I talked. She's promised to marry me. She'll do whatever she has to do for Mattie."

"Did you explain it wasn't just for Mattie? Did you tell her that it was for you, too? That you love her?"

"No, not exactly." Graham's insides twisted. There was no way he could put into words how he felt about Caitie. Whenever she came into a room, it felt like the sun came with her, warm and bright. But was that love? She said she'd marry him, and at the time, it had made his heart bang against his chest proudly. But she'd said yes because she loved Mattie, not him. And the fact that she made Graham's life bearable in an unbearable situation said something. But he didn't know if it was love. If it wasn't, it had to be something damn near it.

Duncan stared at him patiently, too wise for one so young. "Do it, Da. Tell her that you love her. Life is short."

Graham had no real answer for his beloved son.

Duncan turned his head and looked out to the sea as if giving her a last farewell. "I'm ready to go back now."

When they got back to the house and Duncan got settled into his hospital bed, he asked for Mattie to be sent to him.

Duncan stared out at the view of the ocean, grateful Da had pushed the hospital bed by the window. He lay back, at peace with where he was. He could feel the end nearing. He didn't want to go. No, but he knew he had to. He hated leaving Mattie, but surely his son, from good Buchanan stock, would be okay. Kids were resilient that way, and Mattie would be all right. Da and Caitie would see to it.

Mattie came to the door and peeked in.

"Come in, lad," Duncan said.

Mattie shuffled in and climbed into bed with him.

"How is my boy today?"

Mattie snuggled closer.

"'Tis time for us to have a man-to-man talk."

Mattie looked up at him with big solemn eyes.

"You are the love of my life. You know that, don't you?"

Mattie nodded his head.

"I would never do anything on purpose to hurt you."

Mattie nodded again.

"But, son, I'm going to be leaving. God is calling me to Him, and I need to know you're going to be okay."

Mattie shook his head and gave Duncan's chest a hard squeeze, an I'll-never-let-you-go squeeze.

"It's not anything to be sad about. You'll see me again in heaven one day. We could go fishing."

Tears fell down Mattie's cheeks, soaking Duncan's nightshirt.

"I know you feel sad, son. I'll miss seeing you grow up, but I know you're going to grow into a strong and honorable man. The only thing I wish for before I go, I wish I could've heard your voice just one more time." Duncan squeezed Mattie, holding back his own tears for the loss of his son's words.

Mattie leaned up and looked into Duncan's eyes. He opened his mouth, but nothing came out. Panic filled his face. Then terror. But determination came into his eyes, and he twisted up his face, opening his mouth again. This time a small, scratchy sound came out.

"Da."

Duncan grabbed his shoulders. "Mattie?"

The boy placed both of his hands on Duncan's stubbly cheeks and gazed into his eyes. "Love you, Da."

Duncan clutched him to his chest, burying his head in his son's neck. "Oh, Mattie."

That night, Duncan slipped into a coma.

Chapter Twenty-four

The townsfolk kept a vigil at Duncan's side, the schedule organized by Deydie and posted at the store. Cait liked to get up in the wee hours of the morning and sit with him until the sun came up.

Today was Monday of Holy Week, the week before Easter. Cait fixed her customary cup of coffee, extra cream, and made her way into Duncan's room.

"Why don't you take a break?" Cait said to the nurse on duty. "I'll call you if he needs anything."

"Thanks," she said and left them alone.

Cait took a seat and sipped her coffee. Not five minutes later, Deydie showed up and sat in the other chair at the end of Duncan's bed.

Deydie cleared her throat, regarding Cait closely and looking hesitant.

Cait waited for her to speak, and it took her a few moments to get it out.

"I need to say something." Deydie's voice sounded like gravel this early in the morn. "It's about you and me and that article for *People* magazine."

Cait braced herself. Enough harsh words had been said already. "I should never have agreed to do it. I was just desperate to get my life back, and I believed my career was the only way." All the emotions she'd been feeling since she arrived in Scotland swelled up inside her and spilled out like water over a flooded dam. "I'm sorry I've been such a disappointment to you. I never do the right thing. Do you think if I try harder that you'll be able to like me again?"

"Hesh up," Deydie said kindly. "I told ye I've something to say. I can be a terrible ole biddy, and I never should've said those things to ye. I shouldn't have. And I'm sorry for it." She nodded her head like that was that. "And ye know, Caitie, I like ye just fine. Ye're family, and I'm right proud of you. I knew that any granddaughter of mine would do the right thing when it came to writing that article. Did that snooty Margaret Pincher, or whatever her name is, did she take the news all right?"

"No, not really. But I don't blame her," Cait said.

"Maybe you could do something nice for her in the future," Deydie offered.

"Maybe," Cait concurred.

And it hit her. She and her gran were finally getting along. A certain kind of peace came over her. It was the only thing she'd really needed since she'd come home.

"In a while, after ye've finished yere coffee, we should go to the cottage. I've some things to show you." Deydie adjusted the blanket about Duncan's feet.

"What things?" Cait asked.

"Never you mind," her gran said. "Ye've always been a curious one. Just like my Nora." Cait wasn't sure, but she could've sworn that Deydie swiped at a tear.

"Well, I'd better make some fresh scones for those coming through today. Do ye want me to freshen up yere coffee?" Deydie had a sheepish look on her face.

Cait didn't answer but carefully set her cup on the nightstand and went to Deydie, wrapping her in her arms. "I'm grateful for you, Gran. I love you so very much."

Deydie didn't swat her away but hugged her back with the strength of an old grizzly.

Cait kissed her cheek. "Get on, now, and get those scones made. I'm getting hungry, you ole bird." She wiped at her own tears.

"Cheeky lass," Deydie said, stepping lightly from the room.

"I take after my gran." Cait's voice broke, but it was just loud enough to get in the last word.

An hour later, the smell of scones filled the house. Deydie brought two to Cait on a beautiful stoneware plate and left to go clean up the kitchen. When the nurse came in to check Duncan's vitals, Cait went in search of Deydie for their walk to the cottage. Her gran was folding laundry in the room off the kitchen.

"I'm ready." Cait grabbed the last bath towel and folded it into thirds.

"Moira just got here and went up to see about Mattie." Deydie grabbed her coat. "We won't be gone too long."

They walked down the bluff in silence, the good feelings still flowing between them. The crisp air had something in it that spoke of spring, but in truth it was still quite cold. The sea, though, looked calm, at peace with the coastline.

When they got to the cottage, Deydie went to her bed. "You get some tea going while I get these out."

Cait went to do as she was told but was still curious. "What are you doing over there?"

Deydie pulled the stack of quilts from her bed, lugging them to the dining room table. "You asked me before what quilts I'd worked on. If you want, I'll show you now."

This was not the same grandmother she'd dropped in on four months ago. Cait helped Deydie position the stack across the table.

Deydie lifted up the first quilt, a Sampler. "Every few years, I take time to make meself a quilt. This is the one I made in 2009, when the winter seemed to go on forever. I hand stitched it."

Cait took it, imagining the love her gran had put into each pull of the thread.

One by one, Deydie revealed her quilts, nine in all. Each one had a story, and Cait lapped up every one. When she pulled out the final quilt, one wrapped in tissue paper, her gran's eyes misted over.

"This is the last quilt that my Nora ever made. She called it Walking with My Daughter." Deydie adjusted the quilt so Cait could see. "Up here at the top, that's supposed to represent me and Nora, walking along the seashore." Sure enough, Cait could pick out the abstract figures of a woman and a child.

Deydie pointed to the middle section. "This part is supposed to represent the world." Blue, brown, and green blocks came together to make the earth, the sea, and the sky. Her gran moved her worn-out hand to the bottom of the quilt. "And this is where Nora is walking with you."

Two more abstract figures were stitched there. The woman was made from the same fabric as the little-girl block up above, but bigger now. Cait's fabric was the same cheery yellow gingham as in the picture with her mama. Lovingly, she touched the image first of the mother and then the little girl.

"Nora always said you were her little sunshine, the reason for every new day." Deydie's old eyes found Cait's. "I think it's time you take this quilt. Nora gave it to me, and I knew one day I was to give it to you."

Cait hugged the quilt to her. "Thanks, Gran. This means the world." She teared up.

Deydie grabbed for it. "Don't go wallering all over it. You want it to last for yere own little girl one day, don't you?"

Cait handed it over. "I won't be having a little girl. Mattie's the closest thing I'll have to my own bairn."

Deydie shook her head. "I don't think so, lass. That's not what Bethia says is written in the stars."

The walk back to the big house was freezing. After she hung up her coat, Cait headed upstairs to put on a sweatshirt, peeking into Duncan's room as she passed. She saw Mattie and Dingus lying in the bed beside Duncan, while Graham sat in the chair beside the bed, holding his son's limp hand.

Dr. Tsang walked past her and into the room. "Can I have a word with you?" he said to Graham.

"Sure. Mattie, take Dingus outside so he can go to the bathroom."

As Mattie walked out, he looked up at her and she ruffled his hair.

She stayed where she was, even though Ms. Manners wouldn't have approved of her eavesdropping.

"Do we have any news?" Graham sounded half hopeful, half dreading the doctor's answer.

"I think it's just a matter of time. If you want your

pastor to deliver last rites, he should do it now," Dr. Tsang said gravely.

"Then Duncan won't wake up again?" Graham asked.

"No. I don't believe he will."

Cait peeked in again and saw Dr. Tsang put a hand on Graham's shoulder.

"The only thing we can do now is to make him comfortable." Dr. Tsang stayed a moment longer, then turned and left.

Cait went straight to Graham then, hugging him to her body as he sat with his chin to his chest.

"I'm so sorry," she said.

Graham held her tight. "I've been honored to have him as my son."

"I know," she said. *You're such a good man. And you don't deserve this.*

They stayed like that for a long while. Finally, Cait pulled away, and Graham stood, stroking her bare arms.

"God, Caitie, you're an ice cube."

"I was on my way to get something warm to wear," she said.

He kissed her forehead. "Let me. What do you want?"

"There's a hoodie in my bottom drawer."

He left, and she settled into the chair he'd occupied. Poor Duncan lay lifeless in the bed, so pale, so fragile. What a raw deal he'd gotten. A shiver ran through her, and she rubbed her arms.

And then panic hit her. She jumped up. Had she just sent Graham to her room to go through her things? Her hoodie concealed the stack of notebooks where she'd written about him, the movie star.

About him, the philanthropist.

About him, the loving father.

"Oh crap," she hissed. She started toward the door. And stopped.

Maybe she was overreacting. Maybe he wouldn't notice the notebooks. Maybe he'd grab the hoodie and rush back to her. *Yeah, and maybe two-ton pigs would up and fly.*

She ran out of Duncan's room and crashed into Graham. Unfortunately, the stack of notebooks he'd been holding went flying, one smacking him square in the face.

"I'm sorry," she began.

He glowered at her. "For what? For betraying me? For getting caught? Or for not making a fast enough getaway?"

"It's not what you think," she cried. Then she frowned at him. "Well, it is what you think, but you've got it all wrong."

"Oh, I have it wrong," he said sarcastically, picking up the red notebook and flipping open to the first page, jabbing at the heading. "List of publications for the Graham Buchanan article," he read. "*People, Entertainment Weekly, Us.*" He stopped and glared at her again. "Shall I go on?"

"It's . . . Well, I . . ." She floundered.

He went stony on her, all emotion wiping itself from his face. "I want you gone. Now. Leave Gandiegow and don't come back."

Indignation replaced her contrition of a moment ago. "You can't tell me what to do. I'm not going anywhere. This is my town. Besides, Duncan asked me to be here for Mattie."

Graham put his large hands on his hips, glaring down, trying to intimidate her. "If Duncan knew what you were up to, he never would've come up with such an asinine request."

"Then lucky for me he's in a coma." As soon as she'd said the words, she wanted to take them back. But they hung in the air like a noose. "I'm sorry," she said desperately. "That was an awful thing to say. I didn't mean it."

Graham turned his stiff back on her. "Aye, like a lot of things you say."

Great timing, Caitie. She threw her things into a suitcase. She wasn't leaving Gandiegow, but she would have to leave his house.

It was going to be tricky. She hadn't figured out yet how she was going to care for Mattie and keep her distance from his irate grandfather.

If only she'd come clean with Graham first, laid it all out for him in a logical manner. He still would've been upset with her, but he would've forgiven her. Especially since she'd decided not to go through with it. Now he didn't even want to be in the same country as her.

She sank to her knees and laid her head on the bed. "Why? Why?" she whispered to the comforter.

Deydie stuck her nose in. "Come to Duncan's room. Father Gregory is going to deliver last rites."

Cait did her best to straighten her emotions up so Deydie wouldn't see.

"Graham said it's getting to be Duncan's time." Deydie eyed her closely. "What are ye doing with yere things?"

There was a clatter from downstairs.

Deydie turned around. "Dammit. That sounded like the sandwiches."

Before Cait could explain anything, her gran was gone.

Downstairs, the house was filling up with Gandiegowans. Cait made her way to Duncan's room. *For Mattie's sake.* She stepped in and clung to the back wall. Graham, Mattie, Deydie, Rhona, and Bethia surrounded the bed. Dingus sat respectfully at the end, by Duncan's covered feet.

It was hard to be in the same room with Graham, knowing how he felt about her—*a traitor, a backstabber.* If only he'd give her the chance to explain.

She bowed her head as Father Gregory began. The packed room became eerily quiet. It was a prayer of safe passage, one appropriate for a fisherman such as Duncan. The prayer also spoke of love, mercy, and forgiveness. How she needed to hear those words right now! They comforted her as her own life twisted and was once again transforming. Cait glanced at Mattie. Though sad, he held his head high, remembering to be brave and strong for his da.

When the prayers were over, a collective sigh went up to heaven and slowly people began whispering, then talking and milling about again. Deydie shooed most of the villagers out so Graham and Mattie could have some privacy.

"Come to the store with me," Deydie said. "To honor Duncan, I'm making his favorite—fisherman's pie and Aberdeen butteries."

"Sure." Cait grabbed her coat and followed her outside.

In silence, they trudged down the bluff and headed toward the store. Along the boardwalk where the sea kissed the coast, Cait and Deydie came across a dead gannet. Without a moment's hesitation, Deydie picked up the lifeless bird by the tail feathers and flung it into the ocean.

Cait stood there shocked and amazed. "How can you do that? You didn't even think twice about sending that poor thing to its watery grave."

"Just tidying the walkway." Deydie gestured to the water. "I'm sure that old bird has led a long life."

The bird had washed out a ways by now. "But to sling it into the ocean like that?" Cait said.

"Life. Death. It's the way of things. One has to accept it." Deydie flashed a smile at her. "Or go wonky worrying over it."

It started to seep in—Death and how it really was. All along, Cait had had it wrong. She'd given Death too much authority. He wasn't in charge. He was just doing his job. It was the living that mattered. How much of her life had she wasted worrying over Death? Too much. But not anymore.

"Ah, Duncan." Cait sighed.

"It's a sad, sad thing about that lad." Deydie stopped and stared into Cait's eyes. "Do you know how we get through the sadness? We have one another, lass. When we share the burden, it lightens the load, eases the pain."

To Cait, death had always meant isolation. She'd gotten this wrong, too.

"I've got a lot to learn," Cait said.

"Stick with me, girl." Deydie cackled. "I'll teach you the right of it."

Cait put her arm around her short gran, and they walked the rest of the way to the store. Together.

Cait moved back down to the cottage with Deydie. She'd no other place to go that didn't belong to Graham. She'd given Deydie no explanation, and her gran hadn't asked, only shaken her head.

In the wee hours of Thursday morning, Deydie woke Cait. "We best be getting up to the big house. Duncan's time has come."

Cait saw the backside of Nurse Ann heading out the cottage door. Cait slipped on some jeans and grabbed her coat.

For the next hour, Graham, Mattie, Cait, and Deydie gathered around Duncan, watching his labored breath. Doc, Dr. Tsang, and the nurses stood in the corner of the room. Cait was in agony. She longed to comfort Graham, and be comforted in turn, but he refused to even look her way.

As the minutes passed, Cait found she was holding her own breath while waiting for the next rise and fall of Duncan's chest.

Suddenly, Mattie crawled up next to his da and touched his cheek with his small hand. "You go," he whispered with tears in his eyes. Mattie leaned down and kissed his da's cheek, then laid his head down and closed his eyes.

They were all shocked speechless.

Graham recovered first, kissing Duncan's forehead. "Goodbye, my lovely son."

As if he'd only needed permission, Duncan's body relaxed. He wasn't gone, but he was different. His next breath came, and it wasn't as deep. A long time lapsed, then another small breath. For a few more minutes, the breaths got further and further apart. And then Duncan stopped breathing altogether.

That night, while the town gathered for the wake, Graham's house murmured with the miracle of Mattie speaking. His grandson hadn't said another word since this morning, but the village rejoiced that Mattie had made headway. Graham left them to their speculations and fled out the back door.

He climbed to the pinnacle, feeling sad, betrayed, and lonely. In the last twenty-four hours or so, he'd lost a son and a friend, or at least he'd thought she'd been. Not a friend like Sid or Colin or Hugh, but something to him. Something he hadn't wanted to name. But it'd all been a lie.

The wind at the top raged against Graham, and he welcomed it. It angered him and at the same time dulled the pain of the losses. At exactly seven o'clock, he pulled his bagpipes to himself and began "Amazing Grace" for his son, letting the song reach up to heaven so Duncan could hear. When he hit the last chord and ended the song, a drum cadence rang out from the ocean. Graham peered hard at where the sound came from. Just off the point, Duncan's boat was anchored with a group of locals aboard, beating their drums in honor of one of their own.

Chapter Twenty-five

The next day, Good Friday, Deydie honored Cait's request and gathered the quilting ladies together at the cottage. Mama's urn sat in the middle of the dining room table, her last quilt, Walking with My Daughter, resting beside it.

When all the ladies stood around the table, Cait took Deydie's hand. "I know you're wondering why I brought you here."

They all started to speak at once. Cait held up a hand.

"I've something to tell you." She wasn't going to make the same mistake twice. She'd decided to beat Graham to the punch and tell them all what she'd planned to do to him and to them. "I'm going to ask in advance for your forgiveness. Keep in mind that I've been mixed up. But I'm not anymore."

She looked to Deydie.

Her gran whacked her on the back. "Go on, now."

Cait took a deep breath and told the ladies everything—how she'd discovered Graham accidentally, planned to betray him, and how she'd thought Gandiegow would eventually see it as a good thing to have him exposed to the world.

"I was blind to what I was doing. I was wrong," Cait said, finishing. "And I'm sorry for it."

The women stood there in stunned silence. The clock on the wall ticked.

"Well," Deydie said, dropping Cait's hand, sounding cheery. "We've gotten that over with, and now it's time for a drink." She pulled a bottle of Scotch off the shelf. "Amy, get the shot glasses."

Rhona looked skeptical. "What are we drinking to?"

Cait wanted to know, too.

Deydie gave them all a grin. "To making mistakes and being honest about it."

Cait's chest got warm, her heart thudding loudly. She grinned at Deydie and helped fill the glasses.

The women lifted their drinks to Cait, and Bethia gave the toast. "To eating crow."

They knocked back their drinks. Cait enjoyed the burn of it. She wasn't naive enough to think they'd forgive her right away, but they'd follow Deydie's lead and, in time, they wouldn't hold it against her.

Moira set her glass down and pointed to the table. "What's this all about?"

"Yes," Cait said. "That's the other reason I called you here today. I need your assistance." She knew it was a lot to ask, especially after what she'd just told them, but she went on anyway. "On this journey to figuring myself out, I've realized something else." She looked around at them. "I've been hanging on to the past. Not in a healthy, reminiscing way. But in a morbid, obsessive-compulsive way. I thought my first step in healing myself would be to give Mama a proper send-off. I hoped you all could help me, give me the strength to move on."

Bethia nodded toward her. "Nora would've wanted you to move forward with your life."

The rest of the women agreed.

Deydie, always impatient, firmly thumped her glass on the table. "Stop lollygagging and tell them what the plan is."

Cait smiled at her. "Yes, Miss Bossy." She turned back to the group. "I thought we could walk down to the pier, one last walk with Mama, and scatter her ashes to the sea."

"That's a fine tribute," Bethia said.

"Well, come on, now," Deydie barked. "Daylight is burning."

Cait grabbed the urn, and the women filed out of the cabin. They walked down the boardwalk, past where Deydie had flung the bird in the ocean, on past the store, finally gathering on the pier in a semicircle.

The day was bright, just the right chilliness to let the bones know you were in Scotland.

Cait opened her mama's urn. "Would anyone like to say anything?"

Moira stepped forward. "I would. It's the poem that was said at my own ma's funeral."

"That'd be fine, Moira," Cait said.

Moira began,

> *I will not say goodbye, for this is not the end*
> *Not adieu but au revoir to my mother and*
> *   my friend.*
> *I held you close to me, but now I let you go*
> *As I set you free, know I love you so.*

As Moira's lilting voice began to speak, Cait sprinkled the first half of her mama's ashes. She handed it to Deydie, who did a sprinkle and then handed it to Rhona and then to each one down the line.

> *You'll fly upon the wind and sail across the*
> *sea*
> *Yet in my heart of hearts, you'll still be close*
> *to me.*
> *We'll meet again someday, this I know is*
> *true.*
> *Until that day arrives, I will remember you.*

Moira had the jar last and tapped the bottom so the remaining ashes fell out. Bethia said wistfully to the breeze, "Nora's finally home."

"Nay." Deydie touched her breast. "She's always been here with us. Right here."

Later that afternoon, Cait and Deydie went to Duncan's house and chose Duncan's favorite shirts and a stack of his jeans to use in making quilts for both Mattie and Graham. Then they met the quilting ladies at the old wool factory, now Gandiegow's Quilting Central, and began work on the Buchanan quilts. Father Gregory stopped by with a bundle that turned out to be a quilt, too. He left it with Rhona without explanation.

"What's that?" Cait asked.

Rhona spread it out. "Gandiegow's cemetery quilt. It documents where everyone is buried."

Though tragic, it was beautiful. The medallion in the middle held the cemetery with small casket blocks positioned throughout, names and dates embroidered on each. Around the medallion were alternating blocks of stars and crosses.

"It's our way of remembering." Rhona pulled out a piece of brown fabric, fashioning it into a casket block. "Father Gregory stores it at the church for safekeeping."

"I expected Duncan to have his ashes put out to sea," Cait said.

"Nay," replied Deydie. "Duncan wanted to be buried in the cemetery overlooking the ocean. For Mattie, ye see. If Mattie ever feels like he needed to talk to his da, he could go to the cemetery and have a chat."

"That's nice," said Amy.

"Our Duncan has always been a thoughtful boy," Bethia agreed.

Cait knew Graham was busy with arrangements, but she worried about him just the same. *Like I could help him feel better. If only.*

Everyone in Quilting Central sat in silence, each in their own thoughts, when the door opened and the bell over it rang.

Bonnie stood there in a tight black sweater, but instead of it being low-cut, it properly covered her enormous boobs. "Excuse me?" This was the most demure she'd ever been.

Cait and Moira rose, as did Amy. "Yes?" the three of them said together.

Bonnie kind of twisted her hands and didn't look nearly the bitch that Cait had encountered before. Finally she spoke. "I—I was wondering if you guys might teach me how to sew."

Deydie and the rest jumped up and rushed her. Bonnie stepped back. Cait worried the poor girl might get trampled.

Rhona got to her first. "Of course we'll teach you how to sew."

"Have you ever cut anything out or used a machine before?" Deydie wanted to know.

"Sister and I will show you how to do our signature stitch," Ailsa said.

"Yes," Aileen agreed, nodding her head fervently.

Bethia guided Bonnie to the chair next to Cait's. "There's always room for one more."

On Saturday, Cait gathered with the other women in Graham's kitchen, feeling strange about being in his house again. He'd been clear about her staying out of his house and out of his life. He hadn't thrown her out when she'd shown up at Duncan's deathbed, but she wasn't so sure what he would do today when he saw her. But dang it, Deydie had insisted Cait be there, and she knew not to cross her gran. Cait still felt weird and jumpy, and on top of that, anxious to see him, needing to know how he was.

"What's wrong, lass?" Deydie asked.

Cait shrugged and pulled a fresh ham from the refrigerator for tomorrow's funeral. Just before putting it into the oven, Mattie handed her an extra potholder. All morning, the ladies had taken turns involving him in everything from the bread making to the pie baking. Just when Cait started to relax, thinking Graham was too preoccupied to discover her there, he wandered into the kitchen.

Cait's heart stopped. She couldn't breathe. He looked her way and frowned but didn't throw her out on her keister.

"I've come to rescue Mattie from estrogen overload," he said to the room. "Come, lad. We need to pick out flowers online. The florist in Inverness will deliver."

Mattie looked to Cait for permission. "Go on, now," she said.

Graham gave her an exasperated roll of the eyes. She understood. It must be hard to have his own grandson defer to her—the one person he couldn't trust. She set the timer for the ham and got busy chopping the romaine.

The next day, Easter, there was no sign of the Easter bunny, no brightly colored eggs, no special chocolates. Only Easter lilies surrounding Duncan's casket, the centerpiece resting near the altar for the funeral Mass. The whole town had gathered, and it seemed surreal that with death in their midst, the sermon would center on rebirth.

After the service, the parishioners followed Graham, Ross, and four others as they carried Duncan's casket up the bluff path to the cemetery. Father Gregory said a few words and a prayer for Duncan. Then loud horns blared simultaneously from a group of fishing boats just off the point, giving Duncan a joyous send-off. It brought tears to Cait's eyes, and she wished Duncan had been there to see it. Mattie squeezed her hand, and she looked down at him. He nodded his head in agreement.

The townsfolk headed back down the path, the quilting ladies at the head of the pack, hurrying to get the food on the table at the big house before the onslaught of people.

Alone at the grave site stood the three of them—Cait, Mattie holding her hand, and on Mattie's other side, Graham holding his hand. She peeked over at Graham and saw tears flowing freely down his face. She pulled a clean tissue from her pocket and handed it to him. He stared at it for a moment and then finally took it.

Cait leaned down to Mattie. "Do you want to go back to the house now, or do you want to stay here for a while?"

He nodded toward the path, so the two of them headed out, leaving Graham at the grave site alone.

Graham stayed with Duncan for a long time, not wanting to leave his son. He'd done that too much in his lifetime. So many lost days.

He ran a hand through his hair. A little voice inside his head told him not to berate himself. Caitie's voice. His career had been a blessing. And in the end, Duncan had seen it that way, too.

Graham didn't know what he was going to do about Caitie. He said he'd wanted her gone. But having her there in the room when Duncan had slipped away had been a comfort to him, and he didn't understand why. She'd lied to him, deceived him, betrayed him. Yet he still wanted her near. His only explanation—grief.

Finally, Graham knelt down and laid his hand on the dirt over the grave. "I'll be back to see you soon." He knew Duncan wasn't really there. He'd gone to a better place, one where illness didn't exist. But the thought that his son was only at the top of the bluff, looking down on the village, consoled Graham. He left to join the others.

When he got home, Deydie had the kitchen running smoothly with the rest of the house packed with funeral-goers.

"Where's Mattie?" he asked.

"In the parlor," Moira said. "With Caitie."

He strode down the hallway, intent on asserting that

Mattie was his. But when he came around the corner, he stopped himself from entering. The three of them were on the couch—Mattie, Caitie, and Dingus—having a cuddle.

Caitie brushed back his grandson's hair. "At first, everyone feels like they have to say how sorry they are. And you have to let them, even if it makes you want to scream. Saying they're sorry helps them to grieve, that's all. We're going to get through this day. Then, I promise, it's going to get better."

Mattie laid his head on her shoulder.

"And when your grandda gets here, you need to give him extra love. He needs it." Caitie swiped at a tear running down her cheek. "We're all going to be okay."

We're going to be okay.

Graham's chest ached and warmed and sort of melted all at once. *Caitie.* She'd double-crossed him, but he still needed her.

Moira and Amy came up behind him, squeezing past him with plates of food and drinks. "For Caitie and Mattie," Moira explained.

As Caitie looked up, he slipped back into the hallway out of sight.

For hours, people roamed about. Finally, everyone said goodbye and drifted out of his house.

Graham went into the parlor and stood by the fireplace next to Precious's fluffy pillow, now Dingus's bed. Caitie and Mattie still sat on the couch but now with a Curious George picture book between them. For a long time no one said anything. He warred with himself about what to do about Caitie, and he needed time to think it through. It was impossibly hard to make any decisions with her so near.

Finally, he went to Mattie and picked him up. "Come sleep with me tonight, lad?"

Mattie nodded his head. The boy looked to Caitie to see if she were coming with them, but Graham didn't trust himself to speak. If he did, he'd want Caitie beside him, comforting him. Instead, he walked from the room, leaving Caitie all alone.

That night, Graham dreamed of Duncan. They were on his boat, pulling in the nets. Duncan had sad eyes and said only one thing. "What about Caitie?"

The next morning, Graham got up before the sun rose and made himself coffee.

The back door opened and in walked Caitie. She jumped in surprise when she saw him and grabbed her chest.

He wanted to reach out and calm her but didn't.

"Sorry," she stammered. "I'm not barging in. Deydie's under the weather. Asked me to get the breakfast going and start a load of laundry. I'll be out of your hair as soon as I can."

"Caitie." He wanted to both yell at her until she left forever and kiss her so she never would. "We should talk."

She looked startled. She pushed back her hair uncomfortably, her eyes darting from side to side. "Let me get some coffee first."

He couldn't help but memorize her every movement. How she latched onto her coffee mug for dear life, how generously she took her cream and sugar, but mostly how lovely she looked this morning.

She seemed to be taking her time, stalling. Gathering her thoughts or gathering her courage—he couldn't tell which.

Stiffly, as if she'd been filled with concrete, she plodded across the room and took the chair opposite him. She sipped her coffee, not meeting his eyes.

Finally, she looked up. They both spoke at once.

"Caitie—"

"Graham, I—"

He motioned for her to go first.

Frowning at her coffee cup, she ran her finger along the rim. "I never wrote that article." She expelled a long breath. "Don't get me wrong. I meant to. But when I got to know you . . . and, of course, Mattie and Duncan . . ."

Her forehead furrowed into deeper lines. He wanted to reach out and console her, but didn't.

She stared at her coffee mug, almost talking to it instead of him. "I was going to confess everything to you. I just needed a little courage. And then, well, everything got worse. Duncan . . ." She trailed off. "I never meant for you to find the notebooks the way you did. I never meant to add to your pain." Her voice broke, but she went on. "You and Duncan and Mattie have been so good to me." She looked up at him then, a tear sliding down her cheek. "I just couldn't betray you. Not even to save myself."

Something inside him split open. She'd sacrificed herself *for him and his family*?

She swiped at a second tear. "I'm so sorry, Graham. Can you ever forgive me?"

He reached over to only touch her hand, to give her comfort and to stop her tears. But he couldn't help himself. He pulled her over onto his lap.

She gasped. For the second time this morning, he'd shocked the hell out of her. She wrapped her arms around him and buried her head in his neck with a little sob.

God, she felt so good. So right. He savored her for a long moment.

He leaned her away so he could see her face. He pushed her hair behind her ear, forcing her to look at him. "Nay, lass. 'Tis partly my fault. I should've let you explain. I know you tried. I was a jerk."

She opened her mouth to defend him.

He laid a finger across her lips. "Shh. I was grief-stricken. Still am."

"I know. Me too."

"But we're going to get through this. We're going to be okay. Just like you told Mattie." Her words had soothed him then, even though they'd been meant for his grandson.

"Then you and I are okay?" she whispered, searching his eyes. "Are we friends again?"

"Nay," he said. "I don't need more friends."

Surprise and hurt registered in her whole body. She tried to pull away. "But—"

He cupped her face and kissed her deeply—trying to show her what he felt, how his feelings went way beyond friendship. However, the kiss wasn't enough. He stood, pulling her to her feet, wanting more of her body pressed against him. She clung to his neck, kissing him back, and then she wrapped her legs around his waist.

"Aye," he growled into her lips. He would carry her upstairs and he would show her how much he cared for her. And he'd finally tell her that he loved her like Duncan had told him to. In time, Graham knew he could make her love him back.

As he started for the stairs, his mobile rang with his agent's ring tone. Graham let it go to voice mail, ignoring the fact that Sid wouldn't call him at this hour and certainly not the morning after Duncan's funeral.

His phone rang again. "Let me shut it off."

Caitie reluctantly slipped from his arms. "It's okay if you need to take the call."

"Nay. I've more important things." He shot her a smoky look. *Much more important.* But the phone stopped ringing. As he pulled it from his pocket, it dinged with a text. He read the message:

Urgent! Call me now!!!

"Dammit." Graham sighed heavily. "I have to call Sid." He gazed over at Caitie. He was already missing her body.

"It's okay." Her face was bright, her lips rosy from kissing him.

"Just give me a moment. I promise." He grabbed her hand, not letting her go too far away, and rang up his damn agent. "Your timing stinks."

Sid cleared his throat. "I didn't want to bother you, but there's news that couldn't wait."

"Get on with it," Graham said.

"It's the last script."

He couldn't imagine why Sid would bring it up now. "I turned it down, remember? That ship has sailed."

"Not exactly," Sid said. "Craig backed out and shooting has already begun. The studio wants you. They've always wanted you."

A million thoughts converged in Graham's head. *But Duncan was buried only yesterday. Caitie and Mattie. My life here.*

Sid read his mind. "I know it's a lot to ask. Especially with . . ." He let the words die off. "But the studio is losing a half mil a day in New Zealand. They could really use you now. Can you get to Inverness and fly out in a few hours?"

Mattie wandered into the kitchen wearing his Thor pajamas and sat at the kitchen table, rubbing his sleepy eyes.

"I'll need to talk to my family first." Graham left it at that and hung up.

He wrapped his arm around Caitie's shoulder and turned to his grandson, frowning, no time to put a good face on it. "Mattie, how would you like to go with me on location to New Zealand?"

Mattie shook his head, mirroring his frown back to him.

Graham couldn't walk away and leave him and Caitie, not now. "It's a beautiful country. We'll get you a tutor. We'll be together all the time."

Mattie ran to Caitie and anchored himself to her with his arms.

Caitie let go of Graham and hugged the boy back, looking at Graham with curiosity. Suddenly, the light came on in her eyes.

"Ohmigosh." She was so excited. "It's the script you turned down, isn't it?" Her smile channeled the sun. "Oh, Graham, you have to take it."

He grimaced. "I can't leave." *Not without Mattie, and not without you.*

Mattie unlatched himself from Caitie and walked over to him and tugged on his hand. Mattie's little eyes were filled with encouragement.

Caitie tilted her head to the side. "I think he's telling

you, Grandda, that you can't turn this down. You have to do it."

"But what about things here?" Graham said. "I have responsibilities." *And you.*

Caitie put her hands on her hips, reminding him of an irate Deydie. "Exactly why Duncan asked me to be your backup." She cringed a little at saying Duncan's name but then screwed a smile on her face and turned to Mattie. "I've been asked to take the best job in the world—hanging out with you—and he"—she pointed at Graham accusingly—"has a problem with it. Doesn't he think I'm capable of doing a good job?"

Mattie went back to her and hugged her protectively this time.

To see his grandson so attached to Caitie . . . His heart swelled. He was attached to her, too.

"Well," said Graham. "I see things are under control here. I best go pack." He wanted to tell her how he felt about her, but he couldn't just drop the *L* word and walk out. It wouldn't be fair to her. He had to show her that he meant it. He had to do it right. His need to tell her would have to wait.

Chapter Twenty-six

Cait sat with Mattie at the breakfast table in their pajamas with bowls of oatmeal in front of them and a calendar between. Five weeks and one day had passed. She tapped next Wednesday. "So, let's see if we're on the same page. Grandda told you he might get to come home next week, too, huh?"

The boy nodded and pointed to Wednesday, also.

She nodded back. "Just checking. Making sure he's telling us both the same story."

Mattie took her hand and smiled with a glint in his eyes. If he wasn't her silent kiddo, she was sure he would be outright laughing at her nervousness. Since the day Graham left, she'd been jumpy and anxious, her life so unsettled.

"I'll be fine," she said, trying to convince Mattie. Or maybe she was trying to convince herself.

Oh, sure, Graham called most days. She would put Mattie on first. Her boy would nod or shake his head but had said nothing since Duncan's death. Cait wasn't going to press the kid on it. She knew when he had something to say, he'd say it. After his time with his grandda on the phone, Mattie would hand it back to her. And then she would stupidly waste every second of her precious time with Graham, trying to decipher his words, looking for hidden clues.

"I miss you." *He loves me.*

"The shooting schedule is gruesome." *He loves me not.*

"The sunset this morn reminded me of you." *He loves me.*

"I don't know when I can come home." *He loves me not.*

She was a ridiculous emotional wreck. She didn't know where she stood with Graham, and it made her batshit crazy. Why couldn't she just be happy and let the rest go?

Last year at this time, she'd had nothing. But now she had a true family—her gran and Mattie. She had her community, too. The quilting ladies and the whole darn town had embedded themselves in Cait's heart and were a treasure to her now. She didn't dare put Graham into the mix. She wasn't a superstitious person, but she wasn't taking any chances either by making assumptions.

She had also found the one thing that had eluded her for so long—real love. Not that use-and-abuse crap she'd sold out for before. What she felt for Graham went way beyond anything she'd ever experienced or expected. She should be happy that he'd forgiven her. But she wanted more. It took every bit of restraint she had not to yell at Graham whenever he called. *I love you, you idiot. Do you love me back?*

She touched the calendar again. "Besides Grandda coming home, next week is our first retreat. We'll have to make sure he stays out of sight. Hopefully, in the future, we can plan better. I'm worried about the food, too, Mattie. Just that part of it is a lot of work. It might be time for Gandiegow to get a restaurant. Then, during quilting retreats, the restaurant can do the catering and we can worry about keeping the quilters busy."

The poor kid. He had listened to her ramble on about the retreat for the last five weeks. But thank God for Kilts & Quilts. It had kept her mind occupied—up to a point. Deydie, the quilting ladies, and all of Gandiegow had pitched in, and it looked as if the first retreat would be a success. She was grateful the arrangements had been time-consuming; they'd kept her from fixating on her love life. Or non–love life. Without Kilts & Quilts, the town would've had to institutionalize her for fretting and worrying over where she stood with Graham.

She'd even made a quilt for him and called it the Gandiegow Star. It reminded her of him—masculine in its earth tones. The star center was surrounded by rugged log cabin blocks, a layer of protection for him from the outside world. In the evenings, when she got too lonely for Graham, she'd give in and pop in one of his movies. Then, for two hours, she'd let herself wallow in loneliness. Never longer than two hours and never when Mattie was around.

Cait jumped out of her seat to grab another cup of coffee. She should cut down on the caffeine, but she had little willpower these days. Halfway to the Keurig, she got sidetracked. "I'd better get the stew started in the Crock-Pot," she said to Mattie.

He took another bite of oatmeal while she went to the fridge and pulled carrots from the crisper. The back door opened and she hollered from the other side of the fridge door, "Gran, can you pull out the Crock-Pot while you're there?"

But when she closed the door and saw who held the slow cooker, Cait dropped her carrots. They scattered all over the floor like pickup sticks.

Graham set the appliance down while she soaked him in. Every last glorious bit of him. He'd gotten sun, his tan bringing out the gold flecks in his brown eyes. His hair had grown, and she longed to run her fingers through it. She wanted to run into his big strong arms, but the little squirt beat her to it. Which was probably best. If she'd learned nothing else, it was best to test the waters first before jumping in. *Less likely to get pulled under and drowned.*

Graham held the boy tight, closing his eyes. Finally, he looked up and found her. Mattie wiggled out of his arms and pulled Graham to Cait.

They stood toe to toe, an electric current flowing between them. Self-preservation kept her rooted to her spot. She had the most to lose because she was the one who loved.

"And you, Lady Caitriona, don't you want to give this lost actor a big hello hug?"

Her heart lurched. *Wanting a hug doesn't mean he loves me.* Instead of flying into his arms, she knelt down to deal with the sprawled carrots. She kept her eyes to the floor but spoke to him, giving him a little of Deydie's attitude. "Why didn't you call and let us know you were back? We could've planned a homecoming."

"The only homecoming I need, lass, is to see the two of you."

She rose with her pitiful carrots and met his eyes. "Does this mean you're done filming?"

"We finished three days ago," he announced.

Both she and Mattie frowned, but Cait spoke for the

both of them as she dropped the carrots into the sink. "And you didn't think to come home sooner? There are people here missing you."

"Are there, now?" He chuckled.

Cait corrected herself. "I mean Mattie. He needs his grandda. Where have you been?"

"Top secret." Graham winked at Mattie and then grabbed Cait and kissed her soundly.

Before she could completely register the fireworks igniting all over her body, he set her back on her wobbly legs and stepped away. She couldn't even sputter out a coherent response.

Graham grinned at her as if he were the laird, acting as if he owned her, the castle, and the keep. "I suggest you get ready for the day."

She glanced down at her Care Bears pajamas absentmindedly. He'd befuddled her for sure. There was something she had to do today, something important.

He carried on, smiling at her. "You have a quilting retreat soon. Don't you need to run along?"

Her brain cleared and she felt stupid. "Well, that was a fine hello," she muttered. She didn't like being dismissed but left graciously, taking her coffee mug upstairs with her. While she showered, she worried over how all of this would play out. Would her heart ever quit skipping beats when Graham was near? Sometime today though, she'd have to corner him for a talk.

After drying her hair and spending more time on her makeup than she had in the last five weeks, she went looking for the men of the house, her stomach in a twirl of nerves. She found them in the upstairs den. They both jumped when she opened the door, and Graham slammed the desk drawer shut.

"What do you have there?" she inquired.

"A gift for Dingus," Graham said, and the dog's ears perked up.

"Fine. Don't tell me. I'll be at Quilting Central with the other ladies."

"Take your time," Graham singsonged. "Don't worry about us."

Mattie giggled.

He'd never done that before.

"Well," she hedged. "I'll be going, then."

"Don't let the door hit you on the—"

She closed the door, so she couldn't hear the rest.

Cait sat next to Deydie at Quilting Central, trying to concentrate on the lunch menu for the retreat. It'd been an hour since she'd seen Graham and Mattie, and with every passing minute, she became more and more obsessed with what might or might not be happening with Graham.

There'd been a lot of buzz about his return, all the quilting ladies questioning her twice as to how he looked, what he'd said, and what his plans were now. Cait had wanted to yell, *How the hell should I know?* The seconds ticked by on the wall clock, going way too slowly for her anxious emotions.

Through Mattie, she was tied inextricably to Graham. But what did that mean? Would they marry like Duncan had requested? *But what about love?* her heart cried.

She took a deep breath and went through it all again in her mind. She now had a good life here and a new career with Kilts & Quilts. Quilting Central had plenty of tables for sewing machines and enough room for any- and everyone to stop by and sew—lots of good old-fashioned community in progress. Cait put her pen down and gazed around the room, shaking her head at the funny truth of it all. While she had been trying to restore the village back to its former glory, Gandiegow had restored her.

And if today had been any other day, if *himself* hadn't materialized out of thin air, Cait knew the buzz of women around her would give her great satisfaction. But she was way too jumpy. Graham had turned her into a mess.

Cait laid a hand on her gran's shoulder to ease her nerves. Deydie glanced over at her and didn't even attempt to swat her hand away.

"I'm grateful for you, you know. You're my rock," Cait said.

"Aye, I'm that and more. This old Rock of Gibraltar, though, is feeling a bit of her age today. This chilly May weather has seeped into me bones. Can ye get me a fresh cup of tea?" Deydie shot her a craggle-toothed smile, the smile Cait had waited for since she'd come home to Scotland.

Before she could get the tea, though, the door to Quilting Central blew opened, and all the women looked up. It was Graham and Mattie. The ladies launched out of their chairs to greet him.

"It's great to be home," he said to the crowd. He'd traded in his khakis and polo for a kilt, a light wool sweater, and a pair of heavy black boots.

Cait stayed in her seat but had zero self-control. She blurted out her question when she should've kept her mouth shut. "What's the occasion? Why the kilt?"

Graham *tsk*ed at her. "Can't a Scot be a Scot?" he countered back.

"I guess." She put her head down and concentrated on the lunch menu, trying not to overheat because of him in that Buchanan kilt.

"Caitie, I'll have a word," he drawled.

She frowned at him. "I'm in the middle of something." She went back to her work.

"Go for a walk with me."

She had two choices—keep her butt glued to the seat or bound out the door after him like she was Dingus.

"Oh, all right." Dingus she would be, dammit. She capped her pen and grabbed her jacket.

Outside the door, she expected him to get right to it, the reason for the walk, but he remained silent. Out of the corner of her eye, she peeked at him. He made her feel warm and cozy despite the cool breeze off the ocean. She still didn't know where she stood, and it was driving her crazy. He led her onto the weathered dock.

Graham looked out to the sea and cleared his throat. "I've got a project for you to do."

His smug expression annoyed her.

"Could you get someone else to do it?" she said. "I'm swamped with the upcoming retreat."

"It's a writing project," he enticed.

Her face went hot with shame. A writing project had gotten her into a whole lot of trouble with him before.

"Aren't you even a little curious?"

"Go ahead and tell me if you must." But he had piqued her interest.

"I need my official biography written."

"Really?" She was more than a little shocked. He'd always kept his personal life personal, as far away from the media as possible.

"Aye. And I want you to be the one who writes it. Call it *Lost Actor—Found*, if you want. Isn't that what you were going to call the article about me?"

A little more guilt hit her, but she recovered. "I think the cool wind under your skirt has you a bit cracked. No pun intended," she added.

He acted like he hadn't heard her and grabbed her hand, dragging her farther out onto the pier while talking over his shoulder. "Sid thinks it should be about my struggle to come to grips with my life and my profession. I think it should be about my roots and what it took for me to get real with the world."

She frowned and felt a smartass comment coming on. "Seriously, you'd better go in and warm up in front of the fire. Or lie down. I'm worried about you."

"I want to dedicate it to Duncan."

"Oh." That shut her up. She tugged back at his hand, and they stopped.

He turned and gave her a sad, knowing smile, like he knew what she felt. He tucked a stray curl behind her ear, grazing her cheek with his fingers. An innocent touch, but it had her body sizzling just the same. God, she'd missed him so much.

He went on. "I thought the proceeds from the book should go into a scholarship fund for all the fishermen's kids of Scotland. Help give them a leg up."

"I love the idea, but when—?" she started.

He cut her off. "But we can't start on it until after the wedding."

Her breathing came to a complete stop. No words would come out. Finally, she regained control over her vocal cords. "What wedding?" *Just to be clear.*

He shook his head. "You know very well, Caitriona Macleod, what wedding I'm talking about."

"But—"

He bent down on one knee, and she about fell off the edge. *This is really happening.*

Cait glanced over, and sure enough, the quilting ladies had all squeezed in the doorway of Quilting Central, ogling them, the twins even pointing in their direction.

"I see them, too." Graham pulled a small box from his pocket, opening it up. It was a diamond ring, set in a substantial band, Celtic knots cut into either side of it.

"Oh my gosh," she got out.

"You can't say no. Not with the quilting ladies watching. They'd string you up." Graham gazed deeply into her eyes. "Caitie, my darling lass, I shouldn't have kept you waiting. Should've told you long ago how I felt. I love you. You're my clear sky, my calm waters, my life." He kissed her hand. "In time, after we're married, do you think you can love me back?"

Her heart skipped a beat and then soared, finally satisfied. She felt calm and at peace, standing here by the ocean.

"Get up, you goof." She pulled him up. "You got your pretty knee all dirty."

"Name-calling?" he said, unfazed.

"It's something I do to remind you that you're just one of us mortals," she said.

"You're always concerned with my welfare, aren't you?" He laid his hand on her cheek. "But you haven't answered my question."

"I've always loved you," she admitted. "And Mr. Darcy,

of course, but that was only a wee crush." She moved her hands to his chest. "It's the real Graham Buchanan, not the movie star, whom I love with all my heart."

His eyes lingered upon her with warmth and wonder. "You really do love me?"

"Aye." She spread her arms wide. "I love you more than the ocean." She laughed, overjoyed. "I love you more than Deydie's cherry cheesecakes. And that's saying something!" Then she wrapped her arms around his neck. "I love you more than the finest quilt I've ever held."

"Will you marry me, then?" he asked, his eyes searching hers.

She glanced over at the white steeple of Gandiegow's church. "Yes, I'll marry you, and it'll make me the happiest woman on the planet."

He picked her up and hugged her. "You've made me verra happy, too."

She swatted him. "But for the luvagod, you could've told me how you felt sooner. You've made me absolutely crazy."

He set her down and smiled. "A little crazy isn't a bad thing. It just means you fit in here in Gandiegow all the more."

"I fit in?" she said softly and then nodded her head. "I really am home, aren't I? I'm so done with being scared and alone."

He took her into his arms. "I promise you'll never be alone again. And you'll always be safe with me, Caitie."

"I know that now. It just took me a while to figure it out." She wrapped her arms around him, too, and kissed him.

It vaguely registered that little footsteps were running

on the pier. Until a small body slammed into theirs, jarring their kiss. Little arms wrapped around their waists, hugging them tight. Graham and Cait looked down and found Mattie. Cait marveled at the little boy's progress. A few months ago, he couldn't get near the pier without trembling, let alone run out on it. But here he was. He'd taken another step toward recovery.

"What do you say, little monkey?" Cait ruffled his hair. "Should I marry your grandda?"

Mattie beamed up at them with happy tears in his eyes and nodded emphatically.

Whoops and hollers came from Quilting Central.

"Well, that's good enough for me. I guess it's a done deal." She gave Graham a sparkling smile and reached for the box in his hand. "How many karats is that thing?"

Later that night, after they got Mattie to bed, Graham spread his new quilt—the Gandiegow Star, she'd called it—in front of the fireplace. He loved that she'd made it especially for him. She'd prepared a plate of cheese and fruit plus two glasses of wine, but at this moment, Graham wanted only to soak her in.

Cait threw a couple of pillows on the floor, her eyes darting up to meet his and then back away. She was a little shy now and quiet. But all afternoon she'd chatted away about Mattie, the retreat, and everything that had gone on while he was away. He knew when he listened to her that she considered it foreplay. But he'd missed her voice and hearing her had made him smile.

He stepped in front of her and toyed with the top button of her blouse. "Are you happy, lass?" His voice sounded husky, even to himself. He was anxious as hell to get her naked, but he needed to know she was okay first.

She laid a soft hand on his cheek. "No one has ever been happier."

"Do you think now I can show you how happy you've made me?" He ran a finger under her top button as he undid it.

She sucked in a breath. "Aye." Her brogue was thick. "I had hoped you'd planned to."

"Aye, plans." He dipped his head down and kissed her neck. He was so turned on, but there were plans they needed to discuss and it had nothing to do with the quilting retreat. He switched to nibbling her ear. "I have to know, Caitie, will you be wanting to have a baby with me?" God, he loved this woman so much.

Her breath caught again, and he kissed her magnificent lips. It took a while for her to answer.

"I would love to give Mattie a brother or a sister." She pulled his sweater over his head and ran her hands over his chest. "Or would it be an aunt or an uncle?"

Graham wrapped her in his arms and kissed her as he pulled her to the floor. "Aye," was the last thing he said as he lost himself in her and the life that lay before them.

Continue reading for a preview of the next book
in Patience Griffin's Kilts and Quilts series,

Meet Me in Scotland

Coming from Signet Eclipse in January 2015!

Just as Emma Castle's plane landed in Scotland, she pulled out her phone and viewed the incriminating evidence once again. *Bollocks.* The damned video had gone viral. Exactly as her boss back in Los Angeles—or now her ex-boss—had feared. She still couldn't believe it. *Fired.* Egghead Emma had been fired.

She watched the forty-eight-second clip for a third time. How superior her British accent sounded, how smug she looked, like she had all the answers. Those forty-eight seconds had irrevocably changed her future. *Thirty years old and already a washup.* Oh, bloody hell, what would she do now?

Well, that was why she was here sitting on the tarmac— hoping to figure things out with her best friend, Claire.

As the other passengers pulled down their bags and left the plane, Emma stared out the window at what looked like midnight. It was only seven p.m., but a blizzard was brewing. An accurate metaphor for her life. She slid her phone back into her pocket.

When the aisle cleared, she hurried off the plane and searched the waiting crowd. God, she'd missed her best friend. She'd hesitated only a moment when Claire had invited her to come to Gandiegow. Running away couldn't fix the predicament she'd gotten herself into, but it would give her a respite, and oh, how she needed a best-friend booster shot to help make things better. Then she could head to London to face Mum. Hopefully, by then she'd have a few things worked out, maybe even a plan of what to do next.

Emma's mobile rang; it was Claire.

"Where are you?" Emma scanned the faces around her. "Are you waiting at baggage reclaim?"

"Nay." Claire paused, producing a long yawn. "I sent Gabriel to pick you up."

"No," Emma cried. The people around her turned and stared. At the same time, her mother's voice rang in her ear: *Losing one's temper is not in a proper Englishwoman's repertoire.*

Hissing wasn't either, but Emma did it into the phone anyway. "For your sake, Claire, I hope you're speaking of Gabriel the archangel and not the other one."

Claire gave her attitude right back. "Don't grumble at me. It's not my fault your flight was delayed. You know how early I have to get up."

"Why couldn't your husband take the morning shift for you?"

Claire *tsk*ed. "The scones are *my* specialty. The restaurant depends upon them."

Emma sighed heavily. "Yes, I know. But still . . ."

"Gabriel was a saint to offer," Claire defended.

Yeah, right, Emma thought.

Her friend went on. "Is he there yet?

"I don't know." Gabriel would be the perfect end to her perfectly horrible day.

"Buck up, Emma. You're a grown woman. You can handle a few hours with him." With that, Claire said good-bye and hung up.

Emma's temples began to throb. Claire was testing her patience as only Claire could. Gabriel MacGregor was incorrigible, plain and simple. Claire *knew* she couldn't stand being around him.

When Claire and Dominic had first coupled up, Emma had spent a fair amount of time in Gabriel's presence. Dominic and Gabriel were inseparable, closer than most brothers she knew. They were not biological brothers, but Gabriel's father had taken Dominic in when he had been orphaned.

Emma had visited Claire often back then and had been thrust into Gabriel's path over and over. He'd made a lasting impression but not in a good way. He had a way of flustering her that was very uncomfortable. For years now she'd successfully avoided him, making sure she had plenty of excuses at the ready if Gabriel was to be present. The last time she'd actually seen him was at Claire and Dominic's wedding, ten years ago. He'd shown up late, roaring in on his motorcycle, wearing a leather jacket, leather pants, and an earring. Undignified and unrefined, especially for the occasion. Even worse, he had stirred something deep inside her that she couldn't name. Ten minutes later, decked out in a tux, he'd smiled at her, tucked her arm into his and walked her down the aisle, best man to her maid of honor. He'd behaved appropriately during the ceremony, but then at the reception, he'd flirted with all the bridesmaids and had taken most of them back to his room for a pajama party. Emma sniffed. *Certainly no pajamas had been involved.* And Egghead Emma hadn't been invited, either. Gabriel MacGregor with his deep Scottish burr was a scoundrel—a rake.

She sighed heavily. There would be no helping it. She'd be forced to spend the next several hours with him in the car, but thankfully, it would only be that. Surely he wouldn't be staying in Gandiegow.

Emma stowed her phone and realized she was being stared at by an extraordinarily handsome man. As a trained psychologist, she recognized within herself all the telltale signs of instant attraction. Her pulse raced, she involuntarily licked her lips, and she brushed her hair off her shoulder.

Then recognition hit. *Dr. Gabriel MacGregor.*
Bugger me.

At twenty he'd been handsome, and she'd thought him a man. But now she saw she had been wrong. Dead wrong. He made the twenty-year-old Gabriel look young and wiry and inconsequential. This man had muscles filling out his long-sleeved polo, the breadth of an American football player, and the stance of a Scottish warrior. She did it again. Licked her lips. *I'm in deep trouble.*

He made his way through the crowd to her, not smiling, not happy to see her, either. In truth, she couldn't blame him. She had been a pill at Claire's wedding, but she had wanted everything to run smoothly for her friend's big day. Emma might've crossed the line by scolding Gabriel at his tardiness. And she'd definitely given him plenty of attitude during the reception about his *tart-iness.* All those women, indeed.

"Do you have more luggage?" he said in his firm baritone burr.

It ran over her like warm syrup. No, butter. No . . . She fanned herself. She was incensed at her own visceral reaction. *And he hadn't given her a proper greeting.* At least she could be civilized.

"Hello, Gabriel." She felt her nose lift higher in the air. It might have been misconstrued as snooty, but seriously, the man was six-three if he was an inch. She cranked her head back to inspect his face.

He gave her a one-sided frown and seemed to be inspecting her, too. But not her face.

"You filled out," he said.

Instinctively, she put a hand over her breasts. Her cheeks burned. She started to give him a piece of her mind, but then she got angry with herself for letting him provoke her.

Defiantly, she put her hand down and stuck out her chest. "Look all you want. They expanded all on their own. Without surgical intervention."

"No reason to get your panties in a twist. I only meant it as a compliment." He continued to feast his eyes on her.

She put her hands on her hips and glared back. "Are you done yet?"

"For now." He gave her an unrepentant grin. *Still the rogue.*

"Yes, I have more luggage," she said, answering his earlier question.

"Fine." Without permission he reached for her carry-on.

She grabbed his arm, stopping him. In the process, her fingers landed on an anvil-hard bicep. She yanked her hand away and snipped at him. "I have it. Thank you." She tugged her bag back. "Your hands are filthy."

As he glanced down at the grease under his finger-nails, she took the opportunity to head off to the bag-gage reclaim, all the while giving herself a stern lecture. Getting grease off her Louis Vuitton luggage wasn't the issue. He was a dog and not the harmless type, either.

I can't be attracted to Gabriel MacGregor. Not again. I just can't. What self-respecting woman would want to get involved with a cad like him?

And those hands. His hands didn't look like doctors' hands—soft and delicate. He had the hands of an oil rig mechanic.

She also noticed he didn't wear a wedding band.

Of course, Claire would've told her if Gabriel had married, wouldn't she? She'd told Emma when he'd sud-denly gone off to medical school. Emma hadn't believed it at the time, assuring herself that he would certainly work in a grimy garage for the rest of his life.

Oh dear. Her thoughts did sound priggish, didn't they? But Gabriel seemed to bring the worst out in her. She'd treated him abominably back then, and she felt herself heading down the same path now. She would never be as serene and proper as her mother would like—all that etiquette training down the drain. Over the years, Emma had tried to be the person her mother wanted her to be, but she'd fallen short. She'd also fallen short of the person she wanted to be. Hell, she was still trying to figure out who that person might be.

With his long legs, Gabriel caught up to her; she auto-matically glanced over. He was all hard lines and phero-mones.

"Why are you frowning?" he asked.

"I'm having a difficult time seeing you as a physician." She probably should have kept her sentiments to herself, but they'd always spoken their minds to each-other, the truth flowing easily between them. *Each of us giving the other more candor than Mum's society friends would approve.* "Unless, of course, you use your title primarily as a way to pick up women."

He frowned at her. "Princess, are we going to get off on the wrong foot again?"

"That depends on you," she spouted. She did her best to sound assertive and unruffled, even though she felt unraveled and unsure. Seeing him didn't help. The last thirty-six hours had left her more than a little battered and bruised. She'd been fired and displaced. If he could have seen inside her—see the real Emma Castle—he'd know she wasn't such a snob. She didn't have all the answers. In fact, he'd see how she was questioning every aspect of her life and every choice she'd ever made.

She put the focus back on him to take it off herself. It helped her feel less uncomfortable. She raked her eyes over him unabashedly. Doctors were supposed to be old and nerdy. Doctors were supposed to instill a sense of calm and trust. Doctors were not supposed to conjure up all sorts of vivid images of a steamy nature. Yes, she could definitely imagine Dr. Gabriel MacGregor in his lab coat *playing doctor*. Just the thought sent a warm, nervous tingle zipping through her veins, throwing her limbic system into a tizzy. *Gads.*

It rankled her that he, a former grease monkey, had made something of himself. Her only claim to fame was that she'd succeeded in becoming a huge failure. But she couldn't let him see how vulnerable she felt. No doubt he'd take advantage of it. She had to admit that he had every right to fling one of her past sermons back into her face. *It's time to become an actual adult and contribute something to society.* The amount of bull she'd dished out regularly to him in their younger days was embarrassing. Especially since, by anyone's standards, she was the screw-up now.

At the baggage carousel, she intended to corral her own luggage, but she'd packed too heavy. In the end, Gabriel stepped in and hoisted her bag off, acting as if it were nothing more than cotton balls in his surgery. "Saint Gabriel," she muttered under her breath.

He raised a superior eyebrow at her. "*Thank you* is the *proper* response. Has Miss Manners forgotten how to comport herself?"

Him and his bloody burr.

And accuracy.

Yes, she should've taken the high road and been grateful. But he made her forget she was supposed to be a lady.

With a huff, she pulled the handle up on her bag.

"What's in there, by the way?" He pointed to her rolling suitcase. "It weighs at least ten stone."

"Books." She would make no apologies. She'd packed as many books as clothes, planning to use reading as her escape from her disastrous life.

"Well, we'd better get a move on. There's a winter storm blowing outside," he offered. "I was afraid you might be diverted to London. But you made it just in time." He looked up at the board as the announcement came over the loud speaker. All flights were canceled.

As they hurried through the terminal, she couldn't stop peering over at him. He was so damned good-looking. A proper English deb did not swear, not even in her own thoughts, but once again, Gabriel had her behaving quite horrendously.

"Emma," he said impatiently, "why are you staring?"

"I . . . uhhh." She sounded like an imbecile. Had his hair always looked this enticing? Enough so that she wanted to run her hands through it? She wondered if Gabriel was in a relationship.

"Well?" he said impatiently.

"Well, what?" She felt stupid for zoning out.

He frowned at her as if disappointed she couldn't keep up.

"Listen," she countered back, "I've been traveling for the last twenty-four hours. Cut me some slack." She'd been in America for far too long, adopting some of its terrible language habits.

"Fine. *Slack cut*," he said.

Emma felt like they'd been trekking for miles through the terminal. Maybe she'd been rash by not allowing Gabriel to help. Her arms felt like deadweight, tired from maneuvering both her carry-on and the checked bag behind her.

Before they stepped outside, Emma stopped to button her suit jacket. But when she left the terminal, she found her effort was in vain. It was bloody miserable—cold as freezer frost. Wind blew up her long pencil skirt and froze both her legs and her nether regions. Her lined suit jacket couldn't keep out the cold either as the snow whirled all around them. "This is quite an adjustment," she hollered above the wind.

"Which? The cold weather or the darkness?"

"Both," she answered.

"The Highlands are extreme, princess. If you think the short days are something, wait until the endless summer nights."

"I don't plan to be here that long." She pulled her

scarf more tightly around her neck, clung to her cases, and hurried along.

He led her to his ancient Land Rover.

"The same auto you had ten years ago?" She wondered if he still had his motorcycle, too.

"Aye. I recently restored the interior." He unlocked her side of the car. "Get in."

Even though she was colder than permafrost, she waited at the back with her bags.

He opened her door, waiting. "I said get in. It's freezing."

"Just open the back." She was stubborn. She intended to prove to Gabriel she wasn't the pampered princess he thought she was.

He came around to the back and unlocked it. She started to lift her bag.

"Here, I've got it." He reached for her luggage as well.

A small tug-of-war ensued. Determined to win the battle, she yanked as hard as she could, but the handle broke, sending her backward into the snow. If she'd thought it was cold before, she was mistaken. Immediately, she was crushed-ice cold from head to toe.

He offered her his hand to help her up, but she swatted him away.

"I've got it." She stood and shook the snow out of her hair. When she bent over to get her carry-on, Gabriel started brushing snow off her bottom.

"What are you doing?" She scooted away from him. "Stop!"

"I'm just trying to help." He gave her a grin and one more brush.

"Don't," she cried and slid into the car.

He got in as well and cranked up the heat. He glanced

over at her. "You should probably take your gloves off and blow on your hands."

"Great medical advice," she said:

"Hey, I'm here to help."

When he got back in, he rubbed his hands together. "Brrr."

Emma's teeth chattered a little, but she needed reassurances. "Are you sure we're going to make it to Gandiegow?"

"Aye. We'll do fine." He patted the steering wheel. "Her engine is newly rebuilt, and she's purring like a kitten."

"So the car's female?" She expected him to make a lewd comment, something about *All sweet rides are.*

He gazed through the windshield up at the sky, which was white with blizzard-like snow. "It is damnable weather. How's your body temperature?"

"I'm fine." But sitting next to him made her nervous. "How long does it take to get there?"

"I don't know. We'll have to take it slow. Just sit back and relax."

Not even possible.

"Don't worry, Emma," Gabriel said, misreading her uneasiness and shocking her by using her name. "I promise to get you to Claire safely."

Then he did the weirdest thing; he reached out and dusted the last of the snow from her shoulder.

She sat there, stunned. He looked a little embarrassed himself. He jerked his head forward and put the car in gear. Without a word, they made their way out of the airport. The streets beyond were relatively empty and even the highway had little traffic.

After a time, she felt safe to secretly peek over at him. Mr. Perfect handled the auto with ease, his large hands resting on the steering wheel, his uneasiness from a while ago gone. Maybe she'd imagined it. When they slid a bit on the curvy roads, he stayed calm, even then exuding confidence. His medium-length coffee dark hair was perfectly styled to fit his perfect head. When he was younger, his hair had been long and wild and out of control. He'd tamed it, and it seemed to suit him now. The only part that spoke of rebellion was the beard stubble. But it wasn't a full rebellion, like he hadn't shaved in days. No, he must have trimmed it carefully this morning. Emma ached to run her hand over it to see if it felt prickly or soft or maybe a little of both. She turned away and shifted uncomfortably in her seat.

"Are you all right?" Concern pinched his eyebrows together.

"Sure. Why wouldn't I be?" The look he gave her made her feel vulnerable. "Did they teach that compassionate look in medical school?"

The doctor shot her a scowl.

Much better. That she could d⁓   ⁓ ⁓ ⁓⁓
for several more miles, but she c⁓ ⁓⁓⁓ ⁓ help sneaking another peek at him.

He sighed heavily. "Emma, ye're staring again."

She turned back to her window but saw only darkness. "You've filled out, too," she said quietly.